FAMILY TREES

A Pine County Mystery

D1165148

Dean L Hovey

Moose Town Press

ISBN: 1545145229
ISBN 13: 9781545145227

Pine County Mysteries by Dean Hovey

Where Evil Hides
Hooker
Unforgettable
Undeveloped
The Deacon's Demise
Family Trees

Two Harbors cozies by Dean Hovey

Whistling Pines
Whistling Sousa
(coming in 2017) Whistling Wings

To my sister, Lynn Hovey. Thanks for your support and encouragement.
To Robert Dennis Arnold (1947-2017)

March 15, 1934
Minnesota State School
Owatonna, Minnesota

It was Margaret "Pixie" Lane's birthday. Tears streamed down her young face and her hands shook. Mrs. Finnegan, a dour woman with a short fuse and an eagerness to use corporal punishment, handed her a wicker suitcase with leather straps and watched as Pixie packed her few pieces of clothing and donned a threadbare woolen coat. The other girls in the dormitory watched in stunned silence; they were conditioned not to show any emotion. With suitcase in hand, Pixie looked at the dozens of girls who had been her family for the past four years, hoping someone would rush forward to rescue her. Most stared at their shoes. A few cheeks were stained with tears.

Pixie was led to the administration building. She'd never been there before but knew it was where students were sent for the most serious infractions, like striking a teacher. Few returned to the dormitory after "seeing the director" and there were whispers about the fate of the rest. The cemetery had graves marked only with numbers and rumors abounded.

Mrs. Finnegan had her hand on Pixie's back as they walked the hallway of the administration building. Muffled voices could be heard behind closed doors with names stenciled on the frosted glass, and their footsteps echoed on the tile floor. Finnegan knocked once on the last door on the right side of the hallway, then opened the door without waiting for a response. She pushed Pixie across the room until she was standing directly in front of the director's immense desk.

Director Engel was an imposing man, with a bulbous red nose and strands of gray hair that were combed from his left ear over the top of his bald head. He continued to write as Pixie quaked in front of him. When he set his pen aside, he blotted the paper and finally looked up. His expression was neutral as he looked her up and down.

"Miss Lane," he said, clasping his hands and setting them on the desktop, "it is your sixteenth birthday and you've graduated from the eighth grade. You're a woman now and no longer a ward of the State of Minnesota." He carefully folded the note he'd just written and slipped it into an envelope with another piece of paper. He reached across the desk, holding the envelope out to Pixie.

"Good heavens, girl," Mrs. Finnegan said, pushing Pixie's shoulder, "take the envelope."

With trembling hand Pixie took the envelope and stared at the writing.

Abigail Corbett
Pine City, Minnesota

"We're not in the business of providing employment for our students," the director said, "but I was recently contacted by an acquaintance who is in need of domestic help. He has paid your way to Pine City, so there is a railroad ticket in the envelope. His assistant, Miss Corbett, will meet you at the station. Give her the enclosed letter when you arrive."

The director leaned back, apparently expecting Pixie to show gratitude, or leave. Either would've been acceptable.

"Sir, what's domestic help?" Pixie asked.

A blow across her shoulders knocked her forward where she banged her knees against the desk. "Show some respect, girl!" Mrs. Finnegan said.

The director lifted his hand, waving Mrs. Finnegan back. "I imagine it will involve housecleaning, making beds, and washing dishes. If you're good, they may offer you training to be a seamstress or cook."

Pixie's eyes glazed. She'd been cleaning and making her own bed for years but hoped adulthood would bring more. Cringing in anticipation of another blow, she asked, "Where is Pine City?" When no blow came, she relaxed a bit.

"It's north of Minneapolis. The train stops at many towns along the way. Be sure to stay in your seat until the conductor announces the Pine City stop. I encourage you not to talk with any strange men." The director looked over Pixie's head and said to Mrs. Finnegan, "Have Mr. Olson drive Miss Lane to the train station."

From the time Pixie left the director's office, the world was a blur. She sat on a bench inside the Owatonna train station while a stark sun shone on the snowy landscape through the window. The ticket agent came out of his cage once to stoke the cast iron stove and tell Pixie the train was on time. She watched in amazement as the clattering train arrived, billowing coal smoke and spewing steam. She walked onto the train platform as a conductor stepped off the train and placed a stool at the bottom of the steps. A nicely dressed man and woman stepped off the train. Terrified, Pixie froze, not sure what she was supposed to do. The conductor pulled a pocket watch from his vest and flipped it open, then replaced it. He looked at Pixie, who was wide-eyed and shaking.

"Are you boarding the train, Miss?" he asked. His voice was kind and he smiled at her. She nodded, regained control of her legs and walked across the platform. The conductor took her hand as she stepped onto the stool, then climbed aboard carrying her wicker suitcase. She found a row of empty seats and took the one nearest the window, clutching her suitcase to her chest.

"May I see your ticket, please?" the conductor asked after she sat down.

She froze for an instant, then remembered the director's envelope. She unstrapped her suitcase and took out the envelope, handing it to the conductor. He opened the envelope, removed the train ticket and used a tool attached to his belt by a chain to punch the ticket.

"You are ticketed to Pine City," he said as he slipped the ticket back into the envelope and handed it back to Pixie. "We stop at several stations before then, including Minneapolis. You just stay on the train until I call the Pine City stop. Do you understand?"

Pixie nodded.

"Let me put your case in the overhead rack," the conductor said, reaching for her suitcase. At four-feet ten-inches tall, Pixie couldn't reach the overhead storage racks.

A man sitting across the aisle, wearing a bowler hat and a black overcoat, eyed her in a way that made her skin crawl. Seeing the undue attention Pixie was receiving, the conductor took the man by the elbow, moving him further down the car, while scolding him in hushed tones. The conductor returned and knelt beside her.

"If anyone bothers you, find me." He glanced down the car at the man he'd just moved.

She nodded.

In Minneapolis, the train had a tumultuous change-over of people. Pixie stayed in her seat and watched as the train emptied and the greatest diversity of humanity she'd ever seen loaded onto the cars from the platform. Well-dressed men carrying briefcases followed women holding crying babies and leading strings of children. Scruffier men left an unpleasant odor in their wake as they shuffled down the aisle. With the riders came a cacophony of voices, the noise of boxes and briefcases being loaded overhead, babies crying, and laughter. The smell of sweat mingled with tobacco smoke, perfume, and Bay Rum aftershave.

One of the scruffy men stopped at her row and took the seat next to her. Pixie glanced at him in horror, sliding as far toward the window as she could. She looked for another seat, but realized the car was completely full, with a few people standing in the aisle.

"Where you going, girl," her seatmate asked.

"P-p-p-pine City," she stuttered, violating the director's admonition against talking to strange men.

"I'm going to Hinckley," the man said. "I got me a job at a farm there."

Pixie finally looked at the man and realized he was probably no more than sixteen also. His face was bright but dirty and he smelled of sweat and coal smoke. "Where's Hinckley," she asked.

"It's up beyond Pine City a bit." The boy paused and gave her a funny look. "Haven't you ever seen a state map before?"

Pixie shook her head. "I guess they didn't teach us that at the State School."

"You been in a State School?" The boy asked. "What's that?"

"My mom died and my dad married a new woman. She didn't want his old family, so I got sent to the State School with my brothers and sister."

"I suppose that's better'n me getting beaten up by my dad when he drank. And he drank every night."

Pixie stared into her lap in silence.

"What?" the boy asked. "Did they beat you at the school?"

"I don't want to talk anymore," she said, thinking of the many beatings she'd endured. And she'd seen worse.

After announcing the Pine City arrival, the conductor lifted Pixie's suitcase down and carried it to the platform. "Is someone picking you up?" he asked.

"I think so." She climbed down from the train, opened the suitcase on the frosty platform and took out the envelope. "Abigail Corbett is supposed to meet me," she told the conductor.

The prettiest woman Pixie had ever seen walked over, knelt down beside her and touched her shoulder. Pixie reflexively pulled away. No one at the school ever touched her gently unless they wanted something from her. Most contact had been punishment liberally applied with a yardstick.

The conductor tipped his hat to the woman. "Good day," he said, as he stepped away.

"I'm Abigail Corbett," the woman said, still kneeling. She looked into Pixie's near empty suitcase. "Girl, are those all the clothes you brought?"

Pixie blushed and closed the suitcase, buckling the leather straps. "I've only got these two dresses and some bloomers." She stood up and looked at Abigail, who wore a touch of rouge to make her cheeks rosy. She smelled like a flower garden and her blonde hair was pulled into a bun on top of her head. She wore a high-necked white blouse and a plaid dress that came below her knees. Her hands were dainty and her nails neatly trimmed. Pixie looked at her own nails, which were gnawed to the quick.

Abigail reached down and took Pixie's hand. "Come with me," she said. "We have to get you some more clothes before we drive out to the Tuxedo Inn."

"What's the Tuxedo Inn," Pixie asked as they walked away from the station.

"It's a restaurant where people come to eat fancy meals and dance to piano music. They call it Tuxedo Inn because men are required to wear tuxedos and women all wear long dresses. You'll share an upstairs room with three other girls, and you'll be cleaning, making beds, and washing laundry."

They walked about a block, then Corbett stood aside and looked Pixie up and down.

"You're such a tiny thing. I suppose that's why they call you Pixie. With those pigtails in your hair, you look like you're no more than twelve." Corbett smiled.

Pixie was stuck on the concept of the Tuxedo Inn. She'd never heard of a tuxedo before, but if Abigail Corbett thought they were classy, they must be fabulous, and by extension, she'd be working in a classy place. For the first time she thought that leaving the State School might not be such a bad thing.

CHAPTER 1

FRIDAY, OCTOBER 1

Floyd Swenson, a sergeant in Pine County's Sheriff's Department, was standing in a farm field in Royalton Township, at the southwest corner of Pine County. A farmer was showing a conservation officer a half-eaten calf carcass he thought might have been killed by a timber wolf. While the conservation officer was getting an earful about wolves, their protected status, and the idiots in Congress as he filled out the forms so the farmer could get state reimbursement for the lost calf, Floyd heard the dispatcher.

"Two deputies request backup at the west entrance to the Nemadji State Forest."

Waving to the farmer and officer, Floyd jogged to his cruiser. The deputies requesting backup were near the Wisconsin border, in the northeast corner of

1

the 1,400 square miles of Pine County. He couldn't be further away.

Nearly an hour later, he crested a hill and snaked his cruiser between trucks loaded with heavy logging equipment and a line of cars on the opposite side of the narrow gravel road. He noted an aging Volvo station wagon, a Toyota Prius, and a blue VW van with a peace symbol painted on one side. Stickers from a dozen environmental groups were plastered to the tailgate. He saw the flashing lights of two Pine County cruisers where the road ended.

Past the end of the county road a narrow logging road disappeared into a veil of pines shrouded in fog. At the mouth of the road, standing next to a green "State Forest," sign, deputies Pam Ryan and Sandy Maki were standing strategically between two groups of people.

On one side were men wearing flannel shirts and quilted vests over bluejeans or tan Carhartt canvas pants. Each was wearing a green or yellow hard hat. Their body language said they were ready to start throwing punches. The opposite group could best be described as young and shaggy. Dressed in North Face, Columbia, or Under Armour rain gear, they appeared to be holding hands while yelling at the loggers. The male protestor furthest from the loggers was shouting into a cellphone, trying to have a conversation over the commotion.

Sandy Maki was the senior deputy on the scene by virtue of his five years with the sheriff's department. As Floyd walked toward the group he could see that Sandy's face was red. He was standing next to the young people who were ignoring his repeated orders to disperse. Pam Ryan, a petite blonde deputy with barely three years in the sheriff's department, was quietly talking to one of the loggers and smiling.

Floyd put a hand on Sandy Maki's shoulder, slowly turning him away from the confrontation.

"What's up?" Floyd asked, as the invectives from the protesters flew behind him.

"These damned hippies chained the gate to the state forest, then they handcuffed themselves to each other and blocked the road," Maki replied. "Mattson's Forestry Servce has a contract with the state to cut trees but they can't get their equipment past these . . . people to do their work."

Floyd recognized Orrin Johnson, the foreman of Mattson's Forestry Service, among the loggers and gave him a discreet nod that was returned with a dip of the chin. Orrin was talking to the loggers, who nodded and stayed by their trucks.

The oldest male protester, who appeared to be in his late twenties, sported a scraggly beard and an obvious attitude. He frowned at Floyd when their eyes met and didn't look away. The male protestors wore stocking caps or backward facing baseball caps. Each had a day's growth of beard. The three women looked younger, two possibly close to twenty, and the third still in her teens. Their eyes refused to meet Floyd's gaze. Every protester wore jeans with ragged holes and scarred hiking boots that contrasted with their expensive waterproof jackets.

Floyd walked up to the most vocal protester and asked, "Why are you blocking the road?" He scanned the scene, noting a chain across the logging road affixed with locks at both ends. It appeared that the entire group had handcuffed themselves together and then looped a handcuff through the chain at each end.

"Are you a local cop?"

Floyd unzipped his jacket, exposing the badge and the holster on his hip, thinking it an odd question since he'd arrived on the scene in a sheriff's department cruiser. "I'm Sergeant Swenson. Who are you?"

"It doesn't matter who I am." The man looked up the road expectantly before returning his attention to Floyd. "We're here to stop the rape of another forest by the money-grubbing logging interests."

"You mean these guys?" Floyd asked, indicating the loggers with a nod of his head. "They're hard-working guys with families to feed and mortgages to pay. Why don't you and your friends unlock yourselves and go home before someone does something stupid?"

"We're staying until the timber is saved. Aren't we?" he said, imploring his cohorts to respond.

"Damn right, Jeremy!" the others replied as they looked up the road again.

"Are you expecting someone?" Floyd asked.

"The media will be here soon," Jeremy said, "and that will put an end to all this. No one will allow this rape of the land to go on once they see it on television." He paused, and then added, "It's convenient that all the timber contracts were negotiated and signed behind closed doors. It was all railroaded through without public comment."

A buzz in the forest drew everyone's eyes to the tree line. The buzz quickly turned into the roar of three ATV engines as three four-wheelers sped out of the timber. The helmeted riders barely slowed to bypass the chained gate. They bounced through the ditch, then sped away down the gravel road. Their jackets were splattered with mud and their faces obscured by the darkened plastic face shields. The protesters had quizzical looks on their faces as the ATVs sped past. The loggers watched in disdain. In seconds they were gone, leaving a trail of dust behind them.

"Orrin!" Floyd yelled to the foreman. "You guys got a contract with the state to cut in here?"

"We got a contract," Johnson shouted back, "and we paid the state up front." The foreman edged his way through the other men and past Pam Ryan. "You want to see it? All the trees that are being harvested are marked and the state forester verified the boundaries."

He handed a copy of the contract to Floyd, then added, "The state solicited sealed bids through a legal notice in the newspapers, and we were the winning bidder."

"Jeremy, where are the keys to the locks and the handcuffs?" Floyd asked as he scanned the cover letter on the contact.

The protester looked up the road again. "I think they're lost," he replied smugly.

In a stage comment, the foreman said. "We could help you restrain these . . . people." The comment brought a murmur of assent from the loggers who had edged closer to the protesters despite Pam Ryan's efforts to keep them back.

Floyd shook his head. "Have your guys get in their trucks." He looked up the road as a white van with a television dish came over the crest of the hill.

"Everyone lay down in the road!" Jeremy instructed, seeing the television van.

Pam, Sandy, and Floyd watched helplessly as the protesters quickly lay down across the gate area. Sandy rolled his eyes and reached for his can of Mace. Floyd put up a hand and walked to the nearest woman. She had light brown hair and blue eyes and was the smallest and youngest member of the protest group. She also looked the most nervous. Floyd knelt next to her.

"You know," Floyd said quietly, "I could leave you chained to the gate until tomorrow."

"Don't let him mess with your mind, Susan," the nearest male protester said. Floyd noted a "Save the Whales" button pinned to his jacket collar.

Susan looked nervously in Jeremy's direction. "Jeremy said we'll only be here until the television crew leaves. He'll unlock us once he makes a statement to the media."

Floyd stood up and walked to Jeremy, who was craning his neck to see if the news crew had their camera set up yet. He cringed as Floyd reached down, expecting to be either hit or lifted up roughly. Instead, Floyd stuck his hand into Jeremy's shirt pocket and pulled out the keys to the padlocks and handcuffs.

"Hey!" Jeremy protested. "You can't touch me! Police brutality!" He looked to see if any of the news people had heard his protest, but they were still behind the van fifty yards away, deploying camera equipment and raising the satellite dish.

"All right," Floyd said to his deputies as he slipped the keys into his pocket. "Let's go." He walked to Orrin Johnson.

"The news crew is here, and I don't want to make this a circus. The girl told me that they're only planning to stay until the news crew leaves. If there's no story, the TV talking heads will be gone. Tell your guys to pull out and have a cup of coffee in Duquette. Come back in an hour and I think our protest will be over and these kids will be on their way back to their political science classes with stories about how they saved the forest."

The foreman nodded. "Got it," he said, although he didn't look happy. "We'll go without making a scene in front of the camera."

As the foreman passed the word to his drivers the protesters started chanting, "Save the forests!" The news crew started filming a reporter as the first of the logging trucks pulled away from the gate.

Floyd huddled with the two deputies as the trucks lumbered past. "Pam, here are the keys to the locks. Let's drive off with the loggers now, so it looks like the protesters won on the news tonight. You come back in a couple hours and let them loose."

Sandy Maki frowned. "Shouldn't we arrest them?"

"Nah," Floyd said, "it would just get them the publicity they want. I figure they've been chained to the fence for a while. Most of them will be ready to make a break for the nearest bathroom as soon as the camera crew clears the road."

Pam smiled. "I've been here almost two hours, and I'm ready for a bathroom." She pocketed the keys. "I'll check in with the truckers in Duquette." She walked to her cruiser.

"I'll hang around until the loggers come back, just to make sure there isn't any more trouble," Maki said.

"I don't think there will be any trouble. These guys will get their faces on the news and they'll leave." Floyd leaned close to Sandy Maki. "Record the license numbers on the cars and run them through DMV. Most of them are from out of state. Then start checking local motels and campgrounds to see if they've got any of these folks registered. I've got a feeling this is set up on the outside somewhere," Floyd said. "I've heard about groups of professional protesters who travel around the country, protesting whatever is fashionable. I'd like to know who's paying the tab."

Sandy nodded toward the sad-looking woman on the end. "My guess is that daddy is picking up the tab for her. She's wearing five or six hundred bucks worth of distressed denim, Merrell hiking boots, and a Columbia jacket."

CHAPTER 2

Floyd drove to the tiny town of Duquette and parked around the corner from the tavern. Highway 23 was lined with the logging trucks and every table in Lobo's was jammed with loggers drinking coffee and eating pastries.

"Hey, Floyd," a voice boomed from the rear of the café. "Why don't you let us take care of those tree huggers for you? We could save the taxpayers a lot of money."

Floyd waved toward the direction of the voice. "Yeah, and we'd be prosecuting you for assault."

"Nah," another voice responded. "We'd just make them happy to leave and not come back."

"We could reduce the herd of ATVs at the same time," another voice added from the back. "When's the season on them anyway? Can we shoot one a day?"

That comment brought a chuckle from the loggers. "We're tired of them racing around like they own the land, cutting ruts down the logging roads. There ought to be a law..."

He spotted Orrin Johnson in the corner booth and pulled a chair from the nearest table. "I wonder how those protesters knew you were going to start cutting today?"

Johnson shrugged. "Who knows? It's been in the paper. The forestry guys in the Department of Natural Resources knew. Every guy in the room told his family and friends there'd be steady work for a few months. I suppose that means that the bankers, bartenders, and shopkeepers knew too." Johnson paused. "What difference does it make?"

Floyd signaled for a cup of coffee, and then said, "I don't know. It just seems strange that a bunch of protesters show up on the first day of cutting. How many other cuts have you done without any problems? Five? Ten? All of a sudden, we got protesters chaining themselves across a gate and calling in the newspeople. Like I said, it just seems strange."

"We don't do much cutting on state land," Johnson replied. "I'd guess that ninety percent of our cuts are contracts with landowners or paper companies. This is different. Not only are we in the state forest, but this is a stand of old-growth hardwoods. The pines were logged out back in the early 1900s when lumber was in demand to build Chicago and the Twin Cities. One forester told me this parcel was left due to a surveyor's error, but I think it was left because the hardwoods didn't make good building material. The forestry guys have been keeping it quiet for decades, but with budget pressure and the ongoing fear of fires, they decided to take them down."

"How big are the trees?" Floyd asked.

"I imagine you see our trucks pulling loads of pulp wood with a hundred logs on the trucks," Orrin said. "If we get three of these logs on a truck, we'll be doing well. McGregor has the only sawmill with equipment large enough to handle these logs, and they'll be cutting thousands of board feet of lumber out of each log. They've got buyers lined up all over the country for the wood. These trees grow slow and straight, making the wood dense and fine-grained. None of these trees will be going into building lumber. I heard the Amish furniture builders in Iowa contracted to buy a million board feet they'll use for furniture. There are a few hickories in there, and they're going to a piano company. One of the forestry guys told me this wood will give superior sound resonance for concert pianos because of the dense grain."

Floyd let out a low whistle. "McGregor is a long haul from here. That's got to be a three-hour drive."

"That's part of the value of this contract to us. We're putting a lot of people to work for several months.

We've invested in specialized equipment and sent some of our guys for training to operate the digital GPS on the equipment. We'll digitize the location of every tree, then follow the tree through cutting so we know exactly how many board feet of lumber we get off every spot in the forest. Not one extra tree will be cut or damaged."

"I'm impressed," Floyd said. He looked around the room at the hardened men who were laughing and slogging down coffee. "I can't imagine that many of these guys would care if a tree they cut was used to build a piano or was burned for heat." He looked at Mattson and asked, "What did you do before you started working for Mattson?"

"I was a history teacher," replied the foreman. "One round of budget cuts and music, art, and history were no longer required and I was looking for a job. I worked my way through college cutting wood, so it seemed like a natural transition to go back."

"Other than the size of the trees, what's special about this cut?" Floyd asked,

"We're cutting 'the grandfathers.'"

"Grandfathers?" Floyd asked, stirring cream into his coffee.

"Here's your history lesson for the day," said Orrin, setting his coffee aside. "Back around 1900, when the original surveys were drawn to allot the timber-cutting grants, the railroads left several tracts out of the grants because the surveyor couldn't determine who owned the land in the plats he was drawing. On top of that, the timber companies wanted the giant white pines that made millions of board feet of lumber. With millions of acres of prime pine, the lumber companies weren't interested in the five small tracts of hardwoods with questionable standing, and might involve Indian treaties. All the acreage around the five hardwood tracts were clear-cut. Four hardwood tracts burned during the 1918 Moose Lake fire. The last tract is included in this contract."

"And that's a big deal?" Floyd asked. "If you don't cut them they'll burn or get blown down in a windstorm."

"Many of them are already down and within a couple years all the ash trees will be killed by emerald ash borers," Johnson replied. "I guess it's more of a symbolic thing. We took bore samples of some trees that are close to three hundred years old. They were seedlings when the Pilgrims landed at Plymouth Rock. Some of the nature people think they should be left standing."

"So, a lot of the trees are already dead, the ash will be dying anyway, and the state gave you a contract to cut everything," said Floyd.

"The forestry guys estimate that in ten to fifteen years the grandfathers will all be dead and they'll have to pay someone to remove the fire hazard." Johnson hesitated, and then added, "But, letting the ash borers kill them is natural, so I guess it's okay with the environmentalists if they die and rot on the ground."

Floyd looked at his watch. "The eco-nuts should be gone by the time you get back to the gate." He drained the last of his coffee and threw a dollar bill on the table to pay for his fifty-cent cup of coffee.

Pam Ryan drove to Duquette and used the restroom before filling her gas tank. It was nearly an hour later when she made it back to the forestry service gate and met Sandy Maki. The protesters were all sitting and straining at the chains to get close enough to talk to each other. The television vans were gone and the only cars left parked on the edge of the narrow gravel road belonged to the protestors. From a distance it appeared dissention was brewing. She stopped a few feet from the gate and stepped out of the car as the protesters stood up.

"The natives are getting restless," Maki said, nodding toward the protestors.

"Okay, folks. I'm going to open the locks so you can leave. I'd prefer to do this without a lot of problems, and I assume that the women would like to be set free first." Pam looked at a dark-haired woman who was now holding her handcuffs out for the first release while she shuffled uncomfortably from foot to foot.

"Let Susan go first," said one of the older women.

Pam unshackled Susan and watched her run to some bushes near the edge of the road, unzipping her jeans as she ran. Pam unlocked the second girl who ran in the same direction. She could see from the wet spots in the gravel that a few of the men had already obtained relief.

When the last person was unlocked, Pam gathered the handcuffs and locked them and the chain that had blocked the gate in the trunk of her squad. The protesters had gathered around Jeremy in a rough huddle and were mumbling something unintelligible.

"All right!" Pam said, "You're free to leave. Please go to your cars and get out of here!"

Jeremy stepped forward with the others loosely following behind.

"Where did the logging trucks go?"

"I don't know," Sandy replied with a shrug. "They probably went to get coffee. It really doesn't matter much, because if you find them, they won't greet you with open arms. You're taking bread out of their mouths and they don't take kindly to that when they only get seven or eight months of employment a year."

Jeremy glanced back at the others and one of the other men shrugged.

"I think we'll hang around awhile, just in case they decide to come back."

The three women rejoined the men. Susan jammed her hands into the pockets of her jeans. "Aren't we leaving?" she asked. One of the other women rubbed her wrists where the handcuffs had chafed them.

"This was too easy," Jeremy replied. "I think it was staged so the truckers came back after we clear out."

Pam smirked and said. "Either that, or they're going in through the other entrance."

Jeremy shook his head. "The south entrance won't hold those heavy trucks, I checked it out yesterday. That road cuts through a swamp. This is the only way they can get the heavy equipment close to the cutting area without getting mired down."

"You guys do whatever you want," Pam said with a shrug. "Deputy Maki and I have warrants to serve and roads to patrol. Just don't go wandering around in the forest so we have to send out a search-and-rescue team to find you. I think we might have a hard time coming up with a dozen people who would care if you were found or not."

Susan looked confused. "What would make you say something mean like that? We're here to save the forest. There should be lots of people around who would support that."

"Get real," Pam scoffed. "Half the people in this county live below the poverty level and get barely seven months of work a year. Most of that is either trying to farm the rocky swamps or cutting wood. The farmers don't have much time for city folks, and I don't think you've made any friends with the loggers today. Did you look at those guys? Their clothes are worn, their hands are calloused from hard work, and they mostly drive beat-up used pickups." She paused. "Now look at you, with your distressed jeans and two-hundred-dollar jackets. Here you are, making their lives miserable while your daddy makes the payments on the AmEx card he gave you." Pam bit her tongue and didn't call them leeches, but the word went through her mind.

Pam radioed that she was back in service as Sandy pulled away. As the protesters returned to their cars, Pam noticed Jeremy staring at her. His expression was blank, but his eyes disturbed her. After holding his gaze for a minute, she looked away and involuntarily shivered before starting her car.

CHAPTER 3

SATURDAY

The phone jarred Floyd Swenson from sleep. He focused briefly on the alarm clock and saw that it was programmed to ring in two more minutes.

"Swenson," he said, trying to blink the sleep from his eyes.

"This is dispatch," the male voice announced. "We have a disturbance in Duquette. Pam Ryan was dispatched and she called for all the backup we can find."

"Where in Duquette is she?"

"She's at the state forest gate outside of Duquette. The loggers are trying to get to their equipment and she says there are a bunch of protesters blocking the road again."

"I'll be on the road in two minutes."

Mary Jungers rolled over and watched Floyd pull on a uniform shirt and pants. "What's the matter?" she asked.

"Pam Ryan is in Duquette and needs backup."

Mary said, "Be careful," to Floyd's back as he walked out of the bedroom door.

By the time Floyd arrived, Sandy Maki had joined Pam Ryan, again separating the two groups. The loggers' heavy trucks, having delivered the heavy equipment to the cutting site the previous day, had been replaced by a line of four-wheel-drive pickup trucks and flatbed semis ready to be loaded with logs. The same array of cars lined the opposite side of the road. ATV engines whined in the distance. The same television van was capturing the images from the middle of the road.

The protestors weren't chained together, but sat shoulder-to-shoulder across the state forest entrance. The loggers were standing back, clustered around Orrin Johnson, the foreman. As Floyd walked from his car, Johnson approached him.

"We can't sit around every day waiting for these idiots to go back to their liberal arts colleges. We're losing money."

"I hoped they'd lose interest after the first confrontation," Floyd said. "Keep your men under control and I'll see what I can do."

Sandy Maki met Floyd halfway to the protestors. "The protesters are professionals," he said. "I checked the license numbers yesterday. They're from Oregon and Washington and almost every one of them has been arrested for criminal trespass or civil disobedience of some variety. From the looks of it, they're pretty well set to be here for a while. They're staying at the Willow River campground, and they've pre-paid for thirty days."

A fourth sheriff's department cruiser pulled up and Kerm Rajacich, a huge deputy known for breaking up bar fights, stepped out of his car. Several of the loggers smiled and talked among themselves, assuming Kerm would knock some heads.

Floyd listened to Sandy and glanced at the television crew, who continued to film the encounter. "I'd like to find some way to get them out of here quietly without being the lead story on the evening news. Have you got any ideas?"

Pam joined the other officers as Floyd looked at the protestors and said, "They're prepared to be arrested and we'll have to carry them to the squads."

"I'm too old to carry protestors," said Floyd.

"Pam has all their chain and handcuffs in her trunk," Sandy said. "Let's cuff them together and just pull them to the side."

Floyd studied the group. "I don't think we'd win a tug of war with them either."

Rajacich walked up to the deputies and hitched up his gun belt. "Let me move them. Please?"

"Hey!" A voice from the group of loggers called out. "I think the middle one with the black hair is kinda cute. Can I take her home?"

"That's a guy, Hank," one of the other loggers said.

"Oh, I can't tell. They all got ponytails." The loggers laughed.

"Let me drive my truck through, Floyd," another voice called, "They wouldn't be more than a speed bump."

Pam studied the protestors, "You know," she said, "if these kids think that we've got some sort of a backwoods vigilante thing going, we might be able to convince them that we need them to move for their own protection. One of the girls is already looking a little nervous."

"Kerm," Floyd said, "quietly stir up the loggers a little while the rest of us protect the protestors. Tell Orrin to have them put on their game faces and look threatening."

Catcalls and jeers started to flow from the loggers as Floyd approached the protest leader. "Listen, you're looking at every law enforcement officer on duty in Pine County. If those loggers start getting ornery, we won't be able to protect you. I suggest that you step aside and let them through."

Jeremy looked at Floyd with disdain. "Get off it. We're perfectly safe here as long as the television camera is rolling."

"Pam," Floyd said, "Tell the television crew they have to clear the road. They've probably got enough video footage for tonight anyway." In the background the commotion among the loggers was getting more vocal, and the group was drawing closer.

The most petite female protester, who was closest to the loggers, got up and retreated toward her car. Two of the men and another woman quickly followed her.

Floyd, Sandy Maki, and Kerm Rajacich moved quickly to "encourage" the remaining protesters to move aside and open the gate to the narrow logging road. The loggers made a run for their trucks as Jeremy yelled encouragement to the remaining protester.

By the time the first truck got to the gate, four of the protestors had moved aside and Pam Ryan and Sandy Maki were handcuffing the one still in the road while Kerm Rajacich stood akimbo, visually daring them to step forward. With a physical lift from Sandy and Floyd, the last protestors were pulled aside and the trucks rumbled through the gate bumper-to-bumper, their diesel engines roaring, while the protestors jeered from the ditch.

As the first logging truck reached the edge of the timber, about fifty yards past the gate, a deafening roar split the air and a shock wave swept over the area, knocking several people off their feet. A huge pine wobbled and crashed on top of the lead truck.

Floyd turned away from the spray of wooden splinters, throwing his arm up to protect his face and head as he was knocked to the ground. Splinters pelted him and a sharp pain seared his shoulder. When the hail of wood stopped, the back of his shoulder was wet with blood. He could feel a wood sliver the size of a penknife sticking through his jacket.

As he stood up, he looked around, seeing that most of the protesters had been flung to the ground. They looked dazed, but were stirring. He scanned the area for the brown uniforms of his deputies, and saw that all three were moving and checking each other.

"Kermit!" Floyd yelled. "Get to the trucks and see if anyone's hurt! Pam, grab your first aid kit and check on the protesters!" He looked around and saw the television crew filming the entire event. "Sandy, get the video! Impound it as evidence!"

Floyd fumbled for the microphone that had been attached to his shoulder. He found it dangling from its cord, bumping against his thigh. "Dispatch, we need an ambulance at the Nemadji state forest entrance. I have several injured people. Let the sheriff know what's going on, and tell him that news crews are already on site."

Pam was back with the first aid kit as the protesters sorted out their cuts, scrapes, and puncture wounds and complained about the dirt and splinters on their expensive jackets. Floyd pulled out his handcuffs and grabbed the arms of two protesters who appeared to be uninjured. They watched without resistance.

"Why are you cuffing us?" the woman asked.

"You're under arrest for attempted murder," he replied. "You have the right to remain silent..."

CHAPTER 4

All four county cruisers were filled with protesters by the time the fire department sirens wailed
in the distance. Jeremy, the leader, had screamed at
the KDLH news crew, demanding that they record the
"Nazi tactics" being used on them. The news cameraman recorded the event, but seemed indifferent. Most
of the protestors went to the sheriff's vehicles quietly,
some smiled at the cameras, resigned to their arrest,
but enjoying their thirty seconds of fame. Two of the
women and one of the men were less pleased, turning
their faces away from the news cameras.

Pam walked among the loggers offering first aid
to those with significant scrapes or wounds. Floyd
pressed his way through the dozen bloodied loggers
who were jammed around the smashed truck. Most

had been peppered with glass fragments when the windows in their vehicles shattered. Using pry bars and chains, they swarmed the crushed truck. Kerm Rajacich coordinated a group of three loggers who attached a chain to the tree lying atop the pickup cab. With the other end attached to the trailer hitch of the largest F-250 Ford pickup, and a lift from the loggers around the cab, the tree trunk began to roll. With a cracking of branches, it slid across the truck's hood to the ground just as the Moose Lake Rescue Squad pulled through the state forest gate.

Floyd and Pam pushed through the truckers. Floyd looked through the narrow opening that had once been the windshield. "Hey, buddy, the firemen are here. Hang in there for me," Floyd said softly. The truck's interior was covered with dust and shards of glass. The logger's lunch box had been thrown open, spreading sandwiches, candy bars, and potato chips all over the interior of the cab. A thermos had been thrown onto the dashboard and coffee was trickling from its cracked lid. He could barely make out a bloodied human figure among the mess.

Orrin stood behind the deputies. "It's Larry Odegaard," he said quietly.

Pam, her uniform dotted with blood and wood chips, climbed over the tree and slid across the hood of the truck until she could reach through the windshield. "Larry, are you OK?" she asked as she reached across the dashboard and touched the driver's shoulder. "Can you say something to me?" His head was resting on his chest. Blood oozed from his scalp, ran down his face, and dripped off his nose and chin. His breathing was shallow and irregular.

Pam was stretching hard while she offered soft encouragement to the trapped man. "Stick with me, Larry. Help is almost here." As she wiggled through the windshield and partially slid inside the cab, the driver drew a deeper breath that he released as a rattle, and didn't inhale again. It took Pam another minute to wriggle close enough to put her fingers against his neck. Tears were streaming down her face as she climbed back out and slid off the hood.

She shook her head and wiped tears with her arm.

Floyd led her away from the truck as the firemen rushed to unpack their first aid gear and rescue equipment. Floyd gestured for them to slow down, and slowly shook his head. The firemen stood silently for a moment, watching Floyd and Pam walk away. The tough loggers stood quietly, looking emotionally drained.

"We should make those damn tree-huggers watch when we tell his wife that he won't be coming home," Pam said as she walked to the road.

The three female protesters were in the back seat of Pam's car, watching the action around the crushed pickup with curiosity. Pam got in the driver's seat, slammed the car door, and reached for a packet of tissues from the glove box.

"What's going on?" the tallest girl asked.

Pam blew her nose and was about to throw the tissue onto the floor when she saw that it was stained red. She looked at her fingers as if they were attached to someone else's hand, and then wiped the blood off them. Once sure that she wasn't bleeding she held the tissue up for her passengers to see.

"This is blood from the guy in the pickup," she said. "He's not bleeding anymore, though. He's dead."

The faces Pam saw in the rearview mirror were shocked.

"I'm sorry; we didn't know," a voice whispered.

Pam stared at their images in the mirror for a few seconds, then said, "You'll probably be very sorry by the time this is over. I expect that you'll all be indicted for premeditated murder."

"We didn't know anything!" the smallest woman protested. "Jeremy does all the planning and we just go where he tells us."

Reacting to a knock on her window, Pam rolled it down.

"Are you okay?" Floyd asked.

Pam drew a deep breath and let it out slowly. "Sure."

"Get the women out of here," Floyd said, looking at the loggers who were now gathered into a scrum and throwing looks toward the protesters in the squad cars. "Take them to Pine City right now. The crowd is getting ugly."

The smallest woman started to cry.

"God," the oldest female protestor said. "I feel like I'm in *Deliverance*. The banjos are going to start anytime now."

Floyd bent down so he could see her face. "Miss, did you think you'd be met with open arms? Like I said before, you're taking food from the mouths of these guys' children and now one of them has been killed. His kids no longer have a father."

"But, you have to look at the bigger picture," the woman replied. "We need to save these resources!"

The group of loggers started moving toward the cars. Floyd thumped his fist on top of Pam's car. "Go! Now!"

As Pam pulled away, the loggers rolled the Volvo into the ditch. It came to rest on its top.

"Hey! They can't do that!" one of the women protested. "We're exercising our right to free speech!"

Pam threaded her squad through the trucks, cars, and news vans. "Could you please shut up for a while? I'm trying to make sure you make it to the jail alive." The young women looked stunned as a second car was pushed into the ditch and the loggers moved toward the other car.

CHAPTER 5

CHANHASSEN, MINNESOTA
SATURDAY

Barb Skog's trip to the Minnesota Historical Society in St. Paul yielded a gold mine of information. She'd located her father's records and those of his three siblings, providing her with a history of their arrival at the State School in Owatonna and their eventual placement. She knew her father had been adopted later, but the school records had given her additional insight into the Lane family's four children and their original placement in the orphanage/school by their father. Edward Lane had listed hardship as his reason for giving up his children. Barb had frozen when she'd read that. "How bad was your life that you had to put your children in an orphanage?" she'd asked herself.

She'd examined each child's records, discovering a health history and a record of each eventual departure from the school, through adoption or adult release. After making copies of those records, she'd raced home and logged onto the Ancestry.com genealogical website and the family tree she'd created. Barb Skog filled in the birthdates of the four siblings, creating a profile for each of them. When they were loaded, little leaves started popping up above the names, indicating that additional information about that person existed in the database, just as shown on the Ancestry.com television ads. She clicked her computer cursor on the leaves as the genealogy website offered possible matching records for her relatives. In a few hours she'd filled in some of the gaps in her father's biological family and learned where they'd gone. One sister had moved to a farm in North Dakota and the other had been indentured in Pine City, Minnesota. A brother had joined the Marine Corps.

She clicked on a leaf and looked at a new record that appeared under the name of her aunt, Margaret Lane. She clicked on the 1940 census records and waited in anticipation for the page to load.

The large file filled her computer screen and there, in handwriting, were the records of the residents of an unfamiliar address in Pine City, Minnesota. Most of the names meant nothing to her, but her eyes lit up when she saw the highlighted name she's been searching for: Margaret Lane, 22 years old. Parents born in Minnesota. Occupation listed as maid. There were eleven other female residents at the address, with occupations listed as cook, maid, domestic help, waitress, and dishwasher, followed by eighteen other names whose occupation was listed as "Patient."

"Bingo! I finally found you, Aunt Margaret!" Was this the Tuxedo Inn mentioned in your placement record?"

Barb saved the census file to Margaret Lane's online genealogical profile. She pondered an address where women were living together as domestic help with patients. "Hmm. Were you working at a small hospital?"

Barb typed the words "Pine City Minnesota Tuxedo Inn." Google offered her several possible matches. She opened the URL for the Tuxedo Inn. A picture of a two-story structure with several cars in a parking lot topped the page, followed by:

"Once noted as the finest nightclub in central Minnesota, the Tuxedo Inn was a restaurant overlooking Lake Pokegama, in Pine City. The name derived from the requirement that Gentlemen arrive in tuxedos and Ladies wear long gowns.

Connected to both Duluth and the Twin Cities by at least three rail lines, the Tuxedo Inn became a getaway location for people both famous and infamous, and openly served liquor throughout Prohibition. The clientele were reputed to have included Minnesota governors and rail barons, as well as gangsters. It was rumored that gentlemen without dates were able to obtain female companionship on the premises."

She typed in the address from the 1940 census, expecting to find it listed as the Tuxedo Inn, but instead saw the listing as the Pokegama Sanatorium. A second Google search brought up a story about the sanatorium with period pictures of women looking at the entrance sign and more modern pictures of a building in ruins.

She went to a *Pine City Pioneer* newspaper archive and entered Margaret's name, with little expectation of a meaningful connection. Dozens of Margaret Lanes showed up, all over the United States, and the articles spanned decades. She narrowed the search to the 1940s and Minnesota and waited. Several Margaret Lanes were mentioned, but an article in the March 19, 1943, edition of the *Pine City Pioneer* jumped out at her.

Due to the falling number of tuberculosis patients, the privately owned Pokegama Sanatorium had been sold. The remaining eighteen patients would be moved to other locations, with many moving to the Nopeming State Hospital near Duluth.

Following the statement, the names of the remaining occupants, patients and staff, were listed. Margaret Lane was the fifth name on the list. Barb returned to the Pokegama Sanatorium search and found a history of Pine County including the Pokegama Sanatorium's opening as a private tuberculosis treatment facility in 1905. The 35-acre site provided housing for 36 patients and had its own farm. It was purchased by the Redemptorist Fathers for use as a seminary in 1943.

Barb printed the page and returned to the genealogy search, looking for a 1950 census record for Margaret Lane. She was disappointed that the 1950 census wouldn't be released until April 1, 2022. She searched for the Nopeming State Hospital, but couldn't find a mention of Margaret Lane. She tried Minnesota marriage and death records. There were lots of suggestions, but none that matched Margaret's birthdate and the geography. Barb moved to a website specializing in headstone records, but found nothing. Social Security death records didn't help. She hit another dead end in searches of military and municipal records. Phone books never listed her name. She wasn't listed as a mother in anyone's birth records. A search of Pine County obituaries elicited no results. Margaret Lane seemed to cease to exist after 1943.

She knew that during World War II the country was in flux. Had she married a soldier and moved out of state? Was she destitute, so was buried in an unmarked pauper's grave? So many questions thought Barb.

"Wait!" Barb said as she re-read the historical information about the sanatorium. "It was a private institution, so someone had to be paying for Margaret to be there. In 1940 she was working as a maid and wouldn't have accumulated enough funds to pay for a private hospital. She was an orphan without a family to pay for her to be a patient there. Or, could she have been a maid at the sanatorium too?

Barb re-read the Tuxedo Inn information and she froze when she read the last line. "It was rumored that gentlemen without dates were able to obtain female companionship on the premises."

Barb leaned back from her computer desk and stared at the screen, trying to think of another avenue to search. She looked at her father's picture hanging on the wall above her computer. He was handsome in his WWII Army uniform and she felt heartsick. His last request at the hospice had been that she use her computer skills to find his siblings. Her father, the youngest of four siblings, had been adopted from the State School by a farm family in Fairmont. He'd grown up on the Skog farm and joined the Army near the end of the war. He'd returned to Owatonna where he married his high school sweetheart, Clara. Barb was their only child. He'd farmed until he was in his sixties and died of emphysema when he was eighty-eight, one year after Clara.

She clicked on the leaf over Karl Lane's name. She knew that Karl "graduated" from the State School in 1941 and immediately volunteered for the Marine Corps. The leaf led her to a military cemetery site. Karl died on Iwo Jima.

Through Ancestry links she discovered that her Aunt Esther had married a North Dakota farmer, Franz Henkel, who was twenty-five years her senior. The records were sketchy, but it appeared that Esther died after suffering a farming injury.

Barb closed her eyes and took a deep breath. She pulled up the picture she'd downloaded from the State School records. Margaret was the oldest, but she appeared smaller than her two brothers, who were two and seven years younger. Her sister was barely past being a toddler in the State School picture. Margaret looked like the runt of the litter. She was cute and petite, even as a 12-year-old.

"Aunt Margaret, where are you?"

A chill came over Barb and she glanced at the grandfather clock in the corner. She'd lost track of time, as she often did when delving into genealogy. The clock would chime midnight in a few minutes. She looked at the picture of Margaret again and tried to enlarge it, but got a pixilated image that revealed nothing.

"An orphan, taken from a State School and sent to a Pine City inn with a shady reputation. You'd probably been exposed to heaven-knows-what diseases, including tuberculosis." Barb stared at Margaret's picture again and shook her head and sighed. "An aunt indentured at a brothel is just what everyone hopes to find in their family tree," she said to the computer.

The clock started to chime and Barb closed down the computer. She looked at the grainy picture and asked, "What happened to you after the sanatorium closed, Aunt Margaret?"

CHAPTER 6

PINE COUNTY COURTHOUSE, SUNDAY

After getting a cup of coffee, Floyd walked to his desk and rubbed his shoulder. He could feel the bandage where the wood splinter had punctured him. "I'm getting too old for this stuff," he said to himself.

From several feet away he could see his desk was strewn with dozens of pink message slips. He hoped it was a cruel joke, but when he picked up the first one he knew it wasn't going to be a top-ten day. He stared at the message to call the county attorney and thought about walking out the door and filling out the retirement papers that had been on top of his dresser for two years. Maybe it was time to make the call to find out if he could live comfortably on his pension.

Shaking off that thought temporarily, he leafed through the other slips as he sipped coffee. Near the bottom of the stack, one of the first slips deposited there, was the simple message, "See me." It was followed by the sheriff's scrawled signature.

"Maybe a really, really bad day," he said to himself as he set down the coffee cup and steeled himself for whatever hell the sheriff had stirred up.

The hallway outside the sheriff's office had the slightest hint of cigar smoke, making Floyd wonder if it was residual from the sheriff's clothing or if the office had better exhaust fans than the rest of the courthouse. Floyd knocked on the doorframe and walked in.

"Close the door," the sheriff said.

"What's up?" Floyd asked as he sat in the wooden guest chair across from John Sepanen, the Pine County sheriff.

Sepanen, a burly dark-haired man with a gravelly voice from decades of cigars, was the ultimate politician, crafting his department strategies carefully to ensure garnering at least 51% of the votes in each election. He reveled in the limelight and publicly supported his deputies without reservation. Privately, he made it clear to each of the sergeants and senior officers that their job was to enforce the law *and* get him re-elected. The order of those directives changed from time to time.

"You look like hell," the sheriff said as he stripped the cellophane wrapper off a cigar.

"You're no spring chicken either, John."

"Look at your uniform," the sheriff said with a smile.

"Crap," Floyd said, surveying the smudges on his pants and arms. "Mary's car had a flat tire when I left for work. She was running late, so I changed it and didn't think to look in a mirror."

"Mary's sleeping over now?"

"Yeah, well." Floyd searched for words, staring at his knees like an embarrassed teenager. "It didn't seem to make much sense to always be driving back and forth between our places."

"Easy, Floyd. I wasn't making a judgment. I was just asking," he said as he pulled a lighter from his top desk drawer and lit the cigar. When he put the lighter away he brought out a crystal ashtray. "You're adults and you've both been through enough of life's hard knocks that you deserve some happiness."

"I appreciate that," Floyd said as he watched the cigar smoke rise and thought once again about mentioning the state law forbidding smoking in public buildings, but reconsidered once again. Especially since the sheriff was being a nice guy at the moment.

"Did you see the news last night?" Sepanen asked.

"We went out for supper and I was too tired to turn on the television when we got home. How did they cover the logging protest and murder?"

"They were amazingly evenhanded," the sheriff said, batting at the smoke to disperse it. "But even with the talking heads making supportive sounds, the cameras caught the medical examiner's truck leaving and the loggers flipping over the protesters' cars."

"If one of my deputies had just been killed by a bunch of idiots, I might've been tempted to go further than flipping over a few cars," Floyd said.

"Yeah," the sheriff sighed. "But they're innocent until proven guilty. I've got a press conference at ten o'clock and I'm planning to say that we're reviewing the video of the incident with an eye to prosecuting the lawbreakers."

"We're going to arrest loggers?" Floyd asked.

"We're going to analyze the tapes. By the time we get through that, and turn the information over to Tom Bakken, the furor should've cooled off and we might get the county attorney to plea bargain down to some minimal fines and let the guys walk."

"How about the protesters?"

"Judge Meyer is overseeing bail hearings this morning. I tried to convince Tom to ask for no bail until we get through the tapes and finish processing the crime scene. As we speak, there are a dozen federal agents combing the woods around the explosion. They've got dogs and metal detectors out there and I hope they find something." The sheriff stubbed out his cigar and returned the ashtray to the drawer. "Somebody should hang for this and I'd really like to see those tree-huggers get what they deserve."

Floyd was about to stand when the door flew open and the county attorney stalked in.

"You won't believe this!" Bakken ranted. "I got a call from a Washington D.C. law firm telling me to delay the bond hearing until their man gets here tomorrow. They put him on a private plane and he's flying into Minneapolis as we speak. I asked who he was representing, and was told he is representing all the protesters. When I asked who was paying, they said that was a matter of client-attorney privilege."

"Who called him?" Floyd asked.

"I checked the phone logs in the jail. None of the kids called a lawyer. All but one called friends or their parents. The last one called the Forest Conservancy, whatever the hell that is."

"Tom, you look unhappy," the sheriff said.

"Unhappy! I'm past unhappy," Tom said. "I'm about ready to chuck this two-bit job and go back to real estate and wills." He threw his head back and stared at the ceiling. "This is insane. My office doesn't have the resources to fight a Washington law firm. Hell, we hardly have the budget to prosecute the DUIs!"

"Didn't you ever see the movie *My Cousin Vinny?*" Floyd asked.

"That was fiction! We're talking about a big-time lawyer flying in here on a private jet, with investigators and expert witnesses. He can bury us in motions and delays until I throw in the towel out of frustration."

"You've got one huge advantage," the sheriff said, trying to lower the tension. "The big-time lawyer doesn't know Pine County and he'll be unprepared to deal with a local jury."

"This will never get to a jury. He'll drain my budget and I'll drop all the charges to stop the financial hemorrhaging."

"Don't throw in the towel before the opening bell rings," Sepanen said. "Let Floyd and Pam Ryan dig into this a little."

The sheriff turned to Floyd. "Pull Pam off whatever she's doing and see what you can learn about the Forest Conservancy in the next hour or two." The sheriff thought for a moment, then added, "And re-examine all the numbers the defendants called last night. See just who we're dealing with."

"Are you okay, Tom?" Floyd asked.

"Just peachy," the lawyer said as he turned and walked out the door.

Floyd stood and put a finger into the air, ready to say something. "Pam and I aren't going to be able to chase down all the contacts these kids made. And if we do, we won't know the significance of the names we uncover. We'll be running an investigation by Braille."

Jodi Houck, the dispatcher, stuck her head in the door. "Is the county attorney gone?"

"Yes. You can probably reach him in his office," Floyd replied.

"I don't need him. I wanted to make sure I wasn't interrupting. A Barb Skog is on hold for you, sheriff."

"Take a message," Sepanen replied. "We're up to our butts in alligators."

"I think you need to talk with her. The caller ID says DEA."

"Now what?" the sheriff asked rhetorically. He lifted the phone and selected the blinking line. Floyd started to leave but was waved back to the chair. Sepanen switched on the speakerphone.

"This is Sheriff Sepanen. How can I help you?"

"First of all, I apologize. I'm sure your caller ID says DEA and your dispatcher probably tripped over herself running to your office. My name is Barb Skog and I need some Pine County detective work."

"If you saw the news last night, you know things are rather . . . chaotic right now. Are your needs urgent, or can we get a brief overview and get back to you when things settle a bit?"

"I may be able to scratch your back while you scratch mine." Skog paused. The rustling of papers could he heard. "I have a list of the protesters you arrested. Because I have some leverage in the DEA—I'm the deputy director of the Minneapolis office—I ran background checks on your detainees. The man who identified himself as Jeremy Pyle is actually Jeremy Pike, which is why you probably didn't get any hits on the NCIC search you ran last night," she said, referring to the FBI's National Crime Information Center database.

"Jeremy is a known eco-terrorist with arrests in five states but no convictions except one federal arrest and conviction in Oregon for vandalizing a Bureau of Land Management research facility. He completed one year of his sentence in a Utah federal prison, and is currently out of contact with his parole officer, which will put him back into prison for another three years once we get him in front of a federal magistrate."

"Hang on," the sheriff said, grabbing a notepad and pen. "Please repeat that. Sergeant Swenson is with me and I'd like him to get up to speed."

"The person you know as Jeremy Pyle is actually Jeremy Pike, who is in violation of his federal probation. I can have a federal marshal pick him up within two hours if I have your permission."

"Hell yes!" the sheriff replied.

"Done," Skog said. "I just sent an e-mail request to the U.S. Marshal and marked it priority." She paused, then went on, "Jeremy has been in possession of controlled substances every time he's been arrested. I can send you that documentation. You should be able to get a search warrant for his motel room. If you've got a baggie of meth or coke with fingerprints, you've got a whole different case than if you're just pressing trespassing charges until you get information from BATF on the blast materials," referring to the Bureau of Alcohol, Tobacco, and Firearms.

"They've pitched tents in a small campground," Floyd said. "I don't think the courts would have a problem with evidence we found behind a zipper."

"Give me the campground address. I'll assign a DEA team to do a search."

"We're able to handle that, Director," said Floyd. "There's no need for you to send agents."

Floyd scribbled a note and passed it to the sheriff. "We don't really want any more feds in the middle of this, do we?"

"Actually, Sergeant," said Skog, "I was hoping to recruit you for a special project. I've read up on your cold cases and I'm very impressed with your results. Solving the mystery of the lost camper who was found in the trunk of a car was brilliant!"

"Flattery will get you everywhere," Floyd said, chuckling, but with a sudden feeling of dread.

"I've got a cold case of my own and I've hit a dead end in Pine County. My father's family was put into the Owatonna State School in the 1930s and they were split up. I've found all his siblings except for a sister. She left the school and became an indentured domestic worker at a place called the Tuxedo Inn, but she disappeared from public records in 1943. The last documentation I can find indicates she might have been a patient or worked at the Pokegama Sanatorium. Her name was on the roster when the hospital closed."

Floyd gave the sheriff a pleading look, emphatically shaking his head. "No!" he mouthed.

"I hate to be negative," the sheriff said, smiling, "but our mission is to protect and serve the residents of Pine County, not to solve genealogical mysteries."

"Sheriff Sepanen," Skog said softly. "I've tapped out every genealogical research option I've got and they're all dead ends. I was hoping that someone like Sergeant Swenson, with local knowledge and contacts, might be able to dredge up something I can't even imagine."

"Director, I don't have a large department. All my day-shift deputies have been dealing with these eco-idiots, and yesterday we had a murder. I'm sorry, but I can't justify sending Floyd on a seventy-year-old cold case that may be nothing more than some records that didn't get entered into a database."

"Hang on for one second, Sheriff." Music started playing over the phone.

Sepanen pushed the mute button on the phone and rubbed his hand over his face. "I hate to burn this bridge, but neither of us wants you doing genealogy for the DEA."

"It's beyond a cold case," Floyd replied. "We're talking iceberg cold with wind-chill. I don't think there's any chance that I'll be able to 'dredge up' something after seventy years. And, to what end? There's probably a simple reason her aunt disappeared and it might have nothing criminal involved. Hell, she could've eloped and been married by some Wisconsin justice-of-the-peace who never filed the paperwork."

"Sheriff Sepanen, are you still there?" Skog's voice sounded clear and confident.

The sheriff punched the mute button and leaned close to the phone. "I'm still here. As a matter of fact, Floyd and I have been talking and . . ."

"Hold that thought for a second, if you will," Skog said, interrupting. "I just spoke with my lead agent, who's on the elevator to Judge Aspen's quarters with a request for a search warrant covering the protesters' tents, vehicles, and personal property. The scope will be cellphones, phone records, drugs, drug paraphernalia, firearms, explosives, timers, and remote detonators. We'll seize the cellphones to check the call history and to determine if any of them may have been used to remotely trigger the bomb." She paused. "I have a message in to my counterpart at Alcohol, Tobacco, and Firearms. His assistant said they already have a team in Pine County and we'll work with them on the explosion investigation and the eco-terrorists. Is there anything else I can possibly do to supplement your department in this investigation?"

Sepanen leaned back and took a deep breath. He looked at Floyd, who was staring at the floor and shaking his head. "There's one more thing. The county attorney was notified that some big-shot lawyer from Washington D.C. is coming to represent the eco-idiots. He's apoplectic about the prospect of using his meager resources to take on a large law firm."

"I'll call the Assistant U.S. Attorney. At the risk of stepping on your toes, I can turn this into a federal case. We have explosives, drugs, and probably some interstate phone coordination of the assault. I see that one of the three women is from Oregon, and she's only a teenager. Hell, we might even be able to go after one of more of the guys for taking a minor across state lines for sexual purposes. That never gets prosecuted anymore unless there's prostitution involved, but it's one more thing on the table for a plea bargain." The DEA director paused, then asked. "Is there anything else I can do to ease the strain on Pine County resources?"

Floyd stared at the phone looking defeated. He shrugged and shook his head.

"I'm comfortable turning this case over to the feds as long as we don't get cut out."

"Sheriff, get your best white shirt pressed and polish your gold badge. I promise that you'll be in the front row of every press conference, and you'll have the chance to brag about the great cooperation between our agencies and how bringing the full force of the DEA and ATF helped move the investigation faster than you could have managed with your limited resources."

The sheriff broke into a smile. His name recognition would jump 100% and he'd be a shoe-in for re-election. "Director, we have a deal."

"I'd like Sergeant Swenson's cellphone number," Skog said. "I'd like to keep the cold case investigation out of the limelight, if possible."

"This is Sergeant Swenson," Floyd said, leaning close to the phone. "First of all, call me Floyd. Can you send me a list of the items you've identified in your investigation? I'll look through them. I might be able to find some old-timers who can fill in some of the blanks about the Tuxedo Inn and the Pokegama Sanatorium. Beyond that, I'll just have to follow my nose."

"Perfect! I'll scan the documents I've got and put them into an e-mail."

After reciting his phone number and e-mail address, they hung up. Floyd said, "You know this is going to be a fiasco if anyone hears I'm chasing down genealogy while we step back from the murder investigation."

The sheriff picked up a pen and started tapping it on the desktop while he stared into the distance. "I need a credible reason to have you off for a while." The sheriff tapped the pen some more. "Did you get treated for your shoulder injury at the blast?"

"I went to the clinic. They shot me up with Novocain, pulled out a few splinters and gave me a tetanus shot."

The sheriff smiled broadly. "You're on mandatory medical leave for a week."

"But, I'm not . . ."

"You've received skilled medical care, including two injections. You're out of here for a week. Make an appointment with Doc Bergstrom for Friday and have him give you a 'Return to work' slip."

"He'd give me a release today if I asked," Floyd protested.

"Make the appointment for Friday." Getting no further argument, the sheriff said, "I'm sure you understand the conversation with the DEA is confidential and will not be shared. Now get out of here while I call the county attorney to tell him the feds are taking over the case and he won't have to deal with the big shot from Washington."

CHAPTER 7

PINE CITY, 1934

Pixie clutched the boxes of new clothes tightly to her chest as the Ford sedan bumped along the washboard gravel road out of Pine City. The downtown quickly gave way to fields of amber oats and hay stubble. They met a buckboard stacked with burlap sacks being pulled by a pair of draft horses. The car passed over a rickety bridge and followed a narrow road that provided occasional glimpses of the river. Abigail Corbett rode in the front seat and chatted casually with the driver as Pixie took in the new landscape from the back seat.

The black sedan turned toward the river and followed a narrow driveway through the underbrush, which gave way to an open lot overlooking Lake Pokegama. Huge willows leaned over the water beyond the white two-story building that dominated the lot. Above the entrance door was a simple sign that said, "Tuxedo Inn." Surrounding the building were gravel parking spots defined by railroad ties set back a few feet from the building. A wooden door opened as Pixie got out of the car and a young woman, almost as pretty as Miss Corbett, stepped out and watched with her arms crossed.

Pixie saw Miss Corbett cup something in her hand and slip it to their driver as she pecked him on the cheek. He pocketed what he'd been given, doffed his bowler hat, and bowed. Miss Corbett was obviously a powerful woman, Pixie thought. The only powerful women she had seen were mean, angry women who exacted power through physical means. Miss Corbett smiled and had people bowing and running to do her bidding. What was this woman's power? Was it her beauty? Pixie wondered.

As the car left, more people spilled out of the building and stood on the steps, looking at Pixie with curiosity. They were all young women, some as old as Miss Corbett, who might've been thirty, but it was hard to tell with her makeup. The older women wore their hair up in buns, and each wore lipstick and rouge. Their dresses were each unique, but attractive. Two of the women's dresses had low-cut necklines that Pixie thought exposed an inappropriate amount of bare skin. Three of the girls, who looked as young as

Pixie, were dressed in black dresses worn over high-necked, long-sleeved white blouses, making them look like they were in uniform. It was the same outfit that Pixie was soon to unpack.

Miss Corbett carried one box and Pixie's suitcase. Pixie clutched the other boxes of new clothing. One of the girls broke from the crowd and rushed to help Pixie. Before the first box was out of Pixie's hands the rest of the uniformed girls spilled from the inn and swamped Pixie with girlish chatter and excitement.

Pixie's first reaction was to recoil from the mob. At school, no one rushed unless they were under threat of punishment, and there was never idle chatter. Pixie had learned to speak only when spoken to. These girls were out of control. She tried to grab back the precious packages as the girls took them from her arms. "No!" she shouted.

Miss Corbett rushed to the group and put her hand on Pixie's arm. "It's okay, Pixie, the girls are just happy to see you. They'll help you carry your packages inside." She turned to the tallest girl and said, "Florence, please take Pixie upstairs and show her to her bunk."

Florence reached out and took Pixie's hand and led her toward the front door. "Our room is in the attic," she explained. We each have a bunk and a closet rod to hang clothes. There's a drawer under your bunk to keep your bloomers and personal things." They pressed past the older women on the steps, who stood back politely and smiled, but didn't seem as openly welcoming.

"She's awfully young," one of the women said. "I wonder if she's even reached her teens yet."

"Pixie is sixteen," Miss Corbett said.

"You'd better keep her out of sight when Charles comes around," another said. "He likes his girls young."

"Are you afraid of the competition?" Corbett asked.

The woman shook her head. "I just don't want to see her get hurt. She's just a kid."

CHAPTER 8

PINE COUNTY SHERIFF'S DEPARTMENT
MONDAY

Floyd poured another cup of coffee and returned to his desk in the bullpen. He entered his password and sat back, waiting for his e-mail to load. At the end of the usual housekeeping e-mails was an unusual return address. He almost deleted is as spam, then recognized it as Barb Skog's personal e-mail account.

The e-mail had multiple attachments and it took several minutes for them to download and print. While he waited he read the text.

> "Floyd, please accept my personal thanks. I hope this doesn't put you into a bind, but I know you're good, and I'm at wits' end. Please feel free to call my personal cellphone number when you find anything. Barb"

Floyd leaned back and stared at the computer. Barb. No federal agent ever offered their first name. She was letting her guard down, meaning this was way off the books. The printer stopped and Floyd retrieved the pages. The 1940 census record was amazing. Floyd looked at the handwriting and tried to envision someone walking to every door in the United States and writing down the line-by-line information about address, birthplace, parents' birthplace, language spoken at home, and occupation. There, in the middle of two pages was Margaret Lane's name with no parents or siblings listed. A kid all alone and thrown into the cruel world with no family, he thought. The file from the State School was thin, with little more than information about her arrival at the school, a picture of her as a child, and a note about her indenture at the Tuxedo Inn.

The following pages were internet sites with information about the Tuxedo Inn and the Pokegama Sanatorium.

He was sliding the pages into a file folder when Pam Ryan walked in and sat in his guest chair. "What's up?"

"Have you ever heard of the Pokegama Sanatorium?" he asked.

"I overheard someone mention it once, but I've got no idea what they were talking about."

"The building remnants are still standing out by the lake," he said, "and there's a nearby dump site that's a favorite spot for necking teens. I've driven

through the dump occasionally and found people digging for old glass prescription bottles."

"Oh yeah, I was through there once when I spotted
a car parked down an overgrown road. An old guy told
me the bottles he'd found were a hot item in antique
shops."

"Um, I heard there was a coffee pot up here," Bruce
Swanson, the jailer, interrupted. He looked Pam up
and down, then smiled when their eyes met.

Floyd pointed to the carafe sitting on the warmer.
"Help yourself."

Bruce shuffled to the counter and found a stack of
Styrofoam cups in a cabinet. Pam and Floyd watched
him pour. "Sorry," he said, realizing the conversation
had stopped. "I didn't mean to interrupt."

"No problem," replied Floyd.

"That was some mess out at the state forest," Bruce
said, stirring sugar into his cup.

"You've got the prime suspects locked up downstairs," Floyd said.

"Yeah. I hope that's the end of it. Looks like the
loggers are going ahead with the cut." Bruce stood
awkwardly for a few seconds, waiting for the conversation to go on. When it didn't he said, "Well, thanks for
the coffee." He smiled at Pam then walked away.

"He gives me the creeps," Pam said when the jailer
was out of earshot. "Every time I run into him he
gives me a look like he's mentally undressing me, then

he hangs out waiting for me to start a conversation. I really don't want to chat with him." Pam shivered. Changing the topic, she asked, "Why the sudden interest in the sanatorium?"

"It depends," Floyd replied.

"It depends on what?'

"Whether I'm talking to Deputy Ryan or my friend Pam."

"Why would that matter?" she asked, her eyes narrowing.

"Deputy Ryan," he said, tucking the file under his arm and standing, "I'm on medical leave while I recuperate from the injuries suffered in the explosion yesterday." He reached over his shoulder and touched the spot with the bandage.

"Okay," Pam said, putting her hand on Floyd's arm. "I'm asking as your friend. What's up?"

Floyd nodded toward the exit and Pam followed him to the parking lot. The afternoon sun was shining and one of the last days of Indian summer, the pleasant days after the first hard frost, was blanketing the region with warm dry air. Floyd leaned against the fender of his cruiser.

"Not a word to anyone. Agreed?"

"Sure," Pam nodded.

"I've been assigned a confidential cold case investigation. No one but the sheriff knows."

Pam asked, "Why is the investigation confidential?"

"A woman living in Pine County in 1943 disappeared from the face of the earth. Someone very influential would like to know what happened to her."

"But we've got a murder investigation . . ."

Floyd put his hand up as a black Ford Taurus rolled to a stop beside them. Two somber men stepped out, their U.S. Marshal badges hanging from chains around their necks.

The driver nodded to Floyd and Pam. "We're here to pick up a federal fugitive. Where's the county jail entrance?"

"Go in the pedestrian door on the lower level. The dispatcher will buzz you in."

"When did we arrest a federal fugitive?" Pam asked, watching the two marshals walk away.

"It seems our protest leader is a federal parolee. He's been out of contact with his parole officer so he's going back to Utah to face a federal magistrate and will probably finish the remainder of his sentence in a federal prison."

"I thought his record came back clean."

"Turns out," Floyd said, "that he gave us a bogus name. He's a well-known eco-protester with a long rap sheet.

"Doesn't he need an extradition hearing to be taken to another state?"

"Apparently not when you're a federal fugitive. It trumps all the state-line jurisdictions."

"But he's our lead suspect in the murder investigation."

"He'll be safely locked away in a federal prison and at our beck and call. Better yet, there won't be a bail hearing for him where a lawyer might find a compelling argument that he's no longer a threat to society."

"I suppose that's a good way to get him jailed, but it seems a little anticlimactic."

"When did you start wearing lipstick" Floyd asked with a frown. "Or am I not supposed to notice?"

"You shouldn't notice. But as long as we're sharing secrets," Pam paused to let some courthouse employees pass, "I heard that the Cohen brothers are going to set their new movie in Pine County."

"Seriously?" Floyd asked.

"No. I just decided to look a little less like a tomboy."

"You feel like a tomboy?"

"I was okay being a solitary tomboy, but having company at supper is nice."

"Are you dating someone I know?"

"Probably not, but I'm not ready to 'out' us just yet." Pam looked off at the I-35 traffic passing by the courthouse. "He's a nice guy, never married, no criminal record, and he has a steady job."

"I hope it works out," Floyd replied. "When the time is right, let me know. I'm sure Mary would love to have you over for dinner."

"Since you seem to be the man with all the answers, what else is going on that I don't know about?" Pam asked.

"The DEA is on their way with a federal warrant to search the campground for drugs, guns, and explosives. There will be an army of ATF agents checking into the motels in the next few days, and there will be a person from the Department of Justice here shortly to talk with the Washington D.C. lawyer who has been hired to represent the protesters. I'll be off on this cold case."

"I'm missing something," Pam said. "When did the feds decide to pour resources into our investigation? Is it because the lead protester is a known felon?"

"My lips are sealed, other than to say they were very appreciative of my interest in pursuing this cold case." Floyd waited, then added. "Now, my friend, you know too much and you can't tell anyone what I just said."

"But. . ."

"Let me know when you can come over for supper," Floyd said, climbing into his car.

CHAPTER 9

THE TUXEDO INN
1934

Three girls led Pixie up two sets of creaking wooden stairs to an attic that had been remodeled into a small bedroom. Florence set Pixie's boxes on a narrow mattress near an open dormer window that let in a mild breeze.

"This bed is yours. Is your name really Pixie?" Florence asked.

"My name is Margaret, but everyone calls me Pixie," she answered quietly.

Pixie looked around the dimly lit room that was crammed with four beds, four wooden chairs, a small desk, some shelves, and two wardrobes with colorful fabric strung across their openings. It was cozier than the dormitory she'd lived in at the State

School, but it was cramped and she felt claustrophobic. She looked at the other three beds, each made up neatly with white sheets and cream-colored wool blankets.

The smallest girl, six inches taller than Pixie, took sheets from a cupboard and set them on the bare mattress. Her hair was blonde and tied back in a ponytail. Setting the clothing boxes on a chair and spreading the sheets over the mattress, she said, "You know I'm Florence. That's Mary, with the mousy brown hair," nodding toward another of the girls.

"My hair is chestnut!" Mary said, "Calling it mousy brown is insulting."

"That's Carol," Florence said, pointing, "she's the thinker." The mid-sized girl smiled but said nothing.

"Where are you from?" Mary asked as Florence finished tucking the sheets with hospital corners.

"I was in the State School," Pixie said, looking at the clothing boxes and unsure what to do with them. "I graduated from the eighth grade and turned sixteen, so I had to leave."

Florence, who was carrying a blanket, stopped. "You're sixteen?"

Pixie nodded. "Today is my birthday."

The three girls looked at each other in disbelief. "You can't be sixteen," Florence said, spreading the blanket atop the sheets and smoothing it. "You look like you're twelve."

Pixie shrugged. "I guess I'm just little." She set her two boxes on top of the blanket and untied the string. "How old are you three?"

"I'm eighteen," said Florence. "Carol and Mary are nineteen."

Mary pulled open one of the wardrobes. "You can share my closet if you want to hang up your clothes."

Pixie carefully unfolded the black dress and put it on a hanger. The next box held two white blouses with high necks and lacy ruffles. From other boxes she unpacked a white dress with bright printed flowers, a pair of shoes, anklets, and a white sweater, the first sweater she'd ever owned.

"Mary is from Duluth," Florence went on. "Her family is big and they didn't have much food, so they found her this job that includes this room and meals. Carol is from Sartell. Her parents were killed in a train derailment and Miss Abigail took her in. I'm from Bruno. My father was . . . um." Florence stopped and stared out the window, then said, "Miss Abigail took me away after my aunt called her."

"Where are your parents?" Carol asked Pixie softly.

"My family had a farm by Hastings. My mother died and then my father married another woman. She wanted to have her own family, so I was sent to the State School with my brothers and sister when I was 10."

"That stinks," said Florence. "You didn't do anything wrong. Your father just didn't want you anymore."

Pixie shrugged, like it was not a big deal. The State School was all she'd known. "It was okay," she said. "Lots of the kids came from worse situations." She untied and opened the last box. Under the tissue paper was underwear. She'd worn bloomers before, but the box held silky shirts to wear under her blouse and a slip. As she fingered the fine fabric she became aware that the room was silent. The girls were staring at her. Not sure what was wrong, she blushed, pushed the underwear back into the box, and closed the lid.

"What is my job?" Pixie asked, shoving the box under her bed.

"You don't know?" Carol asked. "Why would you come here not knowing?"

"You'll do the same as the rest of us," said Florence, pushing her way past Carol. "In the morning we change linens and bring water up to the second floor rooms. In the afternoon we set tables and clean the first floor."

"And in the evenings?" Pixie asked.

"We're neither seen nor heard," Mary offered. "The customers start coming in for dinner about six and we're supposed to be up here. Mostly, they want us to be invisible, like elves."

"What are elves?" Pixie asked.

"An elf is supposed to be Santa's helper at the North Pole," Mary said. Seeing no recognition in Pixie's eyes, she added, "The legend is that a man called Santa has a workshop at the North Pole where he and his help-ers, called elves, build toys for children. The elves help Santa load them on his sleigh on Christmas Eve, then Santa flies all over the world delivering toys to chil-dren who are well-behaved."

"The Santa story is a fairy tale," Mary explained. "There are no real elves. The work gets done magi-cally. That's what Miss Corbett wants here. She wants us to keep things clean and orderly, while making it look like the work is done magically."

"So when we're hiding up here, what do we do?" Pixie asked.

"We sometimes read books or we play cards," Mary explained.

"Cards?"

"Really?" Florence asked. "You don't know what cards are?"

Pixie shook her head.

Footsteps on the stairs scattered the girls and when the door opened, each was sitting on her own bed. "It's time to set tables," Miss Corbett said. "Florence, show Pixie how to dress. When you're downstairs, all three of you can show Pixie around and have her help you."

The door closed and the girls scrambled. Mary pulled out Pixie's blouse and skirt, while Florence set the rest of the boxes on shelves. Pixie stripped off her old dress and stood naked next to her bed, her immodesty shocking the other three.

"You can change in the closet," Mary said, staring at Pixie. Part of their shock was that Pixie was unconcerned that she was standing naked in front of three strangers; another part was that Pixie was skin and bones, with her ribs pressing against her skin. The third shock was the array of bruises and welts that covered her arms and legs.

"Who beat you?" Mary whispered, reaching out and touching a blue bruise on Pixie's upper arm, causing her to recoil in pain. Pixie snatched the blouse off the bed and quickly pulled it on, fumbling with the many tiny buttons.

"The people at the school had to keep us in line, so sometimes they'd smack us with a yardstick."

"What kind of things were out of line?" Florence asked, as Pixie stepped into her dress.

"I don't know," Pixie said with a shrug, buttoning the skirt. "Sometimes we were walking too slow or sometimes too fast. If you talked without raising your hand, they'd smack you. If you did something really bad, you got the switch."

"What's the switch?" Mary asked as she led the group to the stairs.

"They'd cut a willow switch and they'd whip your behind with it until you said you'd behave. Most people said they'd behave before they ever got the switch, but most times they didn't sound sincere enough so they got the switch anyway."

"Did that hurt a lot?"

"I think the boys got the switch harder than the girls. Sometimes the boys would stand in class for a few days after they got the switch because they couldn't sit down."

Carol, Mary, and Florence looked at each other like they'd never had the switch.

"We've got to work," said Florence, who led them downstairs.

Carol grabbed Pixie's hand and led her downstairs, then pulled her to a sideboard on the farthest side of the dining room. She pulled open a drawer and removed crisply starched linen tablecloths from the top drawer and stacked them on Pixie's arms.

"This is the easy part," Carol whispered. "We spread a tablecloth on each table, then we get a flower vase and put a flower on each table."

"What's the hard part?" Pixie whispered as they spread and smoothed the first tablecloth.

"The dishes," Carol replied. "They're heavy and if you break one, they deduct if from your credits." Pixie had no idea what a credit was, but decided to ask later.

Pixie helped with the tablecloths while sneaking looks around the dining room. On the side opposite the entry door a long wooden counter ran the full width of the room. It was lined with wooden stools. Behind the counter was an elegant mirror that reflected the whole room. Bottles and drink glasses lined the glass shelves in front of the mirror. A middle-aged man, bald and with a significant paunch, stood behind the counter polishing glasses with a white towel. When he caught Pixie staring, he winked at her.

"Who's that?" Pixie asked, as they gathered cut-glass vases from the sideboard and slipped a cut flower into each vase.

"That's Hank, the bartender. He's nice and in the morning he sometimes lets us taste wine if there's some left over from dinner."

"What's Hank do?"

Carol stopped and stared at Pixie. "That's the bar, where they serve liquor," she explained. "The customers sometimes sit on the stools and Hank serves them liquor or beer. Most of the time the waitresses take orders from the people sitting at the table and Hank fixes their cocktails."

"How many people work here?" Pixie asked, following Carol around the dining room. Florence and Mary were setting out sterling silver place settings and carefully folding linen napkins.

Carol shrugged. "There's Hank, and Willy, who's the cook. Willy's got a couple of women and young men from town who help until the guests arrive, and there's Mrs. Marty, the baker, and Greta, who washes dishes."

"Who were the women standing on the steps when I got here?"

"They're the waitresses and hostesses. They stay in the rooms on the second floor until the customers start to arrive."

"I don't know what a hostess is," Pixie said.

"They dress nice and take people to their tables. If the waitresses are busy, sometimes they serve wine and drinks." Carol looked around, then whispered in Pixie's ear, "and, sometimes, if a customer didn't bring a date, the hostess will take him up to her room and we can hear them laughing through the floorboards."

Seeing the confusion on Pixie's face she whispered, "They have sex. That's why we have to change the bed linens every day and bring fresh water for their wash basins."

Pixie's head swam. What was sex, she wondered. What did that have to do with changing bedding and washbasins? She hoped she would catch on, but this was a strange place, she thought.

CHAPTER 10

THE PINE COUNTY
HISTORICAL SOCIETY
MONDAY

Pondering potential genealogical sources, Floyd drove to the historical society located downtown in the old Courthouse. He parked past Nicoll's café, walked across the street, and climbed the sandstone steps to the first floor. The historical society was halfway down the hall.

As soon as he walked through the door he heard, "Floyd Swenson! I don't believe I've ever seen you in here before." Edna Purdy, easily ninety years old, was a dynamo, slowed only by the walker she pushed toward him across the museum floor. She'd taught high school history for forty years and knew the names of at least half the people in Pine City and the surrounding area.

"Miss Purdy, how are you today?"

Edna pushed her walker close and grabbed Floyd's upper arm. "You need to put some meat on your bones. I heard Mary Jungers is feeding you and she's a fine cook. You'd better start eating seconds when she fixes you a meal."

"Where did you hear that Mary Jungers was cooking for me?" Floyd asked, amazed that she not only remembered his name, but knew about his relationship with Mary.

"I don't reveal my sources. If I flip my confidential informants, my grapevine would dry up. Besides, no one is anything but happy for both of you. You both waited a respectable mourning period, you're both consenting adults, and it's nobody's business what goes on behind closed doors."

"I suppose if you know about Mary, the whole county knows we're sharing meals."

Edna smiled. "It's not just meals you're sharing, Floyd. Why don't you set aside the pretense and move in together?"

"What?" Floyd asked, the conversation suddenly uncomfortable.

"Quit pretending you're not shacking up and move to one house," Edna said. "Think economics. Why pay taxes and utilities on two places when you're only living in one?"

Floyd's stomach clenched. "I wasn't looking for a life coach when I came in," Floyd said. He suddenly felt like a teenager, being badgered again by his old high school teacher.

"The advice is free," Edna said, flipping her hand and shuffling toward the information counter. "Beware, free advice is usually worth what you pay for it."

"I wanted to pick your brain on some historical information," Floyd said, hoping to totally change the conversation.

Edna backed herself up to a chair and sat, briefly catching her breath. She started the canned speech she gave to visitors. "Pine County was named for the endless stands of white pines that the first settlers found when they arrived. The logging started almost immediately and Pine City was built because of its location on the Snake River. The logs, some five feet in diameter, were rafted on Lake Pokegama while waiting to be cut into lumber.

"The Great Hinckley Fire took place on September 1st, 1894. The conflagration consumed over two hundred thousand acres, and there were four hundred eighteen confirmed casualties, although it's assumed that some of the bodies were never recovered. The towns of Brook Park, Mission, Pokegama, and Hinckley were consumed, with only the brick walls of a few structures to mark their location. The fire came as far south as Pokegama, but Pine City was spared, probably due to the prevailing winds and the firebreak provided by the river and Lake Pokegama.

"A Canadian train engineer, named William Bennett Best, was at the controls of the lead train engine blocking the only track out of Hinckley. Despite the approaching fire and the threats from the other engineers on the trains blocked behind him, he refused to leave the station until the wooden train cars were smoldering and on the verge of breaking into flames. He's credited with saving over five hundred lives. Although it was among the most heroic deeds of the era, the Canadian Government refused to acknowledge his heroism because he saved Americans."

She paused to take a breath and Floyd jumped in. "That's a great refresher, but I need some different history," Floyd said. The lumber and Hinckley fire information were scripted and probably hard-wired into her brain. He hoped her memory extended beyond those facts.

"Well, if I can still remember it, you're welcome to it," Edna replied.

"Back in the 1930s there was a fancy nightclub near Pine City."

"That would be the Tuxedo Inn," Edna said, jumping in ahead of the question. "It was known to be quite a place in its day. They served booze all the way through Prohibition. There were all kinds of rumors about which city and county officials were paid to look the other way, and no respectable man or woman would admit they'd been there."

Floyd smiled. "You're amazing."

"I know. There's no point in being humble at my age. What's your question?"

"I have an acquaintance who traced one of her relatives from the Owatonna State School to the Tuxedo Inn, in 1934. From there, she shows up at the Pokegama Sanitarium, but she disappeared from all records when the sanitarium closed in 1943."

"Firstly, it was a sanatorium, not a sanitarium. A sanitarium is a facility where people are treated for mental health issues. A sanatorium is a hospital-like facility where people with infectious diseases, like TB, were quarantined while being treated, or isolated until they died. Secondly, the Pokegama Sanatorium didn't close. It was converted to a seminary by some Catholic sect," Purdy corrected.

"Thanks for the clarification. I assume the missing woman moved when the seminary took over. I need to find some way to track her down. Perhaps there's something only someone in Pine County would know about her."

"Did you talk to the family who used to run the sanatorium?" Edna asked.

"It's been closed for seventy years. Whoever owned it is dead and gone."

Edna gave him another dismissive wave. "I know that! But his kids or grandkids might have the records sitting in an old steamer trunk somewhere. Another thing to check is the cemetery. Some cemeteries were diligent with their recordkeeping and others less so. If I remember correctly, the Lutheran cemetery had a scandal back in the '60s when their custodian took off with the trust money and destroyed all the records. You might have to walk through the cemetery to look for a headstone." Edna thought for a second. "Actually, you might start there."

"Do you have any other suggestions, Miss Purdy?"

Edna's toe started tapping the leg of her walker and she stared at the floor. There was a deep sadness in her eyes when she looked back at Floyd. "I hate to be negative, but there are a couple aspects of this story I find disturbing.

"Firstly, the women employed at the Tuxedo Inn were local pariahs. Even if they weren't ladies-of-the-evening, everyone in town assumed they were. Your acquaintance's relative had a tough life and lived among some tough people.

"Secondly, she might've caught tuberculosis from someone at the nightclub. There are all kinds of ways to catch TB, most often from someone coughing on you. I'm not a medical expert, but I'd assume you could catch TB and all kinds of other nasty diseases working in that place. When TB patients were diagnosed early, they went to a sanatorium to rest and soak up fresh air. Many recuperated and went back to their lives. The more advanced cases were sent to other state-run sanatoriums to protect the public and to die. In the early 1940s there was no streptomycin, which was the first antibiotic that was really effective at treating TB. The sulfa drugs of that day were the only treatment for infections, and they weren't effective at treating TB. They had all kinds of issues with purity, dosage, effectiveness, and length of treatment. I'd give you 50:50 odds that the person you're looking for died of TB and is buried in an unmarked pauper's grave."

Floyd drew a deep breath and blew it out, puffing his cheeks, overwhelmed by the information coming from this old woman with such an incredible memory. "Wild goose chase is the phrase that comes to mind," he said.

"Genealogy is challenging and rewarding," Purdy said. "I spent years, starting with my mother's family Bible, and later requesting birth, marriage, and death certificates from counties all over the U.S. It's much easier now with the Church of Latter Day Saints reading rooms and the internet. Almost all of the U.S. records are now online and the databases are searchable. The only problem I've stumbled across is the computerization of the handwritten records. There are lots of spelling issues and I've found Purdy spelled wrong and transcribed into the databases incorrectly.

"The people at Ellis Island did the genealogists no favors. If there was a boatload of Swedes, and the Ellis Island people thought there were too many Johnsons, the immigrants were told to pick a new last name. Sometimes that was recorded as a change and other times it wasn't. Lots of the immigrants were illiterate, and the people at Ellis Island had only slightly better capabilities. I met a man whose name was Wellumsum. I'd bet a Social Security check that he's English and his family name was Williamson. I suppose his illiterate forefather mumbled the name when he arrived and the transcriptionist put down the phonetic spelling." Purdy paused. "It happened a lot."

"And you waded through all that?" Floyd asked. "Where did you find the patience?"

"Genealogy is a mystery awaiting a solution," Purdy said with a smile. "It's addictive, and when you start making connections, it's euphoric. I stumbled across a Purdy family history in the Minnesota Historical Society Library and I was able to fill in seven generations of my father's family in one afternoon. I had to call everyone I knew to tell them the exciting news. Have you researched your family, Floyd?"

"My father eked out a living on a rocky farm near Sturgeon Lake. His parents were from Sweden. My mother's family name was Fjeldheim, and they spoke Norwegian at home. I don't have much interest in pursuing the family history further than that. I don't have any children, so there's no legacy to pass on to them. Besides, my job provides enough mystery without spending my off-hours reading about dead relatives."

"Suit yourself," Purdy said, "but you might be pleasantly, or unpleasantly, surprised. I've found some heroes in my family tree, a few skeletons, and a few black sheep. It's all interesting."

"I want to find one person in Pine County who might remember the inn. Who would you suggest?"

Purdy drew a deep breath and let it out slowly through pursed lips. "I suppose there's no harm in sharing this anymore, especially since you're a cop and will hold information in confidence." She paused awaiting acknowledgement. When Floyd nodded she went on. "Tilly Crown used to be Tilly Westberg. She worked at the Tuxedo Inn, unbeknownst to anyone in Pine City. She mysteriously blew into town one day and was married to Fred Crown within the week. Everyone thought she was a mail-order bride, but she and I talked a little about the old days and she let it slip that she'd been an assistant cook at the inn. Fred used to ferry groceries and supplies there. They struck up a friendship and when Tilly paid off her indenture, she was free to leave."

CHAPTER 11

PINE COUNTY COURTHOUSE
MONDAY, OCTOBER 4

Pam was writing a summary report from the notes she'd taken at the protest. Her lapel-mounted radio came to life, and at the same time she could hear the dispatcher's voice through the office area.

"Any unit near the courthouse, please respond."

"I'm in the bullpen," Pam yelled, walking toward the dispatcher's cubicle. She was joined by Dan Williams, the undersheriff, and Kevin Parr, one of the lieutenants. As they arrived, Sandy Maki radioed his position, near Sandstone, 40 miles away.

The dispatcher spun in her chair, her face flushed. "The county attorney just dialed 911 from his office and hung up."

Pam bolted for the stairs with the two men close behind. When she opened the door to the first floor she could hear shouting. She stopped just outside Tom Bakken's office door with her hand on her Glock and spun around the corner. Williams and Parr stopped behind her, ready to follow her lead. She stepped into a heated argument between the county attorney and a large man dressed in an expensive dark suit and a red tie.

"Get him back!" the stranger yelled. "My office called and told you I was representing him. You are legally obligated to hold my client until I arrive."

Tom Bakken leaned to the side to look at Pam and the two other deputies. "Please remove this man from my office," he said.

The man spun around and glared at Pam. "If you lay a hand on me, I'll sue you for everything you own and your first-born child."

"Meet Mr. Rosen," Bakken said. "He's from Washington D.C. and he apparently thinks that the world is at his command. Get his butt out of here."

"Who are these bozos?" Rosen asked with a sneer. "They look like the rural version of the Keystone Kops."

Pam stepped forward and put out her arm, gesturing toward the door. "You may exit this way."

Rosen's eyes narrowed and he glared at her. "Get your lapdogs out of here," he said to Bakken over his shoulder. "Barnette Fife and her merry band of hicks have no horse in this race. This is between you and me, you arrogant, incompetent ass."

"Leave now, or I'll remove you," Pam said, slipping a can of Mace from the holder on her belt.

Rosen, close to six-four and probably weighing three hundred pounds, sized up Pam and the two men. "You three would be lucky to remove a whimpering puppy."

Pam removed her handcuffs with her other hand. "Turn away from me and put your hands on your head. You're under arrest."

"Fuck you, blondie." Rosen grabbed a briefcase from Bakken's guest chair and stepped toward the door.

"Sir," Dan Williams said, "a licensed law enforcement officer just placed you under arrest. Unless you want to end up face down on the floor in handcuffs, I suggest that you set down your case and comply with her commands."

Rosen spun and faced the county attorney. "The fun is over. Get these hicks out of here and let me explain what you're going to do next."

"What I'm going to do next is watch Deputy Ryan put you in handcuffs and book you into the jail for assault."

Pam sensed the presence of someone entering the room, but kept her eyes locked on Rosen, assuming Williams and Parr had her back.

"Are you the legendary Ira Rosen?" a female voice asked.

"Who are you?" Rosen asked, turning to the woman. "Are you the dogcatcher? We seem to have every other minor official in this hick county here."

The tall slender woman in a tan woolen suit stepped past Pam and handed a business card to Rosen. "I'm Jane Simmons, Assistant U.S. Attorney."

Rosen studied the card briefly and looked past Pam. "Finally, we have someone with actual power. Tell these rednecks to bring my client back for his bail hearing."

Simmons smiled. "I directed the U.S. Marshals to remove a federal felon from the county jail. He was in violation of the terms of his parole. He's been returned to Utah to complete the balance of his prison sentence or until we put him on trial here."

"The hell you have," Rosen said, fingering the business card before slipping it into his shirt pocket. "My office notified the county attorney that I was representing the protesters and they were obligated, by law, to hold them without further questioning, until I arrived."

"Who is your client, Mr. Rosen?" Simmons asked.

Rosen took out his cellphone and punched buttons. "Susan. Jeremy. Clarke."

"What's Jeremy's last name?" asked Simmons.

"Pyle. Jeremy Pyle."

Simmons leaned around Rosen so she could address the county attorney. "Is there a prisoner named Jeremy Pyle in the county jail?"

"Not to the best of my knowledge," Bakken replied, trying not to smile. "We had a prisoner, who gave us an alias. During our attempts to ID him, Ms. Simmons called to tell me they had a fingerprint match for a wanted felon. We were never told his name. The U.S. Marshals removed him several hours ago."

"What kind of stunt are you pulling?" he asked. "This is bullshit and you've crossed a line. I want my client returned immediately."

"I think you have a fictional client, Rosen," Simmons said. "The man you told the county attorney you are representing doesn't exist. You were lied to by whomever hired you." Simmons paused. "Who did hire you?"

"That's a matter of attorney-client privilege."

"The other clients you were hired to represent are in the jail downstairs," Bakken said, evenly. "If you agree to behave, I will ask Deputy Ryan to escort you to the interview room. If you prefer to be belligerent and uncooperative, the deputy will arrest you and then you'll have hours to talk with your clients in a shared cell. Which will it be?"

"This is not the end," Rosen said, picking up his briefcase.

"I think it might be," Dan Williams said. He called up the video he'd just taken on his cellphone. "I just recorded your rant and attached it to an email to Ms. Simmons. You may want to share it with a magistrate, Ms. Simmons. I suspect the judge might ask for Mr. Rosen to be replaced when they see it."

"Take me to my clients," Rosen said, displaying greater control. He pushed past the deputies and the U.S. Attorney.

Dan Williams stepped forward and directed him down the hall. They waited silently for the elevator, the lawyer thumbing through the screens on his cellphone. When the elevator arrived, Dan stepped in and punched the button for the first floor. Rosen stepped in without looking up from his phone.

"Your clients—" Dan said as the elevator doors closed.

"My clients are innocent until proven guilty."

"Patience isn't your long suit, is it?" Dan asked.

"I don't suffer idiots well. I offer no apologies." Rosen stabbed at his phone several times, then looked around at the elevator walls. "This place is so far into the boonies I can't even get 4G on my phone. How do you guys communicate with the outside world? Pony Express?"

The elevator doors opened and Dan stepped out, directing Rosen to a small window next to a door without an outside knob. "Push the button and identify yourself to the jailer. He'll put you into an interview room and deliver your clients."

Rosen pushed the button and a minute later a weathered male face appeared at the window. "How can I help you?" Bruce Swanson, the head jailer, asked.

"I'm Ira Rosen, here to meet with my clients."

"Who are your clients?" Swanson pulled out a clipboard and put a nicotine-stained finger on the top of the page listing the last names of the current prisoners.

Rosen stabbed at the phone again, then lowered it, obviously frustrated. "I can't get in touch with my office in this cellphone desert. My clients are the protesters who were arrested yesterday."

"I'm sorry, Mr. Rosen," said the jailer. "The rules say I can't admit you unless you tell me who you want to see."

"Didn't you hear me? I said I don't have their names!"

Swanson smiled. "Our procedure bars the admission of anyone who can't provide the name of their client." Swanson paused, then added, "Who am I to say that you're not a reporter or even an accomplice?"

Rosen pulled a business card out of a pocket and pushed it into a slot under the window.

"Business cards are cheap," said Swanson, holding the card at arm-length to read it without his glasses. "I need to see a picture ID, like a driver's license, and the name and birthdate of your client."

"Hang on a second," Dan said, walking away, leaving Rosen arguing with the jailer, who was reveling in his power. Pam watched in amusement from the furthest corner of the small room.

Dan returned a few minutes later carrying a piece of paper. "Here's your client list."

Rosen snatched the paper from Dan's hand and read the first name and birthdate to Swanson. He pulled a wallet from his suit jacket and removed a driver's license that he slipped through a small slot under the window. Within seconds, a solenoid clicked, signaling the release of the door lock. Swanson held the door open for Rosen. Dan hung back until Rosen passed.

"A word of caution, Rosen," Dan said, "Bruce has PTSD. Don't piss him off. He might snap."

The jailer smiled and twitched theatrically a couple times.

"God save me from these hicks," mumbled Rosen as the door closed behind him.

"Bruce seemed a little too happy to stick it to Rosen," Pam said as they left the room.

"He's always been a little edgy, but lately I think Bruce is a little over the top," said Dan.

"I've only been here for a couple years, but I have to admit he makes me uncomfortable," Pam said as they walked into the bullpen. "Were you serious about the PTSD?"

"I remember Bruce before he went to Viet Nam. He was a quiet kid, but as normal as any of us. He was a different person when he returned. As I recall, he crawled into a bottle for a while and I think he got some help from the VA before he was ready to resume his life."

"Maybe he's off his meds," Pam said as she poured coffee, "because he's a bit creepy."

"I'll mention it to the sheriff. Bruce must be close to the mandatory retirement age."

"Why would he continue working if he's eligible to retire?" Pam asked.

"You saw him. He's the big fish in his little pond," said Dan. "Away from here, he's just another old guy. He's never married and I don't think he has any hobbies. I think this job is his entire world."

CHAPTER 12

STATE FOREST ENTRANCE
MONDAY

The Nemadji State Forest entrance was strung with crime scene tape and the county road leading to the gate was lined with dark-colored sedans and Suburbans, all bristling with antennae. Beyond the tape an army of people in black windbreakers were milling around. Most said BATF; others had US MARSHAL, BCA, or HOMELAND SECURITY in large yellow letters across their backs. Most of the people seemed to be grid-walking the area west of the crushed pickup, walking shoulder-to-shoulder through the thigh-high grass. A few small red flags dotted the field and an evidence team, in dark blue coveralls, was huddled around one of the flags. Another evidence team was climbing around the pickup, and a third team was examining the shattered tree. Dan Williams, the Pine County under-sheriff, was talking with the team examining the truck that had been crushed by the tree.

As she pulled up to the scene, Pam said, "Holy shit, I've never seen this many cops from this many agencies."

Pam also saw a newer Cadillac with two people inside parked near the gate. As she walked down the road she could see that the license plates were from the Fond du Lac Chippewa Nation. She knocked on the window and it rolled down with a hum.

"Can I help you?" she asked.

The weathered face of a woman stared back at her. Although her skin was deeply creased from years of sun exposure, there was a youthful look to her face, and very few gray hairs were interspersed in her long, black hair. Pam estimated that the woman could've been eighty, or maybe sixty. Top end estimation would be closer to ninety, but Pam really couldn't tell. A handsome Native man, around twenty, sat in the passenger's seat and smiled at Pam.

"You're kind of puny to be a cop," the woman said, eyeing Pam up and down.

"It's okay. I carry this big old gun," Pam said, patting the butt of her Glock, then feeling stupid for the flippant answer.

The woman's sad eyes didn't soften. "Honey, you're in Pine County. Most everyone carries a big old gun."

"Can I help you?" Pam asked again.

"Not really. We're just here to see what's happening with our timber."

"This is a state forest, ma'am," Pam replied. "I'm afraid this isn't your timber."

"I'm Mary Marcineaux," said the woman. "I'm the president of the Mille Lacs Chippewa band. Get a copy of the 1837 White Pine treaty, read it, and then tell me this isn't tribal timber."

"You'll have to take that up with the Minnesota Department of Forestry."

Marcineaux shook her head. "It's a matter for the federal courts. They've been pretty good about seeing the treaties from our standpoint lately."

The window hummed closed, leaving Pam standing in the road feeling like she'd just lost a debate. The engine started and the Caddy pulled away as a tow truck came over the hill. A slender middle-aged woman broke away from the team examining the truck and nodded to Pam as she jogged to the tow truck. Her jacket said DEA. She waved to the trucker, who climbed out of the cab. Pam walked over to join them.

"We want all three of these cars taken to a secure impound lot," the DEA agent explained.

The truck driver looked at the protesters' cars, including a Taurus and a Volvo tipped onto their sides, along the north side of the road. "I'll start with the

Taurus and work my way down the line. It's going to take me a couple hours to haul them down to Pine City."

"Do whatever it takes," the woman replied.

As the truck driver climbed into the cab, the woman turned to Pam and put out her hand.

"I'm Barb Skog." She had a firm handshake.

"Pam Ryan. It's amazing to see the number of people working this crime scene," Pam said, gesturing toward the scene.

"I was lucky to catch some help from Homeland Security. Once they heard there might have been a terrorist attack, they were climbing over each other trying to get their people on the road. I think they've had a team staged at the Mall of America and the sports arenas around the Twin Cities for years, thinking those would be the likely targets of opportunity in Minnesota. The director thought I was crazy when I said we'd had a logger killed in a terrorist attack in Pine County." Skog pointed to the team huddled around the red flag. "I think I've been vindicated now that they've found a detonator."

Pam looked at the team, then back at Skog, who was wearing bluejeans and a plaid blouse under her dark windbreaker. Her badge, with the word Director etched across the top, was hanging from a lanyard around her neck. "You're the deputy director of the Minneapolis DEA office?"

"Yes."

"But . . ."

"They let me out from behind the desk on occasion," Skog said with a smile.

Pam saw the crow's feet at the corners of Skog's eyes when she smiled, and guessed that she was about sixty years old. They stood and watched the methodical work going on across the crime scene.

"Were you here when the bomb went off?" Skog asked.

"I was next to the protesters," Pam replied, pointing to the entrance. "They'd handcuffed themselves together over there."

"From the size of the debris field, it must've been quite a blast. One of the ATF guys said the bomb was way too big to just bring down the tree. He suggested that the bomber was either an amateur or someone intent on injuring a lot of people."

"They found the timer?" Pam asked.

"It wasn't a timer," Skog said, shaking her head. "It was remotely detonated. ATF thinks it was triggered by an electronic device used by someone nearby who knew when the logging trucks were rolling past."

"There was a news team taking video of the protest when the bomb went off. We got the card out of the camera, so there might be a picture of the person who triggered the detonator."

"I have a Minneapolis team examining that recording at this moment," Skog said.

The whine of the tow truck winch distracted them, and they watched as the Taurus rolled upright, then slowly slid up the tow truck's ramp. Skog's cellphone chimed and she stepped away, talking in hushed tones.

A few minutes later she returned. "My team at the campground could use some help," Skog said, slipping the phone into the back pocket of her jeans. "They've got a warrant to search the protesters' tents and personal belongings, but I guess the campground is full and the natives are restless. Could you give them a hand keeping the crowd back while they search?"

Pam looked at her watch and did a calculation. "Sure. I can be there in about twenty minutes, if they can hold out that long."

Skog laughed. "I only sent three investigators and it appears there's some kind of Rainbow World convention there. They said the whole place reeks of marijuana smoke and half the campers are naked."

Pam nodded. "They like to come here after the freeze so the mosquitoes don't eat them alive. That's the derivation of the phrase, 'Busier than a nudist in a Minnesota swamp.' There's a lot of body surface to defend from the little buggers when you're naked."

"That paints a picture," Skog said, smiling.

"It's not pretty to watch," Pam replied. "Most of the Rainbow People are gray-haired hippies and, well, let's say the view isn't like watching people work out on Venice Beach."

"Oh dear," Skog said, laughing.

Pam looked at her watch again. "I'd better run to the campground before your agents pluck their eyes out."

Pam drove past the park owner's house as she entered the park. The mom and pop owners were sitting on their porch, rocking, and taking in the spectacle. They waved to Pam as she passed.

The scene at the campground was comical. Three agents with "DEA" printed on their jackets were standing in the center of a campsite surrounded by crime scene tape. The DEA logo made them unwelcome among the twenty people milling outside the tape yelling insults. The hecklers were a ragged bunch, ranging from the naked Rainbow People to a few people in motorcycle jackets with their club affiliation emblazoned on embroidered patches. Other campers were sitting around small fires.

"Okay, folks, the show's over," Pam announced as she stepped out of her cruiser. A slight tinge of marijuana smoke hung in the air mixed with the wood smoke from a dozen campfires. Northern Minnesota was enjoying a warm front, with the temperature in the 70s, after a late September hard frost. The locals took vacation days, drove around looking at the turning leaves, golfed, fished, or rode their ATVs on the miles of trails, calling it the last hurrah before snow season. Pickups with boat, motorcycle, or ATV trailers were parked at every campsite.

One of the male feds gave Pam a pleading look. A second rolled his eyes. The lone female agent was studying her shoes, deliberately avoiding the nude male hippies pressing against the yellow crime scene tape in front of her. She glanced at Pam, then turned her gaze to the campers further away. A group of ATVs roared down the driveway and stopped alongside a camper trailer. They removed their helmets and watched with amusement.

Pam approached a large biker on the fringe of the crowd. "Get out of here and leave the feds alone." She'd dealt with the same man at a bar fight a few weeks earlier and she'd learned he was an accountant from the Twin Cities. He liked to hang around with the bikers, but she knew he was unwilling to put his job at risk with an arrest.

"Aw, man," the big guy said. "We never get to play with feds."

"You're Clarence, right?" Pam asked him. His gray hair was covered in a red bandana and his considerable girth was contained by greasy jeans and a leather jacket that looked like it might've zipped when he'd been forty pounds lighter. A bleached blonde woman, wearing a halter top and short shorts, glided to his side. "Go back to your campsites," Pam said in a commanding voice. "The show is over."

Clarence took a deep breath and turned his girlfriend away from the feds. The three bikers followed behind, grumbling and looking over their shoulders, before joining a larger group of leather-clad people hunkered around a smoldering campfire. The group took up several campsites with an RV, tents, and an assortment of pickups, motorcycles and ATVs. A few hushed words were exchanged and two of the leather-clad bikers strapped on backpacks, got on their ATVs, and roared away in a cloud of dust.

The Rainbow People were less inclined to disperse. A hirsute man stepped forward in his naked glory. The look on his face said he knew Pam would back down when confronted with his nudity.

"We were here first," the man said, putting his hands on his hips, effectively displaying his pubic hair and its neighbors.

Pam fixed her eyes on his forehead and reached to her belt. She removed an asp and snapped it, extending the spring-loaded nightstick tipped with a metal weight. She tapped it on her shoe and took a step toward the man.

"Return to your campsite or you'll be curled in the dirt clutching your bruised nuts."

The man's eyes grew wide and he flinched slightly, then turned sideways. "Violence is never the solution to a problem," he said angrily. Then he stepped away, apparently going to a distant campsite where a large group of nudists were sitting around a campfire passing a home-rolled cigarette, or maybe a joint. The rest of the naked people followed, but not until the female fed looked up in time for one of the men to wink at her. She rolled her eyes and quickly changed her focus to Pam, who retracted the asp and put it back on her belt.

"I'm Agent Spelling," the older male agent said, offering his hand to Pam. "These are Agents Prince and Allen." The other agents also shook Pam's hand.

Allen, the female agent, shook her head, "That was ugly on so many levels." She wore khaki slacks and a black t-shirt under her black DEA jacket. Her badge was hanging from a lanyard around her neck. The two men were in jeans and button-down shirts. All were young and fit.

"I recognized the red-headed guy from the undercover sting we did in Bloomington last year," Allen said. "Luckily, he didn't seem to recognize me in a DEA jacket with short brown hair."

"I'm surprised you recognized him," Spelling said. "Did he flash you during the bust?"

Special Agent Prince was drinking from a water bottle and choked as he tried to stifle a laugh.

"He has a snake tattoo on his neck," Allen replied, rolling her eyes again.

Spelling got close and whispered, "Did you see that exchange between the bikers? I wonder if the two that left took their stash with them in case we decided to search their campsite too?"

"Maybe they have outstanding warrants," Pam said.

"Or maybe just guilty consciences," said Agent Price.

The ATV riders hunkered around their campfire were not making eye contact with the agents. The largest guy took a drag on what appeared to be a marijuana joint and then flicked the roach into the campfire while the agents watched.

"I'll bet the last of their contraband just went into the fire," said Snelling. "They're not stupid kids. I'll bet they've all been busted and now know all the tricks to stay out of our reach."

"Have you been in the standoff since you got here, or have you been able to search?" Pam asked.

Prince hefted a backpack. "We've got pills, weed, white powder that smells like meth, maybe some Ecstasy, and a Ruger Redhawk revolver that was rolled up in a sleeping bag. We've got a hundred pictures documenting the location of all the contraband."

"Really?" Pam asked. "The protesters left all that in the campground when they drove away?"

"Trusting, naïve, or stupid," Allen said, setting the bag on the ground.

"You arrested three men and three women?" Spelling asked.

"Right. They'd chained the state forest entrance shut and cuffed themselves together."

"It looks like two of the girls were sharing a tent," Spelling said. "We didn't find any contraband in their gear. Two of the guys were also sharing a tent, and the third tent had the couple. The guys' tent had a baggie of grass and some cigarette papers. The coed tent had the gun and the drug assortment."

"Do you have any idea who was paired up?" Allen asked Pam.

"It wasn't obvious at the protest," Pam replied. "If I had to guess, I'd say the leader was probably with one of the women, but I couldn't' tell which one was his tent-mate."

"We'll bag up their gear," Spelling said, "then we'll send the drugs for analysis. There appear to be fingerprints on the containers and that should link the suspects to each drug container and the gun. The quantities make it look like the drugs might've been for distribution. We didn't find any cash here, but I imagine they'd have that locked in a car somewhere rather than leaving it in the campground."

"I would've said the same thing about the pistol," Pam replied. "That's not a cheap piece and it's as good as cash in a private sale or pawn shop."

Agent Allen walked close to Pam so none of the nearby campers could hear her. "We'll turn the pistol over to ATF. I suspect these guys aren't the original owners and it may be stolen. They'll be able to track the wholesale buyer in an hour or two."

news. Jeremy figured a day of local coverage, then he thought at least one of the networks would pick up the feed from a local affiliate and we'd bug out. I don't know where the whole bomb-in-a-tree thing came from, but it wasn't us."

"The yokels should have a bail hearing today. I'm sure they don't have anything to link you with anything but the peaceful protest, so I should be able to argue for your immediate release, or at worst, a small cash bond. Either way, I can write them a check or wire the bond money to them and you should be on a plane before dinner."

"I'll need to take a shower and put on some clean clothes. They left us chained and there wasn't a bathroom . . ."

Rosen made notes. "What size pants and shirt do you wear? I saw a Walmart one exit back."

"Walmart? Are you serious?"

"Hey, I'm only the messenger," Rosen said, holding up his hand. "This is rural Minnesota. There isn't a Brooks Brothers or Nordstrom's on every corner here."

"What a fucking nightmare."

"Just to be clear," Rosen said. "You guys had nothing to do with the explosion. Right?"

"We had absolutely nothing to do with the explosion."

"Is there anything else that I need to know about?"

Parrish pushed the granola wrapper away and leaned back. "You probably want to dash out to our campground. We scored some marijuana from the Rainbow People and it's stashed in a tent. Other than that, we're clean."

"Where's the campground?" Rosen asked.

"In some town named after a tree. Oak something or Elm something. I remember thinking the name should be Nightmare on Elm Street because the place is such a shithole. Jeremy liked it because it was busy with all those Rainbow People who were running around naked and smoking pot. He felt we would blend in there, even if we were wearing clothes. Then we saw these old bikers and it felt even stranger. Add to that a communal shower and rustic toilets with spiders and you've got every childhood nightmare."

Rosen picked up his cellphone and punched in a search. "Does the Willow River Campground sound familiar?"

"I guess. If you find a bunch of wrinkly-skinned old hippies running around naked, you've got the right spot." Mike shook his head. "There should be a law about public nudity once you're past thirty unless you work out twenty hours a week in the gym."

"I have to bail the others out at the same time or it's going to raise red flags." Rosen said.

"Whatever. Just get me out of here."

"Is there anything else I can do for you before the bail hearing?" Rosen asked, flipping the pages of his legal pad."

"I'm done with this shit," Parrish said. "It's someone else's turn to save the forests, whales, and other animals. This was scary and stupid."

"I'm sure your uncle will be pleased to hear that," Rosen replied. He rose from his chair and knocked on the window. "Hang in there," he said as the female jailer took Parrish's elbow and led him away.

Rosen packed his legal pad, recorder, and pen into his briefcase and left the Fiji water bottle and granola wrapper on the table. The jailer was back within a minute with the teenaged girl.

"Here's your last client," the jailer said.

"I've got all I need," Rosen replied to the jailer. "I'll have you bailed out in a few hours," he said to the girl barely looking at her as he pushed past them and walked quickly down the hallway.

⟩⟨ ⟩⟨

In the sheriff's department offices, down the hall from the jail, Pam was transcribing her written notes into the computer. The sheriff walked into the bullpen area with another man and poured two cups of coffee before leading the guest to Pam.

"Deputy Ryan," the sheriff said, "meet Special Agent Randall Ash, from BATF. He's got a lead and needs our assistance." With that intro, the sheriff walked away.

"What's up?" Pam asked the tall, well-dressed black man as he sat down in the steel guest chair.

"We analyzed the blast residue and have a lead on the dynamite supplier."

Pam picked up a pen and slid her notebook from a pocket. "You got dynamite residue? I mean, it wasn't all consumed in the explosion?"

Ash shook his head. "An explosion is a chaotic event that propagates from the ignition source across the explosive. Some trace amounts are always blown clear of the explosion without ignition. So, we analyze for taggants that the explosive makers put in each batch. These taggant materials are a mixture of rare chemicals, and the specific chemicals and ratios of those chemicals are as unique as a fingerprint. We take the analysis back to the manufacturer and they tell us who bought a particular lot of material. We can then follow the lot to the end buyer."

Ash handed Pam a printed sheet. "At the top is the analysis, followed by the name of the manufacturer, then the distributor. It appears that the only local buyer of that 1998 lot of dynamite was Pop's Pond Excavations."

"Pop is Billy Davidson, a local character," Pam replied. "He's like eighty years old and spends most of his time in Peggy Sue's Café, in Willow River, drinking coffee and telling lies with his cronies. He owns

Pop's Pond Excavations, but I think he only does it as a hobby to supplement his Social Security."

Pam closed down the computer and put on her jacket. "C'mon. We're going to Peggy Sue's for coffee."

The muddy pickup with Pop's Pond Excavations logo painted on its doors was parked in front of Peggy Sue's Café amidst a half dozen other pickups and beaten-up old cars. Pop's truck was rusting along the rocker panels and wheel wells. The windshield had multiple spider webs of cracks.

A group of octogenarians sat around a table by the far wall of the café, each with a coffee cup. In the center of the table was a dinner plate with the residue from shared cinnamon rolls. The loudest of the group was a gray-bearded man wearing a tan flannel shirt over faded jeans that looked like the owner had a habit of wiping his dirty hands on his thighs. When the bell over the door rang, the whole group turned to see who had entered. A quizzical titter ran among them. Pam smiled because they were all hard of hearing and they had all asked, "Who's the black guy?" loud enough to be heard across the room.

Pam recognized most of the men and nodded to them as she got closer. "Pop, this is Special Agent Ash, from the Bureau of Alcohol, Tobacco and Firearms."

Ash stepped forward and shook Pop's hand, noting the liver spots and the bruises on his arms. "Could we talk in private for a minute?"

A smile spread across Pop's face as he turned and pulled a chair over from a nearby table. "C'mon and sit, sonny. Whatever we talk about will be the talk of the town within an hour and these guys might as well hear the real version of it before my embellished story gets around."

Ash was uncomfortable with the response but took a seat after he saw Pam get her own chair from an adjoining table. She sat down across from Ash as the old men leaned close so they could hear. One man put a fingertip to his ear to turn up his hearing aid volume.

"There was an explosion at the state forest gate Friday," Ash said.

Before he could go on, one of the men said, "We heard those hippies killed Larry Odegaard. Hoppy said the explosion was just to cover up the gunshot."

Ash closed his eyes and silently counted to three before putting forth his best professional smile. "I really can't comment on an investigation."

"You don't need to," another man said. "We got the details from the hardware store."

"How would the hardware store have such great information?" Ash asked.

"Well, Grant, he's the hardware store owner, his nephew was one of the first responders. The nephew,

Willy, told his mom about the explosion and the gun-shot guy in the big logging truck. I guess it was pretty well destroyed. They took all the protestors to the Twin Cities to keep them from getting lynched."

A third man leaned forward. "We know the protesters were really deep cover Al Qaeda operatives, and this was just a prelude to an attack on the Prairie Island nuclear power plant. That would've put half of southern Minnesota in the dark and probably started a war with Pakistan, where those guys were trained."

Ash was almost ready to respond when Pam interrupted. "All the protesters looked pretty much Caucasian to me. I don't think they were affiliated with a Middle Eastern terrorist group."

"That's why they can slip in and do so much damage," the first man whispered. "After they escaped from Guantanamo Bay, they had facelifts in Miami so they'd fit in better."

Ash went from confused to amazed, then to amused. "How many of these terrorists were there?" he asked.

"Well, we heard there was seven of them at the protest . . ."

"Naw, I saw at least nine of them on the news," the final man interjected. "But, that's just the tip of the iceberg. I heard the whole Willow River Campground was filled with terrorists. I guess most of them are nekkit. That's how they keep the cops from shooting them outright. If they don't have clothes on, the cops can't claim they have hidden weapons. Then there's the bikers. They're the money guys. They sell drugs to finance all the terrorist attacks."

Ash stifled a laugh and grinned. "Actually, we're here to see Pops. Where do you buy the dynamite you use for blasting ponds?"

"I don't use dynamite much anymore," Pops said, tugging at his ear. "It's too darned expensive for blasting ponds. ANFO is cheaper and works well. I gotta dig a deeper hole, that takes more time, but all I've got is time. I used to just mix up the fertilizer and fuel oil, put a blasting cap in the mix and light the fuse. A minute later, boom! There's a new pond."

"ANFO?" Pam asked.

"It's a mix of ammonium nitrate fertilizer and fuel oil" Pops explained. "It's a little tricky to get the mixture right, but it's cheap and easy to make. What keeps everyone from getting it on the 4th of July is the need for a blasting cap. Those are regulated and hard to come by. Now I buy it premixed, saves the mess and the sore back."

Ash was jotting notes, then asked, "But you do have some dynamite too, right?"

"I've got some old stuff I keep around for blasting rocks. It has a faster propagation rate so it shatters the rock rather than throwing it into the air."

"Can you account for all your dynamite?" Ash asked.

"It's in a locked trunk in my barn. I haven't had the trunk open for a couple years."

Ash stood. "Can you take us out there, now, to see if it's been disturbed?"

Pop drained his coffee cup, set a dollar on the table and slowly rose from his chair. He was stooped over and limped badly the first few steps before hitting his stride.

"I get the impression you're not a fan of the government," Ash said as he held the door for Pop.

"Politicians are all thieving idiots." Pop said, stepping through the door. "I truly believe that they'd sell their mothers into prostitution if it'd raise a hundred bucks for their campaigns." Pop got to the bottom step and hesitated, waiting for Pam to catch up. "But, if you're asking if I'd blow somebody up over being angry about whichever party is in power, the answer is no."

Pop climbed into his truck and cranked over the engine, which caught with a puff of oily exhaust smoke. "Follow me!" He yelled out of his window.

They followed for thirty miles past farms, swamps, and stands of timber. Pop operated out of an old farmhouse on a township road off Highway 23, near Duquette. A sign at the end of the driveway advertised

Pop's Pond Blasting and Gun Sales. The two-story house had peeling white paint. A stack of storm windows piled next to a propane tank showed the beginning of the autumn swap of screens to storm windows.

Pam followed Davidson into the driveway and Agent Ash brought up the rear in a tan Ford sedan. Pop parked next to an old barn with weathered siding that showed only hints of the red it had once been painted. In contrast to the shabby siding, a brand new steel door. It appeared that the large barn doors had been reinforced, but still looked ready to fall off. A large lock was attached to a substantial hasp on the barn door. The hayloft had windows, and behind them were the shadows of bars. Pop had turned his barn into a secure fortress, without making it obvious.

Pop met them at their cars and said, "This is where I store all my supplies." He pointed at the barn with his thumb over his shoulder.

"Looks like you've fortified the place pretty well," Ash said as he closed his car door.

"I figured the one sure way to attract attention would be to put up a spanking new building and set up all kinds of security systems and motion detector lights," Pop said, leading them to the steel side door. "Nothing invites unwanted curiosity more than something new showing up or old stuff getting painted and spiffed up. The only security system I rely on is a Winchester shotgun behind the door in my gun shop up at the house."

They rounded the corner and Pam reached for her Glock. Ash, lagging behind Pam, pulled his windbreaker aside and unholstered his pistol. "What's up," he whispered.

"The door is ajar," Pam whispered. "No cars around or signs of activity." She took a quick peek through the small opening and pulled back. "Too dark inside to see anything. Pop, when were you last inside?"

"I blew a stump for Ron Iverson in July. I don't think I've had it unlocked since then."

"So, it may have been open for the past three months, and you might not notice?" Ash asked.

"Haven't needed anything in it since then."

Pam pulled the five-cell flashlight from her belt and held it over her shoulder. "Follow me," she said to Ash. "I'll go left. You go right."

Without hesitation, Pop pushed past them, threw the door open, and flicked the light switch. "If you're in here, get the hell out before I start shooting!"

Pam glanced at Ash, who rolled his eyes. They burst in behind Pop and methodically checked every nook and cranny as Pop looked on with amusement before walking to the rear of the barn and pushing open a steel door that looked like it had come from a jail cell.

"Well, shit-the-bed. Somebody stole my dynamite!" Pop was looking at an old metal army footlocker that had been emptied and upended. "I wonder when that happened?"

Ash was punching numbers into his cellphone as Pam led Davidson out of the barn. "So, Pop, you think this could've happened any time between July and now?"

"I mowed back here about a month ago, no, two weeks ago. If the door had been open I would've noticed it." Pop shook his head. "There was a lot of blasting material there. A lot."

"Deputy Ryan, please string crime scene tape across the door," Ash said. "When the teams get through at the blast scene, they'll come here and process the barn." He turned to Pop. "Let's look at your records and see just how much is missing."

"Not unless you let me back in the barn," Pop said. "All the records are locked up in the desk you saw inside the cage. It looked like a lot of them were all over the floor. It's going to take awhile to sort it all out."

Ash looked toward the wooded area beyond the barn, obviously trying to keep his cool. "All right, then. Come along with us to the blast scene. I'd like your opinion. You've blasted stumps and most of our teams are ex-military or have industrial experience. You might have some insight into the explosion that we'll miss."

As Pop walked toward Ash's car, Pam pulled Ash aside. "I've never heard a fed admit they didn't know everything. Are you really with ATF?"

Ash smiled. "We do know everything. But, with Pop along with me, we don't need to leave anyone here to keep an eye on him. He'd be rooting around in the barn as soon as we left the driveway if he's not with us."

"Jerk," Pam said, smiling back.

"That's the nicest name I've been called this month."

Pam radioed for a backup deputy to monitor the newest crime scene until the federal agents arrived.

CHAPTER 14

THE TUXEDO INN

The girls hustled up the stairs and closed the attic door behind them. The other girls stepped out of their dresses and hung them carefully in the wardrobes before putting on older dresses. Pixie noticed that they were wearing slips under their dresses and their bloomers had lace along the edges. Pixie followed their lead and slipped into her old dress.

Florence pulled a folding table out of a small space alongside the wardrobe and set it up while Carol and Mary dragged chairs to the table. Pixie watched, curious about the activity. Her stomach rumbled, not having eaten since breakfast.

Footsteps on the stairs preceded a knock. The door swung open and a teenaged boy with deep acne scars and black hair handed a tray to Florence. It held four plates of food that smelled sumptuous.

"The cook made sunnies and peas tonight. I think there might be some cherry cobbler later," the boy said. He looked at Pixie with an open-mouthed stare. "Who . . . who are you?"

"She's Pixie," Florence said as she closed the door. "Get out of here so we can eat."

The girls set plates in front of each chair, took the flatware from the tray, and unfolded napkins. Pixie stood near her bed, unsure of what to do. Carol waved her over to the table while taking a bite from a steaming dinner roll.

The girls dove into their supper, chatting about the people who might be downstairs and what the cooks or waitresses said about the world. Pixie started nibbling the small brown triangles on her plate and decided to eat some peas.

When the conversation slowed, she asked, "What are sunnies?"

All three girls looked at the untouched fish on Pixie's plate and smiled. "They're sunfish," Carol said softly. "A local guy catches them and brings them to the cook. It's a big treat."

Pixie poked at the brown crust and the fish crumbled into nuggets. She picked up a small nugget on her fork and put it into her mouth tentatively. As she chewed her eyes grew wide.

"Butter! They taste like butter." She took another forkful and started to chew, then looked scared. "Something poked my tongue!"

"They have little bones," Mary explained. "Spit it out and do this." Mary demonstrated how to peel the meat off the bones with her fork. "See, no bones."

Pixie ate her way through three sunfish, two bread rolls and a small bowl of peas without another word. She was the last to finish and was surprised to see the other three girls staring at her.

"What?"

"You didn't say anything during supper," Florence said.

"We weren't allowed to talk at school. Besides that, I didn't have anything to say."

"Did you hear Connie talking about the Germans and the Jews?" Mary asked.

"What about them?" Pixie asked.

"The Germans are running all the Jews out of their country. I guess they blame the Jews for all the problems there. What do you think about the Jews?" Mary asked.

"What's a Jew?" Pixie asked as Florence started stacking the plates and collecting the silverware.

"Didn't they talk about the Jews and Germans in your school?" Carol asked.

"No. We learned about arithmetic and English. Sometimes we talked about science, but that was complicated and the teacher didn't understand it very well." Pixie thought for a second, then added. "We learned about the Revolutionary War and George Washington."

Mary brought a small package from the closet and opened the flap. Pixie watched her shuffle the cardboard rectangles. Sensing Pixie's curiosity, she said, "There are cards. We usually play a game called rummy."

Pixie shook her head.

As Mary dealt, she explained, "We start out by dealing each of us seven cards . . ."

CHAPTER 15

NEMADJI STATE FOREST
MONDAY

Pop followed Agent Ash through the gate to the edge of the crime scene tape. The team that had been collecting evidence from the truck was packing up their gear and a technician was taking pictures of the red flags in relation to the other landmarks around the area. A short woman, wearing dirty blue coveralls, approached Ash. She held out a clear plastic bag sealed with red tape. "Look what we found."

Ash held up the bag and examined the fragment of a computer board. Several gold solder points gleamed in the sunlight. He held it out for Pop to see.

"Have you ever used one of these as a detonator?" Ash asked.

"Naw, I use fuses and blasting caps. They're cheap and reliable," Pop replied, cocking his head and looking at the black fragment of electronics. "Whatever that thing was, it probably cost more than I charge to blast a pond."

"What's your professional opinion of the blast that took out the tree?" Ash asked, pointing to the splintered tree above the crushed pickup.

"Do you have blast residue all the way out to the end of those flags?" Pop asked.

"That's as far as we've found splinters," Ash replied. "The fragments go about twice as far on the opposite side of the tree."

"You've got yourself an amateur, son, or else someone was trying to impress you with the blast."

Ash cracked a smile. "Why do you say that? He dropped that tree right on top of a pickup truck."

"Well, sir, there's a whole science to blasting trees. There's a British Columbia tree-blasting school where they teach you how much product to use, where to place it, and how to pack it. If you know what you're doing, a tree can be dropped exactly where you want it to fall with a minimal amount of expensive dynamite. Whoever set up this blast probably used half a dozen sticks of dynamite when half a stick would've dropped that tree. One thing you learn in this business is that dynamite is expensive and you don't use more than you need for the job you're doing.

"Second, if your blaster wanted to take out that specific truck, he should've placed the charge in a drilled hole, with packing behind it, door-high, on the truck side of the tree. If the debris hadn't killed him the blast wave would've turned the driver's innards to Jell-O.

"Three, he put the charge on the wrong side of the tree. An amateur would think that a blast on one side of the tree would topple the tree away from the explosive charge. What really happens is you blow the wood out from under the treetop and kick the lowest part out, which brings the tree back toward the charge.

"I think your bomber was trying to send a message and through his own stupidity and bad luck, dropped the tree on the unluckiest truck driver in the world. I'm thinking he wanted to scare everyone, but never intended any physical harm."

"You keep referring to the bomber as him," Pam said. "What makes you think it was a man."

"Women don't do bombs. Plain and simple. Dynamite is a big boy's toy. We like to hear the 'BOOM!'" I heard women like poison because they can kill off their target, but not actually watch him die."

"Do you agree?" Pam asked Ash.

"I'd say that's true 99.9% of the time. I've arrested one female bomber, and she was only involved because of her boyfriend." Ash nodded to Pop. "My team agrees with most of your hypothesis. The bomber used too much product, placed it ineptly, and was more likely trying to scare people than kill anyone. But the lack of intent doesn't mitigate the death."

"Do you think it was the protesters?" Pam asked.

"Maybe one of them was in the military or has explosives experience. We'll see if any of them have been on bomb-making websites. Every call they've made in the past year will be noted and trailed back to the caller or recipient. We'll know if they snore and the size and shape of every birthmark before we're through."

"My mind starts to reel when I hear you talking about having enough resources to follow all those leads," Pam said. "It'd take me years just to make the phone calls."

"It's all computerized. Once we get the search warrants, the data flows electronically and we can do database searches for keywords and names. We'll have the results in a few days."

"Big brother is always watching," Pop said, shaking his head.

CHAPTER 16

CARING ARMS SENIOR CARE CENTER
MONDAY

Floyd approached the young woman at the Caring Arms reception desk. She perked up when she saw Floyd's uniform.

"How can I help you?"

"I'd like to talk with Tilly Crown," Floyd replied.

The woman, whose nametag said "Mae," picked up a laminated sheet and scanned through the names with her index finger. "Matilda Crown lives in apartment 312. Would you like me to call and let her know that you'll be visiting?"

"Yes, please."

After a brief phone chat, the receptionist gave Floyd directions to Tilly's apartment on the third floor. The directions took him to an apartment with a gold star pennant on the door that told him Tilly's son had been killed in Viet Nam. The door was ajar so he pushed it open as he knocked.

"Mrs. Crown, may I come in?"

"Please do," a pleasant female voice said. "Forgive me if I don't get up."

Floyd walked past a small kitchen. The hallway opened to a bright living room decorated with quilts in fall colors. A small woman, was sitting in a wheelchair. Her gray hair was curled and she wore a touch of perfume that fragranced the room.

"Mrs. Crown, I'm Floyd Swenson."

"Yes, I remember your name from the *Pine City Pioneer*. You're the one who solved the case of that little girl who was missing from the summer camp. That was such a sad story."

"I've got another cold case like the missing girl. I hope you can help me."

"I don't know that I'll be of any help to you," Tilly said, "but I'd be happy to hear about your mystery. Make yourself comfortable," she said pointing to the couch. Floyd sat, carefully avoiding the quilt draped over the back of the sofa.

"Back in the '30s, a young woman was sent from the Minnesota State School to the Tuxedo Inn as a domestic worker. At some point she was moved to the Pokegama Sanatorium where we think she may have been a staff member or one of the remaining patients when it was turned into a Catholic seminary. Her name was Margaret Lane. I was contacted by her niece, who is trying to determine what happened to her after she left the sanatorium."

Tilly listened intently, nodding when appropriate. When Floyd finished she said, "I'm sorry, but I don't think I've ever met anyone named Margaret at the sanatorium."

"Do remember the Tuxedo Inn and the Pokegama Sanatorium?"

"Everyone in Pine City knew of the Tuxedo Inn," Tilly said with a smile. "No one from town would ever admit to having been there, but we all knew of it. Some called it a fancy eatery and others called it a den of iniquity. Like many things, I imagine the truth lies somewhere in between."

"Were you ever there?"

Tilly looked out the window and nodded without comment. Floyd waited, letting the silence work for him.

"Do you have any more questions?" Tilly asked.

"Tell me what you saw at the Tuxedo Inn."

"Everyone, from our parents to our Sunday school teachers, told us to stay away. They said it wasn't a place for proper young women. Those warnings only stoked our curiosity. Early on, the only way to get there was by boat, and we didn't dare row across the lake. Once there was a road, we sometimes took our bicycles out there and hid in the bushes, trying to get a glimpse of the people coming and going. There really wasn't much traffic during the day, so most times we saw nothing. There were deliveries from the dairy and bakery. The local farms sold them produce in season. As teenaged girls, we were shocked that those businessmen were actually going there.

"I was there with Lorraine Larson during the early '30s when we saw a big black car come racing down the road, stirring up a cloud of dust. We thought we saw Alvin Karpis, the gangster, whose face was on the Post Office wall. A few other times we saw hard-looking men and women coming and going. Lorraine told everyone and we got in trouble for being out there. But that didn't stop us."

"Did you or your friends ever work there?"

"Good heavens, no." Tilly said. She shook her head. "The Tuxedo Inn workers were pariahs. They shopped in town and we were cordial to them, but there was a line not to be crossed."

"Who owned the Tuxedo Inn?"

"What an interesting question," Tilly said. She looked into a corner and paused. "I never heard anyone mention the owner."

Floyd knew she was lying, but moved on. "What do you remember about the Pokegama Sanatorium?" Floyd asked.

"That was the other forbidden place, for obvious reasons. It was a private hospital overlooking Lake Pokegama where rich people went to get rest and sunshine. Work there wasn't glamorous or lucrative. It was like working in any hospital; there were doctors, nurses, medical aides, laundry workers, cooks, janitors, and maids."

"Did you know anyone who worked there?"

"I knew a few people who worked there, but they've all passed now." Tilly looked out the window again. "Most of the people I knew back then are gone."

"I'm not familiar with TB," Floyd said, changing the topic. "Was the fresh air and sunshine treatment successful?"

"I guess it helped some. I think a few of the patients are buried in the town cemetery." Tilly paused. "The locals mostly lost their jobs when the seminary opened. I think the Catholics had nuns and brothers who did all the work so they didn't need to hire local folks." She paused, then said, "I'm afraid I'm not being helpful."

"I appreciate your time, Floyd said. Rising from the couch, he shook Tilly's frail hand.

"Could you help me up?" Tilly asked, sliding to the edge of her chair. Once on her feet she said, "Please feel free to come by anytime."

Floyd released Tilly's hand and stepped back. "Are you steady?"

"Oh, yes. I use the wheelchair because I can't walk all the way to the dining room. Otherwise, I walk around the apartment by myself."

Floyd was closing the door when he heard, "Officer?"

"Yes?"

"Do you know about the sanatorium dump?"

"I know about the dump."

"There's also a ravine near the old sanatorium, on the south side of the road. They used to dump their waste there and I've heard that people go there to dig up old medicine bottles."

"I don't think I'd get anything from a medicine bottle," Floyd said, "but thanks for the tip."

"More than one person disappeared from the area around the sanatorium."

Floyd shook his head. "There have been rumors about people disappearing around the dump since I was a kid. I think those stories are meant to scare campers more than relating to crimes."

"I'm just saying that if you are searching for one person, you might want to think about a few others, too."

"Do you have names?" he asked.

"Not really," Tilly replied. "It's just common knowledge. Times were tough during the ´30s and through the war. I heard Dillinger came here after he got flushed out of his place over in Wisconsin, and the bootleggers and gamblers from St. Paul liked to get away from the city and enjoy the fresh air and lakes. I heard a rumor that the Bremer kidnapping was planned in a cabin on Rush Lake. That's not very far outside Pine County."

"Thanks," Floyd said. "I'll keep that in mind."

CHAPTER 17

STURGEON LAKE
MONDAY EVENING

Floyd was pleasantly surprised to see Mary's car in his driveway. She'd become a regular guest after he'd cleared a shelf in the medicine cabinet and a drawer in the dresser. She left a few unmentionables in the drawer, just in case she needed something, and she'd hung some blouses in the closet.

Floyd put his Glock on the top shelf of the entry closet and hung his jacket. He could hear a reality courtroom case on the television in the living room. Mary was standing at the ironing board, pressing one of his uniform shirts and focused on the TV drama.

"Hello," he said.

Mary's head jerked around and she nearly dropped the iron. "Are you trying to scare me to death?" she asked.

"I think the National Guard could've marched through here and you wouldn't have noticed." He pecked her on the cheek as he walked past.

"I washed, dried, and folded the clothes that were in your laundry basket," she called after him. "Since I don't know how you sort your clothes, I decided it was better if I just set them out for you to put away."

Neat piles of clothing were stacked on the bed. "You know," he said, "I'm entirely capable of washing and ironing my own clothes."

"I know that," Mary said. "I just had some down-time and decided to do laundry while I watched TV. I only had a little bit here to wash, so I decided to fill up the washer load with your stuff."

She took the uniform shirt off the ironing board and put it on a hanger and carried into the bedroom as Floyd took a tan flannel shirt off the hanger. Mary put her hand on his lower back. A bandage was visible under his white t-shirt.

"Let me take a look at your shoulder before you put that shirt on.

"It's not a big deal," he protested, as he removed the undershirt.

Mary removed the bandage gently, exposing pink tissue and a scab. The small wound was closed with two Steri-Strips. "The gash isn't inflamed or oozing and it looks like there will hardly be a scar when it's healed. Does it hurt much?"

"It aches a little," he said as he pulled his t-shirt down. He buttoned the flannel shirt as Mary hung the freshly ironed shirts in the closet. When she turned around, Floyd was buckling his jeans. He moved his wallet to the jeans and pulled out a key ring and walked toward the front door.

Mary looked at the keys dangling from his index finger. "I guess we're going out for supper."

"You should've been a detective," he said, holding the door for her as she picked up her purse and coat.

"You're home awfully early," Mary commented as she climbed into Floyd's pickup.

"I'm off for a few days."

"You didn't say anything about taking vacation," she replied.

"The sheriff told me to take a week of sick leave because of my shoulder injury."

Mary's eyes narrowed. "Your shoulder injury isn't that bad. What's the rest of the story?"

Floyd repeated the story of the missing girl and the rumors about the Tuxedo Inn. He was just going to explain he was at a dead end when he drove into Ernie's Diner's parking lot.

"Sounds like you're becoming the master of cold cases. Is that what you want to do?"

"I suppose it's fine as long as I don't become the master of lost causes," he replied as he held the diner door for her. Ernie's was decorated like a '50s malt shop with chrome fixtures, 45-rpm records and pictures of Elvis decorating the walls. They sat in a booth with red vinyl-covered seats and a Formica tabletop. "Cheeseburger, fries and a chocolate malt" special was handwritten on a white board over the cash register.

"Can you see which soup they have today?" Mary asked.

"Split pea with ham," he replied, reading a sign.

A teenager, wearing a white apron, brought two coffee cups and filled them. Her nametag said, "Ginger," which fit her coppery hair color. "Hi, Sergeant Swenson. Do you know what you want to order, or do you need a few minutes?"

"I'll have the special," Floyd said, "with grilled onions."

"A bowl of pea soup and whole wheat toast for me," said Mary.

As the waitress returned to the kitchen Mary leaned across the table and whispered, "Does every waitress in Pine County know your name?"

"I eat out when I'm on patrol . . ."

"It was a rhetorical question that doesn't require an answer," Mary said, playfully. "Now, tell me about your case."

"There's nothing more to tell. I talked to Edna Purdy at the county historical society, then visited Tilly Crown. She had some interesting rumors about the Tuxedo Inn, but rumors aren't going to answer my questions. I need to find some written records."

The bell over the door jingled as Ginger brought their food. Mary, facing the door, was buttering her toast when she saw who'd entered. She waved from her seat. Floyd looked over his shoulder and saw Pam Ryan entering with a handsome young man.

"Pam," Mary called, "come join us."

Floyd looked over his shoulder and got a look from Pam that said, "What are you doing here?"

Pam led her friend to the table. "I don't want to interrupt your supper," Pam said.

"You're not interrupting." Mary slid her place setting across the table, next to Floyd.

"Travis, this is Sergeant Floyd Swenson, my boss, and Mary Jungers," The two men shook hands. "Guys, this is Travis Conrad." Travis appeared to be about thirty years old and a little under six feet tall. With his short hair, broad shoulders and narrow hips, even though he was wearing a plaid shirt and jeans, he had military bearing.

"I'm surprised to see you here," Floyd said to Pam. "Ernie's is a long way from home."

"I live in Moose Lake," Travis said, "so, Ernie's is middle ground. There's that, and Pam likes to meet on the fringes of Pine County to hold down the number of rumors about her personal life."

The waitress returned with place settings for Pam and Travis, then took their orders.

"Please, eat while your food is hot," said Travis.

"Do you work in Moose Lake?" Mary asked, before dipping a spoonful of soup.

"I work for the tax assessor, up in Carlton," Travis replied. "I spend a lot of time on the road checking property valuations and looking at recent sales. I'm not the most popular guy in the county."

"You're the one who gets all the irate phone calls when property values are adjusted," Floyd said.

"Oh, not just when valuations are adjusted," Travis said. "I get calls when the estimated tax statements come out, I get calls when the cities adjust their levy rates, and I got a lot of calls when Moose Lake approved the levy to build their new high school and put the addition onto the hospital."

"You're unusually quiet, Pam," Floyd noted.

"She isn't ready to introduce me to her co-workers," Travis said. "She said something about not fueling the rumor mill."

"We went through that period," Mary said. "Actually, we might not be past it yet. I own the flower shop in Pine Brook. By tomorrow morning the girls will know where we had supper and what I ate."

"I think people are more interested about where we have breakfast," Travis said, causing Pam to blush. He quickly added, "Not that we're eating breakfast together."

"Floyd and I met when he was investigating the disappearance of a girl from the Willow River camp,"

Mary said. "He had a lot of questions because the skeleton was found on my family's farm where it had been for decades. After awhile, I noticed that his questions were less and less about the missing girl and more about me."

"No," Floyd said. "I figured out which days you had fresh doughnuts in the shop and happened to stop by on those days. You've got better coffee than the courthouse."

"The gas station has better coffee than the courthouse. How did you two meet?" Mary asked.

"I met Pam in Carlton, at the courthouse." Travis laughed and said, "She was there to pick up a prisoner and I was dealing with an irate taxpayer. She asked if she could help, which calmed down the guy. He left and we talked a little, I noticed she wasn't wearing a wedding ring, and I asked for her phone number."

"Were you in the service?" Mary asked.

"Air Force," he replied with a smile. "Is it that obvious?"

"You carry yourself with confidence and your haircut looks military," Mary said.

"You're a pilot?" Floyd asked.

"Nothing that glamorous," Travis replied. "I was in logistics. You know, making sure all the right equipment, parts, and people arrive at the right place at the right time. I served in Iraq and Afghanistan, but not where the bullets were flying. The closest I came to a combat injury was a case of heatstroke."

"You're being awfully quiet, Pam," said Mary.

"I thought I'd stay on the sidelines until the interrogation was over."

Mary laughed out loud.

"What's going on with our bombing investigation?" Floyd asked, grabbing the hint that it was time for a new topic.

Mary raised a finger while she swallowed. "For Travis' benefit—we have ground rules for work discussions. There will be no discussion of blood, guts, or anything that's going to keep me awake tonight. Now you may answer Pam."

"Pop Davidson was robbed, and we're pretty sure that was the source of the explosives," Pam said. "There's consensus that the bomber was an amateur because he used way too much explosive and put it in the wrong place. It appears that dropping the tree on top of the pickup was accidental. Everything points to an attempt to scare people, but not to do harm."

"Are the protesters the prime suspects?" Mary asked.

"I don't think so," Pam replied. "We're checking their backgrounds, but they're more into publicly ridiculing the establishment than hurting people."

"I saw the explosion on the news," Travis said. "The protesters seemed as surprised by the explosion as you were. If they'd known what was coming, I'd have expected them to duck and cover before the blast."

"That's a good catch," Floyd said. "Most civilians wouldn't notice that."

Travis smiled. "WDIO ran that clip a hundred times. The first time I saw it, I was distracted by the blast. Later, I watched the reactions of the people. Everyone seemed surprised — you guys, the protesters, and the loggers."

"The BATF guys had the same thought," Pam said. "I'm sorry, but this is an active investigation and we need to move to a different topic. Floyd, how's your cold case going?"

"Dead ends. The only avenue I haven't pursued is bringing in a backhoe to search the sanatorium dump."

"There was a sanatorium in Pine County?" Travis asked.

Floyd shared the history of the Tuxedo Inn and the Pokegama Sanatorium as Pam and Travis ate. "So, that's the backstory for my cold case. I've got a young woman working in a questionable inn then apparently moving to the sanatorium. When the sanatorium closed, she disappeared."

The four threw out theories about the missing woman until alien abduction was suggested.

"It was nice to meet you," Floyd said to Travis, shaking hands, while Pam hugged Mary.

"Likewise," Travis replied. "Pam talks a lot about you and I was looking forward to meeting you sometime."

"What did you whisper to Pam?" Floyd asked when they were in the pickup.

"I told her Travis is a keeper."

CHAPTER 18

THE TUXEDO INN

Pixie couldn't sleep. The State School dormitory was silent at night. Even in the attic, she could hear the murmured voices, the clatter of plates, and the closing of doors. When she heard footsteps coming up the attic stairs, she closed her eyes and feigned sleep. The door creaked open and the footsteps stopped at the edge of her bed.

"I'm sure you're not asleep," Abigail Corbett said softly.

Pixie pulled the sheet up tight against her chin and opened her eyes.

"This has been a big day for you. Did you get enough to eat?"

Pixie nodded.

"Good. We need to put a little meat on your bones." Corbett ran her fingers along Pixie's arm until she hit a lump and Pixie yelped. "Florence said you were bruised. Were you beaten at the school?"

Pixie shrugged. "Some. Only because I deserved it."

"I know your world has been upended, but you're safe here. If anyone hurts you, tell me. You'll get used to the routine here and later we'll talk about what's to become of you. Now, close your eyes and get some sleep. You're safe here," she said again.

CHAPTER 19

THE TUXEDO INN
MARCH 16, 1934

Pixie was deep in a dream about school when an aroma intruded. Her eyes popped open and she sat up straight. "Bacon?" she asked.

The State School breakfast was always some sort of hot cereal, usually cornmeal mush or oatmeal, but early in her life Pixie had been part of a functioning family who ate real food and the aroma of bacon was imprinted in her memory.

A large woman was holding a platter of food while Florence and Mary scrambled to clear the playing cards from the table. Pixie threw off her covers and sat on the edge of her bed, not knowing what to do. When the woman set the platter on the table she looked at Pixie and said, "Come child, you've got to eat."

Each of the plates held two strips of bacon, a scrambled egg, and two pancakes so large they hung over the edge of the plates. Carol, who was chubby and perpetually hungry, sat down and ate eggs with her right hand while pouring maple syrup with her left. Florence and Mary were cutting up their pancakes. Pixie stared at the bacon, not sure if she should eat it with her fingers or cut it up and eat it with a fork. She felt a strong arm across her shoulders.

"Honey," the woman said, "just dive in."

Pixie snatched a slice of browned bacon with her fingers and bit it with a crunch. Her taste buds went wild. She scooped up a forkful of eggs and jammed them into her mouth, then reached for the bacon again.

"Honey, slow down. Nobody's going to take this away from you. Savor it."

"Mrs. Marty, you make the best pancakes in the whole world," said Carol, who was sopping up syrup with a wedge of pancake.

The woman sat on the bed nearest Pixie and watched the girls eat breakfast.

"I do enjoy watching someone appreciate my cooking," she said to Pixie. "My name is Mrs. Marty. Who would you be?"

"My name is Margaret, but everyone calls me Pixie."

"Mrs. Marty is the baker," explained Florence. "She comes in early to bake bread and make the soups.

She brings us breakfast before we go down to start cleaning."

"Do you live here, too?" asked Pixie.

"No, dearie, I live in Pine City. I drive out here every morning. Where are you from?"

"I was at the State School, but I turned sixteen and had to leave."

"Looks like you didn't get much bacon at the school."

"We had mush most days," Pixie said, still chewing as she spoke. "Sundays we got a bowl of oatmeal with a pat of butter on top. Then for lunch we'd get oatmeal fried in lard with brown sugar syrup."

Geraldine Marty looked Pixie over from head to toe. Seeing a waif who was nothing but skin and bones, she resolved to put some meat on Pixie.

The girls washed up in a large basin, combed each other's hair, and then dressed. When they reached the first floor, Florence led them to a closet in the back of the kitchen where she handed out freshly laundered aprons from a stack on a shelf. They were nearly out of the kitchen when Mrs. Marty stopped Pixie to straighten her apron. Pixie took a step, then realized there was something in her apron pocket. She stopped and pulled out a doughnut. After staring in wonderment for a second, Pixie looked at Mrs. Marty, who winked at her.

The morning routine was a little different than the evening, and as the girls cleaned and set tables, the waitresses and hostesses came down from their second floor rooms. As each woman appeared, Florence scurried up the stairs and returned a few minutes later. The third time, Florence took Pixie's hand and led her to a room where the door was ajar. Florence handed Pixie a large pitcher. "Take this to the bathroom and fill it with water. And be careful; it'll be heavy."

By the time Pixie returned with the pitcher Florence had stripped the bedding and put on fresh sheets. A dressing screen in one corner enticed Pixie to peek behind it. She saw several nice dresses, a corset, and several pairs of bloomers.

"Pixie!" Florence whispered. "Get out here and help me with this quilt."

As they straightened the quilt, Pixie asked, "If we work hard, will we get to be waitresses, too?"

"Don't even talk crazy like that," Florence said. "Let's get back to the dining room."

CHAPTER 20

NEMADJI STATE FOREST
TUESDAY

Pam Ryan was parked outside the state forest entrance. The excitement of the protest had given way to a quiet autumn day with high scudding clouds crisscrossed with contrails from coast-to-coast flights passing high overhead. Flyover land, she thought. All those people on the two coasts rushing to do business and make money while the center of the country grew food and lived sedate, quiet lives without the drama of New York or Los Angeles. Her wandering mind was interrupted by the honking from a battered blue Ford pickup emerging from the forest.

A man braked short of her cruiser and threw his door open. He had a wild-eyed look.

"I was hoping somebody was still here," he said, almost breathless. "We've been trying to get a cellphone signal."

"What's up?" Pam asked, standing behind the door of her cruiser, not entirely sure what the guy had in mind.

"We started cutting in the timber back there," he said, pointing down the road he'd just traveled. "We found an old building there and were poking around during our coffee break, and well, there's bones."

"Human bones?"

"I wasn't sure until I moved a few boards and saw the skull. They're human all right. It was staring right back at me," he said with a shudder.

Pam radioed in her location and asked for backup. "Can I drive my cruiser in there, or will I need four-wheel drive?"

"I think you'd better ride with me. Some of the ruts are pretty deep when you cut through the swamp." Pam stepped up into the pickup and buckled her seatbelt. "My name's Bill Preston. I've seen you around. You're Pam Ryan, right?"

"Right," Pam said at the pickup lurched through a three-point turn on the narrow dirt road. As they entered the timber the dispatcher radioed that Sandy Maki would be at her location in 15 minutes.

"Ten-four, dispatch. I'm out of my vehicle riding with Bill Preston to the logging site."

Bill's description of the road being rutted was an understatement. The pickup bounced along the dry portion of the road, but when they reached the margin of a marshy area the tires spun and slid from side to side through water-filled ruts and a small pond before getting back to higher ground. After ten minutes of bouncing around, Pam could see yellow-painted equipment through the trees.

They stopped next to a semi that was being loaded with huge logs. A skidder was pulling another log across the ground from where it had been felled. The snorting of the diesel engine and the thumping of the log as it was dragged over stumps and ruts was insignificant compared to the dozen chainsaws whining in the background. Orrin Johnson, the foreman, met them at the truck and handed Pam a scraped and stained yellow hardhat.

"Put that on and follow me." He yelled to be heard over the noise.

A narrow trail had been worn through the thin underbrush growing under the canopy of maples and oaks. They stepped over rocks, roots, and tangles of vines until they were a hundred yards from Bill's truck. Orrin pointed into the distance. Barely visible in the shade of the trees was the geometric shape of an old building, now turned black from decay and covered with patches of green moss. If not for the few straight lines formed by the fallen roof, it would've been invisible until they were upon it.

Orrin stepped carefully around the fallen boards, retracing footprints made during someone's previous walk into the structure. Patches of tarpaper had survived the years of damp rot along with some rusty nails along a rafter that looked rather like the spine of a dinosaur. A lump of the fallen roof was punctured by a piece of metal chimney and a cast iron stove, both rusty and leaning.

They stopped short of the stove and the foreman pointed to a spot where some roof boards had been moved. "Over there."

Pam stepped around him, carefully picking her footfalls. Through the opening in the boards she saw a large bone, perhaps from a thigh, and a portion of a skull with the eye socket exposed. The bone was stained dark and it too had moss growing on parts of it. Pam backed away and rejoined Preston and Johnson.

"Whoever that is has been there a long time," she said, scanning the area around the structure. "It's going to be hard to get a forensic team in here to process the scene. The road's nearly impassable and there's no place to land a helicopter. She looked at the semi and saw the driver securing his load of logs.

"How did you get that logging truck in here?" she asked. "He didn't come in on the same road we drove."

"We put some gravel on the road past that big pine that comes in from the south and cut a trail around the bog. It's more passable now," Johnson replied. "Billy took the shortest route to where we thought he might get a few bars of service when he found you."

Pam looked at her phone and saw the "No Service" message. "Considering the years those bones have been lying there, I don't suppose there's a need to rush a team back here." She looked around at the unbroken underbrush. No one had been near the skeleton in a long time.

"Billy, can you drive me back to my car?" Pam asked. "I'll contact the sheriff's office and we'll secure the scene until we can get a forensics team in here." She looked at the undisturbed remnants of the structure.

"Did you guys look anywhere else under the rubble?"

"Naw," Billy said. "I thought the old stove might be worth a few bucks, but it weighs like five hundred pounds. That was my only interest."

Turning to Orrin Johnson, Pam asked, "Can you make sure no one disturbs this area until I get back?"

Orrin pointed to the workers swarming over a recently fallen oak like ants. "Nobody's going to bother this. They're all too busy making money. I'll bet you that no one has been in this spot since the building fell down, and that might've been a hundred years ago."

Pam looked at the rotting ends of the broken boards. "It's been awhile," she agreed. "This might be a great project for our cold-case guy. He loves digging up old skeletons."

CHAPTER 21

PINE COUNTY COURTHOUSE
TUESDAY

Ira Rosen was sitting in the courtroom with the five protesters, awaiting the arrival of the judge. He'd spoken to each of them. They claimed to be clueless about the organization of the protest and the bombing and each swore to that. Jeremy Pyle, as they had known their leader, had done all the planning. The rest were little more than bodies to show up on the news.

The hallway door creaked open and Jane Simmons, the Assistant U.S. Attorney, walked in dressed in a pin-striped tailored suit with darts in all the right places to make the suit attractive as well as businesslike. She was followed by Tom Bakken, the county attorney, whose wrinkled brown suit looked like it had come off the rack at J. C. Penney just before he'd slept in it. Simmons nodded to Rosen, put her leather shoulder bag on the prosecutor's table, and pulled out a legal pad covered with notes.

"Good morning, Mr. Rosen," she said, after organizing her workspace.

Rosen rose from his chair, trying not to show his intrigue. "I'm a bit confused," Rosen said. "I can't imagine that anything in this case would interest the U.S. Attorney's office."

Simmons opened her briefcase and withdrew a sheaf of papers. She separated a few pages from the rest and handed them to Rosen while Bakken sat at the table. "I'm requesting that your clients be remanded into federal custody."

Rosen grabbed the papers and scanned the top document while the protesters whispered to one another. "I have a hard time believing a judge would even consider your attempted obfuscation," he said, throwing the papers back on the prosecutor's table. He returned to his chair where he whispered to the defendants.

The rear courtroom door opened and two stern-faced men, wearing body armor stenciled "US MARSHAL" took seats in the last row. A new round of anxious whispers rose among the defendants.

A door opened in the front of the courtroom and a bailiff announced, "All rise. The honorable Calvin Morton presiding."

Calvin Morton was concerned about not tripping over his black robe. When he sat down and looked at the attorneys he was surprised to see unfamiliar faces at both the prosecution and defense tables. He looked at his file and was more confused.

"I thought we were having a bail hearing," the judge said to Tom Bakken, "but the cast of characters here makes me think something else is in the wind."

"Your Honor, may I approach the bench?"

"And you are?"

"Jane Simmons, Assistant U.S. Attorney," she replied. Without further invitation, she handed a few stapled sheets to the bailiff, who delivered them to the judge. The judge slipped on a pair of reading glasses and carefully read.

Setting his glasses aside a few minutes later, the judge asked, "And who is the defense counsel?"

"I'm Ira Rosen, attorney for the defendants."

"Mr. Rosen, have you read the federal warrants?" Morton asked. He then saw the marshals sitting in the back of the courtroom and frowned.

"I saw them for the first time just moments ago, and frankly, it caught me unaware."

"Your Honor," Simmons said, smiling, "I gave Mr. Rosen a copy of the warrants as a courtesy. He will have the opportunity to speak with his clients at length in Minneapolis. I will also provide him with further details of the case against his clients prior to their arraignment."

"Mr. Bakken," the judge said, "I assume you're aware of this turn of events and you're prepared to turn these defendants over to the U.S. Marshals."

"Yes, Your Honor. In light of the federal charges, I withdraw the county charges, with one exception." Bakken nodded to the marshals and the man closest to the door stepped out and returned in seconds with a tearful man and a rattled woman.

"Your Honor," Bakken went on, "I've taken the liberty to invite Amanda and Jeffrey Stevenson to the courthouse. Their daughter, Susan, is one of the defendants. Susan Stevenson has been listed on the register of the National Association of Missing and Exploited Children for seventeen months, since her disappearance from a shopping mall in Oregon. Miss Stevenson is now sixteen years old and is the victim listed in the arrest warrant under the Mann Act. Based on the evidence collected . . . "

"No!" Susan Stevenson shouted, jumping up from her seat. "I wanted to be with Mike and Clarke. I wasn't forced to come here."

The judge rapped his gavel. "Miss Stevenson, please return to your seat."

Ira Rosen took her by the arm, whispered to her, and eased her back into a chair.

"It's clear that Miss Stevenson is a minor who's been transported across several states for sexual exploitation," Jane Simmons said softly. "Based on her response, it appears she may need some . . . therapy, and to that end, I recommend that she be released into the custody of her parents."

"Mr. Rosen, would you care to comment?" The judge asked.

Rosen leaned close to the defendants as they whispered among themselves.

"Mr. Rosen?"

Straightening, he looked at the judge and said, "Your Honor, Miss Stevenson doesn't wish to leave with her parents, and it is clear that any contact between the defendants has been entirely consensual."

"Miss Stevenson is sixteen. The male defendants are all more than five years older," Simmons said. "We have collected forensic evidence that shows she has been supplied with methamphetamine and marijuana, and has been intimate with at least two of the male defendants. It is our contention that Miss Stevenson is a victim."

Amanda Stevenson started sobbing and Susan hung her head.

"Mr. Stevenson, are you prepared to provide the services your daughter may require?" the judge asked.

"Yes, Your Honor. With the help of Ms. Simmons, we found placement for Susan at a substance abuse center near our home. We are prepared to do whatever it takes to restore her to a normal life."

"Mr. Rosen, do you object to that plan?"

"I'm at a loss, Your Honor. This information is new and I'd like to spend a few minutes with my clients before answering." The defendants continued to whisper.

"Mr. Rosen, given the nature of the charges, I suggest that you remove Miss Stevenson from the other defendants and take her into my chambers for consultation. I will ask a female bailiff to stand at the door during your consultation."

Rosen leaned over and whispered to Susan, who vehemently shook her head. In an emphatic whisper, he spoke again, and put his hand on her elbow. In tears, she stood and was guided to the judge's chambers.

"Mr. Bakken and Ms. Simmons, please approach the bench."

With the lawyers before him, the judge asked, "What the hell is going on?"

"In consultation with the Federal Drug Enforcement Agency, we were able to determine that the defendants are professional protesters. All, except Miss Stevenson, have been arrested multiple times for trespass, disturbing the peace, terroristic threats, and drug use. When we searched their cars and campsite, under a federal search warrant, we recovered a firearm and drugs consistent with drug distribution, and evidence of sexual activity that . . ."

"Whoa," the judge said, raising his hand. "Tom, you're okay turning this hornets' nest over to the feds?"

"Your Honor, I'm relieved to turn this over to Ms. Simmons. I don't have the human or financial resources to prosecute this mess, especially with Mr. Rosen involved. He is a partner in a large Washington D.C. firm with a history of defending the children of the rich and influential. They have the resources to hire teams of investigators and expert witnesses that we don't. Before that, they'd snow us with motions and petitions until I was ready to scream 'Uncle.'"

"I don't know what Mr. Rosen is saying to his client," the judge said, "but I'm inclined to let Ms. Simmons take this mess out of here and turn Miss Stevenson over to her parents so they can try to get her straightened out, although I don't hold out much hope."

"The Stockholm syndrome," Simmons said. "She's so brainwashed by the group that she doesn't have any idea that she's being used."

The judge tapped a pen on the bench top for a few seconds. "All right. Give the rest of the defendants to the marshals. I'm not sure what Miss Stevenson wants to do, but she's going with her parents."

Simmons nodded to the marshals, who pulled out plastic handcuffs. They started cuffing the men, then the women, who all stood looking dazed. Simmons walked back to the Stevensons and whispered to them.

Mrs. Stevenson started crying again and Mr. Stevenson nodded and shook Simmons' hand.

The door to the judge's chambers opened and the female bailiff held the door as Rosen and his client, whose eyes were red from crying, entered the courtroom. Rosen hesitated a fraction of a second when he saw the marshals standing with his handcuffed clients.

"Your Honor," Rosen said.

"Mr. Rosen, your clients are now federal detainees. Mr. Bakken has dropped the charges against Miss Stevenson and she is now leaving in the custody of her parents."

"But, Your Honor . . . "

"We're done, Mr. Rosen," the judge said, rising.

"But Miss Stevenson has . . ."

"Mr. Rosen, if you continue to speak, I'll have the bailiff remove you from the courtroom. I suggest you get directions to the federal courthouse in Minneapolis and find a nice hotel. You might be there for a while." The judge stepped down from the bench and Rosen turned red with rage.

With the judge gone, Rosen whispered to Susan Stevenson, who looked back at the other defendants. One of the guys nodded for her to go to her parents. Rosen led her to the aisle and her parents, who engulfed her in hugs while she continued to stare back at the other defendants. Rosen turned to Simmons, who was packing her briefcase while smiling broadly.

"You've crossed a line. I will not let this hick judge railroad my clients."

"Have a nice day, Mr. Rosen," Simmons said, closing her briefcase and walking away with the county attorney. The U.S. Marshals ushered the remaining defendants to the exit, checked the hallway, and then led them away as Ira Rosen watched.

With the courtroom empty, Rosen pulled out his cellphone and hit a speed-dial number. The phone rang once, then was answered by a voice announcing the name of his law firm.

"Carole, this is Ira. Is Clarence in his office?"

After a few seconds on hold, "Ira, how are things in flyover land?" Clarence Doherty asked. "Will you be back tomorrow?"

"This has turned into a cluster fuck," Rosen said, keeping his voice low. "I was ready to steamroll the county attorney, then the U.S. Attorney shows up with arrest warrants for all but one of the defendants. The remaining defendant, it turns out, is a juvenile runaway who's been smoking dope and screwing the guys. The U.S. Attorney handed me the arrest warrants and asked the court to release the girl to her parents, who just happened to show up from Oregon. I got a few minutes with her, in chambers, and tried to figure out what the hell is going on. She doesn't know a thing except that they were camping their way across the country, selling meth and Ecstasy to pay the bills."

"A U.S. Attorney showed up?" Doherty asked. "Why wouldn't this be a local arrest? I mean, even with some drugs involved, the local cops never call the feds."

"I know," Rosen said. "When I spoke with the county attorney, he was shaking in his boots. I'm sure I could've inundated them with paper and got the kids off with a fine and time served. This thing with the feds is different. If they've really got the evidence they claim, at least one of the guys is going to be charged with interstate transport of a minor for sex."

"Ira, take a deep breath. Get with the feds and see what they've really got, then we'll decide how to proceed. I'll call Harry and see just how deep his pockets are."

"I don't care how deep his pockets are! I'm in Bumfuck, Minnesota, living out of a suitcase in a Motel 6 that I wouldn't use for my dog's kennel. Hell, the nearest Hilton or Hyatt is seventy miles away."

"Ira, get a decent hotel in Minneapolis and buy yourself a steak dinner with a couple single malts. Then call me tomorrow."

"Clarence, I have an appointment with our friend tomorrow. I can't sit here babysitting these delinquents!"

"I'll have Carole reschedule him. Just take another day or two and see what happens there."

Rosen closed his eyes and exhaled. "Fine. I'll hang with this two more days, tops. Then I'm coming back to civilization. Just so you know, it's only October, and they're predicting snow for tonight. At lunch, the waitress laughed when I asked her how long things would be shut down. They just plow the streets and keep working! It's like I'm in the Arctic Circle!"

CHAPTER 22

TUXEDO INN
SEPTEMBER 1934

The girls were finishing breakfast in their attic room when they heard the stairs creak. Abigail knocked gently, then stepped into the room and closed the door.

"I haven't said thank you enough," she said, sitting on the edge of Pixie's bed. "It's been a crazy time and sometimes I forget the most important things. Is there anything I can do for you?"

All four girls shook their heads. "No," said Florence, "everything is fine."

"Someday you'll all be somewhere else and I hope you think back on this time with pleasant memories. The country is having some tough times and we've been able to get through a lot better than many people in the rest of Pine County."

Abigail stood and smiled at the girls. "I know that none of you has any family nearby, and I hope that I've been able to give you a place where you could grow up, be safe, and feel like you are part of a family. Our family."

As Abigail's footsteps creaked down the stairs Florence looked at the others, who were in shock. "Abigail was crying," she said.

"I've heard people are losing their farms and their jobs, but maybe it's worse than we know," said Carol.

"You girls and Abigail are the only family I've had since I was sent to the State School. Abigail is like our mother," Pixie said.

"She said that someday we'll all be gone," said Florence. "I wonder if something is happening?"

"It doesn't matter," said Pixie. "I think Abigail will look after us no matter what happens."

CHAPTER 23

PINE CITY CEMETERY
TUESDAY

Floyd walked through the cemetery as the sun rose, leaving a trail of footprints in the frosty grass. He started in the oldest section and read headstones from the 1800s that were intermixed with some newer graves scattered in large family plots where several generations of a family were side-by-side. He found a section of graves from the late 1930s to the 1940s and made a cursory search of that area but didn't find a headstone with the name Margaret Lane. He meandered to an area of recent burials and wiped the grass clippings from a flat stone that bore his wife's name, "Virginia Swenson."

"I haven't been out for a while," he said to the headstone. "Things are a little crazy, and well, I've been talking to Mary Jungers a lot. She's been staying over sometimes, and that makes the evenings a lot easier than sitting alone in the empty house. People are talking, but I'm too old to care anymore. It's not like we're going to be raising any children. Mostly we just spoon and talk. She runs a flower shop and that whole world is changing, so her business is a little rocky sometimes. She's talking about selling and retiring, and if she does, well, I might just turn in my badge and spend some time getting that old pickup running. I'm getting too old to chase down a burglar, and shooting that Mexican guy last year rattled me."

A gust of wind rushed through the trees, rustling the few remaining oak leaves.

"Funny, you weren't concerned about me spooning with Mary, but when I talk about retiring, I get a sign." He looked up, waiting for another gust that didn't come. "Now I'm on a wild goose chase trying to find a woman who's been missing since the '40s. She was working at the Tuxedo Inn, then she showed up at the Pokegama Sanatorium. When the sanatorium closed she disappeared without a trace. I'm not sure how that's a police matter now, but I'm on it."

A rusty blue pickup turned in the gate and drove slowly to the small building where the lawn care equipment was stored. Floyd stood and walked over as the man, dressed in a tan jacket and wool stocking cap unlocked the door.

"Hi, Jeff," Floyd said, extending his hand.

"Floyd, I haven't seen you around for a while. How's life?" Jeff Smith, now in his seventies, had been the cemetery caretaker for fifty years. His face was rutted from decades in the sun but his blue eyes twinkled.

"Actually, I need some help. I'm trying to locate a grave."

"Come on in," Smith said, opening the door. He flipped a light switch, illuminating the variety of mowers and trimmers required to keep the cemetery in top shape. Floyd followed him to a wooden door in the rear corner that opened to a room only big enough for a small desk, a file cabinet, and a library table covered with a thin layer of dust. Smith flipped the switch on a computer and the display lit up.

"Who are you looking for?" Smith asked as he doffed his jacket and hung it on the coatrack in the back corner of the office area. The computer flashed a request for username and password, which Smith keyed in quickly.

"Margaret Lane," Floyd replied.

Smith typed in the name and stared at the screen. "I've got no listing for anyone with that name. When did she die?"

"Possibly as long ago as the '40s."

"Ahh," Smith said, pushing away from the desk. "I've only got the last twelve years on the computer." He unclipped a key ring from his belt and unlocked the small file cabinet that looked like an old-fashioned library card index file. "I got two sets of cards: one set is arranged by name and the other is by date of death."

Smith's fingers marched across the cards and quickly found the L section. He pulled out three cards and read, "Lenore Lane, Malcolm Lane, and Theresa Lane. That's all I've got. I can check obituaries, Social Security death records, and death certificates," he said, moving back to the computer.

"I'm pretty sure those databases have already been searched," Floyd replied.

"No harm in looking again and, who knows, I might know a trick or two." Smith logged onto a website of headstone images. He typed in "Lane, Margaret" and waited. Hits started to pop up on the screen. "Looks like Margaret was a pretty popular name from the mid-1800s until the 1950s. I've got headstone records for thirty-seven Margaret Lanes. They span fifteen states and nine decades."

"We can ignore any deaths before 1940," Floyd said, stepping behind the chair so he could read the screen. "And, I know this woman's birthdate was July 15, 1918."

"That wipes out all of these hits," Smith said. He pulled up a fresh search screen and keyed in, Lane, Peggy. "The searches are very specific and if the person was buried with their nickname on the headstone, we'll only find it with the exact spelling. Looks like we've got nine Peggy Lanes, but none of them were born before 1923."

The search for Maggie Lane yielded nothing relevant.

Smith closed down the headstone search and pulled up another website. "This is a more obscure website used primarily by funeral directors. It allows me to put in wild-card characters and initials. It searches and shows me anything close to what I've entered."

"What kind of wild card?" Floyd asked.

Smith keyed in Lane, M*****. "The pound signs tell the database the name is at least that many characters long and it will spit out anything that matches. I put in five stars so we will eliminate all the Marys, which would probably number in the thousands, and will still catch Maggie and Margaret."

Thousands of records scrolled down the screen. "Let me sort this by birthdate," Smith said. "Michael Lane, born July 16, 1923, died June 8, 1944, Normandy, France."

Floyd stared at the screen and quietly surmised. "Two days after the D-Day invasion."

"I suppose so," Smith replied. "Definitely not Margaret. I'll repeat the search with a P and wild card."

Again, hundreds of records appeared. Another sort by birthdate wiped out all but two people, neither were named Peggy, and both were buried on the West Coast.

"Got any other tricks up your sleeve?" Floyd asked.

"Not really," Smith said, pushing back from the desk. "There are a couple situations that wouldn't show up on any searches. If she is buried in a private family plot somewhere, there wouldn't be a headstone record, but there should be a Social Security death record. If she became indigent somehow, she might be buried in a pauper's grave as a Jane Doe."

"Or, she may be in a shallow grave or swamp somewhere," Floyd said. His hands were suddenly cold and he jammed them in his pockets. "Thanks for the help. If you come up with any other ideas, give me a call."

"Sure, Floyd. I'll think about it."

Floyd's cellphone chirped as he walked back to his car. The caller ID said PCSD.

"Swenson."

"I know you're officially on leave," Pam Ryan said, "but you want to put on your uniform and come out to the Nemadji State Forest entrance."

"The protesters are back?"

"No, we've moved on to a whole new chapter of chaos."

"What's going on?"

"I can't talk. Just get out here."

CHAPTER 24

NEMADJI STATE FOREST
TUESDAY

Satellite dishes were the first things visible as Floyd approached the state forest. There were at least three, all elevated high above the news vans to get a direct line to a satellite flying somewhere above. As he came over a rise, he saw nearly a dozen news vehicles lining the road, with several cameras filming live broadcasts using the state forest gate as background. Inside the gate sat a white Winnebago with the Minnesota Bureau of Criminal Apprehension logo.

Pam was trying to keep the Winnebago between herself and the cameras.

Floyd eased between the parked vehicles lining the road, but the ditches at the edge of the gravel left barely enough space for his pickup to pass. Several of the newspeople waved and tried to flag him down, but he waved back and kept rolling. Once inside the gate he drove just far enough down the rutted logging road to pass the BCA van and park out of view of the cameras.

"What is this all about?" he asked Pam.

"Haven't you seen the news today? One of the loggers discovered a body inside a collapsed shack. It's in the middle of the area that's being cleared."

"Are we talking about a current missing person, or have the remains been there for a while?"

"The skull I saw had lichens and moss growing on it."

"Just one body?"

"I saw one skull yesterday. The BCA techs and guys from the state forestry department are disassembling the shack to see what's underneath."

"Has anyone guessed how old the shack is?" Floyd asked.

"One of the forestry guys said they used to lease land to hunters who put up shacks. The records are spotty, and they haven't found any leases for this particular area. I got the impression that the state stopped offering leases in the 1950s, but they didn't make anyone remove their shacks. There was some tacit agreement that removing or burning the shacks would be more harmful than just leaving them standing. Technically, they were state property, so anyone could've walked in and used them, but he said, they're in such remote locations that few people other than the leaseholders and their hunting parties even knew they were there."

"So, they think this is an old hunting shack," Floyd summarized.

Pam looked at the news crews and motioned for Floyd to move behind the BCA mobile crime lab. "We've got to be careful. I saw one of the crews with a parabolic microphone, the ones the networks use to listen to football huddles. I assume they can hear anything we say if we're within their line of sight." Pam leaned against the fender of her cruiser. "I think the hunting shack theory is the official line, if anyone asks. I overheard one of the forestry guys comment that it's one hell of a big hunting shack, if that's what it really is."

"Does the forest service have any buildings out here?" Floyd asked.

"They don't have any structures in the area, nor do any of their maps indicate any structure there. I've heard theories about everything from an illegal logging camp to an old homestead to a gangster's hideout.

"One of the loggers told me that John Dillinger made a run to Minnesota after the shootout with the FBI in the Little Bohemia Lodge in Wisconsin. He supposedly hid out in Minnesota for a few months in 1933 before returning to Chicago. Another one of the guys said a lot of old gangsters and gamblers were in

St. Paul until the police cracked down after a kidnapping. With the police breathing down their necks, and Prohibition making it hard to get liquor, they moved operations to Pine City where there was lots of moonshine and the sheriff's department turned a blind eye to the criminals, either out of fear or because they were pumping money into the local pockets.

"We'll know a lot more once they get the roof off and can see what's inside the shack," Pam looked at Floyd and asked. "How's your unofficial investigation going?"

"Apparently, Margaret Lane ceased to exist when the sanatorium closed. Like we said at Ernie's, it's as if she was abducted by aliens. Or maybe kidnapped by gangsters. That's as likely as any of the other theories I'm chasing. It would make some sense, too, because there's no record of her anymore. If she was recruited into a bordello, she probably wouldn't have used her real name, and when she died she was either buried in a pauper's grave or with a headstone with her working name. And if she worked at the sanatorium she may have contracted TB. If she died from it, she's probably in an unmarked grave."

"So, master detective Swenson, how do you research that seventy years later?"

"I'm sure the bordellos kept excellent records," Floyd said with a snort. "Or maybe she fell in love with one of the male patients at the sanatorium, got married, and moved off without a paper trail."

"or she left with one of the workers. Were there any young orderlies or other single men working in the sanatorium? Or even a single neighbor or deliveryman?"

"I'd like to narrow the field of possibilities, not add to it,"

"It was you, Floyd, who told me to follow the clues as they lead and not lock yourself into solutions that don't fit the evidence."

"That's all well and good, "Floyd said, "but, I don't have any clues to follow. I'm running on conjecture and that's a road to nowhere."

"At the press conference this morning," said Pam, "one of the newsmen asked the sheriff if he had a motive or suspects for this crime. The sheriff said, 'At this point we have no information and no evidence. If I were to comment on that basis, I'd just be another jerk with an opinion.' That's one you should write down and pull out every time some pushy reporter is pumping you for an update on a case that's not progressing."

Floyd peeked around the BCA mobile crime lab at the reporters.

"They're like buzzards waiting for the carcass to die," Pam said, "then they go into a feeding frenzy."

"They're doing their jobs," Floyd replied. "It must be a slow news day in the rest of the world." He stared at his shoes for a moment, then smiled. "I kinda like the alien abduction theory. I wonder if that will sell."

"When pigs fly, as my grandpa used to say."

"I'm going to take a look at the shack," Floyd said. "That'll give the camera crews another shot for the evening news."

He drove his personal pickup down the rutted road, the grass now flattened by the vehicles driving back and forth. The forest opened where the loggers had been working, He could see pickups parked on the far side of the clearing with a half dozen people standing around. Parking at the opening to the clearing Floyd walked to the huddled group who appeared to be strategizing.

"Hi Jeff," Floyd said to the lead BCA crime scene tech he had worked with in other investigations.

Jeff Telker, dressed in a white Tyvek coverall, excused himself from the others and shook Floyd's hand. "Good to see you, Floyd."

"What's your preliminary take on this?" Floyd asked as they stood at the edge of the clearing. Little of the shack was visible except the rusty cast iron stove protruding from tarpaper.

"We've seen the partial skeleton of one body. We're trying to figure out how best to peel back the remnants of the old shack without ruining any trace evidence."

"So it's too early to tell if there's more than one set of remains or the cause of death?"

"Way too early for that. Sonny Carlson is just drawing up the crime scene relative to the landmarks and taking pictures. It'll be awhile before we actually start to dig into the shack. Then, it'll be like an archaeological dig. We'll have to peel back the layers and record the tidbits of evidence we find."

"You're going to be here for days," Floyd said.

Jeff looked over the scene and drew a deep breath. "It depends on what we find, but we could be here days, then spend more days in the lab digging through the evidence."

"Good luck," Floyd said, shaking hands again before returning to his pickup.

At the gate he stopped and told Pam, "I'm off to my next stop," Floyd said. "I'm not sure why, but I feel like I need to look at the sanatorium dump."

"The dump?" Pam said, wrinkling her nose. "The one on the west side of Pokegama?"

"That'd be the one. I can't imagine that I'll find anything, but it seems like someplace I should be."

"There've been hundreds, maybe thousands, of people who've dug through that heap. There's nothing left of value."

"Yeah, I'm not even going to bring a shovel. I'll just look around and check it off my list." As he turned to leave he said, "Send me a text when the crime lab guys find something."

Jeff Telker and Sonny Carlson, the BCA crime scene technicians, were working alongside Dale Palm and Terry Pritchard, two interns from the Minnesota

Department of Natural Resources' Forestry office. The young interns were dressed in jeans and denim shirts and seemed amazingly happy to be helping the BCA dismantle the tarpaper roof covering the collapsed shack. Alongside the perimeter of the shack, the pile of tarpaper and rotten lumber debris being fed into large plastic evidence bags kept growing, even though most of it was being added a handful at a time due to the structure's advanced state of decay.

"This is like being on an archaeological dig," Terry Pritchard, the younger intern said. Although he'd completed his forestry degree, he was baby-faced and looked no more than sixteen.

"Okay," said Jeff Telker, the senior crime scene tech, "We're going to roll out this next ceiling joist and hope it moves intact. Stay outside the area we've cleared, and don't freak out if we see more bones."

"Freak out?" said Dale Palm. "This is way cool!"

"Crime scenes aren't cool," said Sonny Carlson, the younger white-haired crime scene tech. "They're interesting, sometimes, but not cool. Hey, Jeff, remember that one over in MacGregor where the guy was raising tigers? Whew, that was interesting. There was blood evidence spread over acres and it took a long time to determine if we were looking at something more than a tiger rampage. It turned out that a neighbor had been teasing the tiger through the chain-link fence and it jumped on the next person who came through the gate."

"Sonny," Telker said, "could you stop talking and lift?" Jeff asked.

"Sure, I can lift," Sonny said, bending down and grasping the rotting beam with tarpaper tacked across its width. "But I'm not so sure I can stop talking. My mother said it's the clash of my Swedish and Finnish blood. Although, it you look at my Finnish relatives, well, they're all pretty quiet and serious folk. Now the Swedes, well, they talk."

"Sonny, lift and roll."

"I'm lifting," Sonny replied. "But I can do two things at the same time. I'm pretty adept."

"Adept at continuous prattle."

"Now, don't get personal. You get your share of comments in, too."

"Sonny can carry both sides of an argument," Jeff said to Pritchard.

"That's a benefit when you're working with some-one who's quiet," said Sonny. "Sometimes I don't know what Jeff is thinking. When I'm throwing out ideas, he'll speak up and shoot my ideas down. I'm never offended by that, but it sure helps clear the air sometimes."

The four men slowly rolled back a long, rough-cut two-by-four that dated back to the days before lumber was planed smooth. The tacks securing the tarpaper had all rusted through, but the tarpaper followed as if it was still nailed.

"Now," Telker said, "as long as it's holding together, let's move it away from the exterior walls. See if we can just peel it back until the entire interior is uncovered."

"You know," said Sonny. "I've always wondered how long tarpaper holds up. When it's directly exposed to the elements, like this, I suppose it breaks down twice as fast as what you put down under a roof. And that new frost guard, well it's really thick and I'd bet it lasts a hundred years."

The two-by-four was as black as the tarpaper and had the consistency of a sponge, but it held together, supported by eight hands, until they were more than ten feet beyond the shack's perimeter.

"This board is thicker and the surface is rougher than the other lumber I've seen," said Palm.

"It hasn't been planed," explained Sonny. "Rough-cut lumber was common up through World War II, and some small sawmills sold rough-cut lumber long after that. On the other hand, these flattened balsam timbers are throwbacks to the 1800s. The black grit between them is most likely sawdust used as insulation."

"Really?" Palm asked. "Like one spark, and this place would've burned like a butane lighter. Whoosh!"

He started to make another comment when he noticed the two crime scene techs staring silently at the middle of the structure. "Were they sitting around a table?" Sonny asked, looking at scattered ivory bones and bone chips, some covered with moss and lichens as if nature was trying to camouflage them. The discolored skulls looked like giant mushrooms with eye sockets and nose openings. The jaws were all separated from the skulls, either by the force of the falling roof or the scavengers who'd apparently been drawn to the rotting corpses. Bone fragments appeared to be randomly arranged around the perimeter of a dark platform, but closer inspection revealed leg bones, arm bones, ribs, and pelvises, all discolored from their years of lying under the tarpaper and now turning the same color as the dirt beneath them. Glass fragments from the tops of three liquor bottles and pieces of drinking glasses littered the area. Other wood scraps intermixed with the bones hinted at the presence of a wooden table and broken chairs. Rusty screws and nails were still holding some pieces together. A rusty pistol was still in a leather shoulder holster, the leather now green.

As the others stared, a camera flash lit the shadows under the tree canopy. Sonny was taking pictures of the tableau.

"Do you think they were killed when the roof caved in on them?" Pritchard asked.

"We need to get a forensic anthropologist in here," Jeff said, squatting over one area of bone fragments. "But I'd say this guy died of gunshot wounds, maybe during a card game." He carefully rocked an intact skull, until a large hole was visible. Tiny cracks radiated like a spider web around the bullet hole. "The bullet that made this hole was a large caliber, not a modern high-speed load."

Sonny then pointed to black disks scattered around the table. "Those would be silver coins. They tarnish quickly in this environment." He picked up a coin in his gloved hand and gently rubbed the surface, then inspected it, "This is a five-dollar gold piece. Since there's only one gold coin, I'll bet this was after the government recalled the gold coins. We should be able to narrow this down to plus or minus a year when we clean up the coins and check the dates. Since the rest of the coins are all silver, the dollar coins and half-dollar coins are the old, large design, we've bracketed the crime scene between the early 30s and the 60s."

Sonny bent down and took a picture of the coins on what had been the tabletop, and said, "The government took all the gold coins out of circulation in the 1930s, but a lot of folks held onto a few. I've heard a lot of gamblers carried one as a good luck piece." He stepped back and surveyed the scene. "I'm guessing we're looking at five bodies, who all died at the same time, somewhere between 1932 and 1964. Because of the construction materials, I'm leaning more toward the 1930's time period."

"Why would five guys be playing poker in a shack out in the middle of the forest?" Palm asked.

"It wasn't a forest in the 1930s," Jeff said, bagging the gold coin and marking the evidence tag. "You're the forestry guys. How old are the pine trees outside this hardwood grove?"

"I think the CCC planted them during the Depression," said Palm. "Everything was either clear-cut or burned by 1900, so this was probably scrubby oak growth or underbrush."

"Since gambling was illegal and St. Paul was cracking down, a shack in the woods might've been a nice getaway for a traveling card game," Sonny said as he shot more pictures.

"Does anything strike you as odd, boys?" asked Jeff as more flashes popped behind him. "Why would someone kill these guys and leave the money sitting on the table?" asked Sonny.

"I think someone wanted them dead more than they wanted the money," said Jeff.

"At least one of them was shot" said Sonny, as he moved a piece of wood away from a rusty piece of metal entangled with small bones, then snapped a picture. "It appears this guy had a pistol in his hand. I guess this wasn't a friendly card game and whatever happened, took him by surprise because I can still see the lead of all the bullets."

CHAPTER 25

PINE CITY
TUESDAY

The sanatorium dump, which was a few miles west of town, had been abandoned in the 1960s when landfills became the legal means of garbage disposal. The dump itself was only twenty yards off the road, down a narrow muddy driveway. Floyd surveyed the jumble of old appliances, broken glass, and rusting metal cans, furniture, and farm equipment. Small .22-caliber shell casings, now covered with patina, littered the area, attesting to the use of the spot as a target range, which in turn was the reason there was so much broken glass and cans riddled with bullet holes.

"Margaret, were you ever here?" he asked. "If you were, there's no way of knowing it anymore."

A rustling in a nearby pile caught Floyd's attention. As he stared, a pile of cans shifted and a chipmunk hopped on top of them and froze, surprised to see a person in his private domain. The chipmunk flicked its tail a few times, and then scurried back into the cover of a different garbage pile.

"Just like Margaret Lane," Floyd said aloud. "She got thrown out of one garbage heap, at the State School, into another at the Tuxedo Inn. Who knows what she endured there before going off to the sanatorium. What happened to you after that, Margaret? Did you drift off to another garbage heap, or did you manage to pull your life together?

"What am I missing? There have to be records. Did you ever file a tax return or pay into Social Security at some point in your life? Did you collect Social Security? Were you baptized, married, divorced, or buried? Was your name ever in a phone book or listed as a member of a church, Order of the Eastern Star, or Women of the Moose Lodge?"

Discouraged, Floyd returned to his pickup and drove to Tuxedo Point. He walked past the crumbling concrete foundations of several buildings and onto the sandbar that extended into Lake Pokegama. Cement footings, upended by years of shifting ice, were the only remnants of the pier that was once the landing for the passenger boats that brought people to and from the Tuxedo Inn before the roads were built.

A boat was anchored twenty yards from shore and two fishermen were chatting with their backs toward shore, oblivious to Floyd's presence. He left them undisturbed and returned to the large foundation that was once the bustling inn and restaurant and now was nestled among weeds. Human scavengers had removed anything with antique value, which left only broken glass and unidentifiable rusting metal pieces.

"Margaret, I know you were here," he said to himself. "I wish you could tell me about your time at the Tuxedo Inn."

Something caught his eye and he unearthed a small agate, glowing red. Alternating bands of red and gray that had built up over millennia were layered in the rock. "I wonder if you ever walked down this driveway, filling your pockets with agates you picked from the gravel?"

"I should check the churches," Floyd said. "Although I doubt anyone working at the Tuxedo Inn attended church."

Ten minutes later, he was walking up the front steps of the Presbyterian Church on Main Street. A middle-aged woman with blonde hair and porcelain skin was standing at a copier in the church office. Focused on her project, she didn't hear Floyd enter. "Excuse me," he said.

Mary Gilbert spun around with her hand to her chest. "Dear me, Floyd! I didn't hear you." Composing herself, she took a deep breath. "How can I help you?"

"Hi Mary, I'm looking for records of someone who lived in Pine City before World War II. I was wondering if you have membership rolls, baptism records, and such going back that far."

"We have a file cabinet full of ledgers with that type of information," she said with a smile. "None of the records are digitized, so you'll have to page through the ledgers, but they're all chronological, so you might be able to search them pretty quickly."

Do you have a table where I could sit while I search?"

"The files are in the church library and there's a table there." Mary took a key ring from her desk and led Floyd to the library. In the farthest corner, she unlocked an oak file cabinet and opened the bottom drawer. She removed a leather-bound ledger from the center of the drawer, set it on the table, and opened it to a random page.

"Hey," she said, "I was guessing this would be about 1940. This one is," she flipped to the first and last pages, "from January 1932 to December 1944."

Floyd pulled the book in front of him and read the hand-written notations of church events, from baptisms to marriages. "Great," he said, "I'll just sit here and page through the book."

"Would you care for a cup of coffee?" Mary asked.

"I would love a cup of coffee. I like it black."

When Mary returned, Floyd was already fifteen pages into the book. He accepted the coffee and savored the aroma before taking a sip.

"Thank you," he said.

"The pot's in the kitchen. Help yourself if you'd care for more."

Forty minutes later he was back in the office. "Thanks, Mary."

"Did you find anything helpful?"

"I'm afraid not, but that's the way investigations go."

He repeated the unsuccessful search at the Grace Baptist Church, then ate lunch at the Pizza Pub. In the afternoon, he was at Zion Lutheran church when his cellphone chimed. The text from Pam Ryan said simply, "5."

"Five people who've been missing for fifty years," he said to himself, shaking his head.

He moved on to Our Redeemer Lutheran and then to the Immaculate Conception parish. At the Catholic church, he was treated to homemade cookies and coffee by the elderly but spry church secretary, Mavis Cook.

"You know, Mavis, if you feed me cookies and coffee, I may just stay here for days."

"Floyd, you're welcome here for coffee anytime, but the cookies are only here on bingo days."

Completing his search of the volumes of Catholic files, he returned to the office, where Mavis was shutting down her computer and preparing to leave for the day. "Thanks," he said. "I didn't find the record I was hoping for, but I appreciate the coffee and your help."

"Anytime, Floyd,"

He turned to leave and stopped at the door. "When the sanatorium closed, it was taken over by a Catholic seminary. That's gone too, but would you have any idea where their files might have gone, or if they even kept the sanatorium files?"

Mavis smiled. "The seminary was run by the Redemptorist Fathers and Brothers and the sanatorium administration building was converted into a retirement home. We don't have any of those records here, but you could contact the Redemptorists. Catholics never throw anything away."

"Where are the Redemptorists?"

"They're officially called the Congregation of the Most Holy Redeemer. I'm not sure if Minnesota is part of the Baltimore or the Denver Province."

CHAPTER 26

THE TUXEDO INN
OCTOBER 1934

Meal preparations were underway and the girls were busy putting away the lunch dishes and setting the tables for dinner. Pixie, now accustomed to the routine, was intently wiping the spots off silverware when she was startled by a hand on her shoulder. She dropped the butter knife she was polishing and gasped.

"I'm sorry," said Abigail. "I didn't mean to surprise you."

"It's okay," Pixie said, picking up the knife and composing herself. She looked around and saw the other girls were busy with their own projects.

"Set aside your work for a bit. I'd like to talk with you outside."

Pixie followed her out the front door. Abigail took a cigarette from a silver case and lit it with a matching lighter. From the top step they could see across the parking lot to the glimmers of Lake Pokegama peeking through the bushes. A crisp breeze hinted of the winter that hadn't yet released its grip on Pine City.

"Do you like it here?" asked Abigail.

"It's nice."

"Are the girls treating you well?"

"Yes."

"Do you need anything?"

"No."

Abigail blew a stream of smoke into the air over her head. "You're not much of a conversationalist, are you?"

"We weren't allowed to speak unless spoken to. I guess I became accustomed to that."

"What do you know about your position here?"

Pixie looked confused. "I work, and you feed me and give me a place to sleep. Is there something more?" Pixie asked.

"You're an indentured servant," Abigail answered. "Do you know what that means?"

Pixie shook her head.

"A sponsor paid for your trip here. You earn your room and board, and a little cash. The cash goes to your sponsor until they've been paid for your trip expenses.

You don't make a lot of money after room and board are deducted, so it will be a couple years before the indenture is paid off."

"That's okay," Pixie replied with a shrug. "I've got nowhere else to go."

Abigail threw the cigarette butt into the gravel parking lot and stared down at Pixie. "Make sure you stay upstairs when the customers are here tonight. Do you understand?"

Pixie nodded, but wondered why.

Abigail lit another cigarette with the silver lighter and inhaled deeply. "There are some men coming from St. Paul. They are tough people who've done some very bad things. We'll feed them well, treat them royally, and they'll spend a lot of money here. They'll probably make a lot of noise and want the music played loud. Some of the women might scream . . . with laughter. Whatever happens, don't come downstairs."

"Why do you let them come here if they're bad?"

"Their money buys a lot of what you see here," Abigail said, not meeting Pixie's eyes.

"But —"

Leaning close, Abigail took Pixie's arms in her hands. "Honey, promise me you won't come downstairs. Promise me."

"I promise," Pixie said, sensing fear in Abigail's voice. "Mary and . . ."

"They know," Abigail said, throwing her cigarette down and crushing it under her foot. "When you hear cars in the driveway, you stop whatever you're doing and run upstairs."

The tables were set and the inn was eerily quiet except for the clatter in the kitchen as the cooks prepared dinner. The early customers were usually seated by five o'clock. It was nearly an hour after that and there wasn't a patron in the restaurant. The girls tried to look busy, rearranging the table settings and refreshing the flowers, but there was nothing left to do. Abigail stood near the door, smoking and checking the clock. Pixie studied her face, which seemed to have aged a decade since their afternoon talk.

Carol, who was working near a window, shouted, "They're here!" Soon after came the sound of tires on the gravel. The girls ran for the stairs and slammed their attic door shut before the first car stopped rolling. Mary dragged Pixie to a dormer window and pulled back the curtain. Pixie hung back until Carol pulled her alongside. They all crouched down so only the tops of their heads were visible to someone in the parking lot.

Four cars were parked in the lot and men were holding the doors open for the women. Mary pointed at the third car. "That man, the one with the little mustache, he's John Dillinger."

"That guy's got red hair," Florence whispered. "I saw Dillinger's picture in the post office and he's got dark hair."

"Well, maybe he's in disguise."

"Maybe it's one of his gang," Mary said

"Well, maybe it's not Dillinger's gang at all," said Florence.

"Chef Tony said the Dillinger gang called from Hastings and reserved the whole inn for the night," Carol said. "Alvin Karpis and Homer Van Meter will be here with Dillinger. One of the Barker boys might be in that last car."

"Who's John Dillinger?" Pixie asked.

"He's the most wanted man in all of the country," said Mary. "I heard that he's robbed a hundred banks and killed twenty policemen. The G-men are offering a thousand-dollar reward for him."

"They look young," Pixie said.

"Gangsters don't live to be old men," Carol said.

"Oh, look at the guy in the last car," said Mary. "I bet that's Baby Face Nelson. He looks like he's hardly older than us."

"Look at his eyes," said Carol. "They're hard. He keeps looking around, like he's a hunted animal."

"I think he's cute," said Mary.

Carol said, "Look at the women with them. They don't look happy."

"They're not wearing tuxedos and long dresses," Pixie said. "I thought that was a rule."

"I suppose if they've rented the whole place for to-night," Carol said, "maybe they don't have to dress up if no one else is coming."

"Did you see that?" Carol asked. "The last guy was wearing a shoulder holster. I saw it before he put on his coat."

Gathering the supper dishes from their upstairs table, Pixie nearly dropped the stack when a woman shrieked downstairs. There was raucous laughter immediately after the shriek. Pixie stood frozen.

"I've never actually heard voices before," Pixie said. "I've only heard noises before."

Mary, who looked equally rattled, shook her head. "It's the gangsters. Tony says they're loud and they play rough."

Carol motioned for the others to come close. "Arthur said the gang was in a shootout with some G-men last Friday in Wisconsin. I guess they barely got away. He said they came to Minnesota until things cool off."

The clinking of dishes in the dining room signaled the end of dinner and the start of after-dinner drinks. The laughter stopped and the voices softened. The girls played cards and listened, trying to hear snippets of conversation. Footsteps on the stairs brought their game to a stop. The girls stared at the door, expecting to see Tony or Abigail.

The door opened and a hatchet-faced man stared at the girls. "Bathroom up here?" the man slurred.

The girls froze. "Downstairs," Carol whispered.

The man's eyes locked on Pixie, looking her up and down, which gave her goosebumps. "You're cute. Why aren't you at the party?"

Pixie edged back, dropping her cards and knocking her chair over. Footsteps pounded up the stairs and Abigail's face appeared. She took the man's arm and tugged.

"Come along, Lucky," she said, "the party's just getting started."

"Why aren't these girls at the party?" he asked. "I'm partial to young girls like that skinny one."

Abigail's eyes scanned the girls, searching for words. "They're sick. We keep them away from the guests."

The man stared at Pixie, then nodded. "She probably has consumption or something."

"Come along, Lucky. The party's downstairs." As the man started down the stairs, Abigail leaned back in. "Lock the door."

CHAPTER 27

PINE COUNTY COURTHOUSE, TUESDAY

Tom Bakken sat at the prosecutor's table scanning the notes in front of him, preparing for an afternoon court session, when his secretary rushed into the courtroom. She handed him a message slip and said, "Call Jane Simmons immediately."

Bakken glanced at the note and felt his stomach churn. "What are the eco-idiots up to now?" he asked himself.

He walked out of the courtroom and called the U.S. Attorney on his cellphone. "This is Tom Bakken," he said. "What's up? I'm on a short recess."

"I'm holding an injunction to stop the logging at Nemadji State Forest. Please dispatch a deputy to escort the loggers out and have someone, maybe the forestry folks, chain the gate."

"What? The eco-idiots got a judge to stop the logging?"

"Oh, if life were only that simple," Jane Simmons said. "Three Chippewa tribes filed for the injunction based on an 1837 treaty. The treaty they presented to the judge says that the tribes sold the timber rights to the pines, but retained the rights to all the deciduous trees."

Bakken stared at the ceiling. "You're serious?"

"Mr. Bakken, I don't joke."

"This is . . ." Bakken searched for words. "The loggers will go ballistic. I mean, this is their livelihood. If the tribe shows up at the gate, I'll be hard pressed to ensure their safety."

"You'd better figure out how to protect them. I heard the tribal leaders called a news conference at the west forest entrance for this afternoon. Send that blonde deputy. She looks good on camera."

"If the cameras are there, the sheriff will be there. Listen, I've got to run. Do you have any other good news for me?"

"The protesters are meeting with the Washington lawyer right now and they'll be going before a federal judge this afternoon. I told Rosen I'd offer supervised parole to the first person who agrees to testify against the others. I'm pretty sure one of them will throw the others under the bus to get themselves a slap on the wrist."

"Good luck with that," replied Bakken. "My experience has been that young people don't turn on each other."

"You haven't threatened to put them in Leavenworth. Ten years in a federal prison is a long time for a twenty-something kid. They'll come out looking like they're fifty."

Bakken was about to reply when he heard the dial tone. He immediately dialed the sheriff. "John, I just got a call from the U.S. Attorney. Three Chippewa tribes have secured an injunction to stop the logging in the Nemadji State Forest. I'll call the Department of Forestry and ask them to chain the gate. I need you to get a deputy or two out there to escort the loggers out and make sure no one goes in."

"What are you talking about, Tom?"

"The Indians say they hold the logging rights to the leafy trees in the state forest under some old treaty. I assume a federal magistrate looked at their claim and signed an injunction to stop the logging until the lawyers from both sides can argue their positions."

"And why are my deputies involved in this?"

"Because the tribes have called a news conference at the entrance this afternoon, and you need people there to make sure the tribal leaders don't get lynched or shot when the loggers get escorted out."

"Sonofabitch! When's the news conference?"

"Call your buddies at the television stations. I'm sure they'll give you the exact time and they'll have crews out there to capture the craziness," Bakken said.

"You heard that we found an old shack out in the logging lease area with a bunch of bodies?" asked the sheriff.

"Yeah, I caught that on the news," said the attorney. "Who are the victims?"

"We don't know yet. The BCA found five sets of skeletal remains and they're taking the bones to St. Paul for analysis."

"Skeletons. So we're not talking recent missing persons," Bakken said with relief.

"Right. The remains may date back decades."

"Any thoughts on the cause of death?"

"At least one appeared to have a gunshot wound to the head."

"Okay," Bakken said. "Doing the math, I figure a murderer in the 1930s would likely be at least twenty years old. That would make him about 100 today, and most likely dead. I can live with that. An old crime and the murderer is dead. It's the best of all outcomes: solve it and I'll pat you on the back and say what a great job you're doing, and I don't have to prosecute a murderer. It's perfect!"

"A decades-old murder won't be easy to solve," the sheriff replied. "It's not like he left behind a card that says 'I did it.' Chances of us actually identifying the murderer or the victim now are slim and none, and I'm betting on none."

"Put your ace cold-case expert on it," said Bakken. "Floyd has pulled a couple other rabbits out of hats."

"He's busy right now, but that may be a thought." The sheriff paused, then added. "Crap! What if our bomber decides to use this news conference to send another message?" He let out a deep sigh. "I'd better find a bomb-sniffing dog somewhere."

CHAPTER 28

FEDERAL COURTHOUSE, MINNEAPOLIS
TUESDAY

Ira Rosen sat in an interview room with a pile of notes and a paper cup of bad coffee. The third protester came into the room, his eyes brightening when he saw Rosen. The marshal led the handcuffed man to the chair opposite the lawyer.

When the door closed, Rosen said, "Mike, what the hell were you thinking? It's a crime just to have sex with an underage girl, but to bring her to Minnesota . . . that's a federal crime and the feds don't look favorably on child trafficking."

"She told me she was eighteen," Mike Parrish protested. "It's not like I thought I had to see her ID."

"Does she look like she's eighteen?" Rosen said, rising from the chair and pacing in the small room. "Child molesters don't do well in prison."

"Prison?" Parrish's eyes grew wide and he clenched the table edges. "Yesterday afternoon you said we'd get probation and be back in Oregon. This is just bullshit."

"That's not how this is playing out," Rosen said. "I'm on shaky ground here, but let me throw this out to you. The prosecutor offered immunity to the first of you who offers to testify against the others."

"Whoa! I'm not ratting them out!"

"Listen to me," said, Rosen, sitting down and leaning close. "Some of you are going to prison. Not a county jail, but a real live federal prison where there are really bad people who did really bad things. If you are the first person to agree to the deal, you get a wrist slap, you walk out of here, get your shit together, and start living a clean life. If you don't, you're one of the people the prosecutor wants to use as an example."

"What did the others say?" Parrish asked.

"Are you listening to me?" Rosen nearly shouted. "You have to be the first one in line to accept the offer. Your uncle Harry and I discussed it and we think we can slip this by the judge and prosecutor. If you agree to testify against the others, you walk."

"But the others—aren't they going to jump on the offer?"

"How slow *are* you? They're not going to hear the offer. It's intended for the first taker and you're the first one I've told." Rosen stood and leaned on the table. "Get your head in the game. Your future is hanging in the balance. If you're convicted, you'll spend years in a scary federal prison and the rest of your life is shit. Not just for the time you're in jail, which will be bad enough, but the whole rest of your life. Tell me you're going to accept the amnesty offer and we can move on."

Parrish's eyes filled with tears. "This is bullshit! This whole screwed-up thing is bullshit. Jeremy said it was going to be a joyride. He had cash and we were going cross-country with the girls and a backpack full of drugs. We'd camp out and when the cash ran out we'd sell dope to other campers to pay our expenses. It was all going to be fun. Then, he gets a call and we have to go to Minnesota. Minnesota! Mosquitoes as big as Piper Cubs and the whole place is like a time warp of the past.

"We're out at this forest gate and Jeremy gets us all lined up and then these redneck loggers start showing up. I looked at him and I said, 'Cue up the soundtrack from *Deliverance.*' It's like I can see the hatred in their eyes and I can almost hear the banjo. I mean, these guys are Neanderthals with necks as big around as their heads, and they look hard. I was really glad when the cops showed up because I thought we were going to be cut up into pieces and thrown into the forest for the wolves."

Rosen made notes as Mike spoke, then set the pen aside. "There are a bunch of issues here. Where was Jeremy getting money?"

"I don't know. He always paid for gas with a charge card and sometimes withdrew cash from an ATM. I just figured it was his money," Mike said with a shrug.

"Exactly who was selling drugs?" Rosen asked.

"I guess we all did," Mike whined. "I mean, it's not like we were drug dealers; we were just picking up some extra cash."

"You bought large quantities, then sold it in smaller quantities to people you didn't know. Mike, that's the definition of dealing drugs."

"No, we were just selling enough to pay for food and campground fees." Mike started to sob. "I'm not a drug dealer. I was just using the money to buy groceries."

"Mike, focus," Rosen said. "I need you to agree to this plea agreement right now. You'll spend a couple months in jail, maybe even get out on bail until the trial, then you'll be on probation for a few years. I go back to Washington and my paying clients."

"But, we're like family, Mr. Rosen. I can't rat them out, and besides, I'm in it as deep as they are."

Rosen hung his head and stared at the floor. After a minute he started packing his papers into the briefcase.

"What are you doing," asked, Parrish.

"I'm not going to hang around and watch this get sucked into a whirlpool." Rosen snapped the briefcase shut. "I'm going to withdraw from the case and ask that a public defender be assigned to you and your friends."

"But, Uncle Harry . . ."

"Your Uncle Harry doesn't have enough money to keep me here. When I explain that I negotiated a deal to get you released and that you declined it, he'll shake his head and say, 'Ira, you did what you could for the kid, but if he's not smart enough to save himself, well, he deserves to be in prison.'" Rosen took his briefcase to the door and knocked for the guard.

"Wait! That's really it? I either take this or I'm cut off?"

"Yes," Rosen said, as the door opened.

"Okay! You've made your point!" Parrish said. He looked at the jailer. "Leave us alone for a little longer."

Rosen nodded and the door closed.

"So, here's the deal. I call the U.S. Attorney and tell her that I have a defendant who's willing to take the deal in return for his cooperation and testimony. We get a hearing before a judge this afternoon and the prosecutor tells the judge she's offering you probation in return for your cooperation. The judge usually agrees and we can discuss bail."

"And the others?"

"They'll all be at the table with us. I'm sure they won't be happy, but hey, life it tough."

"They'll kill me."

"You'll be segregated from them and probably released on bail. It's not good for them, but someone is going to turn and it might as well be you." Rosen took out a pen and poised it over the paper. "The bimbo from Oregon, Susan, who else was she screwing?"

"That's cold."

Rosen tapped his pen. "Listen, the only way the judge will accept your plea is if she's had sex with at least one of the other guys. Whose sleeping bag has she been sharing?"

Parrish took a deep breath. "Initially, she was recruited by Jeremy, and she kinda fell under his spell, but his militancy grew thin and she came over to my tent just to get away from Jeremy. Then Clarke was hitting on her one night while we were doing meth and she just drifted off with him, but she came back to my tent the next night."

"So, she's had sex with Jeremy, Clarke and you. How about Stephanie?"

"I don't know," Parrish whined. "We were pretty messed up for a while and the girls and the dope just kinda flowed around."

Rosen leaned back and stared at the ceiling. "Mike, it sounds like you guys had a traveling orgy."

"Meth kinda does weird things. I mean, your inhibitions go away and the orgasms are epic. You kinda get going and it gets crazy."

"I need something to tell the U.S. Attorney. If I can tell her that you're willing to testify that the other guys had engaged in sex with Susan, she'd be more willing to let you be the star witness."

"I suppose she probably slept with the other guys, but I can't remember who or when. She was with me mostly."

"Focus on the others. You've got to have a cohesive and repetitive story that Susan was with the other guys. When and where were you when you were all using the meth?"

"We were in the Black Hills after the Sturgis bike rally. There were still a lot of bikers around and we were partying pretty heavily with those guys, so that's probably when we were the most messed up and things were the craziest."

"Give me dates and the name of the campground . . ."

CHAPTER 29

PINE COUNTY SHERIFF'S OFFICE
TUESDAY

Floyd and Pam arrived at the courthouse at the same time and the dispatcher directed them to Sheriff Sepanen's office. Floyd knocked on the doorframe and they walked in. The sheriff, dressed in a white golf shirt with the Pine County Sheriff's Department logo on the chest, motioned them to his guest chairs.

"The Nemadji forest logging is turning into an even bigger fiasco," Sepanen said, closing the office door. "Three Chippewa tribes have received an injunction to stop the logging. They claim that the hardwood trees were granted to them under an old treaty. The U.S. Attorney called Tom Bakken and he's going to have the forestry guys chain the gate shut as soon as we clear the loggers out."

"Forestry can escort the loggers out and lock the gate," said Floyd. "Why do they need us?"

"Because the tribal leaders have called a press conference, and everyone is afraid there might be a problem if we're not there to intervene." Sepanen looked at Pam. "I want you at the west gate. That's where the press conference will be."

"Okay," said Pam, "but I'm not the imposing figure that Kerm Rajacich would be."

"Don't make me say it," the sheriff said.

"Pam is the face of the sheriff's department you'd like to see on television," Floyd said, with a smile.

The sheriff shrugged. "I'll go along and stand in the shadows."

"Thank you," said Pam. "I wasn't excited about being the only buffer between a bunch of angry loggers and the tribal leaders."

"Floyd, are you making any progress on . . . the other project we discussed?"

"I made a few inquiries, but most are dead ends. I have one lead left, to follow with the Redemptorist Fathers who operated the Pokegama Lake Seminary. There's an outside chance they may have the sanatorium records. Other than that, I'm out of ideas."

"Have you talked to Pam about the bodies that were found in the Nemadji Forest shack?"

Floyd shook his head. "When I was out there the BCA had one skull and were about to start peeling back the tarpaper. But now there were five victims."

"Yes, the BCA recovered five sets of human remains that appear to have been there a long time. I had a call from Sonny Carlson this morning. They cleaned up the coins they found on the table inside the shack. The newest coin was from 1934, so we're tentatively assigning that as the time of the murders."

"Are you sure they were murders?" Floyd asked.

"At least one skeleton had an obvious bullet wound to the head, and there's another that looks like a rib was nicked by a bullet.

"Floyd," the sheriff said, "I want you to step up and lead the investigation."

"Really? You want me to take on another cold case?"

"You're the best I've got."

"How do you know that? You've never assigned a cold case to anyone else," Floyd replied.

"You've solved them and that's more than I expected. You've shown creativity and ingenuity in the process."

"Pam is the source of creativity. I just slog through old clues."

"I beg your pardon," Pam said. "I'm the one who slogs through records and reports. You're out interviewing people and doing the interesting things."

"You're my cold-case team," said the sheriff. "I want the two of you to work with the BCA and see where the investigation goes."

"Floyd, you can call Sonny back," Pam said. "The last time I called, he had me on the phone for half an hour! I know that he's half Finn and half Swede, that his wife's name is Betty, and the names of his three children. He's fun to talk with, but man, he can hold up both ends of a conversation. I could barely slip a question in."

"Yeah, he's talkative, but he's good," said Floyd. "I worked with him on a case a few years ago. He processed the crime scene and came up with two fibers he linked to the trunk of the murderer's car. He was dogged and thorough."

"But I needed to get my question answered and it took too long," Pam complained.

"He told me he thinks best when he's talking," Floyd said.

"Then he was thinking for half an hour while I listened. I'll email him from now on." Pam said. She paused, then added, "What if another bomb goes off during the press conference?"

"I thought of that. I called Duluth PD and asked for a bomb-sniffing dog," the sheriff replied. "I want to check the forest entrance area before the press conference to make sure we *don't* have another event."

"There are only a couple of narrow two-lane roads leading into the forest," Floyd replied. "A terrorist could place a bomb anywhere along the roads or on the trails."

"The tribal news conference came up pretty quickly," Pam said. "Let's hope the bomber hasn't had time to get set up before the news conference.

"Okay, let's get out there and make sure no one gets hurt," the sheriff said, rising from his chair. He paused and cocked his head. "When did you start wearing lipstick?" he asked Pam.

"I wear it sometimes," Pam replied, blushing.

"It's very subtle," replied the sheriff, nodding approval.

"You know," Floyd said to Pam as they walked down the hallway, "everyone will hear about your boyfriend sooner or later."

"Later is better," she replied. "This may all be a flash in the pan and over before the rumor mill gets hold of it."

"I think it's too late."

Pam stopped and put her hands on her hips. "Why do you say that?"

Floyd shrugged. "You don't think anyone has noticed your lipstick or new haircut? Even the sheriff noticed and he doesn't notice anything unless he's seeing it in a mirror."

CHAPTER 30

PINE BROOK FLORAL
WEDNESDAY MORNING

Mary dialed the phone and waited. "Carlton County. How may I direct your call?"

"Tax assessor's office, please," Mary said.

Soon she heard, "Assessor's office, this is Travis Conrad."

"Hi, Travis. This is Mary Jungers. Floyd Swenson and I met you at Ernie's."

"Hi, Mary," Travis said, after a second of hesitation. "What can I do for you?"

"I apologize for the short notice, but if you and Pam are free tonight, we'd like you to come down to Floyd's house. We'll throw something on the grill."

"I don't have any plans for tonight, but I can't speak for Pam."

"I'll have Floyd talk to her. Let's assume it will work. If there's a hitch, I'll call back and leave you a message. Floyd lives west of Sturgeon Lake . . ."

CHAPTER 31

NEMADJI STATE FOREST

Floyd and Pam met Orrin Johnson, the logging company foreman, at the west gate. A blue Air Force Reserve pickup was parked next to the gate with a spherical bomb enclosure mounted on a trailer behind it. Further back was a Duluth police department cruiser with a K-9 logo. A Duluth police officer, wearing camouflage fatigues, was walking a grid pattern with a black Labrador who was happily racing through the scrubby brush growing along the edge of the forest.

"I've got to tell you, Floyd," said the foreman," the guys are not happy that they're being pulled off this job."

"I don't expect them to be," said Floyd. "But the court injunction is the law and I'm obliged to enforce it." He turned to the two forestry interns he'd met earlier and said, "You're set to lock things up?"

"We've got a length of chain and a padlock," said Terry Pritchard. "That won't stop a determined trespasser, but a law-abiding citizen will look at the lock and say, 'Someone doesn't want me to go in here.'"

"It looks like your bomb-sniffing dog is having a good time," Floyd said to Pat O'Brien, the Duluth police K-9 officer who joined them at the gate.

"Turbo doesn't get outside much," O'Brien said. He spends most of his time walking the airport concourse, or checking bags at the Duluth Convention Center. I'm sure this is doggy heaven."

A low rumble signaled the approach of the logging equipment. The group stood aside as the parade of pickups and semis passed by. The drivers looked angry or resigned. As they ambled down the logging road, a procession of cars bearing tribal license plates crested the hill. When the two lines met, horns honked and gestures were exchanged. One pickup stopped and the young driver jumped out and approached the lead tribal vehicle.

"Oh shit," said Floyd, jogging to intercept the pickup driver. Pam was a few steps behind, watching the rest of the logging vehicles, hoping the others would stay in their pickups.

"You're taking our income," the young logger yelled. "C'mon out here and tell me how you have the right to take our jobs."

As Floyd approached, he could see a man and woman in the lead tribal car. None of the dozen people in the following cars seemed inclined to get out, which Floyd felt was a good choice.

The young logger stopped at the front fender of the lead car, a newer Buick, and slapped his hand on the fender. "Go back and collect your gambling money and leave us alone!" Floyd reached the logger just as he was about to kick the fender and grabbed his shoulder. "Take it down a notch," he said softly.

The logger spun and glared. "This was going to be my first paycheck in a year, and these Indians are taking it away." He looked back at the car, and then looked at the line of logging vehicles idling behind his pickup. "I don't get it. The tribes claim all these rights, but run big casinos that don't pay any taxes and don't have to follow the state laws. They all get checks from the casinos, then they parade in here like they own this land and get us chased off. We're just trying to make a legitimate buck while they sit here in their new cars. I bet there isn't a one of these guys who's ever had a job. They spend their whole lives sucking on the government teat, griping about how they were mistreated a hundred years ago, and filing lawsuits to spear fish on lakes that don't allow a white man to keep enough fish for his dinner. I don't get it."

Pam was a few yards behind him, staring down the loggers who'd decided to stay in their trucks.

Floyd stepped between the logger and the driver's window, and said, "Get back in your truck and go home. The only thing that will be decided here is whether you go to jail. The courts will decide who has the logging rights and who doesn't."

"I can't go home," the logger said, his voice cracking. "The refrigerator is empty and the cupboards are bare. I'm not sure I even have enough gas to make it home."

"Stay there," Floyd said. Then he walked to the window of the first car. As the window rolled down he knelt and looked at the tired face of Connie Stepan, one of the tribal elders. She was a woman he'd seen around the northern part of the county and on television discussing tribal rights. In the back seat he recognized Mary Marcineaux, the tribal president.

"Did you hear what he said?" Floyd asked.

The women nodded. Ray Marcineaux, sitting next to her, said, "This is about who owns the logging rights and not about us versus them. We've got no beef with them trying to make a living, but they can't cut down trees that we own without our permission and without paying us for the lumber."

"Do you see all those trucks?" Floyd asked. "Every one of them has one or two guys who are ready to drag you out of these cars and beat you to a pulp, or worse.

It's not my place to decide who owns the wood. I'm here to make sure everyone goes home unharmed and that no property is destroyed.

He walked to the back window and Mary rolled it down. He said, "Mary, this will all be sorted out in the courts, not here. In the interest of your safety, will you lead your group away from here and help me defuse this situation?"

"We've called a news conference," Mary replied. "There will be television and newspaper people here in a few minutes to hear our side of the issue."

"Well, if you want them to record a riot, that's fine. But, if you want to make your point and keep everyone safe, you'd best drive away."

"We have no beef with these guys," said Stepan again, "we just want what was given to us in the 1837 treaty."

"Well," Floyd said, looking at the loggers who were fidgeting in their vehicles, "it is personal. Didn't you hear what that kid just said? He's broke. His cupboards are bare, and this was going to be his first paycheck in a year. He's mad because you're here in fancy new cars, paid for with casino profits. In his eyes, you're taking the bread out of his mouth. His buddy was killed by someone who planted dynamite out here, and he's financially and emotionally bankrupt. You may have treaty rights, but this is not the place for that argument. Please leave before someone gets hurt."

"This is a public road and we have every right to be here," said Ray Marcineaux.

"I'll bet that every one of those pickups has a rifle or shotgun behind the seat. If these guys get too mad, they'll start loading their guns."

"That's why you're here," said Mary. "You have a duty to protect us."

Floyd looked at the line of logging trucks. "I see maybe twenty-five angry guys and two cops. Who do you think is going to win that fight?"

"You'd better call for backup," said Ray Marcineaux.

"Are you kidding? This is Pine County. There are exactly two deputies on the road in the whole county right now. The Duluth K-9 officer makes three. You're looking at all the police resources that are available. I can call for backup, but it might be an hour or more before a state trooper or deputy from a neighboring county can get here."

Not seeing any softening in the resolve of the people he was talking to, he added, "Most gunfights are over in less than three minutes."

The car window rolled up and he soon heard arguing. Floyd stepped over to the logger and put his hand on the young man's arm. "Go home. Nothing good is going to come from this confrontation." He could see one of the car's passengers on a cellphone, having another animated discussion.

Orrin, the foreman, jogged over. He took Floyd by the elbow and steered him to the shoulder of the road where they were out of earshot. "We've got to get this moving. The longer my guys are sitting with their engines idling, the greater the risk that one of them will do something stupid.

"I'm trying to get the tribal council out of here. Can you take your guy back to his truck and get him rolling?"

The foreman glared at the car's driver through the windshield. "Do you think they are the ones who planted the explosives?"

"I doubt it," Floyd replied. "They've got too much at risk to pull a stunt like that. If word got out that a member of the tribe was responsible for killing a local guy, the casinos would empty and their bank accounts would be drained. I'm sure they wouldn't risk that. Their tool is the court system and they know how to use it effectively."

Orrin stared at the road, pondering Floyd's words. Pam Ryan was talking to the driver of the lead logging truck. Some of the other loggers had shut off their engines and were gathering around Pam. She seemed at ease and unconcerned about the growing group of loggers surrounding her. Orrin kicked at a rock in the gravel and picked up an agate the size of a walnut, with layers of rusty red and clear stone. He spit on it and rubbed the dirt off on his pants, exposing the translucent red and white layers.

"This is not the time or the place to make a stand," said Floyd. "I don't want to arrest any of your guys, but if they threaten anyone, I will."

Orrin rubbed the agate clean, then dropped it in his pocket. "I'll see if I can get them moving. Then I'll call the forestry guys to see if they have another tract we can log. I've got to get my crew working or some of them are going to lose their houses, and then you'll really see some anger."

Orrin turned away and walked to the young logger, who was staring at the Buick, trying to discern what was happening with the occupants. Orrin pointed at the line of trucks and they walked together back to the lead pickup. As they stepped away, the Buick engine purred to life and it drove away, followed by the other cars with tribal license plates.

"I think it was the eco-protesters who did the bombing," Floyd said. "Some of those groups are militant and they'll do almost anything to promote their case."

"I don't think so," said Pam. "Some of those folks all had arrest records and they've been all over the map with their protests. I mean, one week they were protesting the use of animals in pharmaceutical tests in New Jersey, and the next week they were protesting the destruction of native prairie in Wyoming. I don't think any of them are really committed to saving this stand of trees. They're just protesting for the sake of protesting. I wonder if there's something else at play that we're not seeing."

"Like what?" asked Floyd.

"I don't know. I wonder if someone didn't want us to find the dead gamblers," said Pam.

"Really? That happened like eighty years ago. Who would care about it now?"

"I don't know. I just have this creepy feeling," Pam said, rubbing her arms.

CHAPTER 32

BCA LAB, ST. PAUL
WEDNESDAY

J eff Telker and Sonny Carlson were sorting through garbage bags full of material recovered from the shack. Each bag's contents were being painstakingly examined under a lighted magnifier. Pieces of interest were plucked from the rotting wood debris with forceps, placed into evidence bags, and catalogued.

"You know," said Sonny as he plucked a white piece of metal out of a lump of rotting wood, "this is better than processing that old outhouse from Aitkin County. I mean, there's a lot more here, but at least we're not digging through decades of human excrement. That was a truly disgusting experience."

"Why was that more disgusting than a bloody murder scene?" Jeff asked. "The outhouse hadn't been used in years and everything had composted to dirt."

"Well, it wasn't that it smelled, it's just the idea of digging through someone's crap that got to me. I guess it's a personal thing, but it was just disgusting." Sonny stopped. "Whoa. Look at this."

Telker leaned over to look at the item under the magnifier. "It's an oxidized lead bullet," he said.

Sonny set the bullet on the tabletop and checked the tag on the bag he was processing. He then pulled over a drawing of the shack. He scratched his head and pushed the drawing in front of Jeff. "This bag was taken from the back southeast corner," he said, pointing to the wall furthest from the shack's door. "I started at the northeast corner, here." He pointed to the drawing, indicating the point closest to the door, "and I've been working my way down the east wall. I've found nothing of interest until this."

Jeff removed a caliper from a toolbox and measured the lead. "It's a little dicey estimating the caliber of something this badly oxidized, but this is definitely a large caliber bullet. Based on the diameter and length, I'm guessing this is from a .45 pistol. I'll look at it under the comparative microscope. If I can pull the rifling marks off the bullet, I should be able to tell what type of gun fired it."

"Are any of the pistols we got from the site .45s?" Sonny asked.

"That's interesting, too," said Jeff. "They're all .38 Special revolvers, and besides that, none of them were fired."

"So, no shootout-at-the-O.K.-Corral scenario," Sonny said.

"More like the Valentine's Day Massacre. It looks like someone walked in and shot them all before they could even draw their guns."

"We don't usually get to process whole buildings in the lab," said Sonny as he sifted through more debris. "It's just crazy how much material is here and how much junk I'm pulling out of the debris." Sonny paused and held up a piece of tarpaper.

"Hello. Will you look at this," he said, pointing to a hole in the tarpaper. "Unless I'm mistaken, this looks like a .45 bullet passed through it." He laid it aside and spread more debris over the tabletop. "And here's another. I think the St. Valentine's Day Massacre scenario is looking more likely."

"Was that shot incoming or outgoing?" asked Jeff.

"It's impossible to tell from this fragment without knowing its orientation."

Opening the bag recovered from what had been the door, Sonny carefully spread the contents on a fresh sheet of white paper covering a second worktable. He pushed aside the fragments of rotten wood, a rusted lockset, nails and hinges, until he pulled a shell casing, green with patina, from the pile.

"Hello," he said. "I was hoping you'd show up here. And here's your brother, and another brother."

"What've you got?" asked Jeff, who was carrying the oxidized bullet he'd been examining.

"I've recovered seven shell casings so far," said Sonny, pointing to the row of green brass shell casings now standing in a row. Wait, here's number eight."

Jeff, wearing purple neoprene gloves, picked up one of the casings and examined it under a lighted magnifying glass. "They're .45 ACP," he said, setting the first casing down and picking up a second.

"So," said Sonny, stepping back and pushing up his glasses with his wrist, careful to not get debris on his forehead. "Since there are at least eight shell casings here, they were either fired from a machine gun, or there were two shooters."

"They're from a tommy gun," Jeff said, setting down the second casing. "Look at the twist pattern of the lands on this bullet. I checked with the armorer. The marks are consistent with a Thompson machine gun, as are the ejection pin marks on the casings. It looks like someone probably kicked open the door and sprayed the shack with shots before the occupants could even pull out a pistol, then walked away."

"A gangster murder," said Sonny. "I thought that kind of violence was isolated to Chicago and Kansas City. A shack in the middle of nowhere seems like an unlikely spot to settle a score.

"Look at this," said Sonny. "One of the bullets nicked the hasp on the door. And here's a piece of the wooden door with two bullet holes through it." Sonny stood and looked at the pieces. This wasn't a St. Valentine's Day Massacre. No guns were drawn because the shots were fired from outside the closed shack. Someone walked up and just fired through the door, hoping to kill whoever was inside."

"That's rather cowardly for a gangster," said Jeff. "I had the impression they liked to see the look on the faces of their victims when they shot them."

"There was no honor among the gangsters. They preferred to shoot before the victim could grab a gun. The shooter didn't want to give anyone a chance to pull their guns by opening the door."

"I hope Angela McMillan can identify some of the victims in the U of M anthropology lab. That might get us an understanding of what happened."

Jeff Telker stepped back and crossed his arms, considering the pile of debris on the table. "Actually, the shack was a perfect spot for an illegal poker game. With Prohibition over, the police were turning their enforcement efforts to gambling and prostitution. Here's a cabin, in the one piece of forest that hadn't been clear-cut or burned off, miles from the nearest town. Who would bother them?"

"But what's the motive?" asked Sonny. "Money was on the table, so they weren't robbed."

"Did you recover any wallets?" Jeff asked.

"Not a one. I was thinking they'd all rotted away, but I've found leather belts and holsters."

"Maybe they were robbed and the cash was taken, but the robbers didn't bother with the change," Jeff suggested.

"Or, the robbers took the wallets to get rid of any identification." Sonny thought for a second, then added. "Even back then, tommy guns were expensive and regulated. Only the cops and military had them legally."

"I read that the Dillinger gang raided a National Guard supply depot and got away with several tommy guns," Jeff said.

"It was during the Depression. Tommy guns cost several hundred dollars and they couldn't be used for anything but killing people. Ordinary people had shotguns and hunting rifles, not tommy guns."

"So, they were either killed by a gangster," said Sonny, "or a cop, or maybe someone else who had access to an arsenal."

"I'm going to call Pine County to see if the sheriff's department had a tommy gun back in the day," Jeff said. "You keep sifting evidence."

"Hang on," said Sonny. "I need someone to talk with to sort out all the ideas running around in my head."

"You're entirely capable of arguing with yourself," Jeff said, as he walked to the door.

"That's true," said Sonny. "But when it's only me talking, well, I sometimes get stupid answers to the questions and it helps to have someone else listening to make sure I'm not running down some blind alley."

"Let your Finnish side argue with your Swedish side. They never see eye-to-eye."

"That might work," said Sonny to the closed door.

"Let's see," he said. "The Carlson side would ask why the shooter didn't burn down the shack after he shot the guys. Then, the Aho side would say that would be a waste of a match since no one is going to find the old shack unless they knew it was there. Then, the Swede might agree. No, the Swede and the Finn don't ever agree. Then, the Swede would say, 'It's not because no one would find it. They left it because starting a fire would attract attention. That, and it might set the forest on fire, too.'"

Sonny started sifting debris again and pulled out three hinges and a hook for latching the door, along with assorted screws and eye bolts. A tarnished silver piece caught his eyes as he again loaded the screen. He carefully lifted the piece and dusted the surface. The watch fob was heavy, engraved with the image of a moose, and had a few gold links dangling from its hoop. Sonny carefully pressed the button, to release the latch, but nothing happened. Using the edge of a spatula to pry the lid, he was able to get the case open.

The inside was untarnished and an inscription etched onto the lid clearly said "To Lucky."

Jeff walked in and saw Sonny staring at the watch. "What've you got?"

"This watch was given to someone called Lucky." Sonny stared at the watch, then smiled. "I guess his luck ran out."

"Back then," Telker said, "everyone had a nickname and I'll bet Lucky was as common as Bud or Mac."

"Let's suppose Lucky was a gambler or a mobster. That'd narrow it down."

Telker pulled a chair to the computer table and logged in. He typed in the search box and sat back. Within moments the screen was filled with people nicknamed Lucky, or with Lucky as an alias.

"Wow," said Sonny looking at the screen, "I guess you were right. Lucky is popular. I think it's ironic that all those criminals were named Lucky, yet here they are, all arrested and convicted. I'd think that they'd give up the Lucky moniker after they got caught. Maybe change it to something more appropriate, like Busted, or . . . "

"Sonny. Please stop talking," said Telker, who was typing. "I narrowed the search for the Lucky nickname to prior to 1935 and added the keyword Minnesota. That narrows it down to three names," said Sonny. Looks like two of them are dead, leaving one, Tommy

O'Connor, aka Terrible Tommy O'Connor or Lucky O'Connor."

"What's it say about him?"

"He escaped from Chicago's Cook County Jail in 1921, a few days before he was scheduled to be hung for murdering a Chicago cop. He hijacked several cars, then was never seen again. There's some speculation he came to Minnesota, either as his chosen destination, or as a jumping off point for crossing into Canada. Here's an interesting tidbit. The April before his escape, he got into a gun battle with Chicago cops at his house. He escaped, but was arrested in St. Paul and returned to Chicago for his trial."

"So, he had some sort of local ties," said Sonny.

"It seems like a long shot," Jeff said, rolling his chair back from his desk and running his fingers through his thinning hair. "There must've been a thousand guys in Minnesota called Lucky."

"How many of them would have been candidates for a machine-gun massacre?"

"I don't know," replied Jeff. "St. Paul had a whole crop of gangsters who were either hiding out here or had operations here. One or two of them must've been called Lucky."

"See if you can find a picture of Lucky O'Connor. Maybe the forensics people can see if the picture matches a facial reconstruction of one of the skulls."

"Is there any chance you can raise a fingerprint off the watch?" Telker asked as he searched the computer for a booking picture of Lucky O'Connor.

"The exterior of the case is hopeless," said Sonny as he turned the watch in his fingers. "If the shooting had been a month, or even a year ago, I would've been able to pull prints off the watch and the spent cartridge cases. Now, not so much."

Jeff pushed back from the computer and faced Sonny. "Not so much, and . . ."

"And nothing. I've got nothing else to add."

"I'll have to mark that on the calendar. On this date, Sonny Carlson had nothing to say. It's historical."

"I don't talk that much. There are many times when I'm thinking or have nothing to add to the conversation."

"First of all," said Jeff, "you talk even when you're thinking. Secondly, I can't remember a time when you've had nothing to say."

"I used to listen a lot," Sonny replied. "I learned a lot of things about a lot of things. When people make statements I know to be wrong, I feel obligated to jump in and answer or correct them." Seeing Jeff's grimace, he asked, "What?"

"There doesn't need to be a question for you to start giving opinions. You sometimes prattle on for hours when we're driving between crime scenes."

"That's entirely different. It's my obligation to keep you awake, so I make a personal sacrifice and talk to make sure you don't fall asleep."

"You talk when I've only been up for an hour and we're driving away from the hotel."

"You sometimes eat a pretty hearty breakfast and I can see your blood sugar crashing."

Jeff rolled his eyes. "So, you can't get fingerprints off the watch or the shell casings. What's your plan?"

"I said I couldn't get prints off the outside of the watch. I'm going to fume the interior with cyanoacry-late to see if any prints show up. It's a long shot, but the watch case has been closed and the FBI has been able to lift prints from 40-year-old crime scenes if the surface has been protected from moisture."

Jeff snapped his fingers. "Do you know what's missing?"

Sonny shrugged.

"There's no car. How did they get out to the mid-dle of nowhere without a car?"

"There might've been two killers and one of them drove it away when they left."

"Keep an eye out for car keys as you sift the last bags."

"You know," said Sonny, "a lot of the cars of that vintage didn't use a key. They just had a start button on the dashboard or even a hand crank. There may be no key to find. I'm amazed that' we've recovered as much evidence as we have. I remember a case in Detroit Lakes and all we had was a blanket we found at the crime scene. I pulled so much evidence off that one item. There were fibers and hair all over it and I was able to link that one blanket to the killer, the victim, the killer's living room, and the car that transported the victim. That's quite a case we built off that one blanket."

CHAPTER 33

FEDERAL COURTHOUSE
WEDNESDAY

Ira Rosen was wearing the same suit, which had been dry cleaned by the Hyatt Hotel while he slept. His new underwear itched and his shirt had creases in the wrong places. He'd eaten too many restaurant meals, and spent too much time on his cellphone trying to smooth the ruffled feathers of clients whose meetings he'd missed. The bags under his eyes said he hadn't slept well. He was reviewing notes when his clients arrived, each escorted by a U.S. Marshal. They took seats alongside Rosen at the defense table, whispering to each other and asking Rosen questions.

Jane Simmons arrived and took a seat at the prosecutor's table. She was scrolling through notes on her cellphone when the bailiff entered the courtroom.

"Mr. Rosen and Ms. Simmons, the judge would like to see you in his chambers."

The Honorable Carl Peterson was a heavyset man with a florid face. Having been passed over for more prestigious positions for years, he'd resigned himself to being a good judge who was going to retire in Minneapolis. He was cursed by his Swedish dairy farm upbringing that made him partial to hearty breakfasts, calorie-laden lunches, and meat and potatoes dinners that were always accompanied by bread and real butter. He rarely exercised and drank Scotch to excess. But he was smart and a good jurist.

The bailiff directed the lawyers to leather upholstered chairs across from Peterson's desk.

"I understand that one of the defendants has agreed to testify against the others in return for a reduced sentence?" Peterson said, addressing the question to Rosen.

"Yes, Your Honor. Michael Parrish has agreed to a plea agreement."

"And, Ms. Simmons, that is acceptable to the prosecution?" Peterson asked.

"Your Honor, we've charged Michael Parrish with the most crimes and we have the most evidence against him. However, having an eyewitness testimony to the crimes of the others will probably lead them all to some sort of plea agreements. They'll be punished for their crimes while easing the backlog of cases in this court."

Peterson rubbed his bulbous nose with the palm of his hand, enhancing the red roadmap of veins covering it. "Ms. Simmons, I'd swear you were running for office. All your words said maybe, but your tone and body language say no. Which is it?"

"Mr. Rosen said he offered the plea agreement to all of the defendants, but none of the other accepted it. That being the case, I'm posed with the devil's alternative of letting off the worst of the criminals to get convictions on the rest. It's distasteful, but the best of the bad options."

Peterson turned to the bailiff. "Have the marshal return Michael Parrish to the detention area. He's to be segregated from the other defendants." With the bailiff gone, Peterson asked, "Which crimes is Mr. Parrish pleading to and what are you suggesting for a sentence?"

"We've agreed to drop the charges of interstate transport of a minor and illegal possession of a stolen gun," said Simmons. "He will plead guilty to the drug charges. We're recommending a year of probation."

"Mr. Rosen, it appears that your female clients are charged with very minor crimes that would plea bargain down to nothing. They wouldn't consider a plea agreement?"

"Your Honor, Mr. Parrish was the first to see the virtue of the plea agreement and I didn't press the issue with the other defendants once he'd agreed to accept Ms. Simmons' offer."

Peterson rubbed his nose again. "I smell lutefisk in this somewhere," he said, staring back and forth between the two lawyers. Simmons tried to stifle a smile. Rosen looked confused.

"I'm not sure what Your Honor is saying," Rosen said.

"I'm going out on a limb a bit, and we're doing something unorthodox in an effort to serve justice quickly and fairly." Peterson looked at the papers on his desk and said, "Bailiff, bring in Miss DeCarlo."

"Your Honor," Rosen said, "this is highly irregular."

"Yes, it is," replied Peterson. "But I've got a bad taste in my mouth and I want Miss DeCarlo to clear up a few things."

"Your Honor," Rosen stood. "I request a chance to meet with my client in private."

"You've had time to meet with your clients. Please sit down, Mr. Rosen."

Stephanie DeCarlo entered the room with a female marshal. She hadn't fared well in the federal detention center. Her hair was scraggly and oily. She hadn't slept well in several nights, and she'd refused most of the food because it was "greasy and disgusting, and certainly not organic." She was led to a third chair where she hesitated, then sat.

"Miss DeCarlo, I'm Judge Peterson and I'd like to clarify a few things."

"Your Honor!" Rosen said. "My client wishes to invoke her Fifth Amendment right and will not incriminate herself by answering any questions."

Peterson glared at Rosen. "Miss DeCarlo, the questions I'm going to ask have nothing to do with your guilt or innocence. I only want to understand your refusal of the plea agreement."

Rosen was on his feet. "Your Honor, our discussions are subject to lawyer-client privilege." He turned to Stephanie and said, "Don't answer any questions."

The judge sighed. "Mr. Rosen, your antics are becoming tiresome. If you persist, I'll move this discussion to the courtroom, and there I'll hold you in contempt for an outbreak like this." Peterson paused, composed himself, and addressed DeCarlo. "I understand that you declined a plea agreement that could've reduced the charges against you in return for your testimony against the other defendants."

DeCarlo looked at Rosen who was shaking his head, then looked at Simmons, who cocked her head as if she were interested in hearing the answer.

"I wasn't offered any agreement," DeCarlo said. "What does that mean?"

Peterson looked down at the papers on his desk. "It appears that the only charge against you is possession of salable quantities of marijuana and methamphetamine. I assume that the prosecutor would waive all those charges in return for your testimony about drug sales and the interstate transport of Susan Stevenson for sexual purposes."

Simmons nodded.

"Your Honor, I wish to have an immediate, private meeting with my client to clarify the plea options."

DeCarlo sensed the nervousness in Rosen and stared at the judge. "That son of a bitch never offered me a plea agreement. He told me to shut up and that he might be able to get my sentence reduced to parole."

Rosen stood again. "Your Honor, those discussions were privileged and interrogating my client about those discussions under these circumstances constitutes a serious breach of judicial discretion. I will file a complaint . . ."

"Shut up, Mr. Rosen." Peterson turned to DeCarlo. "Tell me in your own words about your plea agreement discussion with Mr. Rosen."

"There wasn't one," Stephanie said confidently. "We never had a discussion about my willingness to accept a plea agreement, or if I'd testify against the others. I told Jeremy that Susan was jailbait when he picked her up at the mall. The guys all knew that and still passed her around."

"Your Honor," Rosen protested. "Miss DeCarlo isn't under oath, and she's obviously under duress due to her jealousy of the Stevenson girl. We need to end this meeting and I need to sit down with each of my clients and review their options."

"Mr. Rosen," Peterson said, "you are an agent of this court and are bound by a number of ethical canons and the laws of the United States. That said, did you, or did you not, discuss the option of a plea agreement with all of your clients?"

"I refuse to answer the question. I'm protected by my Fifth Amendment right to not incriminate myself."

Jane Simmons' mouth fell open in disbelief. "The hell you say."

"Mr. Rosen, I find you in contempt of court. Bailiff, remove him to a holding cell."

Rosen pulled a cellphone from his pocket and pressed a speed dial number. The bailiff reached over and took the phone from his hand and turned it off.

"I demand a phone call," Rosen said as he was handcuffed.

"You'll get a phone call after you're searched and booked," said the bailiff.

"This is not over!" Rosen yelled as he was escorted out the side door of the chambers. "I have friends in high places!"

"Miss De Carlo, please return to the courtroom," Peterson said. De Carlo's eyes were wide and her mouth agape. It took a second for the judge's words to register. She stood and quickly walked out of the judge's chambers, the female marshal at her side.

With the defendant gone, the judge smiled at Simmons. "I've never experienced anything like that before. Do you think he really gets by with crap like that in DC?"

"It's a different world," Simmons agreed. "I suppose I should find public defenders for the defendants and reconsider Mr. Parrish's plea agreement."

"Let my bailiff know when you're done with that," Peterson said. "While you're on that, I need to call my boss and warn him that I may have stepped on some toes by doing the right thing."

CHAPTER 34

NEMADJI STATE FOREST

The sheriff showed up a few minutes before the first news truck, looking very out of place in the forest. He was resplendent in his white uniform shirt with the gold PCSD emblem on one collar point and a single gold star on the other.

"What happened to the loggers and the tribal leaders?" he asked as he approached Pam and Floyd.

"I persuaded the tribal leaders to leave to avoid violence," said Floyd. "As soon as they were gone, the loggers left."

"I talked to the loggers and we're sitting on a powder keg," said Pam. "They smiled, but they are really angry about Larry Odegaard's death and now being ordered off the timber parcel. There are a few hotheads in the mix who may be capable of doing something stupid. I overheard them say they were going to the Kerrick Bar to tip a few."

The first news truck to show up was from the CBS affiliate in Duluth. While the technician and cameraman set up, Megan Winston, a pretty blonde with a few years of experience on the Duluth news scene, walked toward the deputies. The sheriff put on his best smile.

"Remember," he whispered to Pam and Floyd, "the loggers are our constituents. We have to keep order and enforce the law, but we have to keep them happy if at all possible." With that reminder, he marched over to intercept the news reporter.

"Sheriff Sepanen," Winston said, smiling brightly and offering her hand. "It's good to see you." As they shook hands she glanced around, looking confused. "My producer said she'd been contacted by the Fond du Lac tribal headquarters. They told her they were having a news conference here."

"Megan, there was a short discussion between the tribal leaders and the loggers. We were able to defuse the situation and, in a show of goodwill, the tribal leaders left and everyone cooled down."

Megan took out a recorder, and started to repeat the sheriff's words back into the device while the sheriff stood smiling. The cameraman was still next to the van, unloading his gear while a technician hoisted the satellite dish high over the van. Another white van, one from the Duluth Fox affiliate, topped the hill.

"Megan," said the sheriff, cupping her elbow discreetly in his palm while steering her out of the center of the road, "could you turn off your recorder for a minute for an off-the-record chat?"

Megan was about to protest when she saw the sheriff's smile. She shut off the recorder and slipped it into the pocket of her slacks.

"It looks like there will be several news organizations here," said Sepanen. "You got here first, so I'm going to offer some advice. You listen to me and decide whether to take my advice or not."

Megan's eyes narrowed. "Is this legal?"

"Absolutely!"

"Then talk. I'll decide how to respond."

"There will be a story here. Maybe the tribal leaders will be back. Maybe not. If they don't show, I'll explain what's going on, from the county's perspective, and everyone here will have the same story showing the same forest background while they talk."

"Okay," said Megan, skepticism in her voice.

"But there's another story here. If you act quickly, you can grab it and all the other stations and newspapers will be following your lead tomorrow."

"I think I already know the story," said Megan. "I got a copy of the court injunction, based on the 1837 treaty. It seems pretty cut and dried." Megan's cameraman started walking toward them, looking confused. Megan put up her hand, signaling him not to approach.

"I think the legal issues are probably moot. The tribes have the rights to the deciduous trees and the loggers are shut out. However, there's something more, which might get your face on the networks."

"Tell me, Sheriff," Megan said, with a touch of sarcasm, "what would that other story be?"

The sheriff put up his hands. "I understand if you're not interested. I see Brian Price. I'll talk with him."

"Hang on," Megan said, as the sheriff turned toward her counterpart at the Fox affiliate. "Tell me the about the story and I'll decide."

"The tribal casinos are in the poorest counties in the state. The jobs they provide are a bootstrap for many people but they also create a lot of animosity. We arrested a drunk who was railing about the tribes stealing. He said the tribes get federal grants to build houses and schools, then they run the casinos and suck the Social Security checks from senior citizens who play the slots and card games. As time passes, there is increasing acrimony between the local residents and the tribes."

"You're repeating a lot of old news. What's the story?"

"Load up your gear and drive over to the Kerrick Bar. The loggers are sitting there crying in their beer over losing the first paychecks some were going to get in a year. They're losing their cars, their homes, and their families because they can't support them," the sheriff said. He paused, then said, "You're all set up here to get the politically correct story about tribal rights under the 1837 treaty. While that's all true— the treaty has been upheld by the federal courts—no one is telling the story of the loggers, who are trying to eke out a living, and the little businesses that would benefit from the business the loggers would provide if they had jobs."

"How many families are we talking about?" Megan asked.

"I don't have an exact number. It may be eighteen or twenty guys who have been out of work for a year, maybe more. You could be the only person talking with the loggers. You'll be the only one to record their reaction."

A white minivan with a *Minneapolis Star Tribune* logo pulled in behind Megan's cameraman. Another white van with a satellite dish on top rumbled down the road behind the minivan.

"They don't hand out prizes for doing a competent job of reporting the same story, from the same perspective and location as the competition," the sheriff said.

Megan's foot was tapping. "Where's the Kerrick Bar?"

"Turn the truck around and backtrack to the stop sign. Turn right and follow highway 23 into Kerrick. The bar is on the highway."

"If I find out you screwed me over . . ."

"You won't," said the sheriff.

Megan jogged to her cameraman. After a short one-sided conversation, they packed up and lowered the satellite dish while the other reporters looked on with curiosity.

CHAPTER 35

NEMADJI STATE FOREST NEWS CONFERENCE

Without the tribal leadership, the news conference became the sheriff briefing the media. He commented on the court injunction and the shutting down of the logging operation. There were a few questions, including a request for an update on the explosion that killed the logger. The sheriff said he was confident they were close to an arrest.

Floyd went back to the courthouse and his cold case. He did an internet search for the Pokegama Seminary and found a brief history of the Redemptorist Fathers' ownership of the property. Initially, they used it as a seminary and later converted it into a residence for retired priests.

The Redemptorists were divided into provinces in Denver and Baltimore, roughly split along the Mississippi. "Well, the source of the Mississippi is in Itasca county," Floyd reasoned. "Pine County is east of Itasca county." So he chose Baltimore and called the contact number listed on the website. The woman who answered the phone sounded elderly.

"Hello, I'm Sergeant Floyd Swenson, of the Pine County, Minnesota, Sheriff's Department. I'm looking for information about a seminary operated by the Redemptorists in the 1930s."

"Sergeant Swenson, I'll have to think for a moment," the woman said. "I think you probably need to speak with someone in our archives. Their phone number is . . ."

A few minutes later a male voice of indeterminate age answered, "Redemptorist archives. How may I be of assistance?"

After introducing himself, he explained, "There was a Redemptorist seminary in Pine County in the 1940s. The seminary took over an old TB sanatorium and I'm trying to find information about one of the women who was at the sanatorium in 1943."

"Sergeant Swenson was it?"

"Yes."

"I'm a bit at a loss. We have archives of all Redemptorist facilities and staff, but I sincerely doubt there would be anything in the files about people living in a building before we took over."

"Could you look, please?"

There was a long pause. "Sergeant, you have to understand. Virtually all of our archival material is on paper and is stored in boxes in a warehouse. It's not an automated system that can be searched by computer." The man paused. "Please explain the nature of your interest. Is this a police matter?"

"I was contacted by the woman's family. The family was separated in an orphanage. Through census and newspaper records, we've learned that the woman I'm looking for was living in Pine County. The last mention of her was in a newspaper article about the sanatorium closing and the Redemptorists taking over the building. After that, there is absolutely no record of her. No census record, marriage record, death record. Nothing."

"Sergeant, I understand the difficulty and frustration the family must be feeling, but our seminaries are for priests. There are no women there."

"I suspected that. My primary hope was that the sanatorium records had been taken over by the Redemptorists and those records might lead me to the woman or explain her fate."

The pause lasted so long Floyd was expecting a dial tone. "Sergeant, I have a volunteer who comes in on Thursdays. If you can wait a few days, I'll ask Sister

Mary Katherine to look for the Pine City records. I make no guarantees. I'm certain there will be a list of the priests who taught there and those who were ordained, but I don't expect to find much beyond that."

After giving his contact information, Swenson said, "Thank you. That's more hope than I've had this far."

Floyd poured coffee into a cup sporting the logo of the regional cooperative. The coffee was suspiciously dark. He sniffed. It smelled burnt, which meant it had probably been on the warmer for most of a shift. He poured the coffee into the sink, then emptied the carafe. As he scooped coffee into the filter basket the sheriff walked over with an empty cup.

"I'm glad you're making a fresh pot," the sheriff said. "My last cup tasted like tar."

"I sniffed it and decided to dump out the dregs and start fresh," Floyd said as he poured water into the top of the Mr. Coffee.

"Have you seen the WDIO broadcast?" the sheriff asked. "Megan Winston found the bar and got an earful from the loggers. It was good to get their side of the issue on the record, but their lack of diplomacy was disturbing. I'm not sure airing their tirades will add to the discussion."

Floyd pushed the start button and stepped back. "When you mess with a man's livelihood, you get a primal reaction. Most of the guys are God-fearing family men, but there is an element, four or five, that are more reactionary, especially if you catch them after they've had a few beers."

The sheriff stared at the dark liquid dribbling into the carafe. "You don't think any of them would be crazy enough to plant the explosives, do you?"

"We interviewed them and they seemed as shocked as we were. Besides that, I don't see any of them doing something that would hurt one of their buddies."

"Are you sure?" Sepanen asked. "Maybe it was someone with a beef against the victim."

"Blowing up a tree with dynamite is a pretty unreliable way to create an explosion that would kill someone," said Floyd. "The ATF guys said that there's a whole science to blasting trees. The direction the tree falls is dependent on the type and amount of blast material, the placement, and the timing. A fraction of a second miscue and the tree would have missed the cab of the truck, and maybe even the whole truck. I think someone was sending a message but probably didn't have any real murderous intent."

"Do I smell fresh coffee?" Bruce Swanson, the jailer, asked from the doorway

"Help yourself," said Floyd.

"Do you think it was the eco-terrorists?" the sheriff asked Floyd.

"I think we can rule them out," Floyd said as he poured coffee for Swanson, Sepanen, and himself.

"Do you need something, Bruce?" the sheriff asked the jailer.

"Just coffee. Thanks," he said and slowly left the room.

"I think it's highly unlikely someone from the West Coast would know that Pop Davidson had blasting materials. Granted, a little internet research and they'd be able to find a pond-blasting operation and assume that the business would have blasting supplies on hand. However, Pop has a good view of his driveway. The blasting materials weren't sitting in the open. The thief had to break down a reinforced door to access the storage area. I think it was probably someone local, someone who knows about Pop's business, and who has enough knowledge of blasting caps and dynamite to be able to set up the charge, detonate it remotely, and be confident they weren't going to kill themselves in the process."

"Didn't Pop say that whoever did this was an amateur?" the sheriff asked. "He said the attacker used many times more explosive than was required to topple the tree. I would characterize the protesters as amateurs."

"I watched the video of the explosion several times and the eco-idiots were as surprised by the blast as we were. Besides, explosives don't seem to be their thing. If they'd done it, BATF would've found some trace of the dynamite on their clothes or gear. Additionally, they have no record of using explosives. Their style would be to spike the trees or hang from platforms in the trees and refuse to come down. I think the Fond du Lac tribe is also out of consideration. Their tool is the 1837 treaty. All they needed was a lawyer, a request for an injunction, and they've got the law on their side."

"Okay," said the sheriff, sipping his coffee. "If it wasn't the loggers, the Indians, or the protesters, who does that leave?"

"Someone who doesn't want the trees cut, for whatever reason," Floyd said.

"Or," said Sepanen, "someone who doesn't want people snooping around that chunk of the timber."

"The poker party in the shack?" asked Floyd. "Who would care if bodies were recovered from an 80-year-old murder scene? The murderer has probably been dead for fifty years."

"Unless there's something else out there that someone would like to keep hidden."

"That land has been a state forest since at least the 1930s," Floyd said. "Before that, most of the land in this region was owned by the railroads, and before the railroads, it was owned by the federal government or the Indian tribes."

Pam Ryan walked in and poured herself a cup of coffee. "I overheard the last of your conversation and

I'll throw out another stakeholder. I have a contact in the Carlton County tax assessor's office. He said there is a mining company quietly buying tax-forfeited property, and the mineral rights to other properties. Someone is betting that there are more precious metal deposits, other than those on the Canadian border."

"But the forest is state land," said the sheriff. "If someone wanted to mine there, they'd have to get approval from the legislature and that'd be no small feat."

"I wonder if someone has been doing some prospecting back there, and they don't want anyone to know about it," Floyd speculated. "Maybe they actually found some valuable ore and they don't want the news to get out until they've had a chance to secure the mining leases."

"There was a company who bought up uranium mining rights all over the region back in the 1980s," the sheriff said. "I don't think they ever found ore rich enough to make mining profitable."

With the conversation dying, Pam said, "Mary invited us for supper. What time do you want us?

"I leave all those plans to the social director," Floyd replied. "What the heck. Since I didn't know about the invitation, Mary can be surprised at the time I choose. Come over at six."

"Us?" the sheriff asked, with a smile.

Pam blushed and grimaced, unable to speak. Floyd jumped in. "Mary's set Pam up with a blind date. I think this one has most of his teeth and finally got his license back after the DUIs."

"Good luck with that," Sepanen said, rolling his eyes.

As the sheriff walked away Pam let out her breath and whispered. "Nice recovery. I froze."

"You know," said Floyd, "there are no secrets in Pine County. There may be a few rumors that haven't come true yet, but no secrets. Once Mary buys groceries, stops at the liquor store, and gets her hair done, most of the people in Pine City will know that you're coming over for supper, who's coming with you, what we're eating, and which wine we'll have to complement the food."

"I'd like to live under the naïve illusion that my private life is still private. It's hardly worth it. I go through all the embarrassment, the rumors, and the snide comments, and he'll probably dump me in a month."

"You're starting to talk like my Swedish relatives," Floyd said. "They're reluctant to undertake anything new because it makes the rest of their lives seem dull."

"I get that," said Pam. "My life has structure and I know when and where I have to be. I work a little overtime, but I get regular days off that I use to catch up on television shows I've recorded or I drive to Minneapolis to go shopping.

"Dating is nerve-wracking. First dates are always an endeavor into the unknown. People try to set me up, and the first cut is: Is he a felon? Then, we move on to: Does he have a regular job? Does he have a car? Does he live with his mother? Does he have a personality? Then comes the actual date and the tension is usually palpable while we both do the get-to-know-you thing, then comes the kiss goodnight: Do I want to kiss him or do I want to run to my door and lock it behind me? Do I give him a peck or do we let our bodies touch? Does he expect me to invite him in for a drink and who-knows-what after that?"

"It's been a long time since I've dated and the world has changed," said Floyd. "I got married right out of high school and our big night out was stealing a kiss at the drive-in movie."

"Really?" asked Pam. "No late night texts suggesting a booty call?"

"We had a party-line phone at home, so there was no privacy and certainly no texting. And, I don't even know what a booty call is."

"It's a friends-with-benefits thing," Pam said, blushing and sorry she'd brought it up.

"Travis has passed through multiple filters. He's polite, friendly, funny, and, best of all, he keeps asking me out.

"Have you heard from your DEA contact lately?" Pam asked, wanting to change the topic.

"No. I should give her a call," he said, walking to his desk.

To Floyd's amazement, Barb Skog answered on the second ring.

"DEA, Skog speaking."

"Director Skog, this is Floyd Swenson from Pine County. Can you give me an update on the eco-protesters?"

"Floyd, it's good to hear from you. Please call me Barb."

"Barb, I don't know if you saw the news from WDIO, but we had a standoff between the loggers and the tribal leaders. We managed to defuse it, but the loggers are pretty hot."

"Yes, I watched the report from all three Duluth television stations on the internet. The WDIO interview with the loggers was very good. They did a very nice job of putting a human face on the standoff. That's so much more meaningful, and heartbreaking than hearing a press conference with a bunch of talking heads." Skog paused, then added, "Not that I don't like to listen to your sheriff. He's sometimes colorful."

"Actually, it was Sheriff Sepanen who pointed out the loggers' issues to WDIO and suggested that the reporter could find them at the bar in Kerrick."

"Nice touch," Skog said. "It was very insightful of him to take the story out of the courtroom and put a face to it. Very nice."

"Tell me about the investigation," Floyd said.

"You know most of the pieces. We raided the camp-site and found drugs and evidence of sexual activity. It may take a week or two for our crime scene techs to go through the bags of evidence we seized. They are literally going through it with a tweezers.

"We turned our preliminary information over to Jane Simmons, the U.S. Attorney, and they should be meeting with a judge this afternoon to lay out the charges and let the defendants plead. Jane called this morning and said she had been approached by the protesters' lawyer and one of them is willing to testify against the others in return for leniency."

"I assume one of the girls offered to turn state's evidence," said Floyd. "They were only involved with the use of the drugs and not in transporting the underage girl. One of them would get off with a slap on the wrist versus years in prison followed by parole."

"She didn't say which one took the plea agreement. She wanted to know if we had DNA results back from the condoms and drug containers. That testing won't be done before next week, so she's filing charges based on the assumption that the results will support the charges. "More interesting than that were the cell-phone records. Most of the texts and calls were among the seven protesters. However, one of them exchanged calls with a prepaid phone purchased at a Minneapolis Walmart. The buyer paid in cash and wore a brimmed hat that concealed most of his face, so we haven't been able to identify him, and the phone has been off since we got the number. If, or when, the phone is turned on again, we'll have the location of the cell tower it connects to and we may be able to find the owner.

"Now, it's your turn. What have you found out about Aunt Margaret?"

"I've been looking in closets, but haven't found a skeleton yet," Floyd replied. "I checked all the cemeteries in the Pine City area and I looked at the membership rolls of every church in town. She doesn't show up anywhere. I called the Redemptorists, who ran the seminary after the sanatorium closed. I spoke with an archivist who's going to have a volunteer look for those records on Thursday. It's unlikely that their records will include the sanatorium information, and it's highly unlikely that your aunt was associated with the seminary. I've pretty much run out of places to look."

"You've gone down some pathways I couldn't access, so thanks. Keep me posted when you hear back from the archives."

"Will do."

CHAPTER 36

BCA, WEDNESDAY

Sonny Carlson organized the boxful of evidence, sorting it into evidence bags of shell casings, lead bullets, bone fragments, buttons, and other items. He counted the shell casings then checked a firearms database.

Jeff Telker walked into the lab and saw Sonny sitting at the computer. "What's up?"

"I found eighteen .45 cases and two bullets," he said. "The bullets had a 1:16 twist. Like you said, that's unusual and consistent with a Thompson. I suppose the shooter emptied a tommy gun into the shack. It probably had a box magazine with twenty rounds and a couple of them probably fell outside our search area. Most of the lead bullets went completely through the shack and may be stuck in trees or are a hundred yards away buried under 80 years of leaf litter."

Jeff dialed the Pine County Sheriff's non-emergency number and asked for Floyd. He activated the speaker-phone.

"We finished processing the evidence from the shack. The likely scenario involves a shooter empty-ing a Thompson machine gun into the people in the shack."

"Have you been able to identify any of the victims?" Floyd asked.

"I got a couple fingerprints off the glass in a watch fob," Sonny said. "I checked AFIS, but there wasn't a match, which isn't a surprise. When they created AFIS in the 1990s, the FBI had a million fingerprints, and they didn't include fingerprints from people known to be deceased or those termed as historical, meaning prints from people unlikely to be alive in 1990. I spoke with a tech, who said the old prints are on file, but to speed up the search processes, unknown prints are compared with only living criminals. He can change the search parameters and pull the older prints in. He might have results for me tomorrow if the prints are in the archived section."

"What else can you tell me?" Floyd asked.

"I just spoke with the anthropologists at the University of Minnesota. They're processing the skele-tal remains and it looks like there's definitive evidence that at least four of the victims died of gunshots, which is consistent with Sonny's machine gun theory," Jeff said. "They were somewhat surprised that one of the victims was a woman."

"A woman?" Floyd said, straightening up.

"An adult woman," Jeff replied. "The skeleton was about five feet tall. That's small by today's standards, but it's pretty close to the average woman's height in 1930."

"What else can you tell me about her?" Floyd asked, thinking of Margaret Lane but quickly dismissing it as too improbable. The time frame could be right, though, he thought. "Was there any identification with the remains? Do they know her hair color? Was she wearing a wedding ring?"

"Slow down, Sergeant. The remains were not in good condition," Sonny said. "We didn't find any identification except the watch fob with any of the remains. The anthropologists are piecing together bone fragments to make complete skeletons. They put together the pelvic bones to determine the gender of the remains."

"If I had a relative, could you run a DNA comparison?"

"What are you getting at?" asked Sonny.

"We were recently contacted by the family of a woman who's been missing since that time period. There's been no trace of her since then," Floyd paused. "I know it's a million-to-one shot, but the timing could fit."

"This appears to be the kind of scene that played out in the mob wars in the 1920s and 1930s. I'm more inclined to think the woman was married to one of the guys or was a girlfriend. Do you have any reason to think the woman you're looking for might've been hanging around with mobsters?"

"Probably not," Floyd said with a sigh. "The last trace we have of her was at a sanatorium when it closed in 1943."

"I'll ask the anthropologists if they think there's recoverable DNA. They might be able to pull some from a tooth or large bone but everything we're looking at points to the mid-'30s. I doubt this is your missing woman."

"Is there any chance they can do dental identification?" Floyd asked.

"The art of dentistry in that time period was mostly limited to extractions. People didn't have money for dentists."

"George Washington had false teeth," Floyd said.

"George was rich," said Sonny, "and he wasn't in a sanatorium.

"I'll contact the woman who's looking for her lost relative. I think she'll be willing to pay for the DNA testing if it's possible."

"The issue isn't if someone will pay," Jeff said. "We're a crime lab. We don't do DNA testing unless a crime is involved."

"What about the woman who was killed in the shack?" Floyd asked. "I'd say that identifying the victims is part of the investigation, wouldn't you?"

"Solving an eighty-year-old crime isn't at the top of our list," said Sonny.

"Even if one of the victims might be related to a big shot in the DEA?"

"Aw, man," said Sonny. "I hate when our priorities get shuffled because of politics."

"There's no need to shuffle priorities," said Floyd. "Just set this one high on the list. There's no need to get any of the brass involved. You just do your work, and there's someone high in the DEA who will owe you a big favor."

"IOUs are good," said Sonny. "We might be able to see our way clear to continue our effort on this case. That's assuming some mass murder or high-profile crime doesn't pull us aside."

"Do what you can," said Floyd.

"Sergeant, before you go," said Sonny, "does your department have a Thompson machine gun in the arsenal?"

"We don't have any full-auto firearms," Floyd replied. "Most of our long guns are shotguns and AR-15s. Why do you ask?"

"From the shell casings and bullets we've recovered, the gun used to kill those victims is a .45 and the markings all point to a Thompson machine gun.

Is there some way to check back in history to see if the department owned one at the time of the murders? I did a little checking and there were a few private sales of tommy guns, but nearly all of them went to the military or police departments. If you had one, and it disappeared about the time of the murders . . ."

"I'll check into it, but I doubt it."

After Floyd disconnected, Sonny turned to Jeff and said, "You're not comfortable with this, are you?"

Jeff scratched his nearly bald head. "A crime is a crime, and we work on cold cases all the time. I think I can live with myself as long as we aren't allowing a major criminal to roam free because we diverted our efforts."

Sonny turned on the speakerphone and dialed the number for the University of Minnesota's anthropology lab. When the phone was answered he said, "Hi, Angela. We just got off the phone with the Pine County investigator. He may have a lead on the identity of our female victim."

"Really?" Angela McMillan replied. "Were they able to link a kidnapping to that time frame?"

"Not exactly. They have a missing person and a living relative who's willing to supply a DNA sample for comparative testing. Do you think you can pull enough DNA from the bone marrow?"

"I don't know, Sonny. Nearly all the bones were crushed, either by scavengers or by the roof collapse.

There's a chance I can pull something out of the pelvis, but I make no guarantees."

Jeff perked up and snapped his fingers. "Angela, this is Jeff Telker. Our lab is backed up right now. Can you do DNA testing in your lab?"

"It depends," she replied. "There's a certified lab in Sioux Falls. If you need testing that will hold up in court, I'd use them. If this is never going to court, I've got a grad student who's doing human genome work and I'm sure he could slip a couple samples into his testing. He's been really good about turning the tests around in a few days, versus a month from any police lab or Sioux Falls, but he doesn't have enough experience to be an expert witness."

"I think your grad student would be a great option," Sonny said. "We'll have Sergeant Swenson from Pine County give you a call and the two of you can make arrangements to get DNA from the family of the missing person."

"Actually, we were just discussing facial reconstruction. I have a student who'd like to build a facial model of the decedent, but that'll take time. Running DNA comparisons is far faster and more reliable than having an artist recreate a face from clay."

CHAPTER 37

THE TUXEDO INN
NOVEMBER 3, 1934

The aroma of bacon preceded the knock on the attic door that caused the girls to jump out of their beds. Carol unlocked the door while the other girls cleared the cards from the table and straightened their beds.

Geraldine Marty carried a tray covered with bacon, scrambled eggs, pancakes, butter, and maple syrup to their table saying, "Here's breakfast, but Miss Abigail said you should stay up here until she comes to get you later this morning."

"Why?" asked Pixie.

"Some of the guests are still here, and she doesn't need you until they've had breakfast and left."

"There are still three cars here," said Mary, looking out the window.

"You girls eat. Don't worry about the cars."

When their breakfasts were eaten, the girls dressed and set the dishes aside. They played cards until they heard car engines. Soon there were footsteps on the stairs. Abigail's face appeared in the crack of the door. She said they should come downstairs.

"She didn't open the door," said Mary.

"It looked like she has a black eye," said Carol. "She must've run into a door."

The dining room was disheveled, with plates strewn randomly on the tables. Several empty liquor bottles sat on the sideboard next to an empty ice bucket and dirty glasses. The room smelled of smoke and sweat, so Mary quickly opened windows to air it out. None of the women were drinking coffee or eating rolls. The only noise came from pans clattering in the kitchen.

The front door creaked open and Abigail stubbed out a cigarette before stepping into the room. Her lovely hair was tied back in a severe bun. One eye was nearly swollen shut, her eyebrow and cheek were nearly black. She glanced at the girls, then turned her face away and scurried up the stairs. The girls looked at each other, unsure of what they'd just seen.

"Let's get to work," the cook said. "These dishes aren't going to clear or wash themselves."

With the tables cleared and the liquor bottles in the trash, the girls began spreading fresh tablecloths and putting away the clean dishes. Miss Abigail came down the stairs with the three women who lived on the second floor. Two of the women wore heavy make-up that didn't quite conceal the bruises on their faces. Their brightly colored silk dressing gowns belied their sorry physical state. A third woman hovered over them like a mother hen. Abigail, also in heavy makeup and dressed in a yellow dressing gown with bright red flowers, walked past the girls without saying a word, then out the front door where she lit a cigarette before closing the door. The other women walked into the kitchen. None of them spoke.

Gravel crunched in the driveway as the tables were being reset. A couple minutes later, Abigail walked in with a large middle-aged man who was wearing a dark suit and gray tie. He took off his fedora, exposing a bald head with a fringe of graying hair. Abigail had tears in her eyes.

"Girls," she said, "come here. This is Mr. Adamson. He needs some help running . . . a boarding house. I'm closing the inn for a while and Ted, Mr. Adamson, would like to hire you."

She pulled a roll of bills from her pocket along with a small notebook. She consulted her notebook, then counted out a stack of currency into Mary's hand. She repeated the process until each of the girls was clutching more money than they'd ever seen.

"Your indentures have been paid off, and here's the money I owe you for the time you've worked here."

"But, Miss Abigail —" Mary said.

"Shush. You go with Mr. Adamson. He'll be fair and treat you well. Abigail pulled the girls together and hugged them. "Before you go, there's one other thing you should know." She pulled them close and whispered, garnering open-mouthed looks of surprise. Then, with tears streaming down her face, Abigail turned and walked to the kitchen, never looking back.

The girls watched Abigail walk away with her shoulders sagging and her head hung low, a shell of her former self. Confused and stunned by the secret they'd just been told, they stood stock-still.

"Ladies," Adamson said, spinning the fedora's rim in his hands nervously. "I have a car to drive us into town. Go pack your things and I'll wait for you outside. Quickly, please."

The girls stared at his back as he walked away. Pixie flipped through the money in her hand, realizing she had nearly fifty dollars. When she looked up, the others were already at the stairs.

"What's going on?" Pixie asked, racing to catch up. "Why doesn't Miss Abigail want us anymore?"

"Something happened last night," Mary whispered. "It's not right that those cars stayed overnight."

"Pack fast," said Carol. "Let's get out of here in case the gangsters come back."

Adamson had the trunk open when the girls emerged. He loaded the four suitcases.

The girls sat in the back in silence while Adamson rode with the driver in the front seat. They passed through Pine City, which was bustling at lunchtime, and continued east. The car turned off the county road and followed a driveway until they saw a long building near a lake. A dozen people were sitting on the open veranda, all covered with blankets.

Adamson opened the back door and said, "Welcome to the Pokegama Sanatorium," as the girls stepped out. He handed each of them their suitcases. "You'll be sharing a room next to the kitchen."

The sanatorium building was two stories high, gray and industrial with small windows. It stood in a copse of pine trees with the lake visible through the trees. The gravel parking lot had three dusty cars parked along one side of the building. Wooden stairs led to a concrete-block loading dock with an entry door. The girls shuffled up the stairs and Adamson opened the door to a large, empty kitchen. He pointed to an open door next to the stove.

"There's your room," he said.

Pixie looked around the cold, windowless room and waited for the others to decide which of the four bunk beds they wanted. She turned to Mr. Adamson and said, "Miss Abigail said someone had been my sponsor when I was sent here from the State School. Were you my sponsor?"

"No, dear," Adamson said. "Miss Abigail sponsored each of you. I'm not sure how she knew, but all of you needed to move on from where you'd been, and she gave you a safe, warm place to live. I'll do the same. You'll get room and board, you get Sundays off, and I'll pay you each two dollars a week."

Pixie dug her fingers into the wad of bills in her pocket and squeezed them. "What's going to happen to Miss Abigail?" she asked.

"I think someone is buying the Tuxedo Inn," he replied. "Abigail told me she was moving to Minneapolis."

"But, we could work for the new owners," Pixie said.

Adamson shook his head. "Abigail was afraid . . . Well, she thought you would be in better circumstances here."

"What's a sanatorium?" Carol asked.

"It's a kind of hospital where people come to recover from tuberculosis. The patients get healthy food and lots of clean air."

"What will we do?" asked Mary.

"You'll help the cook, change beds, wash linens, help the patients move around and, well, just be helpful."

"Are we taking someone's job?" Pixie asked.

Adamson shook his head. "I had some guys who just left and Miss Abigail said you ladies were hard working and reliable. To speak frankly, you're lucky. Jobs are hard to find and Miss Abigail has looked out for you very well."

Pixie squeezed the money in her pocket as tears welled in her eyes. Abigail was her surrogate mother and for the second time she'd been ousted from her "home."

The Tuxedo Inn was a scene of similar unhappiness. A black Packard rolled into the parking lot and a thirty-something hatchet-faced man got out. He limped to the door, forever hobbled by childhood polio. Abigail met him at the door with a withering glare.

He handed her an envelope. "Three thousand."

She took the envelope and carefully counted the money. "You know this place is worth ten times this," she said.

"Take it, or you'll get a repeat of last night's party," he said with a grin. "The boys might not hold back next time."

Abigail shuddered.

"Pack your stuff and get outta here," the man said. Looking over her shoulder he saw the three women standing near the door. "They stay, and so do the girls upstairs."

Abigail shook her head. "The women are coming with me."

The smile left the man's face. "That wasn't the deal," he said.

"I agreed to sell the business, but the workers are not anyone's property. They leave like human beings and you do what you want with the building when you take over."

"Whether you like it or not," the man said, "you're a madam and they are your working girls. The girls upstairs may need to be broken in, but the boss kinda liked the looks of the little one."

Abigail looked directly at him and said, "The girls are already gone."

The man pushed past her and hobbled up the stairs. Doors slammed and furniture was tossed aside.

With the man distracted, Abigail shooed the three women away. "Get in the car with Geraldine, and get out of here. Now!"

When he heard the car start, the man limped down the stairs just in time to see the black Ford leave the parking lot in a cloud of dust. He spat out a string of expletives and slapped Abigail.

"You stupid bitch! You have no idea who you've crossed." He grabbed her by the arm and roughly dragged her to his car. He threw open the back door and punched her in the stomach, sending her reeling to the floor. He careened out of the parking lot, leaving the Tuxedo Inn's doors open and lights blazing.

CHAPTER 38

PINE CITY
WEDNESDAY AFTERNOON

Floyd had an afterthought as he pulled out of the parking lot and turned toward downtown. He arrived at the historical society just as Edna Purdy was closing the door.

"Can I sneak in a quick question before you lock up?" Floyd asked.

"You're the only person who's been around this afternoon. Come in."

"A federal judge issued an injunction to stop the logging, citing the 1837 treaty. Can you tell me what bearing that treaty has on the harvest of trees from the state forest?"

Edna smiled broadly and pushed her walker toward a bookshelf in the corner. "I can show you exactly what the judge is considering." She scanned the bookshelf and took down a slender book. "Take this over to the table, please."

Sitting next to Floyd, she flipped through the pages as she explained. "The 1837 treaty is often referred to as The 1837 Pine Tree Treaty. Aside from acquiring the land from the Chippewa tribes, it opened the great tracts of white pines to the logging industry. The eastern forests were nearly barren and the growing Midwest needed lumber. Central Wisconsin and Minnesota had millions of acres of mature white pines that made excellent building material, and the rivers and streams to float the logs and power the sawmills."

She found the page she wanted and spread the book so she and Floyd could read it together. "At the risk of sounding like your teacher again," she said with a smile, "I'd like you to read the bottom of page 14."

Floyd read, "The federal Indian Trade Intercourse Acts prohibited Americans from logging on Indian lands without special permission. A land cessation treaty would provide legal access to these lands." He looked at Purdy and said, "The treaty opened the forests to logging. I don't see how that's relevant to the current standoff with the tribes."

Purdy smiled and flipped a few pages ahead. "Read the second paragraph on page 18."

"The elder Hole-in-the-Day (Pagoonakezhig) from the Upper Mississippi River region and La Trappe (Magegawbaw) from Leech Lake responded to Governor Dodge. Although the chiefs agreed to cede the land requested, they wished to express their concerns. "We wish to hold on to a tree where we get our living and to reserve the stream where we drink the waters that give us life," La Trappe said. After the interpreters translated the chief's words into English, Verplanck Van Antwerp wrote a footnote (one of only a handful) in his record of the proceedings, "This of course is nonsense—but is given literally as rendered by the Interpreters, who are unfit to act in that capacity. I presume it to mean that the Indians wish to reserve the privilege of hunting and fishing on the land and making sugar from the Maple." Meanwhile, to emphasize the kind of tree he meant, La Trappe walked up to the table on which Dodge had set a map of the proposed cessation and placed an oak sprig on it. "It is a different kind of tree from the one you wish to get from us," he commented, adding, "Every time the leaves fall from it, we will count it as one winter past." By this comment, La Trappe declared his willingness to bargain with Dodge over the pinelands in Wisconsin while reserving from any land cession the deciduous forests."

Floyd looked at Edna Purdy's smug smile. "Now you and I understand the federal logging injunction better than anyone else in this county," she said.

"So, the tribes have treaty rights to the hardwood trees, and unless they come to some sort of agreement with the state and the loggers, nothing can be done."

Edna closed the book. "I assume the judge has read the same passage and will uphold the treaty rights." Using the table for support, she pushed herself up and picked up the book. Floyd took it and replaced it in the open slot.

"Now that I understand that," said Floyd, "can you provide any more help with my missing woman?"

"If you've spoken with Tilly Crown, checked the graveyards, and checked the church records, you've covered every option I can think of." She rolled her walker toward the door. "Now, you need to go home for supper. You've got guests coming over."

"I won't even ask how you know that," Floyd said with resignation. He shook her frail hand. "Thanks for the history lesson."

Purdy smiled. "A teacher's work is never done," she said as she closed and locked the door.

＊

The aroma of roasting turkey permeated the truck's cab before Floyd opened the door. Also excited about the fragrances coming from the house, Penny, Floyd's dog, ran circles around Floyd's feet until Floyd was inside hanging his cap on the coat rack.

"You have time to take a shower and change," Mary said from the kitchen. She was stirring a pot and barely looked up.

"I don't even get a welcome home kiss anymore?" he asked, wrapping his arms around her waist.

"Not while I'm stirring seven-minute frosting," she replied. "Get changed and then you can whip potatoes."

"You could've warned me that you'd invited company," he said as he put his holster on the top shelf of the closet. "I stopped at the historical society and Edna Purdy told me to go home because we were having guests for dinner."

"I told you I was going to invite Pam and Travis over for supper."

"Yes, you did. But you didn't say when."

"Well, it's tonight. Change into something more casual, then I need you to help."

Walking to the bedroom, Floyd said, "What would you have done if I'd had an emergency or worked late?"

"I would've had a lovely evening with Pam and Travis. We would've learned about each other and made pleasant conversation."

"Okay," Floyd said, walking back into the kitchen in jeans and a golf shirt. "What can I do to help?"

Mary handed him the electric mixer and pointed to a pot on the stove. "Pour some milk onto the potatoes and whip them," she said. "Anything new?"

"Maybe," Floyd replied. "The BCA determined what type of gun was used at the shack—it was a tommy gun."

"Like the Eliot Ness shows?"

"Same thing. It does terrible tissue . . .'

"Shush," Mary said, waving her arm. "No blood, no guts, and no gore."

"Well, they also determined that one of the victims was a woman."

"Your missing woman?"

"They're going to check the DNA to see if they get a match."

"Is that likely?" Mary asked.

"It's probably a one-in-a-million shot."

Crunching gravel and the barking dog announced the arrival of Pam and Travis. Floyd met them at the door. Travis was dressed in khaki pants and a plaid shirt. Pam was wearing gray slacks and pink blouse, and had mascara and a touch of eye shadow.

"Welcome," Floyd said, holding the door for them. "Can I get you something to drink before supper?"

"I've got a couple bottles of Riesling chilling," Mary said.

"That sounds good to me," said Travis. Pam nodded agreement.

"How are things in Carlton County?" Floyd asked as he took wine glasses from the cupboard.

"Same old, same old," Travis replied. "Cloquet is considering a bond issue for a new middle school and everyone is up in arms over the increased property taxes." He took a wine glass from Floyd and added, "I saw the sheriff on the news and I watched the interview with the loggers. It sounds like things were tense."

"The loggers are really upset about the injunction that stopped their cut. I can't say I blame them. They had a contract with the state" said Floyd. "But, I got a history lesson this afternoon and the tribes ceded the rights to the pines, but reserved the rights to the hardwoods. Unless there's some sort of negotiated settlement, I don't see how the logging will happen."

"The Fond du Lac tribal headquarters are outside Cloquet," Travis said, "so we get a lot of feedback from both sides. I understand that the tribes have hunting and fishing rights from an 1837 treaty. They're trying to live in the 19th century and the world has changed. Every spring they net thousands of walleyes full of eggs and create a huge public relations problem for themselves. Now that the Lake Mille Lacs walleye population has crashed and resorts are losing money, the fishermen and resort owners are really in an uproar."

"I don't think there's a good solution. So far, everyone has lost," said Pam. "One of the loggers told me he's used up all his unemployment benefits, mortgaged his house, sold his boat and snowmobile, and applied for public assistance. He doesn't want welfare, but it's literally his last option."

"I heard the McDonald's in Moose Lake is hiring," Travis said, smiling

"It's a great job for a high school kid or a retiree trying to make a few extra bucks, but it's not much of a career," said Floyd, as Mary pulled the turkey from the oven.

"Okay, Sergeant," Mary interupted, wiping her brow with a kitchen towel. "It's time to take a chair at the table and get ready to carve the turkey."

Mary chattered as they set the table with bowls of Brussels sprouts, creamed corn, cranberry sauce, whipped potatoes and gravy. Floyd presented the carved turkey, neatly sliced on a platter.

"Are you making any headway on the explosion?" Mary asked.

"That's out of our control," said Floyd. "BATF took over the case and it's now their jurisdiction. At some point, they'll either announce an arrest, or dump it back on us if they can't find the bomber."

"Travis and I were talking about your missing woman from the 1930s," said Pam. "He had an interesting thought."

Being caught with a mouthful, Travis put up a finger and continued chewing. After he swallowed and took a sip of wine, he said, "Pam said you've tapped out all the databases and found nothing. We're darned closed to the Canadian border. She may have spent the rest of her life north of the border."

"I hadn't considered that," Floyd replied. "I'll have to give my genealogist a call to see if she searched those records. It's also possible, but a long shot, that the skeleton we found at the shootout scene may be the mystery woman."

"How about those Twins," said Mary, "did you see that they're going to break the team record for the most games lost in a season?"

"Tired of skeletons and explosions?" Floyd asked.

"Anything would be an improvement," said Mary.

"Have you met Pam's parents?" Floyd asked, garnering a glare from Pam and a kick under the table from Mary.

"We've talked about it," Travis said, "but Sleepy Eye is a long drive and we'll have to coordinate it with Pam's long weekend and her parent's availability. Pam and I are going to Bayfield, Wisconsin, for the apple festival in a couple weeks and we're going to spend a night in Ashland with my parents."

The small talk went on for another two hours. Pam helped Mary clear the table while Floyd took Travis to the garage to show him his pickup restoration project.

After explaining the most recent upgrades to the upholstery, Floyd paused.

"Pam's like a daughter to me. Please don't do anything to hurt her."

Travis smiled. "Neither of us are teenagers and we've both been through the hotter-than-the-sun romances. We're feeling our way along and seeing what develops. She's an extraordinary woman, and I respect what she's accomplished." Travis paused. "She thinks the world of you, Floyd. The way she talks, you're her half-brother and half-father.

"So, Sergeant Swenson, as long as we're interrogating each other, what are your intentions with Mary?" asked Pam as she walked into the garage.

"Touché. We're at a very different point in our lives, but the issues are much the same. We're progressing slowly and waiting to see what happens. I think we're both comfortable with our relationship, and I'm in no rush to move too quickly.

"We should probably get back inside. Mary made chocolate cake with seven-minute frosting. That means you're a VIP. She doesn't make seven-minute frosting for every guy Pam brings here."

"Has she made cake for many of Pam's boyfriends?" Travis asked, a bit anxiously.

"You might be the first, but my memory isn't what it used to be."

Mary and Floyd waved as Travis and Pam drove away. She put her head on his shoulder and said, "They're cute. Did you catch his slip?"

"What slip?"

"When Pam asked him to talk about his theory about your missing woman moving to Canada, he said, 'Yes, dear.'"

CHAPTER 39

NEMADJI STATE FOREST
OCTOBER 6, 1934

"Where in hell are we going?" "Terrible Tommy" O'Connor asked the driver as they bounced down a rutted trail. The car's headlights lit little more than a pair of faint lines through the tall grass.

"You wanted a place that's safe," said Bernie Gold. "Nobody's been to this place since it was logged and there ain't nobody going to find us. Since the women ran away and told some folks in town about your party at the inn, the sheriff would like to talk to you, so we can't play there."

O'Connor looked out the passenger window into darkness. His other nickname was "Lucky," because he'd never spent a night in prison despite several scrapes with the law, until his conviction for killing a Chicago cop. The "Terrible" nickname was coined when he started killing off his associates for the slightest transgressions. He had a short fuse, carried a pistol in a shoulder holster, and wasn't reluctant to pull the trigger when provoked.

"This place is perfect," said Bernie. "There's no way the St. Paul cops know about this place, so no one's going to ship you back to the gallows in Chicago."

"You're right," said Tommy. "Ain't no one going to ship me back to Chicago unless I'm in a pine box."

They bounced over a large rock and the woman let out a scream that was stifled by the gag tied over her mouth. With her hands and feet tied, she had no ability to roll with the bouncing car and was thrown into the two men sitting on either side of her. Their response was an elbow jab to her ribs that brought a gasp.

"We should've left her at the inn, Tommy," said Edward Darrow. "She's been nothing but trouble since you picked her up. The locals are going to miss her."

"Can it, Ed, or I'll put you in the hole alongside her."

"I'm just saying. There's no way we can go back and run that place now that we've been seen hauling her away."

"Well, it's no skin off your nose. I got the money back so we're all good. Except for her."

A black structure with gray wooden slats emerged in the headlights. "We're here," declared Bernie.

Grass rubbed against the bottom of the doors as the men stepped out of the car. Bernie scurried to the trunk and brought lamps and a can of kerosene to the front of the car. Using the headlights, he filled and lit them. With the headlights off, the lanterns cast a circle of pale yellow. Beyond their reach, the forest was shadows of pale gray, lit by the nearly full moon.

"I'll take this one," said O'Connor, grabbing the nearest lamp and walking toward the tarpaper shack. "You and Ed grab the beer and food out of the trunk."

James LaPorte, the thin, hatchet-faced man with a pencil-line moustache, grabbed Abigail by the arm and dragged her out of the car. She slid off the seat and fell onto her hip, eliciting a grunt of pain. He flicked open a knife and cut her ankles free.

"Get up and walk, sweetie," said La Porte, "I'm not carrying you."

Abigail struggled to her feet and was pushed roughly into the shack as gnats and mosquitoes quickly gathered around the light cast by the lanterns. Bernie and Ed carried two peach crates into the shack; one with sandwiches wrapped in waxed paper, and one with a variety of liquor and beer.

A rectangular rough-hewn table, big enough to seat eight loggers, was the centerpiece of the small building. One side had a bench and the other some wooden chairs. Hooks hanging from a center beam held the kerosene lamps. The floor was packed earth. A small cast-iron stove, shrouded in spider webs, stood in one corner. Beyond the dining/kitchen area, the walls were lined with bunks that had become home to a variety of mice and other vermin.

"This place is a dump," declared Darrow. "I wouldn't let my dog sleep here."

"It's an old logging camp," explained Gold. "It hasn't been used in ten or twenty years. That's why it's such a perfect place to lie low. No one would ever think to look for you here. It's like you dropped off the face of the earth."

"I've been in nicer jails than this," growled O'Connor, surveying the surroundings.

LaPorte pushed Abigail toward the corner where she cowered. Darrow and Gold straightened the chairs and wiped off the tabletop under O'Connor's gaze. LaPorte pulled beer bottles out of the box and threw a deck of cards on the table.

"I'm cold," whimpered Abigail. Her complaint was met with O'Connor's withering glare.

Chewing sandwiches, the gangsters sat around the table. LaPorte unsealed the cards and shuffled while Gold stood in the background.

The sandwiches were soon gone but the beer kept flowing. The poker game was underway, with laughing and swearing. Gold picked up the waxed papers and threw them into the wood stove. He rubbed his hands together and surveyed the pieces of wood in the box next to the wall.

"I'm going to gather some kindling and light a fire," said Gold, rummaging through the food box for a flashlight. None of the gangsters looked up from their cards as he walked out.

The moonlight cast an eerie glow through the bare trees and the beam of the flashlight was weak. The gangsters were arguing, although their voices were indistinct. Bernie shone the beam down the trail behind the car. He started circling the area around the shack, picking up small tree limbs.

A flashlight winked from behind the car and was gone in a blink. Bernie pointed his flashlight in that direction and flashed it three times, then shined his light into the treetops and waited.

"Took you long enough to get here," Gold whispered as a black clad figure emerged from the darkness.

"Shaddup," hissed the visitor. He stepped next to Gold and doused his flashlight. "Where are they?"

"The table is on the right, by the stovepipe," Gold whispered. "The other half is the bunkhouse."

The visitor nodded and opened his wool overcoat, exposing a tommy gun. Gold's eyes grew wide. "Where's Abby?" the visitor asked.

"She's by the door, sitting on the floor." Gold pointed to the farthest right end of the structure.

Inside the shack, the gamblers were getting drunk and noisier. "Where's that shit Gold? I could use a little heat," said LaPorte.

"Did you just deal me off the bottom of the deck?" challenged Darrow.

LaPorte grabbed Abigail and pulled her onto a chair. He untied her hands and shoved the cards to her. "Here. You deal."

With shaking hands, Abigail picked up the cards and shuffled. There was a noise outside as she started to deal.

"What was that?" asked LaPorte.

"Gold's probably breaking sticks," said Darrow.

With a firm grip on the tommy gun, the visitor pulled the trigger, stitching the door and side of the shack until the clip was empty. The muzzle flash blinded them and the racket of the shooting left them temporarily deaf. He pulled Gold aside, anticipating shots from inside the shack. As their ears and eyes adjusted to the dark and silence, the visitor latched a new magazine into the gun and they stepped to the door.

Facing the door, the visitor braced himself for another burst from the tommy gun. Gold threw open the door and they waited for someone to respond. All they heard were the creaking sounds of the shack and moans.

Gold stepped into the shack, looked at the carnage, then turned and vomited outside the door. The visitor, who'd experienced trench warfare in France, looked at the mayhem dispassionately until he realized that one of the bloody bodies had auburn hair and was wearing a dress.

"No! I thought you said she was in the corner!"

"She was," said Gold, wiping spittle on his sleeve. "She must've moved after I left."

The two men stood in the doorway, staring at the mess in the dim kerosene light. The coppery smell of blood mingled with mildew, urine, and feces.

"Let's go," said the visitor.

"You're not going to bury her?" asked Gold as they walked back to the car.

"I don't see any point," said the visitor. "I can't bury her next to her God-fearing parents. The family's better off thinking she ran away than knowing what she'd become."

"But you would've saved her."

"Only to put her on a train to send her as far away as the tracks run."

"But . . . "

"But, nothing. Drive me to my car. It's about a half-mile back."

CHAPTER 40

PINE COUNTY COURTHOUSE
THURSDAY

Floyd was pouring his first cup of courthouse coffee when his cellphone rang.

"Sergeant Swenson."

"Sergeant, this is Sister Mary Katherine at the Redemptorist archives. Doctor Pittman said you are looking for some specific records. How may I be of assistance?"

"Sister, thanks for calling. There was a Redemptorist seminary here in Pine City, Minnesota, until the early 1940s. The building had previously housed a sanatorium. I'm searching for a woman who's been missing since that transition took place. I've been unable to find the sanatorium records and the last record I have of the missing woman is a reference to her being at the sanatorium when it was turned over to the Redemptorists."

"What is the name of your missing woman?" the nun asked.

"Margaret Lane. Her birthdate is March 15, 1918."

"I promise that I'll look, Sergeant, but our archives are massive and it may take me days to find the Pine County Seminary records, if I can locate them at all."

"Sister, anything you can do will be greatly appreciated. I'm out of ideas."

"This is a rather ecumenical suggestion, but call the Church of Latter Day Saints, in Salt Lake City. They have the most extensive library of genealogical records in the world."

"Thank you, Sister. My contact has tried virtually every legal record available and has found nothing."

"Sergeant, humor an old woman. Call the LDS library and ask to speak with a genealogist."

"Certainly, Sister. I'll give them a call immediately."

Instead of calling Salt Lake City, Floyd called Barb Skog, who answered on the second ring. "Barb, this is Floyd Swenson."

"I hope you have news," she said.

"An update more than news. The volunteer for the Redemptorists that I told you about just called. Sister Mary Katherine will search for the Pine City records. She suggested that I also speak with an LDS genealogist in Salt Lake City, but I assume you've already made that contact."

"Yes, I contacted the Mormons early in my search. They didn't offer anything I hadn't already seen on Ancestry.com."

"I have one other remote possibility," Floyd said. "I spoke with the BCA crime scene techs who are processing the remnants of the shack that was found in the Nemadji State Forest. One set of remains is female."

"How interesting," said Skog with a hint of excitement. "Were they able to identify her?"

"They haven't been able to identify any of the victims," Floyd replied. "There's a chance they may be able to recover DNA from the remains and they agreed to do a comparison if you supply them with a sample. But the time frames don't exactly match up. The murders at the shack look like 1930's vintage and we think we have a record of your aunt at the sanatorium in the 1940 census."

"Of course I'll give a DNA sample. Who is your contact and what's the phone number?"

Floyd relayed Jeff Telker's information.

"Remember how we were waiting for someone to use the burner phone? We got a ping yesterday in downtown Minneapolis. We've got an address in an office building, but there's no way to identify the caller. He might've been in one of the offices, or one of the two restaurants, so that really doesn't buy us much.

I've got two people looking at the security tapes to see if they can match the enhanced video of the Walmart buyer with any of the faces going to the elevators. But a thousand people work in the building and probably another few hundred enter the restaurants each day. It's a long shot. Even if we identify the phone's owner, we've still got to figure out his ties to the protesters and the bombing."

"These investigations are never easy, are they? Good luck and keep me posted."

Bruce Swanson, the jailer, was stirring sugar into a cup of coffee, waiting for the end of Floyd's phone conversation. "I saw the sheriff's press conference. He didn't mention that there was a woman's body in the shack."

"That's new information from the forensic anthropologist," replied Floyd.

"That person you were just talking with thinks the body might have been her aunt?"

"The odds aren't in her favor. We don't know exactly when her aunt disappeared, but we're pretty sure it was sometime later than the people died in the shack."

"So," Bruce said, "you don't know who the female in the shack was, and you probably won't be able to identify her."

"If we had a relative, we might be able to get a DNA match. Otherwise, there's really nothing that will help us identify her."

"Sad," Bruce said as he turned to walk back through the security door with his coffee.

Floyd got up and walked to the Undersheriff's office. Dan Williams was sitting at his desk, apparently reading a report. "Excuse me," Floyd said quietly.

"Floyd, come in. What's up?"

"I had an interesting call from the BCA. They've processed the evidence from the state forest crime scene. They found shell casings and a couple bullets that came from a Thompson machine gun. It appears someone walked in with a tommy gun and shot everyone."

"Were they able to identify the victims?" Dan asked.

"No. There wasn't any ID on any of the victims," Floyd replied. "But they asked me if the department owned a tommy gun. The tech said a few had been sold to private citizens and some had been stolen, but most were either issued to the Army or were in police arsenals."

"I haven't seen one in the gun room," Dan said. "But, you've been around longer than me."

"I've never seen one, either. Do you have any records from the 1930s?"

"I don't know," Dan said. He turned his desk chair and opened the bottom drawer of a metal file cabinet. After looking through tabs, he pulled out several yellowed file folders and set them on his desk. He slid two of them to Floyd and opened one himself.

"These ledgers look like sign-out records from the late 1920s," Floyd said. "The handwriting is nearly illegible. I can read a few of the entries, but the signatures are faded and scribbled."

Dan flipped through a few pages and stopped. "Here's a sheet with dates in the 1930s," Dan said. He followed entries with his finger. "Most of these entries are confiscated guns going in and out on their way to court. Each entry has the brand of gun, the serial number, and the signature of the person who removed and returned it to storage."

Floyd stood next to Dan's shoulder as he scanned the list. After three pages, Dan put his finger on an entry. "Thompson," he said, reading the serial number. "It was removed and returned by Harold, whose last name I can't read, on November 2, 1932."

They leafed through the following pages and saw the Thompson checked in and out once or twice a year by a number of different deputies and bailiffs, starting in 1927. The blue ink was faded and the handwritten names nearly illegible.

"The last entry is January 1934," said Dan, flipping forward into the 1950s. "It was taken out and returned by—" he stopped, trying to decipher the faded, scribbled name, "Jim Zane, all in the same day." He flipped through the following pages without seeing another mention of the Thompson. "Based on this record, it should be sitting in the back corner collecting dust."

Dan pulled a key ring out of his top desk drawer. "Let's look."

They stopped at the security door and waited for the electronic release. When it clicked, they walked in and were met by the head jailer.

"What's up, guys?" Bruce asked. He wore the same brown uniform as the deputies, but without the striped pants leg that denoted a sworn deputy. His face was weathered, his hair thin and graying.

"We're checking the inventory of the gun room," replied Floyd.

Swanson shrugged. "Must be a slow day."

The gun storage room was locked up like a bank vault. Inside, the walls were lined with the department's racks of shotguns and AR15s, with shelves of guns being held as evidence.

"A tommy gun is unique. It should stick out among all these more modern weapons." Floyd said, walking down the rows of long guns on the left wall. "I've got nothing."

Dan opened a cabinet. "This is full of ammo. I've got several boxes of .45 ACP shells but no tommy gun. Let's look at the logs again to see who had access to the gun after the last time it was checked in."

Ten minutes later, Floyd made a list of fifteen names. "So, I've got these names. I assume all of them are dead. What am I going to do with it?"

"Is there a name that jumps out at you as someone who might've had some connection to gangsters?" Dan asked.

"It's more likely I'd identify someone who had a beef with gangsters." Floyd replied. "And, there's still the question: Where's the gun?"

"I imagine it's either at the bottom of a lake or in some private collection," Dan replied. There's little chance we'll find it."

Floyd let out a sigh. "Another dead end."

The jailer was sitting at the security door reading a report when they locked the gun vault. He pushed a button located under the countertop and the door clicked. "Everything in order?"

"Have you ever seen a tommy gun in the vault?" Floyd asked.

"Not since I started here," said Swanson, "and I've been here since the day I got out of the army in '69."

Again sitting at his desk, Floyd pulled a piece of paper from of his wallet and dialed Tilly Westberg's phone number.

"Hello," the frail woman's voice said.

"Ms. Westberg, this is Sergeant Floyd Swenson from the Pine County Sheriff's Department. We spoke last week about the woman I'm trying to track down who worked at the Tuxedo Inn back in the 1930s. Do you remember a woman named Margaret Lane?"

"I thought about it some more after you left, but like I told you then, that was a long time ago, Sergeant. I'm afraid I'm not much help."

"Do you recognize the name Margaret Lane?"

"I really don't remember anyone named Margaret," Westberg replied. "I recall Miss Abigail, but the others were more . . . transient."

"How about someone who was using a nickname for Margaret? Maybe someone who was called Maggie, Peg, or Peggy. Do those names mean anything to you?"

"I'm afraid they don't ring a bell."

"This young woman, named Margaret, left the Tuxedo Inn and was at the Pokegama Sanatorium in the 1940 census."

There was a sharp intake of breath, followed by silence. "Are you still there, Ms. Westberg?" Floyd asked with concern.

"At some point the inn was sold and I heard that all the staff left. There were lots of rumors about what happened, but most were just juicy gossip. Someone told me that the four girls who lived in the attic all went to the sanatorium as domestics."

"Do you remember their names?"

"Well, I think I remember Florence, because Miss Abigail rescued her from an abusive home. But I really don't recall any of the others."

"But you remember Florence?"

"Yes. Abigail doted on all the upstairs girls like a mother hen, but Florence got the most attention and coaching from Abigail. No one ever said anything to me, but the rumor was that Florence had been adopted into an abusive home and Abigail somehow rescued her. I suspect that Florence's residence at the inn wasn't accidental. It seemed like all the women who worked there had some sort of backstory and most of them left some pretty dire situations before they lit at the inn."

"Do you know where I might contact any of the other people who worked at the inn?"

Westberg let out a laugh or coughed. "Sergeant, most of the people who worked there had been cast off, rather like the carnies at the circus. We were close, but not close enough to talk about our pasts. As for the others, I have no idea where they went. It was chaos the day Miss Abigail sold the inn. That morning everyone packed their bags and left in a rush."

"No one stayed to work for the gangsters?"

"That last night, when they rented the whole place, some bad things happened. I wasn't privy to all the activities, but there was screaming and fighting and the rest I'll leave to your imagination. Miss Abigail and several of the second floor girls had bruises they tried to cover with makeup. But makeup can only hide so much, if you know what I mean. Everyone picked at their breakfast like they weren't sure what to say or do. As I recall, Miss Abigail stood up and said, "It's been good working with all of you. Now get out of here before the new owners show up and make a scene."

"And that's the last you saw of any of them?" Floyd asked.

"The four attic girls loaded into Mr. Adamson's car and they drove away first. The rest of us all crammed into the bakers' car and hustled away after them."

"So, Miss Abigail ran away with you?"

"No. The last I saw of her, she was standing on the top step, waving us goodbye, with tears rolling down her cheeks.

"No one ever knew what happened to her. Some gangsters re-opened the inn, but it went from being a classy place to something seedy. The locals never admitted going there before Miss Abigail sold, but once the gangsters took over, nobody ever went out there. There were rumors she was buried in a shallow grave on Tuxedo Point. I think it's more likely that she caught a train to Chicago or Seattle and never looked back."

CHAPTER 41

MINNEAPOLIS FEDERAL COURTHOUSE

Stephanie DeCarlo was surrounded by beige. She was sitting in a small beige room in a beige chair handcuffed to a ring in the metal table in the center of the room. Obviously nervous, she made regular furtive looks at the camera mounted high in one corner and jumped with surprise when the door clicked and a tired-looking young man, dressed in a wrinkled suit and carrying a briefcase, walked in. He was followed by a substantial woman wearing a light blue blouse and khaki slacks with a U.S. Marshal's badge attached to her belt.

"I'm Rory O'Hara. I'm your new lawyer," the man said, extending his hand.

"Uh, hi. I suppose you know I'm Steph."

"Please remove the handcuffs and leave us alone," O'Hara said to the marshal.

As the handcuffs were removed, O'Hara pulled a pen and a legal pad from his briefcase. The marshal left and O'Hara removed his suit jacket and hung it on the back of the chair before sitting down.

"Who's paying you?" Stephanie asked.

"I'm a public defender," he replied. "There's no cost to you."

Stephanie nodded, then pointed to the camera. "Is that recording us?"

O'Hara looked over his shoulder, then shook his head. "No, the red light isn't on. It's illegal to watch or record a private conversation between a lawyer and his client."

Stephanie nodded.

"I spoke with Jane Simmons, the Assistant U.S. Attorney. Then I read through your file." O'Hara leaned back. "Tell me about the logging protest."

"There's not a lot to tell," she said, with a shrug. "Jeremy led us to the forest gate and we chained ourselves together. The loggers showed up and it got kinda scary, then the cops showed up and everything settled back down. When the loggers left, a cop took the keys for our locks, handed us some bottled water, and left us sitting there. Jeremy was really mad, but there wasn't much we could do. We all got nervous and it was like hours before the cops came back. By then, we were all hungry and Susan had wet her pants. The cop turned us loose."

"No one hit you or abused you?" O'Hara asked, taking notes.

"Uh uh. We just sat there, mostly bored."

What happened when the loggers came back?"

"The cops arrested us and they were loading us into their cars. Then the logging trucks drove onto the road."

"Tell me about the explosion."

Stephanie glanced at the wall. "It was, like, surreal. I had my back to the road when I heard this boom! I got knocked down and then I was hit with lots of wood splinters. I heard this crash and then people were running all over the place yelling and screaming."

"Did you see the explosion?"

"I had my back to it."

"Did you know there was going to be an explosion?" O'Hara asked casually.

"What?" DeCarlo said, surprised by the question.

"Did you know there was going to be an explosion? Did you, or one of the others, plant the bomb that exploded?"

"No! We were there peacefully. Jeremy told us we were going to get on the news and then we were going to Wisconsin."

"You never saw bomb-making materials or detonators?"

"No! Everything we did was peaceful. I wouldn't have been involved if I thought someone was going to be hurt."

O'Hara made notes in silence. "Tell me about Susan Stevenson."

"Like what?"

"When and where did you meet her?"

"We were on the West Coast, kinda making our way toward northern California. We stopped at a mall one day to pick up some stuff and Jeremy picked her up in a mall. Next thing I knew, she and Jeremy were exchanging bodily fluids and the rest of us were sitting around the campfire, disgusted, listening to them get it on like dogs in heat inside Jeremy's tent."

"My notes say you and Jeremy had been a couple before Susan came on the scene," O'Hara said.

Stephanie squirmed. "We were, kinda, non-exclusive."

"Explain that to me."

Stephanie stared at the tabletop, then at the camera. When O'Hara didn't say anything she looked at a corner, not willing to meet his eyes. "It's hard to explain."

"Try."

"We scored some meth and it makes you kinda . . . I don't know, kinda affectionate and uninhibited. I guess we just kinda enjoyed each other's company."

"I believe you said, 'Getting it on like dogs in heat.'"

"With meth, you lose your inhibitions and the sex . . . it's cataclysmic."

"So, you, Susan, and Jane, were all having cataclysmic sex with a variety of the guys?"

"You make it sound so bad."

"I'm not judging," O'Hara said. "I'm just trying to understand the dynamics of the group."

Stephanie shrugged. "We were close."

"If Jeremy had bomb-making materials, would you have known?"

"We were living in tents and in our cars. It's not like there was a place to hide anything from any of the others," she replied. "Mike bought a Snickers bar at a gas station and tried to eat it without anyone knowing. Jane saw it, and she pounced on him like a lioness. We all got a bite." Stephanie shrugged again. "If there was dynamite in Jeremy's car, we all would've known."

"Why did you say dynamite?"

Stephanie shrugged. "I don't know. Isn't that what bombs are made of?"

"The file says the group was buying and selling drugs. Who was doing the buying and selling?" O'Hara asked.

"I don't want to discuss it."

"Listen to me carefully," O'Hara said, taking off his glasses and rubbing his eyes. "I'm your lawyer and my job is to defend your rights and to keep you out of jail, if possible. To accomplish those goals, I need you to be completely honest and open with me. Understand?"

Stephanie shrugged.

"Who was buying and selling the drugs?"

"Jeremy had a way to get cash sometimes. We'd stop someplace with Wi-Fi and then money would come. Mike made a couple calls and got some cash, too. They made the drug buys."

"Where did they buy?"

"Campgrounds and truck stops, usually."

"Who sold, and where did they sell?"

Stephanie squirmed and wouldn't meet O'Hara's eyes. "I guess we all sold some. It kinda depended on the situation."

"Did you ever buy drugs for the group?"

"Not really."

"Not really isn't an answer. Let me ask it differently. Did you acquire drugs for the group?"

Stephanie stared at the door. "Yes. We all did."

"And sometimes you exchanged sex for drugs?"

"It sounds dirty when you say it like that. We were high and it just sorta happened."

"Did Susan exchange sex for drugs, too?"

"Sometimes."

"Was she encouraged to exchange sex for drugs by any of the guys?"

"Sometimes."

"Who encouraged her?"

"It was more than encouragement. Jeremy told her we were out of money and drugs and it was up to her to help support us." Stephanie shrugged. "It's not like we did anything for drugs that we weren't already doing with the guys."

"Is that what Jeremy told you?"

"Jeremy and Mike, mostly."

"So, Jeremy and Mike were pimping Susan, Jane, and you out for drugs. Is that a true statement?"

"You make it sound like we were whores."

"Weren't you?"

"They didn't beat us or anything. We were just expected to help provide for the group."

"What were the guys doing to help provide for the group? Were they having sex to get drugs, too?"

"Yuck! No."

O'Hara set the pen aside and took Stephanie's hands. "Jeremy isn't the person you think he is. Pyle is an alias. His name is Jeremy Pike and he's a convicted felon. He was on parole when you were traveling with him, and he hadn't checked in with his parole officer in several months. When he was arrested, the feds returned him to prison to complete his sentence. They'll bring him back here for trial. Do you understand?"

Stephanie shook her head. "He's just connected to the network of anti-government people. They've all been arrested at protests, but it's never a big deal."

"Jeremy pled guilty to arson for burning down a federal forest research facility. In return for his guilty plea, the government dropped other drug-related charges. He's been arrested over a dozen times. Most often, he was released after paying a small fine and for time spent in jail awaiting the judgment. He's considered an eco-terrorist and he's suspected of planting the bomb at the forest explosion."

"He's very committed to saving the environment."

"He's mostly committed to making himself a pain in the ass and dragging along a bunch of unsuspecting and impressionable young people, like you and Susan. The last few months have brought his crimes to a whole new level, with kidnapping Susan and pimping you, Susan, and Jane across the Northwest and Midwest."

Stephanie started to cry. "No!"

O'Hara checked his watch, then took out his phone and checked emails while he waited for her to run out of tears. She wiped her nose on the sleeve of her orange jumpsuit and looked at him through red-rimmed eyes.

"What happens now?" she asked. "Mike already volunteered to testify against us."

"The judge and prosecutor refused his plea agreement," O'Hara said softly, trying to de-escalate the tension. "I spoke to the Assistant U.S. Attorney just before I came in here. She's not aware of the full scope of your exploitation, but she's offered to reduce the charges against you to drug possession. If I come back to her and explain the . . . ordeal you've been through while under the influence of drugs and Jeremy, she may drop all charges against you in return for your testimony against Jeremy and Mike."

Stephanie shook her head. "I can't face them in court."

"I doubt there will ever be a trial," O'Hara said. "Once their attorney understands the nature of your cross-country trip, I suspect there will be some sort of plea agreement that results in Mike and Jeremy staying in a federal prison for quite a few years." He paused, then added, "Susan is in a substance abuse treatment facility, and getting therapy for her mental state. If her parents have any say in the matter, she'll be back to testify to her abuse at the hands of the guys. That, and the consideration of her age, will certainly motivate the guys to accept a plea agreement. Juries aren't kind to men who pimp underage girls. Sexual exploitation of minors is subject to significant penalties, and people who pimp children, like Susan, aren't accepted well in prison society."

Stephanie stared at the tabletop. "What will happen to me?"

"I'll urge the prosecutor to put you into some sort of residential treatment facility and get you counseling. I'm no expert, but I think you're probably experiencing

Stockholm Syndrome, where a captive bonds with her captors over time. Once you recover, you'll be free to return to your family. Where is home?"

"I was born in North Dakota, but I grew up in Mesa, Arizona. I suppose my mom is still there." She shrugged. "I haven't talked to her in awhile and I'm not sure she would be happy to see me. The last time I was home she threw me out when she caught me smoking a joint."

O'Hara pushed the legal pad and pen across the table. "Write her name and address. I'll contact her and let her know that you're okay."

"What do I have to do now?" Stephanie asked as she scrawled a name, address, and phone number on the yellow legal paper.

"I'll write up a statement, based on your account of what's been happening and I'll have you read and sign it. With that in hand, I'll talk to Jane Simmons and we'll work out a plea agreement. If she's amenable to it, you could be out of jail and in treatment in a day or two."

Stephanie sniffled and wiped her nose on the jumpsuit sleeve again. "Okay. But, I don't want to see Jeremy or Mike."

"I can't guarantee that, but it's highly unlikely that you'll ever see either of them again."

As O'Hara stood, Stephanie asked, "Can you get me some decent food that doesn't look like overcooked slop? Maybe something green, with fiber? I mean, even the green beans they serve are cooked until they're almost brown and have the texture of oatmeal."

"There's not much I can do until you're out of custody. But, once you're freed, you should get better food at a treatment facility."

"After our life of camping and moving, I don't think I'll ever be able to eat a baked bean again." She shuddered. "Beanie weenies and herbal tea were kind of our staples."

"Except for the meth," O'Hara added as he snapped his briefcase closed.

"We didn't need to eat much when we were doing meth," Stephanie conceded.

As O'Hara put on his suitcoat he pulled a Snickers bar from a pocket and handed it to his client. "I don't suppose this is particularly nutritional, but it's yours if you want it."

Stephanie grabbed the candy and stripped off the wrapper like a starving person. A look of utter bliss crossed her face as she savored the first bite.

"Before I go," O'Hara said, "is there anything else I should know?"

"I don't know why," she said, around a mouthful of candy bar, "but it was pretty important to Jeremy and Mike that we be at that forest entrance on the first day the loggers were entering the forest. No one said why, but we really picked up our pace to get to the campground in Willow River when we did. I thought maybe we were supposed to meet some other folks, but it's not like we knew anyone there. It seemed kinda odd."

O'Hara cocked his head. "You have no idea why?"

"Not a clue."

CHAPTER 42

PINE CITY
THURSDAY

P am Ryan walked into the bullpen and poured herself a cup of coffee. Floyd was staring at the computer, oblivious to her entrance.

"Thanks for dinner," she said. "We had a good time. Travis really enjoyed getting to know you better. He's hinted about connecting with some of my friends, but I've always avoided the topic."

"He enjoyed having supper with a couple of old fogies?" asked Floyd, looking up.

"You're not that old. You and Mary are just nice, friendly people. I think Travis was a little relieved that I wasn't hanging out with a bunch of kooks or rednecks." She paused, then asked, "What's got you so entranced on the computer?"

"A woman named Abigail Corbett owned the Tuxedo Inn. She's listed in the 1930 census."

"How is that significant?" Pam asked.

"There's no trace of her after the census."

"How about the other people who lived there?"

"I haven't dug very deeply. Some of them were at the Pokegama Sanatorium in the 1940 census and two of them show up in marriage and death records. So, it's not like aliens swept all of them away on a spaceship."

"How about the others?"

"Based on the lack of public records, there's no way to contact them without a séance," Floyd replied.

"I've heard that's a great way to get in touch with people who have passed. I'm sure any information you got would be admissible in court too," she teased.

"What information wouldn't be admissible in court?" the sheriff asked as he walked into the bull-pen, trailed by a dapper man wearing an impeccably tailored suit.

"Floyd's trying to get in touch with some dead people," Pam replied with a smile.

The sheriff rolled his eyes. "This is Agent Barry Hoffman from ATF. He has some news about the bombing investigation."

Pam put out her hand and introduced herself as Floyd shut down the computer terminal.

"Floyd Swenson. I'm pleased to meet you," Floyd said, getting up.

"Let's move back to my office," the sheriff suggested.

In the small office Hoffman pulled a guest chair aside so he could face the others.

"We verified that the bomb materials were all taken from your local pond-blasting business." He looked at his notes and added, "William Davidson, or Pop, as he prefers to be called, isn't much for keeping records. We went through his books, then talked through a few more instances where he used blasting materials but neglected to note them in his records.

Barry closed his notebook. "Between us, if he weren't an old man with a spotless history, we'd arrest him and seize all his inventory."

"But—," Floyd interjected.

"But his poor records don't equate to criminal intent. I've spoken with the Special Agent in Charge. The SAC agreed that we will quietly remove the remaining stockpile of explosives and have Davidson shut down that business. He also has a federal firearms license and sells guns from a shop in his house. His records there are better, but we're going to audit his sales for the last year to see if we can reconcile the sales with his records. Again, there's nothing illegal, just some questionable recordkeeping."

The sheriff nodded. "I see no point in making a federal case out of this." He smiled at the play on words.

Barry grimaced. "There is something that came out of our investigation I'd like to share. We canvassed the area around Davidson's operation to see if anyone noticed unusual activity or vehicles. The results were strange at best."

"Strange in what way?" Floyd asked.

"None of his neighbors have security systems or outside cameras. One woman told us she doesn't own a key to her front door. On the other extreme, we had a guy meet us at his front door with a shotgun and told us to get off his property."

"Ray Pickard," Pam and Floyd said in unison.

"You know about him?" the ATF agent asked.

"Oh, yeah," replied Floyd. "He moved here a few years ago to live off the land. We get a call every now and then that he's either growing his own marijuana or making moonshine."

"You haven't busted him?" Hoffman asked.

"He was growing hemp, a relative of marijuana without the THC. We checked with the BCA and were told it was technically illegal, but anyone smoking hemp would die of lung cancer before they got high. He seemed to be legitimate, because he was spinning the fiber and making cloth on a loom in his barn."

"Hmm," Hoffman said, unimpressed. "We finally found a large house at a crossroads by Pop's operation that had a security camera looking out over their driveway. We made a copy of their images from the time before the explosion."

"That would be the vacation estate owned by that actress," Pam said. "No one actually mentions her name, but I heard it owned by Roberta Mason. She grew up in Hinckley."

"The plat map says it's owned by a corporation," Hoffman said. I didn't feel the need to dig any deeper since the housekeeper was polite and cooperative. When we reviewed the video we saw nothing but cars and trucks, mostly people who lived on the road."

"What's your conclusion?" asked the sheriff.

"On the day before the explosion, three vehicles passed through, going out and returning. Two of the three were gone less than half an hour, which wouldn't be long enough to get to the bomb site and return. Davidson was gone for two hours."

"You think Pop set the bomb?" Floyd asked. "I think that's a stretch. I've known Pop a long time. He's not the bomber."

"I suppose there are three options: Davidson set the bomb himself. The dynamite was stolen more than a week before the bombing. Or the thieves came in cross-country without passing the security camera. Davidson was adamant that he knew nothing about the missing explosives."

"Almost everyone around here has ATVs and can travel virtually anywhere," Floyd said.

"We combed the area around the storage building and didn't see any fresh ATV tracks or grass that had been packed down near the barn, but I suppose someone could have walked in from the woods." Hoffman paused. "We're going to question Davidson again. I'm just not convinced of his innocence."

"Be careful," Floyd advised. "He's a little forgetful and you might not be able to rely on the answers you get. Worse than that, a lawyer would eat you alive, arguing that even if Pop had been read his Miranda rights, he might not be able to give you informed consent without an attorney."

"Really? He's got dementia and he's running a blasting business and selling guns?"

"Oh, I don't think he has dementia. He's got some short-term memory issues so he sometimes misses appointments because he's forgotten which day of the week it is, but he's harmless. But his knowledge of blasting is hard-wired "He used to blast a few ponds every year. Now he mostly drives around drinking coffee and solving the world's problems with a bunch of other old-timers."

Hoffman stared at the corner of the sheriff's desk, mulling Floyd's words, then said, "I'm going to interview Davidson again as soon as we're through here. Based on this discussion, I sense that he's a local character. I'd like your support as we pursue this part of the investigation."

"What do you want from us?" the sheriff asked.

"Let me be clear," Hoffman sat up and straightened the crease in his pants. "This is purely an advisory visit. I was asked to update you on our investigation. All I want is your assurance that you won't interfere."

"Why would we interfere?" Floyd asked.

"It seems like Davidson is an old buddy and you've discounted him as a suspect."

Sheriff Sepanen leaned back in his chair and said, "We are your partners, not your adversaries."

Hoffman nodded and put his notes away.

"I appreciate the update, but why did you come here today?" asked Floyd.

"The SAC got a call from someone up the chain of command and he asked me to brief you on our investigation. I'm not entirely comfortable with that because a leak could compromise the work we've done." Hoffman stood.

"I'd like Sergeant Swenson to accompany you when you interview Pop again," the sheriff said, rising from his chair.

Hoffman eyed Floyd, then said, "I'm leading this interview. You can come along, but I want to be clear: you're an observer."

The sheriff stared at Hoffman but didn't immediately respond. A pulsating vein bulged in his neck. As his face went from red to pink, he said. "Agent Hoffman, I appreciate your willingness to make us part of your investigation. I assure you that Sergeant Swenson will be nothing but professional and that everything you've told us will be held in strict confidence. "Contrary to the common belief in Minneapolis, we're not country bumpkins. We will offer you the same professional courtesy you'll find in any other department. However, Pine County is unique. The county is spread over fourteen hundred square miles, half of that is lakes or swamps. My department consists of thirty people, including bailiffs and jailers. My patrol deputies are spread very thin." The sheriff took a deep breath and went on. "If you were out at Pop's farm, and needed immediate backup, the nearest deputy could be more than a half hour away from you. By sending Sergeant Swenson with you, I'm providing you with immediate backup in case things get ugly. It's a professional courtesy and not an attempt to butt into your investigation."

"I . . . I apologize," said Hoffman. "Thank you for offering Sergeant Swenson's support." He looked at Floyd, assessing the ability of the slender, gray-haired man, obviously nearing retirement, to be his backup.

The sheriff read his thoughts. "Agent Hoffman, do you recall the kidnapping case we solved last year that ended with a chase down I-35? Or, the cold case two years ago when Deputy Ryan chased down a murderer?"

"I vaguely recall reading about them."

"Floyd and Pam were both awarded the medal of valor for their actions. It was the third medal of valor that Sergeant Swenson has received." The sheriff paused to let his words sink in. "I would trust any deputy in my department to cover my back. If I was in a shootout, you're looking at the two battle-hardened people I'd want covering my butt."

Hoffman looked at Floyd and Pam's faces and nodded. "Okay."

The discussion was interrupted when fire tones sounded on Pam and Floyd's radios and the dispatcher called out the Kerrick and Duquette Fire Departments to respond to the report of an explosion on Stevens Lake Road.

CHAPTER 43

POKEGAMA SANATORIUM
OCTOBER 4, 1934

The girls woke to the banging of cast iron doors and a whiff of wood smoke. Their room was cold, an abrupt change from the warm attic of the Tuxedo Inn. As they quickly changed from night-gowns to dresses, the noise shifted to the clatter of pots and pans as the cook started breakfast. By the time they'd made their beds, the aroma of baking bread filled the kitchen and their tiny room. Pixie was the first one into the kitchen. The cook looked at her with surprise.

"Who are you?" She asked.

"I'm Pixie Lane. I'm here to help you."

The cook was a large woman who filled the space between the oven and the island in the center of the kitchen. Her hair was mousy brown with a wide gray streak. She wore a light blue dress under a white apron that was dusted with flour. Beads of sweat sparkled on her forehead as she stood in front of the wood-fired stove.

"No one told me about new kitchen help," the cook said. Carol, Mary, and Florence hovered out of sight near the door. "Stay here," she said to Pixie.

The girls looked back and forth at each other, unsure of what to say or do. From the other side of the door they heard the cook having a heated discussion with Mr. Adamson.

"Just put them to work, Opal," he said. "They're good, reliable help and your job isn't threatened."

"Why did you hire them?"

"Two of the orderlies took off without notice and these girls were highly recommended."

"I've never seen them around town. Who recommended them?"

"A friend, and that's all you need to know."

"I don't want help. I've always cooked alone."

"Put them to work doing the menial things that are bothersome. Have them peel potatoes and carrots. Once the patients are up, I'll have them changing sheets and helping in the dining room."

"Humph," the cook said. "That whore at the Tuxedo Inn blackmailed you, didn't she? I heard she closed up yesterday. I'll bet she made you take her help."

"Opal, please. Just put them to work and it'll be fine."

"You'd better hope that Mrs. Adamson doesn't find out about the new help."

"There's no need to involve her in the details of the operation. She's a busy woman."

The kitchen door swung open and the cook waddled in looking unhappy. "Oh, look. There's more of you." She looked disgusted as she scanned the kitchen, apparently looking for jobs to assign.

"You, Pixie. Get a paring knife and start peeling that pile of carrots and potatoes."

Pointing to the girl closest to their room. "What's your name?" she asked.

"I'm Carol."

"You grab that broom in the corner and sweep up the floor." She pointed at the others. "You two fill the wood box next to the stove. Make sure it's full to the top. When that's done, I'll have another load of bread to bake."

"Ma'am, what should we call you?" Carol asked.

"At least you're polite," said the cook. "You can call me Mrs. Palm." She hesitated, then asked, "What did you girls do at the inn?"

"We set tables and helped in the kitchen," said Carol. "Then, we'd change beds and clean."

"Ma'am," said Mary. "Could we have some breakfast?"

The cook's face softened. "When did you last eat?"

"Breakfast yesterday," replied Carol. "Mr. Adamson picked us up, and we haven't eaten since then."

"There are bowls and spoons in the dining room," Palm said. With Mary in the lead, they brought bowls and lined up in front of the stove where they each got a ladle of hot oatmeal.

"Take a seat at the table by the window and I'll be right with you."

As they sat with hands on their laps, Mrs. Palm returned with bowls of butter and raisins, and a pitcher of cream. "Stir some butter and raisins in, then stir in a little cream." She watched as they dove into the food.

"What are raisins?" asked Pixie, pushing the wrinkled brown pellets around with her spoon.

"They're dried grapes that are extra sweet," said Palm, smiling for the first time. She popped two into her mouth and savored them. "We get them from Fresno, California." She poured herself a cup of coffee and joined them at the table. "Where are you from?"

"I was at the State School in Owatonna," said Pixie. "I turned sixteen and they sent me to Miss Abigail so I'd have a job." She put one raisin in her mouth and considered the flavor before stirring the remainder into the oatmeal.

"We had a big family," said Mary. "I was too small to help on the farm and was one more mouth to feed. Miss Abigail came and got me."

They looked at Carol. "My parents were killed in a train derailment. The day after the funeral, Miss Abigail took me to the inn."

Florence, who was usually the most talkative of the four, stared into her oatmeal and chewed. When she looked up, all four were looking at her. They'd all shared their stories, but Florence had never revealed her history to them.

"Did something bad happen?" asked Palm, softly.

Florence stopped chewing and stared. Then she shrugged.

"Do you remember why Miss Abigail brought you to the inn?"

Florence looked back and forth between the faces. She made an almost imperceptible nod.

"Can you tell us?" Mrs. Palm asked.

Florence shook her head and took another spoonful of oatmeal, staring at the bowl. "My father was bad. Miss Abigail came and yelled at him, then she took me away."

Palm stroked her hair gently. "You girls call me Opal. If you need something, let me know." She stood. "When you're through eating, wash the bowls, then start those jobs."

Pixie leaned close to Florence. "Are you okay?"

Tears welled in Florence's eyes and she nodded.

CHAPTER 44

PINE COUNTY COURTHOUSE
THURSDAY

Pam and Floyd stepped toward the sheriff's door. "Come on, Hoffman. That address is on Davidson's road."

Hoffman rode with Floyd and they raced out of the courthouse parking lot with lights and siren. Pam's squad was close behind. They drove north on I-35 and turned east on highway 23, toward Askov, where a huge sign advertised the Rutabaga Festival on the fourth weekend of August.

"What's a rutabaga?" asked Hoffman.

"It's a root vegetable related to a turnip."

"They have a festival celebrating a turnip?"

"It's a Scandinavian staple, sometimes served with, or instead of, mashed potatoes. Sometimes they're cooked with Swedish potato sausage," explained Floyd.

"So, how do you have a festival to celebrate a rutabaga?"

"They have a parade and there's a kiosk that serves abelskivers, a sort of ball-shaped pancake, and rutabaga sausage. There's even a trailer that makes rutabaga malted milks."

"Are rutabagas sweet?" Hoffman asked.

"Not really," replied Floyd. "They're rather strong tasting. I've never had a rutabaga malt, but I imagine there's a lot more vanilla ice cream than rutabaga."

Hoffman shook his head. "When you live in a small town, I suppose you seize any opportunity to have a party."

Past Askov the scenery changed to forest, interspersed with pockets of alder swamp. The roads intersecting the highway weren't paved, and many had "Dead End" signs. They passed through Bruno, where a sign over a burned-out building announced that the new restaurant would be opening in the summer. In the distance they saw a column of smoke rising over the trees.

Just past Bruno, Floyd slowed and turned onto a gravel road. The dark column of smoke now was directly ahead of them. A small faded sign advertising Pop's Pond Blasting and Gun Sales stood at the intersection.

"This really is in the sticks," Hoffman said, as they passed gravel driveways. A concrete driveway led to a white mansion that looked like it belonged in the Antebellum South. "That's the Roberta Mason's mansion, where I got the video."

A half-mile past the mansion they went over a rise and the flashing lights of a firetruck stood out against the greenery. A sign with Davidson's logo pointed to a weathered farmhouse. Behind the house a number of outbuildings had been flattened. Near the center of the yard was a smoldering pile of wood and another firetruck. Floyd parked next to Pop's pickup, behind the house. Pam parked alongside him. They stepped out into a debris field of wood splinters. Every window in the house had been blown out and the siding had been pelted with splinters, some still stuck in the cedar shakes.

They walked to the firetruck where a pump was howling. Two firemen were directing the flow of water onto the smoking debris that used to be the barn.

"Looks like Pop was home," Pam said, nodding toward his pickup. "I assume he was in the barn or he'd be standing here."

"There's not much we can do here right now. I'll check the house," said Hoffman. "Sergeant Swenson, please cover the back door. Deputy Ryan, please look around the remnants of the outbuildings."

The window shades were shredded behind the blown-out windows and Floyd saw no sign of activity as he circled the house. Hoffman knocked on the front door, and Floyd heard the doorbell ring. The back door was ajar, so Floyd pushed it open and stepped into the farmhouse kitchen.

"Hello! Are you home, Pop?"

The kitchen smelled like cooked cabbage and burned coffee. A cast iron frying pan sat on the gas stove and a Mr. Coffee carafe held black residue that had once been coffee. Tiny shards of glass covered every surface. The carafe was still hot, so Floyd crunched across the broken glass and flipped the switch off. A plate, smeared with egg yolk and breadcrumbs sat in the sink with a cup and dirty silverware. A loaf of bread spilled out of the bag onto the counter next to a toaster.

Floyd walked through the living room, which was also the gun shop. A long case displayed an array of handguns behind cracked glass. Racks of long guns lined the walls around the counter. Some had been knocked from their slots and were scattered on the floor. Floyd kept his hand on the butt of his gun as he quickly crossed to the front door. He opened the door and held it for Hoffman. "No one home," he said. "The back door was open, so I walked in. Someone's been around, but not recently. The coffee pot had burned the residue down to char."

Hoffman looked at the guns arrayed on the walls, in the display case, and on the floor. "Davidson doesn't have much security considering the guns he's got displayed." Alongside the counter was a jumble of cardboard gun boxes with UPS labels.

"There isn't much crime out here and Pop is the kind of guy likely to respond to a break-in with buckshot."

The hinges of the back door creaked. "Floyd? Hoffman?" Pam called.

"In the living room," Floyd said.

"The outbuildings are in heaps and there doesn't seem to be anyone inside them. There's a mess in the barn," Pam said, looking distressed. She turned and walked out of the house without further comment.

The volunteer firemen had knocked down the flames and were standing by with their hoses, ready to deal with any flare up. They looked out of place. A bit of breeze carried the stench of burned flesh.

The fire chief, Otto Bergren, walked over and addressed Floyd. "The state fire marshal is on his way, but I'd say it's pretty clear that an explosion was the cause of the fire. Normally, I'd guess that there'd been a gas leak, but with Pop's blasting business, I'm more inclined to think this was an accident." He paused and looked back at the steaming pile of burned timbers. "There was someone inside. My guess is that it was Pop. He paused, then softly said, "His body may not be intact."

"Let's step back so we don't disturb the scene," Floyd said. Away from the fire chief he asked Hoffman, "Do you have resources to process this scene or should I contact the BCA?"

"Call the BCA. It'll take a day or two for my people to get here."

"For now, we'll treat it as a suspicious death," said Floyd.

"Old professionals don't have accidents," said agent Hoffman. "Davidson's books weren't in the best shape, but his storage and safety were good. There's no way he would've had an accidental explosion like this."

Floyd stared at the remnants of the barn. "You think this was murder?"

Hoffman squatted down and rested his arms on his thighs. "I think it's likely."

"I'll call the sheriff and the BCA," said Pam.

"I'll call Minneapolis and get a team rolling," said Hoffman.

CHAPTER 45

FEDERAL COURTHOUSE
THURSDAY

Stephanie DeCarlo had showered and washed her hair, but was still wearing tattered hip-hugging jeans and a t-shirt. She was sitting in Judge Peterson's courtroom. Her public defender, Rory O'Hara, exuded confidence that had been lacking in their morning meeting.

"What's happening?" DeCarlo asked.

"The U.S. Attorney is meeting with the judge to review the plea agreements. Once she's done, they'll come out to review your written statement and ask if you've agreed to the terms of the plea agreement and whether you are willing to testify against the others, if needed."

"And then I'm free?"

"Not entirely," replied O'Hara. "Part of your plea agreement is parole, which means you'll have to enter a treatment facility, declare a permanent residence, and you'll have to meet with a parole officer on a regular schedule. I'm sure you'll have to get a job and submit to random drug tests. If you stay out of trouble, stay drug-free, find a job, and meet with your parole officer, you'll be a free person in a year."

"Um, I don't have a permanent residence."

O'Hara flipped through the pages of his legal pad until he found a phone number. He took out his cellphone, dialed, and handed the phone to DeCarlo, who looked confused.

"Hello," a woman's voice answered.

"Mom?" There was a pause, then she said, "It's Stephanie."

"Are you okay?" April DeCarlo asked. "A lawyer called and said you were arrested."

"I . . ." Stephanie stammered. "I screwed up, but I think there's a chance I can get back on track."

"I've missed you. I know we bumped heads, but things are different, better."

Stephanie listened silently with tears welling in her eyes, then said, "I want to come home, but I'm an adult and . . . I need some space."

She took a deep breath. "Mom, what I'm saying is I need to come home, but we need a new set of rules."

"The lawyer said you were going to be on probation and that you'll have to stay off drugs. Are you ready to do that?"

"I'm sitting in a federal courthouse with a lawyer and I'm scared. He says I'll have to find a job and meet with a parole officer. But I have to have a permanent address." She took another deep breath, wiped away tears, then said, "I want to hit the reset button on my life and come home. Can I?"

"It sounds like you've hit rock bottom," said April. "Maybe we've both changed enough to make this work. I'll move my quilting out of your old room and you can move back in."

Stephanie wiped more tears on her forearm. "Okay. I'm not sure how I'll get home, but I'll see you when I get out of here."

O'Hara took the phone and switched it off. "It sounds like things are patched up."

"You'd already talked to her," Stephanie said, sniffling. "She sounds different, like maybe we can both be adults."

"I've made arrangements at an outpatient substance abuse center for you. I assume that'll be part of the plea agreement too."

Stephanie nodded her head, took a deep breath, and said, "Okay. I'm ready."

The bailiff opened the door to the judge's chambers and looked at O'Hara, who nodded. A moment later Jane Simmons and Judge Peterson stepped into the courtroom.

From the bench, Judge Peterson asked, "Miss DeCarlo, I've read your statement and spoken with Ms. Simmons. Was your statement given without coercion or reservation?"

Stephanie looked at O'Hara, who whispered, "Say yes, Your Honor,"

"Yes, Your Honor."

"Ms. Simmons said that you've accepted a plea agreement." Peterson put on a pair of reading glasses and read from a sheet of paper. "The terms of that agreement waive a one-year sentence. In return, you may be required to testify against your co-defendants, you will be obligated to take random drug tests, you will enroll in a substance abuse program, and you will meet with a parole officer on a regular basis, the terms to be agreed upon once you are released. If you violate any of those terms, you will be arrested and will have to serve the one-year sentence. Are those the terms to which you've agreed?"

"Yes, Your Honor."

Peterson set the paper down and signed it. "I've accepted the plea agreement. I'll leave you with Mr. O'Hara and Ms. Simmons to hash out the details." The judge stood, and the others rose.

Simmons approached the defense table and sat in a chair. "Here's the situation. The co-defendants, other than Jeremy Pike, have accepted plea agreements, so you won't have to testify against them. My boss is reviewing the case against Pike, and it'll be his decision whether to press charges against Pike or whether to just let him finish the remainder of his current sentence. At some point, you may be called back to testify against him, but I can't say how or when that will play out. I understand Mr. O'Hara has located a safe place for you to live." Simmons paused. "You're free to go."

Stephanie looked scared and confused. "What happens to Jane and Susan?"

"Jane had accepted the same deal as yours. Susan is a minor. She's in a treatment facility and won't be charged with anything. If we have to prosecute Jeremy, I would like her to be the star witness, if she's mentally capable of it."

"How about the other guys?" Stephanie asked.

Simmons reached out and put her hands on top of Stephanie's hands. "Mike Parrish is going to prison for five years and Clarke is going for two."

Tears spilled over and ran down her cheeks. "That's harsh."

"Jeremy and Clarke knowingly sold drugs and pimped you girls out. Mike knew Susan was underage and took her across the country, having sex with her and bartering her services for drugs."

"But it's not like they forced us to take the drugs. They never beat us."

"They put you under mental distress and manipulated you. Basically, you were brainwashed and mentally abused. They deserve to be imprisoned for that."

Stephanie stared into Simmons' eyes. "But they loved me."

Simmons shook her head. "They loved the power and the drugs. They told you they loved you to manipulate you. You were a pawn." Not seeing Stephanie's acceptance, she added. "You aren't the first woman to be taken in by a man's lies. I hope you'll learn from this and treat everyone with suspicion until they earn your trust."

O'Hara nodded. "It's a cruel world. Sometimes, you don't get the lessons until after the tests," he said.

Simmons stood and said, "I've got a meeting and you've got a long trip ahead of you. Good luck."

As Simmons walked away, Stephanie asked O'Hara, "How do I get to Arizona?"

"Your mother wired money to me," he replied, then took out an envelope and handed it to her. "There's a plane ticket to Phoenix and some cash for meals. I'll call and let your mother know that I'm dropping you off at the airport. She'll meet you when you land."

Stephanie opened the envelope and fingered the ticket and the cash. "Do I owe you anything?"

O'Hara closed his briefcase and took her elbow. "I'm paid by the court. All I want from you is the promise that I'll never see you in court again." He steered her out of the courtroom. "Let's go to the airport. The next flight to Phoenix is at 2:40."

CHAPTER 46

MINNESOTA BCA OFFICE
THURSDAY

Jeff Telker was finishing his report, summarizing their findings from the Nemadji State Forest site when his desk phone rang.

"Inspector Telker, this is Colleen Kelly from the FBI fingerprint office in D.C.. I have some results for you."

"I could use some excitement. I'm writing reports and I can barely keep my eyes open."

Sonny Carlson reached over Jeff's shoulder and touched the speakerphone button. "This is Sonny Carlson, Colleen. I overheard Jeff talking to you and wanted to get the unfiltered version of your call."

"I don't think there'll be much to filter," said Kelly. "You have solved one of the FBI's longest fugitive searches."

"Well, that doesn't surprise me. We are pretty bright and diligent. I find that to be a good recipe for success. I was just telling Jeff that we've been . . ."

"Sonny, let Colleen tell us her news."

"Well, I was just explaining how we . . ."

"Let Ms. Kelly speak."

"The fingerprint you sent to us wasn't in the automated AFIS fingerprint database, as you discovered, Sonny. So we had one of our experts search the archives manually. As I said, you solved a very old case. The fingerprint belonged to Thomas O'Connor, also known as Terrible Tommy. Born in Ireland, in 1890, he escaped from the exercise area of the Illinois Cook County jail on December 11, 1921, four days before he was to be hanged for killing a policeman. He escaped with four other inmates. Two of the escapees were apprehended, but O'Connor, Edward Darrow, and James LaPorte disappeared. The three of them were never arrested after they escaped. Hang on a second, I have O'Connor's file.

"The file is a little disorganized, but a witness reported seeing him in 1927 at a Chicago pharmacy robbery where a policeman was killed, but it wasn't ever substantiated. There are also unsubstantiated sightings in Minneapolis, Detroit, Iowa City, Dallas, Kansas City, Quebec, and even South America. The file also mentions a headstone in the Holy Sepulcher cemetery in Worth, Illinois, with the date of death listed as

1951. But, no one has ever excavated the grave to see if there's even a coffin there. For all we know, it might just be a memorial." She paused.

"Here's your trivia for the day. The City of Chicago left the gallows in place, anticipating O'Connor's eventual capture and return. The jail wanted to tear them down, but the City passed a law requiring the gallows be left in place in case he was found. The gallows were eventually disassembled and put into storage, and were apparently turned over to a museum in 1977. They were later sold to Ripley's Believe It or Not Museum."

"Hey, we helped Chicago finally close a case," said Sonny.

"Does the file give you any thoughts about why they disappeared so completely?"

"The working theory was that they crossed someone from one of the South Chicago gangs who killed them. There was also a rumor that a group of Chicago policemen vowed to kill him on sight. If either of those groups had killed him, he'd probably have been at the bottom of Lake Michigan."

"Do you know if O'Connor or the others had any ties to Minnesota?" asked Telker.

"O'Connor was arrested in St. Paul, then was returned to Chicago for the original murder trial. He may have heard about the 1930's St. Paul amnesty program. The St. Paul police chief made it known that if gangsters didn't commit any crimes in his city, he wouldn't arrest them. That brought several notorious gangsters to the city where their stolen money was infused into St. Paul's economy. John Dillinger had a house on Snelling Avenue, in St. Paul, and Ma Barker's gang lived in a house in White Bear Lake."

"There's always been a large Irish community in St. Paul," said Telker. "Maybe O'Connor had friends or relatives locally."

"He had some kind of ties there. A 1932 note from a White Bear Lake, Minnesota, constable asked the St. Paul police chief if he should arrest O'Connor. There's no reply, so I assume Tommy enjoyed a leisurely summer on the lake."

"A forensic anthropologist has the bones we recovered from the state forest," said Sonny. "If you send us pictures and physical descriptions of the three, we'll see if they match the skeletal remains we found."

"I'll email copies of the photos to you as soon as I hang up."

"Thank you," said, Jeff. "We found one set of female remains with the others. Do you know if LaPorte, O'Connor, or Darrow were married or were known to travel with a female consort?"

"I'll check, but even if one or more of them was married, gangsters weren't known for their marital fidelity."

"If you have photos of any of their known associates, who have also been missing for eighty years, please send them too."

"O'Connor seems to have killed most of his associates," said Kelly, "but I'll send you the photos I have in the file."

⊷⊶

"This is Sheriff Sepanen."

"Hi, Sheriff, this is Jeff Telker from the BCA. I have a possible ID on one of the bodies from the shack in the forest."

"Really?" asked the sheriff, leaning back in his chair. "How did you determine that?"

"My associate was able to pull a fingerprint off the inside of a pocket watch and the FBI did a manual fingerprint archive search. The fingerprint matches a guy named Tommy O'Connor, also known as Lucky Tommy and Terrible Tommy. The last is a gangster nickname he picked up for killing anyone who crossed him. He was sentenced to be hung in Chicago, but escaped from the jail four days before the scheduled execution. We've just received a picture and physical description that we can use to compare to the skeletal remains," said Jeff.

"Terrible Tommy has been missing since the 1930s?"

"Actually, Tommy O'Connor has been missing since 1921 when he escaped from Chicago's Cook County jail. The two men who escaped with him, Edward Darrow and James LaPorte, also disappeared. I sent their photos and physical descriptions to the forensic anthropologist."

"Very interesting. Do you have any leads on the identity of the woman?"

"I asked if any of the missing men had wives or girlfriends but that seems to be a dead end. I was contacted by Barb Skog, of the DEA, and a sample of her DNA is being compared to the female remains in case they're her missing aunt. That's if the anthropologist can recover any usable DNA from the teeth or bone marrow."

"Keep me posted," said the sheriff.

After the BCA call, the sheriff dialed a Duluth cellphone number handwritten on the back of the television station business card. "Hello, Megan, this is John Sepanen."

"Sheriff, can I call you back at this number in five minutes?"

"I'll be here."

Four minutes later, Sepanen's phone rang. "Hi, Sheriff. Thanks for waiting. What's new?"

"I appreciate the great background piece you did on the loggers at the bar. It was very nice to see the other side get some air time."

"My producer was miffed at first that we'd driven away before the news conference, but after she saw the edited piece, she was pleased. Once she saw the coverage from the other stations, she was elated."

"I'm glad we didn't get you into trouble," said Sepanen. "I also appreciate your willingness to accept the suggestion." He paused, then added, "I'd like to toss you an exclusive."

"Hang on," the WDIO reporter said, followed by the sound of shuffling papers. "Is this on the record?"

"You can quote me if you'd like."

"Start anytime you're ready, Sheriff."

"I was contacted by the BCA with the tentative identification of one set of remains from the Nemadji Forest murders. One body was identified as Terrible Tommy O'Connor, who has been missing since his escape from Chicago's Cook County jail in 1921. A forensic anthropologist is comparing pictures and physical descriptions of O'Connor, and the two men who escaped with him, to the skeletal remains recovered in the state forest."

"No shit!" Winston said as the computer keys clicked. "I'll do an internet search on O'Connor as soon as we're off the phone. I'll bet the *Chicago Tribune* will be thrilled to get a call about a cold case."

"I'm sure they'll be more than thrilled. O'Connor escaped four days before he was scheduled to be executed. I was told Cook County kept the gallows in place for years, awaiting O'Connor's return."

"Anything else?" Winston asked.

"One of the skeletons was female."

"Do you know who she was?"

"We're pursuing several possible identities."

"It sounds like you have some thoughts about her identity. Would you care to share who she may have been?"

"Not at this time," said the sheriff.

"But I'll be the first to know, right?"

"We seem to have a symbiotic relationship. As long as that continues, you'll be the first call I make on any breaking stories."

"That's okay, as long as you don't feed me lies."

"Who? Me?" asked the sheriff.

"Yeah," said Winston. "You love me today, but will you still love me in the morning?"

CHAPTER 47

UNIVERSITY OF MINNESOTA
THURSDAY

Angela McMillan set the physical descriptions and pictures of the three gangsters on a desk in the anthropology lab. Her grad-student assistant, Bethany Stone, stood at her shoulder, focused on the pictures.

"Interesting haircuts," Bethany said, staring at the booking photos. "It looks like someone put a bowl on top of their heads and shaved off the hair below the edges."

"Simpler times," said McMillan. "People didn't have seventy bucks for a stylist." She took a tape measure from a drawer and laid it on the stainless-steel table next to the first set of remains.

"One hundred sixty-three centimeters."

"Sixty-four inches," said Stone, making the conversion from metric to inches in her head. "Five-seven was a pretty common stature for a man in the early twentieth century, so this is on the low side of average. That doesn't give us a definitive identification."

McMillan made a note and moved the tape measure to the next skeleton. "He's 170 centimeters," said Stone. At the third skeleton, she said. "This one is 161 centimeters."

McMillan took her notes to the desk and compared the measurements to the physical descriptions of the three missing men. "Five-seven and five-three. These match the physical descriptions we received," she said. "But you're right, this doesn't rule out many of the men from that era. Scan these photos and overlay them with the skull photos. That'll give us a better comparison."

One by one, Bethany manipulated the photos on the computer until they were displayed on the LCD screen in proportion, and directly over photos of the skulls. "I'd feel more comfortable making an ID from their dental records, but assuming that their dentists are long gone, these are pretty darned close to a perfect match."

"So, we have LaPorte, Darrow, and O'Connor, and that leaves us with one John Doe and one Jane Doe," said McMillan. "Were you able to get a bone marrow sample from the female remains?"

"I got something. Although it was badly degraded it may be good enough for a mitochondrial comparison."

"How long before we will have the comparison with the sample from the DEA?"

"I took the samples to Leo," said Bethany. "He's backed up about a month, but I told him there was a family member who wanted to know if our skeleton is a long-lost relative and he said he'd move us up in the queue. I left with the impression we'd have the results in a couple days."

"We shouldn't use up our IOUs on an eighty-year-old mystery, but it would be fun to know the answer."

CHAPTER 48

DAVIDSON FARM, NEAR BRUNO
THURSDAY

Jeff Telker and Sonny Carlson drove up Pop Davidson's driveway in the BCA mobile crime lab, a customized Winnebago RV. Pam Ryan motioned them to a grassy spot next to the house. They saw the yard littered with wood splinters and that a large part of the barn was missing. The rest was charred.

Sonny was out of the RV first, looking around and sniffing the air.

"Hi, Deputy Ryan," he said when walking toward Pam.

Jeff joined them, sniffing the slight breeze that was blowing from the direction of the barn. "Do you have any thoughts on the time of death?"

"He's been dead for at least a few hours," she replied. "The fire department responded to a report of an explosion about three hours ago."

Sonny opened the storage compartment built into the side of the RV and removed a toolbox. He took out purple plastic gloves and handed a pair to Jeff. Pam led them to what was left of the barn. The smell of burned hair hung in the air. The sheriff was talking with Floyd and Tony Oresek, the Duluth medical examiner. Ed Paulson, Tony's assistant, and Barry Hoffman were having a discussion outside the barn.

After introductions, Pam led Sonny to a horse stall with charred and buckled boards. He looked inside at the body covered with debris and shook his head. "This is bad. Not as bad as the guy in Pillager who killed himself with the shotgun. That was a real mess. I bet they had to scrub the whole kitchen after that. Now that I think about it, I imagine they replaced the cabinets and wallboard. It was so bad that . . ."

"Um, Sonny," Pam said. "I'd rather not hear the details about the splatter, if that's okay with you."

"Not a problem," said Sonny, taking out a camera. "I'll get some pictures and we can process the crime scene." After snapping a few shots from the gate, he stepped into the stall and took close-ups of the nickel-plated revolver that was lying close to the victim's hand. Everything was coated with fine dust from the explosion.

"Have any of you walked in this stall?" Sonny asked, moving to get photos from a different angle, then taking a photo of the floor near the victim's hand.

"The closest we've been is here, at the gate," Floyd replied.

"If that's the case, someone screwed up their very carefully staged suicide scene by stepping in some bodily fluids." He stepped close to a bloody footprint with a large wood shard on it and took pictures from several angles. "We'll have to clear the debris to get a clearer picture. I can compare it to the shoe database, but the widely spread waffle pattern of the print makes me think this is the tread pattern of a man's hunting boot."

Jeff Telker carefully stepped into the stall and picked up the pistol with gloved hands. "The polished finish on the nickel plate is perfect for recovering fingerprints, but even with all the dust generated by the explosion, I don't see a single print on the gun. It may have been wiped clean after the shot." He carefully opened the cylinder and dumped the shells into an evidence bag. "Only one spent cartridge. None of the brass shows any fingerprints either. I'd say someone carefully loaded the gun with gloved hands."

Oresek, tall, gaunt, and serious, and often compared to the Disney cartoon figure of Ichabod Crane, stepped forward and took in the scene. "We'll check the victim's hands for gunshot residue and his finger-nails for tissue he may have scratched off his killer."

"If there are scuff marks from a struggle, they might be covered in dust" said Sonny. "My impression is that he walked here and was shot where his body fell. There's a high probability the killer was known to the victim. The killer probably expected the entire barn to be destroyed in the explosion or fire so he wasn't too concerned about cleaning up the crime scene other than wiping the gun."

"It was probably someone he trusted," said Floyd.

"I'm not so sure about that," said Sonny. "I remember the woman up in Baxter. It was a home invasion and the intruder had on gun on her and led her to the basement without apparent resistance. She probably hoped he'd lock her in the basement, or tie her up, then leave."

"Did he leave her unharmed?" asked Pam.

"Once she told him where the drugs and money were hidden," said Sonny, "he shot her. We identified him from a handprint he left on the back door and arrested him a few weeks later. Under interrogation, he said he didn't want to leave behind a witness who'd seen his face."

"When you're through in here, we need to process the dynamite storage area," said Floyd. We'd like to know if all of Pop's explosives blew up or if they were stolen."

"If all of the stored ANFO had blown," said Hoffman, "it would've leveled the entire barn and the house. Someone wanted you to think his whole inventory had blown, but I doubt this damage resulted from more than a bag of explosive." Hoffman paused, carefully considering his words.

"The victim's recordkeeping wasn't great, but in my professional opinion, there's more than a dozen bags of ANFO missing. That's not enough to bring down a large structure, like the courthouse, but it's certainly enough to do some significant damage."

"How much damage are we talking about?" asked the sheriff.

Hoffman thought for a moment, then said, "Think of the photos of car bombings. I'd estimate enough to spread car parts over several city blocks and leave a crater in the ground."

"I wonder if we're dealing with a terrorist or just a nut?" asked the sheriff.

"We may not know until it's too late," replied Hoffman.

Pam and Floyd's radios sounded off, announcing a disturbance at the entrance to the Hinckley casino. They ran to their cars, then drove thirty-five miles to the casino. As they approached the north entrance they could see a crowd of people blocking the driveway and spilling onto the road.

Floyd stepped out of his cruiser, leaving the door open. He immediately recognized some of the loggers. They were carrying signs and yelling at the casino security guards who had formed a line across the driveway to the parking lot. Pam ran to the loggers and edged them back from the security officers.

"What's going on?" Floyd asked the security guards.

"These idiots are blocking the casino entrance." The tall, dark-haired guard turned and pointed behind him. "We've got a hundred cars backed up waiting to get out of the parking lot and dozens more are turning away from the entrance rather than face the picketers. You've got to get them out of here."

Floyd looked at the picketers, who were mostly gathered around Pam, still blocking the driveway. A variety of hand-painted signs sported messages of "Logs Mean Jobs" and "No Indians in the State Forest." Some of the protesters were yelling "Logs mean jobs!"

"It looks to me like the protestors are on the highway right-of-way, and are exercising their rights of free speech and public assembly."

The security guard rolled his eyes. "Have them exercise those rights elsewhere. We're trying to run a business and they're interfering with commerce."

As they spoke, a WDIO news van steered onto the shoulder of the road fifty yards away from the protest. Floyd watched as the reporter put the finishing touches on her makeup in the side mirror as her cameraman hoisted the transmission dish and dragged out a video camera.

Floyd looked at the security guard's name tag. "Boyd, I think you've got a PR problem."

"We won't have a problem if you run those yahoos out of here and open the driveway." Boyd ran his hand over his nearly bald heard. "The court has already issued an injunction shutting down the logging."

"I think the tribe is going to lose in the court of public opinion," said Floyd, nodding toward the approaching news crew.

"No," said Boyd. "I will not allow them to film this."

"If they're on a public right-of-way, you can't stop it."

"Bullshit!" Boyd pulled a radio from his belt and eased away from the crowd. He was soon in an animated discussion with someone inside the casino.

Megan Winston, microphone in hand and wearing a blue polo shirt with the WDIO logo stitched on the chest, walked up to the nearest protester and asked, "What's going on?"

The young man, obviously of Scandinavian descent with blue eyes and blonde hair, and sporting a yellow CAT cap said, "We decided to picket outside the casino so the rest of the world can see the magnificent palace the Indians built with *our* dollars. They don't pay any taxes and yet they made us stop logging so we can't make any money."

A dark-haired man leaned over to the television mic, "And we're not going to take it anymore!"

The camera panned across the picket line, capturing the line of white-shirted security guards and the long line of cars waiting to exit the parking lot. The cameraman was about to cut away when a black Suburban bounced across the casino lawn, past the waiting cars.

A large man, red-faced and close to four hundred pounds, launched himself out of the Suburban and slow-jogged to Boyd, who gestured and pointed at the crowd. As they spoke, a Minnesota trooper and another county cruiser stopped on the road.

The huge security guard, with a name tag that said "Sean – Supervisor," stepped up to Floyd. "Either you remove these people from our entrance, or I will."

Floyd nodded toward the news crew. "You might want to hold your voice down. I think they're recording you on that parabolic microphone." When Sean looked at the news crew, he saw the black dish pointed toward him."

Sean put his hand gently, but firmly, on Floyd's shoulder and steered him toward the Suburban. "Get the protestors and that news crew out of here."

"I can't. They're on the highway right-of-way, and they're staging a peaceful protest."

"You don't seem to understand me," said Sean. "Either you get them to leave, or I will."

A second news van pulled to the shoulder of the road and disgorged a reporter and a cameraman, who jogged to the edge of the crowd.

"It looks like one of the news crews from the Cities just arrived. You might want to comb your hair before you remove the protesters. You'll want to look your best on the 10 o'clock news," Floyd said, calmly.

A cellphone chirped in Sean's pocket. He put a finger in one ear and returned to the Suburban to talk. Pam was being interviewed by the camera crews while the state trooper made sure the protesters stayed off casino property and allowed cars to pass on the highway.

Sean again emerged from the Suburban and signaled for the security people to gather around him. After a short discussion, they walked away from the protestors. A few security people walked to the line of cars and spoke with the drivers as they handed out slips of paper. Several minutes later, the line of cars disappeared back to the parking lot and the security people were gone, except for Sean.

Sean turned his back to the protesters and leaned close to Floyd's ear. "We're backing off the confrontation and handing out chits for free dinners. I'm acting in good faith because we don't want anyone hurt. Please talk some sense into these guys and get them out of here."

"Sean, I don't have a lot of influence with these guys. I suggest you talk with the tribal leaders and tell them what they've got on the line. Compare the casino profits with the goodwill they're losing over the timber rights. You might want to suggest a three-way discussion between the tribal leaders, the logging company, and the state. It might resolve the problem for everyone."

"I don't think they want to relinquish their rights to the trees."

"And most of the loggers haven't had a job in nearly a year. Their unemployment benefits have run out."

Sean turned and looked at the protesters. "What a ragtag mob," he said. "I don't think they'll look good on television."

"Look at the guy talking to Megan Winston. He's showing her pictures of his kids. Do you think that'll play well on the news?"

"Aw, shit." Sean jammed his meaty hand into his pants pocket and pulled out his cellphone. "I'll make the call to Mary Marcineaux, but I make no promises. She can talk with the elders, but they make the rules."

"I tell everyone the same thing," said Floyd. "Do the best you can and hope it's good enough."

"Sergeant, you missed your calling. You should've been a philosopher or psychologist."

"Sean, before you go," Floyd said. "We were just at a crime scene where a bunch of explosives were stolen.

I don't know if the tribe and casino are a target, but keep your eyes open."

"Lots of explosives?"

"The ATF guy said it was enough to make a car bomb that would crater the road and spread debris for blocks."

Sean closed his eyes and rolled his head back. "Ah, man. I was in Iraq and saw the damage those little IEDs did, and it was horrible. A car bomb is a hundred times worse."

Sean scanned the crowd. "Do you suspect one of these guys?"

"It's the same material that went off in the forest and killed that logger. I doubt that it was this bunch, but I wouldn't let my guard down."

"We've got very sophisticated security measures. I'll make sure we ratchet them up."

"Most of your security is to stop cheaters and thieves. Are you really prepared to deal with a bomber?"

"We train for every contingency. The security is set up so it doesn't intrude on the casino experience, but believe me, it's tight."

Floyd passed a business card to Sean. "My cell-phone number."

"The casino is outside your jurisdiction," said Sean, fingering the card.

"We're not adversaries," said Floyd.

Sean took out his wallet and handed Floyd a card that was molded to the wallet's shape. "You got anything else going on right now? If not, I'll walk you through the security room."

CHAPTER 49

PINE COUNTY COURTHOUSE, FRIDAY

Floyd did a Google search for the Latter Day Saints and genealogy. He made a call to Salt Lake City and, to his amazement, the phone was answered by a perky woman on the first ring.

"Church of Latter Day Saints Library. How may I be of assistance?"

Taken aback by the perkiness and the quick response, Floyd stammered. "Uh, this is Sergeant Floyd Swenson, from the Pine County Sheriff's Department in Minnesota. I'm trying to locate a missing person."

"I'm sorry, Sergeant, but we only deal with genealogy, not missing persons' issues."

"The person I'm trying to find has been missing since the 1940s."

"Hang on. I'll connect you with one of our genealogists."

After a few seconds he heard, "Trish Brouchard, how may I be of assistance?"

"Ms. Brouchard, I'm a sergeant with the Pine County, Minnesota, sheriff's department. I'm investigating a cold case involving a woman who hasn't been seen since the 1940s. I hoped you might be able to help me."

"Sergeant, I suggest that you start out with Ancestry. com. They have birth, death, marriage, census, and all other sorts of information."

"The person who contacted us started with Ancestry.com but hit a wall. I was hoping you might be able to view something unavailable to us."

"Sure. Give me a name and birth date."

"Margaret Lane was born March 15, 1918, somewhere in southern Minnesota. We found her in census records at a State School in 1930 and again in Pine County in 1940. Other than a newspaper clipping that says she was at a sanatorium, here in Pine County, I can't find a trace of her after the 1940s."

Floyd heard the computer keys clicking. "Okay, I found those census records. Did you look at birth, death and marriage records?"

"I've found nothing but the census records," replied Floyd.

"Hmm. Lane is a pretty straightforward name. Not too many ways to misspell it and it should be easy to read even if the writer was shaky. Did you modify the search to include nicknames, like Peggy and Madge?"

"To be honest, I didn't do the actual search. The woman who sent me on this chase is a diligent law enforcement professional who is the niece of the missing woman and I have to assume she covered all those bases."

"Rather than tying you up on the phone while I run some broader searches, why don't you give me your phone number?"

"Sure," Floyd said before reciting his cellphone number.

"Sergeant, you said that you're in Pine County, Minnesota. Give me the names of the counties that abut Pine County and I'll broaden the search."

"Carlton, Kanabec, Isanti, Aitkin, and Chisago counties in Minnesota and Burnett and Douglas counties in Wisconsin." He had to spell out most of the county names.

"Help me with my geography," she said. "How far are you from Iowa and Canada?"

"Iowa is about three hours away and Canada about four, depending on the route you choose."

"I'll dig in and see what I can find. I'll give you a call before I go home tonight or in the morning if I'm still running down some threads."

"Thank you!"

Floyd was immersed in thought after his conversation with the LDS library and burst into the sheriff's office without noticing Megan Winston sitting in the guest chair. He stopped so quickly that he nearly fell over.

"Sergeant," said Winston, "I'm not that scary."

Floyd regained his composure. "It's not that you're scary; it's just that I've never been fired for something I didn't say to the press, and I'd hate to end that streak today."

Lines creased the makeup at the corners of her eyes as Winston laughed out loud. "I should write that down!" Turning serious, she asked, "What did you say to the giant security goon that had his undies in a bunch?"

Floyd looked at the face he'd seen so often on television. She looked thirty on television but closer to fifty when she smiled. "I don't recall anything specific," said Floyd.

"C'mon," she said. "He went from hothead to pussycat in the span of one minute while talking to you. What could you possibly say that would bring that turnaround?"

Floyd looked to the sheriff, who nodded. "Well, I told him that the casino might win a fight over logging rights in the federal courts, but if they tried to clear the protesters out of the driveway, they'd lose their battle in the court of public opinion. I suggested that he speak with the tribal leaders to see if we could get them to the table with the loggers and the state forestry people before the tension escalates and someone else gets hurt."

"That's brilliant!" said Winston. "I'm constantly amazed by your deputies, John." She pulled out a small notebook and made notes.

"I'd prefer that quote be attributed to the sheriff," said Floyd,

"You're the one who said it. Why not get the credit?"

"I prefer to be behind the scenes. As far as I'm concerned, the best thing I can do is make the sheriff look good."

Winston looked at the sheriff who was trying to look serious, but he gave up and broke into a broad grin. Winston shook her head and continued to make notes.

"You two should be a comedy team," she said, closing her notebook. "Do you think there will be a meeting between those three groups?"

"If they hear it on television, I think they might be embarrassed into talking with each other," said Floyd.

Winston cocked her head. "That would be an interesting lead into the segment. 'An unnamed source suggested that the tribal leaders, the state forestry department, and the logging interests meet to negotiate a solution to the current standoff.'" She reached for her spacious bag and stuffed the notebook into a side pocket. "What can you tell me about the death in Bruno?" she asked, conversationally.

"What death in Bruno?" asked Floyd.

"The one you called the BCA to investigate just before you got called to the picketing at the casino." She looked at their surprised faces and added, "You're not my only sources."

"A victim died of an apparent gunshot wound. His identity is being withheld pending notification of his family."

"Was it a suicide or a murder?"

"Yes," the sheriff said.

"Yes to which question?"

"That determination will be rendered by the St. Louis County medical examiner."

"Even if I play nice and don't report that detail until tomorrow when it becomes public information?"

"I'm afraid so," said Sepanen.

Winston stood and slipped the bag's strap over her shoulder. "Are you any closer to arresting someone for the explosion that killed the logger?"

"We're closer every day," said the sheriff with a smile.

CHAPTER 50

CHANHASSEN, MINNESOTA
FRIDAY

I t was nearly midnight, but Barb Skog was still staring at the bluish glow from her computer screen. She clicked through search screens on Ancestry.com, changing the search parameters to be more inclusive, then a broader range of possible birthdates, then allowing similar spellings of names. Each new search brought dozens of pages of irrelevant data the computer thought would get her close to the person she wanted to find. None of them did.

She went back to Margaret Lane's profile and pulled up the 1940 census. Again she saw the name and the address. She looked at the other names: Mary, Geraldine, Abigail, Florence, Astrid, Carol. None of the surnames were the same. A group of dissociated women living together.

She created a profile for each of the women and started a new family tree, with them all linked as if they were siblings. Using the approximate ages, she entered each name and hoped for the best. By the time she'd finished entering the last name, a leaf was wiggling next to Florence Wagner. When she clicked on it, an adoption record popped up, asking her to accept or reject it. She opened it and found that Florence had been adopted as an infant in Aitkin County.

Barb accepted the file and appended it to Florence's profile. Before she was through, a new leaf wiggled next to Florence's name. Clicking on the link, Barb found two new possible links: a birth certificate in Aitkin County and a member's family tree with the name Wagner.

She opened the Wagner family tree and quickly found Florence, with her correct birthdate, in Aitkin County, Minnesota. Her adoption was noted, as was the death of her adoptive father a few months after Florence's fourteenth birthday. The Wagner genealogist had located the 1940 census records and had also found a marriage record from 1946 in Pine County. That was followed by a Social Security death record from 1955.

"Dead end," said Skog.

She went back to the birth record. The mother was listed as "Abby Brown" and the father, "Unknown."

With a sudden adrenaline rush overcoming her fatigue, Skog clicked back on the 1930 census record and saw Abigail Corbett. Age 23.

Skog changed Abigail's surname to Brown, and relaunched the search. Within seconds she had a marriage to Phillip Corbett and a 1907 birth record in Aitkin County.

"Yes!" said Skog. Her sudden enthusiasm elicited a blink from her tabby cat, who quickly closed its eyes again.

When she went back to the Tuxedo Inn family tree, there were wiggling leaves next to all the names. It took her until nearly 3 a.m. to track down all the genealogical links, but suddenly a pattern emerged. Nearly all the women at the Tuxedo Inn had left their families before their fourteenth birthdays. In two cases, the father had died within days, before or after the girls' move to the Tuxedo Inn.

"Abigail, were you rescuing the girls?"

She looked at the surnames again, preparing to shut down the computer. She was exhausted and her mind was swimming with the new information. The surnames were familiar. She clicked back to her family tree and entered a search on each of the surnames of the "Tuxedo Inn girls," as she'd come to call them.

Three of the five surnames she entered were in Barb's family tree, including the Browns, who lived in Aitkin County.

"What are the odds?" she asked herself as the computer blinked off.

CHAPTER 51

UNIVERSITY OF MINNESOTA
GENOME LAB
FRIDAY

Graduate assistants were often jokingly referred to as academic slaves, often working 80 hours a week to get the education and experience required for the advanced degrees they were seeking, while also being at the beck and call of their advisors to take on other duties as assigned.

Brian Axdahl's 10-hour workday was over and he was loading his backpack when the DNA sequencer chimed, announcing the completion of its analysis. His first thought was to let the information sit until the next day, but curiosity got the better of him. Stowing his backpack behind his desk, he looked at the computer display of the mitochondrial DNA he'd extracted from the Pine County Jane Doe skeleton. He returned to his desk and restarted his computer, finishing a granola bar as the machine slowly booted. He chose an icon on his home screen and then went to the end of the list of files, each a record of a DNA test.

Finding the Skog/Jane Doe files, he clicked and waited for the results to display on his computer screen. With the Skog file open, he imported the Jane Doe DNA test from the sequencer and compared the results. The Jane Doe sample was badly decomposed, so the nuclear DNA was jumbled, but the mitochondrial DNA samples were clean and a perfect match.

"Man, that's impossible," he said to himself as he verified that he'd pulled separate files and hadn't compared the same file against itself. He pulled out his cellphone and called his advisor, leaving an excited voicemail message. He considered calling the man at the BCA who'd left his card with the samples, but hesitated, thinking he'd rather wait until someone else verified his results. Staring at the computer screen, he decided to risk the wrath of his advisor and called the BCA.

"BCA, Agent Telker."

"Agent Telker, this is Brian Axdahl, at the University genome lab. I'm sorry to call so late in the evening, but I've got the DNA test results from the Jane Doe you found in the forest. The nuclear DNA tells me the samples possibly came from distant relatives. The mitochondrial DNA says they have a common female ancestor."

"Let me put you on the speaker. My co-worker is here too. Run that by me again, please?" Jeff said as he activated the speakerphone and waved at Sonny Carlson.

"Okay," Axdahl said, after taking a deep breath. "Here's your DNA 101 class. We each have genes in the nucleus of our cells that are inherited from our parents. Half come from our mother and half from our father. In all, we have 46 genes, arranged as 23 pairs. Do you follow me?"

"Got it," said Telker.

"In addition to the DNA in the nucleus of our cells, there is also an organelle called the mitochondria, which has its own set of DNA. The mitochondria are sometimes called the cell engines. Because the mitochondria have a double cell wall, its DNA is better protected, so we can often get a mitochondrial DNA comparison even when the nuclear DNA is badly degraded, even from ancient samples. The mitochondrial DNA is part of the mother's egg cell, so that set of DNA is the same for everyone who has a common female ancestor."

"Okay," said Sonny. "So we get a blended set of nuclear DNA, half from our mothers and half from our fathers. We only get the mitochondrial DNA from our mothers. I get it. So how does that pertain to the Skog and Jane Doe samples?"

"Like I told Jeff, the Skog/Jane Doe mitochondrial DNA match. The two samples had a common female ancestor. Jane Doe's nuclear DNA is kind of a mess, but I can say with a high probability that they're cousins, but definitely not mother/daughter or sisters."

"Barb Skog is looking for her aunt. Would Jane Doe be that closely related?"

"It's hard to say," said Axdahl. "I'm thinking maybe a great aunt, or a distant cousin."

"I have to call Ms. Skog," said Sonny. "She was very anxious about the results, and she's a genealogy buff."

"I wonder if she'll be able to help," said Jeff. "She contacted the Pine County sheriff to get assistance with her search. If she was aware of another relative in Pine County, I think she would've mentioned it."

"I'll bet the remains are someone distant enough from her immediate family that she may not have made the connections yet," said Sonny. "She's diligent, but tracking down all the leaves that pop up on Ancestry.com takes a lot of time. I spent a couple of late nights looking through my Finnish relatives and I'm just amazed at the number of my relatives who moved to Northern Minnesota after 1900. The Swedish side of the family is made up of five Peterson brothers who moved from Sweden and bought farms around Mahtowa. They have hundreds of descendants now. When I stop off at the sausage shop, it's an unusual day when I chat up someone in line and find out that they're *not* a relative. You know . . ."

"Sonny," said Jeff, "I think he would rather go home than hear about your family history."

"Well, I was just getting to the point. The immigrants tended to group themselves together in ethnic communities and it wouldn't be surprising to find out that Barb Skog's relatives lived in the same town. Back then it was . . ."

"Is there a point coming up soon, Sonny?" Jeff said, leaning back in his chair and closing his eyes.

"I think I forgot the point when you interrupted me," Sonny said, looking disgusted.

"Thanks, Brian. Have a nice evening."

After they closed the call, Sonny said. "My point is, when you get into some of these small towns, the family trees are more like a wreath. The families intermarry, then their children marry cousins. The branches often don't spread very far."

"The family wreath," said Jeff. "That's a good analogy."

CHAPTER 52

POKEGAMA SANATORIUM
1943

"I wonder why Miss Abigail never came here to visit us?" Pixie asked, as she and Florence put fresh sheets on a bed. They wore light-blue dresses that looked like nurses' uniforms. "She was crying when we left, like she was sad about us leaving, but it's like she really didn't care."

"I don't know," said Florence with a shrug. "She's just busy or something. Maybe she moved out of town."

They pulled a quilt on top of the sheets and fluffed the goose down pillows as Pixie thought quietly. Then she said, "It's just not right. She treated us like family and now she's gone."

"My other family is gone too," said Florence. "It just happens."

Pixie froze. "I've wondered many times where my sister and brothers are. I haven't seen them since I left the State School. I hope they got good jobs like we have."

Florence gathered the used linens into a pile and pushed them into a rolling hamper. "You can't dwell on that, Pixie. There's nothing you can do about it, so you might as well just live your own life."

Together, they pushed the hamper to the next room where a pale young man lay on the bed reading a dime novel. Hearing them enter, he looked up and smiled at Pixie. "Good Morning, Sunshine. How is my favorite laundress?"

"I'm okay," Pixie said, ignoring the flirtation. "You have to get out of bed so we can change your sheets."

Billy "Junior" Wickerson set his book on the bedside table and turned back the sheets. He was clad in flannel pajamas with vertical blue and white stripes. His frame was small and his face gaunt after his yearlong battle with tuberculosis. Swinging his legs over the side of the bed and sitting upright left him breathless.

"Help me to the chair," he said to Pixie. He gently put his arm across her shoulders and stood, his weight heavy to Pixie, who weighed barely ninety pounds.

"Here," said Florence, "I'll get your other side." She stepped up and the three of them shuffled to a wooden guest chair in the corner of the room. Billy sat, breathless after the short ten-foot walk.

"I'm getting stronger," he said after a few minutes. "In May I needed a wheelchair to get out of bed."

Pixie and Florence stripped the bed and set out fresh sheets. "I wouldn't call you cured," said Pixie, "but you do have a little more stamina."

"My dad says I should be well enough to go home when the sanatorium sells."

Florence and Pixie froze. "They're selling the sanatorium?"

"That's what my dad says. There are only a dozen other patients, so it doesn't really pay to keep it open anymore."

"Who's going to buy it?" asked Florence.

"I guess there are some Catholics who think it would be a good spot for a seminary," said Billy.

"But this whole town is Lutherans and Methodists," said Pixie. "Why would they want to be here?"

"I only know what my father told me," said Billy.

"Are they keeping us?" asked Florence.

"I don't know what'll happen to the staff. I suppose they'll still need people to cook, wash dishes, and change the linens."

"Don't they have nuns who do that?"

"I don't think so," said Billy. "I think the nuns all go to a nunnery and it's only men who want to be priests that go to a seminary."

Florence continued cleaning the room. "It makes no difference. We'll find jobs somewhere else if the Catholics don't want us."

"My father said I might not be well enough to be on my own at the house, so he told Mr. Adamson that he might need to hire a private nurse for a while, at least until I can get myself up and down the stairs." He gave Pixie a smile. "He might let me choose who he hires."

Pixie blushed. "We're not nurses. We just change beds, clean, and help cook."

"I don't really need a nurse," said Billy. "I just need someone to carry meals up and down the stairs and to help me get up and down."

Pixie glanced at the bathroom, then back to Billy. "I think you need a male nurse, or a married woman, who can help you shower and get dressed."

"Why?" asked Billy.

"People will talk," said Florence. "An unmarried girl can't afford to get a reputation."

"It might not matter if a girl got a reputation if she married the guy." Billy's smile was broad and inviting.

"I think you'd better get well before you start throwing out comments about getting married," said Florence. Pixie blushed and looked away.

"When a woman gets to a certain age," said Billy, "she's got to start thinking about her future. She needs to settle down, get married, and have children. It's easy to become an old spinster."

Pixie scooped up the dirty linens. Without looking back at Billy, she pushed the hamper into the hallway. Florence closed the door behind them.

"He's right," said Florence. "We're practically old maids now. Most girls get married before they're twenty-one. Maybe you should be nicer to him."

"I'm not thinking about getting married," said Pixie, wheeling the hamper into the next room. "I'm just trying to keep my job and be happy."

"There are lots of ways to be happy. Billy's been getting googly-eyed at you for a year and you pretend you don't notice, but I know you like him."

"He's just a patient. I try to be nice to every patient."

"You're nicer to him. Every time he looks your way, you look away and blush. It's not hard to figure out that you're sweet on him."

Pixie pushed the hamper ahead, Florence's words echoing through her mind.

"Billy's father comes to visit him every Saturday afternoon," said Florence. "It might be time for his pillows to be fluffed when his papa is here."

"I don't do things like that."

"Maybe it's time for you to start thinking about your future," said Florence.

"Why don't you go in to fluff his pillows?" asked Pixie.

"He doesn't look at me the way he looks at you."

After the beds had all been changed the girls went to the kitchen where the aroma of fried onions and frying hamburger filled the air. Pixie started peeling a mountain of potatoes while Florence diced carrots. Opal was chattering about the radio news reporting the terrible wars in Europe and the rumor about the Japanese preparing to invade Australia.

"Opal, do you know Billy Wickerson's family?" Pixie asked, trying to be nonchalant.

"They're good folks," said Opal. "Bill Senior is a paymaster for the Northern Pacific Railroad. That's about as good a job as a man can have in these times. They live in a big house up in Carlton, and they live pretty high on the hog. That's how Billy Junior can afford to stay here. All our patients are from rich families who can afford the cost of private treatment."

"Billy said the sanatorium is being sold," said Florence.

"Well, you ladies must've had quite a conversation with Junior," said Opal. "Mr. Adamson is talking with some people about selling. I don't know that they've signed any papers yet."

"Billy said Catholics are buying it," said Florence. "They want to make it into a seminary. I wonder if they'll keep any of us on."

"I wouldn't worry about that," said Opal. "It's hard to find good cooks and domestic help. If they're smart, they'll know how valuable we are and they'll hire all of us."

Florence looked at Pixie and whispered, "You've got to look out for yourself. Think about Saturday."

"What's happening on Saturday?" asked Opal.

"Pixie is meeting her future father-in-law," Florence said. Pixie responded by throwing a long potato peel at her.

CHAPTER 53

DAVIDSON'S FARM

Pop's body had been removed and the floor of the horse stall was swept clean. Sonny was holding a one-sided conversation as they packed up their samples and gear.

"I don't think there's been a horse in this stall for a decade or two. The floor doesn't have any horseshoe scuffs and the urine stains are old."

Floyd interrupted the monologue when he arrived, asking, "Did you guys find anything interesting?"

Sonny replied. "This wasn't a suicide. Whoever tried to set the scene was either inept or hasn't watched any of the CSI TV shows. The gun was wiped clean of prints, but he left boot prints and handprints all over the place. I think I got enough DNA off a handprint to run a sample."

"You can get enough DNA from a handprint for analysis?"

"The new replication technology takes a bit of time, but we can ID a suspect if he sneezed at the crime scene."

"You said the killer left a handprint. Can you run that through the National Crime Information Computer?"

"We can't run the print through AFIS, but the outline of the handprint is distinct," said Jeff, pointing to the gate. "It's on the wooden gate, so the definition of the fingerprint ridges and whorls are lost in the wood grain. But, as Sonny said, we may be able to pull enough of the killer's DNA from the surface to process."

"Where's the ATF guy?" asked Floyd.

"Agent Hoffman made a call, then he and the sheriff left," said Sonny. "They didn't say where they were going."

Wandering away from the two, Floyd stood in the horse stall lost in thought. A pockmark in the wall identified the place where the techs carved a spent bullet from the wood. Sonny started chattering about the auction he'd attended the previous weekend, marveling at the bargain prices for a barn full of woodworker's saws and tools. Jeff was smiling and nodding, so it appeared he was engaged in the discussion. Floyd watched the duo and grinned. A perfect team: a talker and a listener.

The sound of slamming doors signaled the end of the loading process. Floyd took one last look around the stall, then walked to the BCA Winnebago. He leaned on the passenger door.

"How long before you'll know if you have a DNA match?"

"It depends," replied Sonny, who was sitting in the passenger's seat. "If the lab isn't backed up, we might know in a week or two. If they're backed up, it may be a month or more. Of course, that is only meaningful if there is matching DNA in the database. I'd estimate there's no better than a 50:50 chance that the murderer's DNA is in the system."

Floyd watched them drive away, then walked back to what was left of the barn and slipped under the yellow crime scene tape. Staring at the horse stall he said, "Okay, Pop, what happened?" He stood with his hands on his hips and studied every nook and cranny, knowing that the crime scene techs had scoured the place. "Did you catch somebody stealing dynamite? Was it someone you knew?"

Leaving the barn Floyd walked past the buildings and into the woods, hoping to see something he'd missed. After 45 minutes of walking deer trails and skirting swamps, he'd flushed one grouse and surprised one deer. Between the woods and the white fence that ran around an overgrown horse pasture he found a deeply rutted ATV trail. A whine in the distance caught his attention, so he stepped behind a tree and listened as the noise got louder. Two ATVs flew past without seeing him. They were covered with mud and the riders were unidentifiable in their helmets and mud-covered clothes. He returned to his car and drove toward Pine Brook Floral.

"I bet there have been ten times as many ATVs on that trail as there are cars on the road," he said to himself. He pulled to the shoulder of highway 23 and opened a county map. The Nemadji State Forest was crisscrossed with trails entering from all directions. The ATV trail behind Davidson's pasture connected with trails going into the state forest to the east, and going to the towns of Sturgeon Lake and Willow River to the west, where other trails connected taking riders as far north as the Iron Range and south to Pine City.

"There are more miles of trails than there are of road," Floyd said to himself, surprised that he just realized that.

CHAPTER 54

PINE BROOK FLORAL

Chimes sounded when Floyd opened the back door and Jackie Sjoberg, one of Mary's long-time employees, stuck her head around a stack of Christmas ornaments she was arranging for the up-coming season.

"Hi, Floyd," she said. "Mary just ran to the bank. I think she'll be back in a few minutes. You know where the coffee pot is and there might be a caramel roll left." The chime sounded again as a customer entered the front door and Jackie walked to the cash register.

Floyd was barely into his second bite of caramel roll when the back door chimed. He was sitting in the guest chair in Mary's tiny office when she stepped in with an armful of mail.

"To what do I attribute this unannounced visit?" she asked with a smile.

"I ran out of loose ends to chase, so I thought I'd take you out to lunch."

Mary set the mail on her desk. "I won't resist that romantic overture."

"It wasn't meant to be romantic. I need someone to bounce ideas off."

"I was being facetious," Mary replied with a smile. "Being taken out to be a sounding board for your criminal theories isn't at the top of my 'fun things to do' list."

They drove highway 23 to Hinckley and parked at Tobies. The midday traffic was light, but as usual, people were lined up two-deep at the bakery counter. They took a table in the back and the waitress poured coffee without being prompted. She took the orders for his burger platter and Mary's Cobb salad.

"Pop Davidson was killed today. Spouses, family members, and drinking buddies are the usual suspects in a crime," Floyd said. "Pop was a widower. I should check on his kids, but I don't recall any of them ever being in trouble. He didn't hang out much in bars, but was a regular at every café in the region. That pretty much drains the pool of usual suspects."

"Oh, dear. Do you think they were after his explosives?" Mary suggested.

"That's what I'm thinking," Floyd replied. "I imagine he caught someone in the barn. But that doesn't explain why they walked from his explosives storage to where he was shot in the barn. I need a big-picture look at what happened. I imagine Pop saw someone and confronted them. That scenario just doesn't work with him marching off with an assailant. That outcome would likely be a shootout in the storage area."

"I don't suppose there's any reason to look at his customers," said Mary, as their meals arrived. "Everyone in the county knew he had guns and dynamite."

Floyd squirted ketchup on the edge of his plate and dipped a fry. "I walked the farm and there's a heavy ATV trail behind his horse pasture, so whoever stole the explosives might've parked their ATV nearby, snuck up to his farm, and surprised Pop. It'd be pretty brazen to drive up his driveway and back their truck up to his barn when he was home."

"Was there a lot of explosives stolen?" asked Mary. "There isn't a lot of space to carry a lot of anything on the ATVs I've seen."

"There are some newer side-by-side ones with almost as much space as a pickup behind the riders. But there aren't many of those. My gut says it was someone who drove up the driveway."

"Maybe that's it," said Mary, carefully putting aside the bacon bits on her salad. "Whoever it was just drove up the driveway. Pop assumed it was someone who wanted to buy a gun, so he walked out empty-handed and they pulled a gun on him."

Floyd took a bite of burger and chewed while he considered Mary's scenario. "That might be the most logical scenario," he said, wiping a dribble of mayo from his chin. "But that would take some balls. I mean, not many people have the nerve to just walk up on their victim. Most criminals prefer to sneak around in the dark, and they usually run if they're confronted."

"Maybe your killer isn't a normal criminal," suggested Mary. "Maybe he showed up in a car or truck that Pop knew."

"Or, maybe he showed up in some sort of vehicle that wouldn't arouse suspicion." Floyd said, then added, "maybe a tradesman, like a plumber or the propane deliveryman."

Floyd stood and reached for his cellphone. He patted Mary on the shoulder as he walked past. "I'll be right back."

Mary had finished her salad when he returned. "Your fries and burger got cold," she said, dipping a soggy fry into a puddle of ketchup.

"I had to call Pam," he said, sitting down and taking another bite of burger.

"Why the rush?"

"Mmm," he mumbled, then put his finger up to pause the conversation.

"Because we may have a video of the killer's vehicle," he said after wiping his chin.

"Pop had video surveillance?" Mary asked. "He seemed old-school, born before all the doo-dads were popular."

"Roberta Mason's house has a surveillance camera overlooking her driveway and the dead end road to Pop's house. The BATF got the video that was taken before the forest explosion. Knowing when the attack on Pop occurred, we should also be able to identify any vehicles driving to Pop's place."

CHAPTER 55

BRUNO

The concrete driveway to Roberta Mason's estate seemed out of place as Pam turned off the gravel road. The white two-story house was palatial, and more than out of place in this corner of Pine County that time had mostly bypassed. Bright white fencing that could've been in Kentucky defined the paddocks where horses grazed. The barn and other outbuildings were all clad in two-tone green and tan with white trim. Pam was barely out of her car when the front door opened and a middle-aged, ruggedly handsome man wearing khaki pants and a plaid shirt greeted her. His teeth were perfect and so white they seemed to gleam.

"Good morning, Deputy," The caretaker said. "would you like a cup of coffee?"

"I would love a cup," replied Pam as she mounted the steps.

"I'm Jerry Barker, the caretaker," he said, offering his hand after closing the door. "My wife, Bridget, is in the kitchen."

"I'm Pam Ryan. I'd like to talk about your security camera."

Barker led Pam through the house, which looked like something out of *House Beautiful* with its vaulted ceilings and architectural flourishes along the ceiling and windows from floor to ceiling. The entryway was tiled with Italian marble, as was the staircase behind the entrance. A huge chandelier with what looked like a thousand crystals lit the two-story entryway. To the left was a living room carpeted in white, matching the white furniture and white brick fireplace that filled the entire back wall. They walked down a hallway past a den filled with red leather furniture and an office dominated by a walnut desk and a wall of books. No matter where she looked, everything shined.

Acres of well-groomed grass, dotted with mature maples and oaks, came into view through massive windows in the back wall of a kitchen as large as Pam's apartment. A small stream meandered through the lawn into a pond. Next to the pond a wrought iron bench sat under a gazebo. The lawn ended abruptly in underbrush a hundred yards behind the house.

"Bridget," said Baker, "we have a guest." Pam stood in awe at the kitchen entrance, having never seen so much stainless steel in one room.

Bridget was rummaging in the refrigerator, which appeared to be six-feet wide. To one side of the refrigerator was a six-burner professional stove with stacked double ovens next to it. Bridget closed the refrigerator door and turned. She offered her hand to Pam. "Deputy Ryan. I think I've seen you at the grocery store in Pine City."

Bridget spoke with a heavy German accent. She was blonde and blue-eyed, and wore no makeup to hide the laugh lines at the corners of her eyes. The lack of makeup made her natural beauty even more striking.

"Yes," said Pam. "I've seen you in town." Pam reflected on the times she'd seen Bridget. Most shoppers were casual. Bridget always wore a dress, which made her stand out from the average Pine City shopper.

Jerry brought three cups to a butcherblock table, then carried a carafe from the stainless steel Cuisinart coffeemaker sitting on the countertop. "Please pull up a chair," he said, pouring the coffee. Bridget brought cream and sugar, then put poppy-seed pastries on china plates.

"The coffee is plenty," said Pam.

"No, no," said Bridget, setting a pastry in front of Pam. "Jerry can't eat all these by himself or he'll look like Otto von Bismarck.

"What can we do for you, Deputy Ryan?" Jerry asked, as he took a bite of his pastry.

Pam bit into the pastry and it melted in her mouth. The sweetness was subtle, complemented by the poppy seeds and almond butter. She suddenly realized that Bridget was staring at her.

"I see that you like the pastry," Bridget said, with a smile.

"It's heavenly," Pam said, wiping the crumbs from her lips with a linen napkin. She straightened up, then said, "ATF said you have good security systems. I'd like to look at the security camera recordings from yesterday."

"I understand that you can't comment on whatever's been happening at Davidson's house," said Jerry, graciously. "I'll take you to the security center when we're through and you can look at the digital history. I'll put a copy on a flash drive for you."

"Thank you for your discretion," said Pam. "Before the firetrucks and police arrived, did you notice any unusual activity?"

Bridget gave Jerry a nod of encouragement.

"There's always a fair amount of activity on the road and we have ATVs racing down the trail on the back of the property daily. I assume the ATVs are usually going to the state forest trails, but I keep an eye on them."

"Did the ATVs go down to Davidson's?"

"I can't see them once they're past our property, but there were a few buzzing around before the explosion."

"Do you have video of them?"

"Was Hitler German?" Jerry said, rising from the table.

"Darling," Bridget said, "Hitler was Austrian."

"That depends," said Jerry, who winked at Pam and smiled. "The borders are redefined after every war. I'm sure his hometown was in Germany at some point."

"He was Austrian," Bridget whispered to Pam.

Pam followed Jerry to a locked door in the hallway. He removed a small key ring from his pocket, unlocked the door, then led Pam inside. The lights clicked on as they passed the threshold. An array of LCD screens showed the areas around the house and the perimeter of the property and a series of green lights blinked in rhythm on a large control panel.

"Wow," said Pam.

"The owner likes to make sure things are secure."

"The owner being Miss Mason," Pam said.

"The owner cherishes her privacy," the caretaker said, taking a deep breath. "I rely on your discretion to honor her wishes."

Pam nodded. "I understand."

"The control panel monitors all the doors and windows, plus the array of remote infrared motion detectors mounted on trees along the property perimeter.

The cameras display continuously, but only record if they're triggered by motion."

"Like deer hunters use on their trail cameras?" Pam said.

"It's the same principle, but the systems here are much more sophisticated, and the images are uploaded to a remote cloud location as they're recorded. The interior motion detectors are on a timer, and if I don't key in the code within two minutes of an event, a call goes directly to your switchboard."

Pam smiled. "That's really interesting, but we might not have a deputy within forty miles when the call arrives."

"We're aware of that," said Jerry. "I lock down all the doors and windows every night, and I can press a panic button that will lock them during the daytime, too. If the owner is here, we will move her to this room, which is like a bank vault, with its own ventilation and fire protection systems. I've been assured that the whole house could burn down and the people in this room would survive."

"I assume you know how to use a firearm?"

"I have a concealed carry permit." He lifted his shirttail, exposing a small flat pistol clipped to his belt. "My PPK doesn't have a lot of firepower, but it'll make someone think twice before rushing in, and I keep a riot gun loaded with buckshot here in the panic room."

Jerry slid a keyboard tray from under the counter and typed in commands. A screen blinked and the light underneath it started to pulse. "Here are the recordings from the past couple of days." He rolled a desk chair to Pam and sat down next to her.

The images went by quickly. First was a garbage truck, going toward Davidson's then returning. The exact date and time flashed on the bottom of the screen. The garbage truck had been out of sight for eleven minutes and the mailman for seven.. Pop's pickup left a few minutes after the garbage truck and didn't return for four hours. A car pulled into the concrete driveway and looped back out.

"That's our newspaper delivery," Jerry said.

Later that day, Pop drove out and returned. Pam noted the date and time. The next vehicle was a UPS van."

"Davidson gets deliveries several times a week. I assume it's part of his gun business. There's a fair amount of car and pickup traffic, probably customers."

They looked at each passing vehicle in freeze-frame, trying to identify the driver or the vehicle. Most were unremarkable. A dark, full-sized sedan without any markings passed. The next video segment showed a firetruck passing, followed by another firetruck, then the Pine County cruisers.

"Go back to the shots just before the firetrucks arrived," Pam said.

Jerry clicked the mouse and they watched a dark sedan driving away from Davidson's.

"Do you recognize that car?" asked Pam.

"Like I said, cars and pickups come and go. I don't pay much attention unless they pull into our driveway."

The video showed the dark car and the driver. "Can you stop that and replay it slowly?" Pam asked.

The image disappeared and then a jerky image of the dark car crept slowly into view.

"Look at the spotlight," said Jerry as the car jumped a few feet ahead in each recorded image. "It looks like an unmarked police vehicle."

"Stop it there," said Pam. The car was broadside with the driver's arm obscuring the view of his face. "Do you think he just happens to have his arm across the window," asked Pam, "or do you think he knows he's being recorded so he's hiding his face?"

Jerry toggled the images back and forth, watching the series several times. "I can't see the driver's face," said Jerry, "but I can see he's got some sort of shoulder patch on his left sleeve and there may be a tattoo on his forearm."

"That's not one of our cruisers," said Pam. "It's an old Crown Victoria. They've been out of service for years. The patch is shaped like Pine County's, though. Can you zoom in on it?"

Jerry centered the image and zoomed, but the result was grainier than the original picture, making it unrecognizable.

"I don't suppose you have an angle that will show the license plate," said Pam.

Jerry shook his head. "Not really. Our concern is someone driving up our driveway. When that happens I get the full front of the car, with the license number and the face of the driver."

"Let's look at the rest of that day," said Pam.

Jerry cued up the camera. The next images were police vehicles, the coroner's Suburban and the firetrucks leaving. After the police vehicles left, there wasn't another recording until the newspaper delivery.

"Please make a copy of that dark car coming and going," said Pam. As Jerry plugged a flash drive into a port on the control panel, Pam wondered if someone was impersonating an officer.

Jerry removed the flash drive, marked the time and date on it with a Sharpie, and handed it to Pam. "I take it that the explosion wasn't an accident?"

Pam weighed her words, then decided Jerry could be an ally. "Pop was dead before the explosion. We're trying to develop a list of suspects."

"Let me pull up the video camera from the rear of the property," said Jerry. "Maybe I got a shot of someone on an ATV."

The screen blinked on as a doe, then two fawns walked onto the backyard. The next image looked like it had been taken through night-vision goggles.

"Whoa. What's that?"

"That's infrared," Jerry said. "It's a raccoon. You can see the heat image given off by the center of his body."

The next image was a ghostly glow flying through the edge of the trees. "ATV," said Jerry. "The engine and exhaust are very hot and appear white in the IR."

"So there's no way to identify the rider?" asked Pam.

"If he stops and steps away from the hot engine I can make out facial features, but they look more like a negative than a photo."

The next video was a pair of ATVs racing through the trees. They were gone for nearly an hour, two raced back, away from Davidson's.

"Can you tell if the same ATVs came back?" Pam asked.

"All I get on the infrared is a white spot from the heat of the engine."

"It must be annoying to have the ATVs racing around all night," said Pam.

Jerry shook his head. "They rarely operate after dark. I assume they can't see the scenery or the dangers on the trail."

"Download that series, too, please," said Pam, handing the flash drive back to Jerry.

CHAPTER 56

PINE COUNTY COURTHOUSE
SATURDAY

Floyd was pouring a cup of coffee when his cell-phone chirped. "Swenson," he answered.

"Floyd, this is Barb Skog. I just got a call from the BCA. The Jane Doe is a relative. She's not Aunt Margaret, but she is at least a cousin."

"That's exciting," said Floyd. "I hope you can take that back to your family tree and find that branch."

"I made another discovery last night."

"Great. I'm just hitting dead ends."

"I was searching for background on the women who were listed as residents of the Tuxedo Inn, from the 1930 census, and I hit the mother lode. It appears Abigail Corbett had a baby girl out of wedlock when she was a teenager, and she gave the baby up for adoption."

'I'd say that was pretty common in the day."

"Yes, but that's not the exciting part. That child was adopted, then when she was a teenager the adoptive father died and the child showed up at the Tuxedo Inn as a domestic helper."

"How interesting," said Floyd. "Does that have anything to do with your missing aunt?"

"Maybe," replied Skog. "I've got to spend some more time checking family trees, but there's a possibility that all the women at the Tuxedo Inn may have been related. They were all orphans or adoptees and when they reached their teen years they left their adoptive homes and showed up at the Tuxedo Inn. Margaret Lane appears to be the last in a line of several girls. It makes me wonder if our Jane Doe could've been one of those girls."

"That would be a huge coincidence."

"I'm still digging for records," said Skog, "but in one case the adoptive father's date of death was within a day of the girl moving to the Tuxedo Inn. I don't have access to the death certificate, but it makes me wonder there's a connection to Abigail."

"That sounds like a long stretch," said Floyd. "Times were tough and people died young. Maybe she picked up the girl after her father died," suggested Floyd.

"I have to admit that's more plausible," said Skog. "About the case, I'm going to the U's anthropology lab. The tech took photos of the skulls found in the shack and he is going to do a virtual reconstruction of the faces. They have the photos of O'Connor, Darrow, and LaPorte you got from the Chicago P.D. They're going to use them for comparison."

"Do you have pictures of any of the Tuxedo Inn girls to compare to Jane Doe?"

"I don't even know where to start looking for those pictures. I suppose they might be in someone's attic, but I don't even know who to ask about them."

"Good luck," said Floyd. He ended the call and said to himself, "I think you'd have better odds of winning the lottery than finding matches with the remains from the shack."

With coffee in hand, Floyd returned to his desk and found the slip of paper with the Redemptorists' phone number. After a few transfers he connected with Sister Mary Katherine.

"Sister, this is Floyd Swenson, from Minnesota again. I was wondering if you've found any records from the Pine City seminary."

"Ah, Sergeant Swenson," the elderly nun replied. "I found a record that indicates where the records may be located, and I sent a request to have that box of files delivered to me. But, as of this moment, I haven't seen the box. Remind me of your phone number and I'll call you as soon as the records arrive."

Floyd recited his cellphone number to the nun. As he hung up, Pam walked into the office area. She sat in the guest chair next to Floyd's desk.

"I have the surveillance video from the movie star's house," Pam said. "I think I know why Pop Davidson didn't put up a fight."

Pam plugged the flash drive into Floyd's computer and let it boot up. "We've got video of a car arriving and leaving just prior to the explosion."

The computer screen went black, then the video showed the dark Crown Victoria roll across the screen, going left to right, in the direction of the Davidson farm. The screen flashed, and the next video showed the same car going the opposite direction.

"The driver appears to be wearing a Pine County patch on his left shoulder," said Pam.

"Back that up and freeze the frame with the car centered on the screen."

Pam picked up the mouse and clicked a few times. Within seconds they were staring at the side of the dark car and the obscured face of the driver.

"That's a Crown Vic," said Floyd. "We haven't had a Crown Vic in the fleet since they quit making them in 2011." He stared at the image, wracking his brain. "Sometimes there's an old Crown Vic in the employee parking lot."

"That's not any of our deputies," said Pam, pointing to the screen. "I don't think anybody has a tattoo on their forearm."

"C'mon," Floyd said as he suddenly stood. They walked quickly to the jail entrance and waited to be let through the locked door. Amy Smith, the newest jailer, let them through.

"What's up, guys?" she asked.

"Where's Bruce?" Floyd asked.

"He just rotated to afternoons, so he's probably home sleeping," replied Amy. "Is there something I can do for you?"

"Where does Bruce live?" asked Floyd.

"I have no idea, and I don't really want to know," said Amy. "It's not like we socialize."

"Have you seen his car?" Pam asked.

"Big old black thing," said Amy. "I think he bought it at an auction of old police vehicles."

"Thanks," said Floyd. "Let us back out. I need to get upstairs to the personnel office."

Pat O'Brien, the county manager, was also the human relations department for the county. He was sitting behind his desk when they knocked. "Hi, Floyd and Pam. What can I do for you?"

"I need Bruce Swanson's home address," said Floyd. "We have video of a car that looks like Bruce's going to and from a crime scene. I need to ask him a few questions."

O'Brien hit some keys on his computer. "He lives at a fire number on Stevens Lake Road, in Norman Township," O'Brien answered, looking at his computer screen.

"Bruce talks about being in Viet Nam," said Floyd. "Was the army his last job before becoming a jailer?"

O'Brien paged down the file. "It looks like he came directly from the army to his current job. He was honorably discharged in May 1969 and started with the county in September. There's no indication of any employment in between."

"Does his file list any distinguishing features, like maybe a tattoo?" Pam asked.

"He has a tattoo on his left forearm," said O'Brien.

"Does his file indicate his MOS?" asked Floyd.

"What's an MOS?" asked Pam.

"That's an army acronym for Military Occupation Specialty," replied O'Brien. "He keyed in an MOS search. "His MOS was 18c."

"What's an 18c?" asked Pam.

"Let's find out," said O'Brien as he opened Google and keyed in MOS and 18c. "That would be a Special Forces Engineer Sergeant. I guess Bruce was a green beret."

"Explosives?" asked Floyd.

O'Brien read from his computer screen, "'Perform and teach tasks in demolitions, explosives, field fortification, bridging, rigging, reconnaissance, and civil action projects.' Below that it says, 'Carry out demolition raids against enemy military targets such as bridges, railroads, and fuel depots.'"

"Uh oh," said Pam. "I bet he knows how to blow up a tree."

"Thanks, Pat," said Floyd, "And please don't say anything about this to anyone."

They hurried out of the office. Floyd was punching numbers into his cellphone as they walked down the steps to the sheriff's office. The phone was answered on the second ring.

"Agent Hoffman."

"Barry, this is Floyd Swenson. We have a hot lead on Pop Davidson's killer, and he may possibly be the bomber. Are you still in Pine County?"

"Actually, I'm on the interstate, passing Harris."

"Turn around as soon as you can," said Floyd. "I'm going to brief the sheriff right now."

"Who is your suspect?" asked Hoffman.

"It's not a phone topic," said Floyd. "We'll be waiting at the courthouse."

The sheriff was on his phone when Floyd and Pam charged into his office. He ended the call and asked, "What's going on?"

"The pieces are starting to fall into place," said Floyd, taking a guest chair. "Pam found video from Davidson's road that shows a dark Crown Vic coming and going before the explosion at Pop's place. The driver appears to have a tattoo and a Pine County shoulder patch. Bruce Swanson, the jailer, has a black Crown Victoria, a tattoo on his left forearm, and wears a uniform with a Pine

County shoulder patch. He would probably look like a deputy to Pop, which would've put him at ease so he could be walked to the barn where he was killed."

The sheriff leaned back and stared at the ceiling while making a steeple with his hands. "Are you saying one of our jailers may be a killer?"

"It gets even more complicated," said Pam. "Swanson's army specialty was demolition."

The sheriff closed his eyes, then pulled a cigar out of his desk drawer. He stripped off the wrapper and clenched the unlit cigar between his teeth. "Is Swanson working now?"

"He's on the afternoon shift," said Floyd, "so he's most likely asleep at home."

"What do you suggest?" asked the sheriff.

"I called Barry Hoffman from ATF. He's on his way back and should be here in minutes. Considering Hoffman's opinion that the killer probably took a bunch of explosives when he blew up the barn, I'm inclined to let ATF take the lead. We're unprepared to deal with a suspect who might be barricaded in a house full of explosives."

Sepanen shook his head. "The siege at Waco comes to mind. We really don't need a Branch Davidian kind of ending to this mess." He paused. "Where does Bruce live?"

"His address is a fire number on a tiny road east of Willow River. I've been down that road a few times and there are hardly any houses there. Any vehicle driving through doing surveillance would be suspicious."

"Let's wait for our ATF friend. Maybe he can get a plane or helicopter to do a flyover so we at least know if Bruce's car is at the house."

CHAPTER 57

HOMELAND SECURITY
WASHINGTON, D. C.

Devon Smith was a nerd. He'd been valedictorian
and president of the Arlington Virginia, High
School chess club then, after graduating with hon-
ors from MIT, was recruited by Homeland Security.
The recruiter had hinted at cutting-edge computer
programs and capturing spies. His first project was
re-writing a commercial facial recognition software
program to speed it up and to make it more robust.
The next project was beta testing to demonstrate the
efficacy of the program.

Initially, he'd tasked the program with recognizing
photos of co-workers wearing different caps, beards,
moustaches, and hairdos. Because the program focused on the proportion of facial features, it ignored

those changes with 100% success. The next step was moving to pictures of known criminals, some taken decades apart. Again, the program performed without flaw.

Even with that history, the wheels of the federal government move slowly and Devon was forced to take baby steps ahead by having the computer look at hundreds, and then thousands, of pictures salted with a few known criminals, to demonstrate that program's ability to find matches.

After that he started scanning airport security camera files and he'd been able to identify all the criminals known to be on the videos, then surprised his bosses by picking out two additional criminals wanted by the U.S. Marshals and one person on the federal no-fly list. His confidence rose with each test, as did his boredom with the tedium of looking at hours of security video while the computer tried to match federal fugitives with the faces that flashed by.

Devon was "tweaking" the program to speed it up when his supervisor, Addie Moore, stepped into his cubicle. Sensing a change in the airflow he turned around, surprised to see her pecking at her smartphone.

"What's up, Addie?" he asked.

"I'm forwarding an email I just received from the Minneapolis BATF," she said without looking up. After sending the message she slipped the phone into her pocket. "The BATF sent a couple photos," she said as

Devon's computer chimed, announcing arrival of the message. He immediately turned to the computer and opened the email and attachments.

"The guy in the security camera photo bought a burner cellphone. Several phone calls were exchanged between that phone and another that was used by some people who may be tied to a fatal bombing. The phone has been off most of the time, but ATF was able to get a GPS location on it twice, both times from a building in Minneapolis. They got the building security video files for the days the phone was active."

Devon looked at the security camera photo briefly, then loaded it into the program. The computer chirped, acknowledging receipt of the picture and a "smoking gun" icon started to spin, showing that the computer was working. He then went to the zip files attached and unzipped them.

"Addie, do you have any idea how big these files are?" Devon asked as the files opened and loaded.

"I didn't touch them," she replied. "I wanted you to receive them as soon as I understood the context of the request.

"These files marked Foshay are half a terabyte. That's a hundred times larger than any airport file I've ever examined. The coffee shop files are 25 gigabytes."

"How long will it take to go through them?"

Devon leaned back and stared at the computer as he thought. "If I set it up to run through the night, we might get through them in a couple weeks." Devon ran his fingers through his sandy hair, then spun around to face his boss. "What are the odds that this guy is on any of the security tapes?"

"His phone has been there at least twice," she replied. She watched Devon, who lived in his own world, oblivious to the turmoil and politics around him. She'd admonished him once when he'd arrived at the security desk wearing torn bluejeans, a Megadeath t-shirt, and tennis shoes without laces. He'd never noticed that the unwritten dress code was at least a button-down shirt and khaki slacks. When she told him that, he looked around like it was the first time he'd ever noticed other people, much less what they were wearing. It was then that she realized how special he was, and that she'd have to make an extraordinary effort to keep him away from the big bosses who were more concerned about budgets, politics, and appearances than nurturing a computer genius.

Devon took a deep breath and leaned back, closing his eyes. "Can this wait a week or so? I was just making some changes to the program that'll speed it up and enhance the graphic displays. Look at this!"

He turned the computer monitor so Addie could see and typed a few commands. A screen popped up displaying the title "THEA," which spun slowly on a blue sky hologram. Wispy clouds drifted across the screen.

"Thea?" Addie asked.

"She's the goddess of sight. I thought she'd be the perfect symbol of what this program does. The blue sky represents her role as the goddess of the clear blue sky and truth."

"How long did it take you to create the hologram?" Addie asked.

"That's what I need to complete. If you watch closely, the clouds kind of jump around as they traverse the sky behind the logo. A couple more days and I think I'll be able to make them flow smoothly."

"How long, Devon?"

"You told me that the deputy director wanted visually appealing presentations. I've been working on this off and on for a couple weeks and this is about as visually appealing as I can make the graphics."

Addie closed her eyes and bit her bottom lip while she counted to ten. When she opened her eyes, Devon was back at the keyboard, typing in commands.

"I think the graphics are good enough for now. Please jump into the Foshay files and see what Thea can do."

Devon spun around and shrugged. "You're the boss, but I'm really close on the graphics."

"Do the recognition analysis first," Addie said. She walked away in a daze and nearly bowled over an analyst rushing down an intersecting row through the cubicles. She closed the door to her office and leaned against the door, tempted to bang her head. "He just doesn't have a clue," she said to herself.

Devon was into day two of the security video taken in front of the Foshay Tower elevators. The program keyed on a dozen points on each face, and was able to scan three faces a second. Even at that speed, the going was slow. The computer stopped the frame as the elevator arrived and looked at the dozen or more people ready to load.

He'd identified three people with bench warrants for minor traffic violations or overdue parking tickets and passed those along to the Minneapolis Police. The computer chimed and he sat up, staring at the face the computer had identified as a match with the Walmart photo.

"Gotcha!" Devon said as he sat forward. "Now we need to know if you work here, are a client, or if you're transient.

He quickly found a list of the business offices in the tower on the internet. With quick keystrokes he went to each company's website. Within a few minutes he was into every company's servers downloading pictures of their employees. A second later it displayed an image and name of each employee. He quickly loaded them into Thea and started another search.

Devon froze the search and reached for his phone. "Addie, I've got an I.D. on the Walmart photo. His name is Garth McLeod. He's a lawyer with Peabody and Marsden."

"What's your certainty?" Addie asked.

Devon rolled his eyes. There was always the chance of an error, but the odds of a miss were lower than the interest rate on his savings account. "I'd say 99.4% sure," he said, not really having a number, but knowing his boss wanted a number to put on the request that would go to a judge when they requested a search or arrest warrant.

"That's good work Devon. Thanks."

Devon leaned back in his chair. "I wonder how many attaboys I need before I can move to a challenging job?" he said to himself. As he mulled that question the computer chimed again. It had just found another picture of McLeod time stamped 12:16. Within seconds there was another chime, this one stamped 13:08. The latest face looked just like the man in the Walmart photo. "Raise that to 100% confident," he said to himself.

Barb Skog's cellphone chirped while she was driving home. She activated the Bluetooth and spoke to the speaker located next to her rearview mirror.

"Director Skog, this is Addie Moore, from Homeland Security in Washington. Garth McLeod is the Walmart cellphone purchaser. He's a lawyer with one of the mid-sized law firms in the Foshay Tower.

I've got a Minneapolis ATF agent on his way to get a search warrant for McLeod's cellphones, cellphone records, computers, e-mail records, financial records, and computer search history from his office, home, and car."

"Is McLeod anywhere on our radar?"

"Not that we can determine. We're starting to dig deeper, but it appears that he's never been arrested."

"Hmm. How certain are you that he's our guy?"

"My analyst said there was a 99.4% chance that McLeod is the guy in the Walmart picture."

Skog smiled. "Call me when you get the warrant. I want to be in on the arrest and search."

CHAPTER 58

CARLTON, MINNESOTA
JUNE 18, 1946

The stately Wickerson house overlooked the Great Northern Railway tracks, which seemed only fitting for the railroad paymaster. With an elegant entryway, a huge kitchen with a butler's pantry, a formal dining room, a library, and a parlor, it was one of the town's grandest homes. A small addition housed a toilet with running water. The second floor had four spacious bedrooms and a single bathroom.

Hanging in the front window was a small red, white, and blue banner with a blue star in the center. Through listening to dozens of family discussions, Pixie knew that Billy Junior's younger brother, Robert, was in the Army Air Corps and had been wounded in Europe. In the months Pixie had been living with the Wickersons, telegrams had arrived randomly telling the family that Robert was slowly making his way back to the United States, from one military hospital to another. Twice, they had received handwritten letters from Robert, and each time Mrs. Wickerson read them tearfully to the family, then rushed to share them with the neighbors. Pixie found the letters sitting on a desk in the entryway one day while cleaning. The stilted prose was carefully edited by military censors and just said, "I'm alive. I'm all right. I'll be home when they let me out of the hospital." Robert never mentioned the specifics or extent of his injuries, and in whispers, everyone assumed his wounds were grave, disfiguring, and debilitating. Dozens of wounded men were coming home from the war. Veterans in wheelchairs and on crutches, missing a leg, or with empty sleeves pinned to their tunics, were too common. In hushed whispers, Bill senior discussed hiring a carpenter to remodel the pantry into a small bedroom in case Robert was unable to climb stairs when he returned.

Pixie had been given the bedroom next to the parents. Two other spacious bedrooms were on the opposite side of the bathroom and stairs. At first, Pixie had been a private duty nurse for Billy, but as he'd recuperated she slowly became a part of the household, even though she kept rebuffing Billy's amorous advances.

She cleaned, often cooked, and served meals, eating with the family at the dining room table.

They were in the middle of dinner when the door-bell rang. Blanche jumped from her chair and nearly ran to the door. "Maybe it's a telegram," she said as she passed Bill senior. When she opened the door, Blanche yelped and broke into sobs, which caused the rest of the family to quickly run to the entryway. A tall man in an army aviator's uniform, was being smoth-ered with hugs from Blanche. Pixie stood back, taking in the excitement and trying to discern the nature of Robert's injuries. From what she could see, he had an unscarred, handsome face two hands and two legs.

She was staring at those legs, wondering if one of them was wooden, when she was brought back to real-ity. "And you are Pixie?"

Her eyes flew from his knees to his smiling face and she felt the crimson rise from her neck to her face. Tongue-tied, she nodded.

Robert stepped forward and reached down, ex-tending his hand. He was more than a foot taller than her four-foot eleven-inch stature, and he had to bend down. "It's nice to finally meet you," he said. "Based on the letters Billy sent me, I thought you'd have wings, because he described you as an angel so often."

"Nice to meet you," Pixie said. When she shook his hand, she realized that the skin was taut and too pink.

The sight of the burn scars jarred her, but she managed to not pull her hand back. Instead, she gently touched the scars with her left hand.

"A fire inside a plane is never a good thing," he said. "I'm lucky I'm still alive."

Mrs. Wickerson grabbed Robert's good hand and pulled him toward the dining room. "I'll bet you're starving, she said. "Pixie, be a dear and grab a place setting for Robert. He can sit next to Billy."

That evening was a blur. Pixie had expected Robert to talk about the war and his wounds. Instead, he talked about anything else, from the airfields in England to the Dutch hospital where he'd been treated after his plane crash. Pixie never said a word, but listened intently, occasionally catching Robert staring at her before she looked away.

After clearing the table, Pixie and Blanche met the men in the sitting room where Bill senior had poured dark liquor from a dusty bottle that had set on the top shelf of the bookcase. The men swirled the liquor and laughed, loosening up from their more formal dinner discussion. Bill waved Pixie over and handed her a snifter.

"This is French cognac that I've been saving for Robert's return."

Pixie accepted the snifter and Bill Sr. said, "To our health!"

Everyone touched their glasses together and took a drink. Pixie took a deep swallow and broke into a coughing fit, which brought peals of laughter from the men. Robert patted her back, which ignited a deep blush.

They laughed and told stories late into the night. Pixie, with little to add, listened and marveled at Robert's confidence and good looks.

⊰⊱

The next morning, Robert slept in and everyone whispered and tiptoed through breakfast. Robert came down the stairs well after 10 a.m. and apologized for his tardiness. He ate oatmeal and seemed to relish the flavor of something that was so very common.

The family fell into a routine in the next weeks.

A month later, Pixie was washing dishes when Robert walked into the kitchen and asked, "Have you been to Jay Cooke Park?"

Pixie shook her head.

Robert grabbed her hand and pulled her toward the door. "Come along."

They walked for miles alongside the St. Louis River as it roared through a narrow gorge, eventually coming to a swinging bridge that spanned the river. Standing on the swaying bridge, they watched the tannin-stained water as people strolled past. When Robert's arm fell across her shoulders her knees felt weak. They returned in time for supper and sidelong looks from Bill junior, who made all kinds of smart remarks. Robert was tired after supper and begged off another round of cognac in favor of sleep.

CHAPTER 59

PINE COUNTY COURTHOUSE
SUNDAY

Agent Hoffman, Sheriff Sepanen, Floyd Swenson, Pam Ryan, and Dan Williams were strategizing in the sheriff's office. Hoffman was on his cellphone with his Minneapolis office while the Pine County deputies pored over a topographical map of Norman Township.

"Bruce lives in a swamp," said Floyd. "Every side of his house is alder brush or cattails."

Pam was on the sheriff's computer. "Here's a Google Earth view of Norman Township." She said. Everyone but Hoffman stepped behind her to look at the image as she zoomed closer and closer to Swanson's house. She stopped when the clearing around his house filled most of the screen.

"That's what I was saying," said Floyd. "It's all swamp except for the driveway to the house. There's no way to approach the house unobserved unless you drop in by helicopter."

Hoffman put his phone in his pocket and joined the group. "That was the State Patrol. They have a fixed-wing aircraft coming this way and they'll fly over the house. We should know if the Crown Victoria is at his home in a few minutes."

Pam shook her head. "Not necessarily. He's got a couple outbuildings that might be garages. If we see a car, we can assume he's home, but it we can't see a car, he might've parked in a garage."

Hoffman looked at the computer image over Pam's shoulder. "Is that his house? It looks like he lives on an island."

"An island would be more approachable," said the sheriff. "There's no way we can slog through the swampy underbrush without making a racket."

"Do you have a hostage rescue team or someone skilled at armed entry?" asked the sheriff.

Hoffman shook his head. "I have a few officers on their way and we're talking with the Air National Guard about a bomb-disposal unit from Duluth, but I don't have access to any sort of invasion force."

Dan Williams, the undersheriff, had been listening quietly. "I don't think we can take him out of the house. It's way too risky. I think our best bet is to set up an ambush and grab him when he drives out. It's noon now and he'll be coming in for his shift at three."

Hoffman looked at the topographical map again. "I concur. We can sit outside these two corners," he pointed at the map, "and when he heads for work we'll grab him on our terms, instead of attacking the house on his terms."

Hoffman's phone chirped and he stepped away from the group and had a hushed conversation in the corner. Within minutes he was back. "The state patrol verified that there's a Crown Vic parked in the yard. There's no sign of other vehicles, nor any activity."

"He's scheduled to work the afternoon," said Floyd. "He's probably home watching television."

"How crazy is this guy?" asked Hoffman, "Is it likely that he'd booby trap the driveway so anyone driving in would be blown to kingdom come?"

"I'm no psychologist," said Floyd, "but the bits I know about Bruce make me think he's unstable. He lives with his mother in a rundown house. He likes to exert excessive power within his span of control. He drives around in an old police vehicle, maybe to make people think he's a deputy."

"He makes me nervous," said Pam. "He's been hanging around the bullpen since the bombing, asking questions about the case. I don't think I've ever seen him in the ready room except on two other occasions when he escorted a prisoner to an interview room. It's not like he's said anything offensive, but he just gives me the creeps."

"What's the motive?" asked the sheriff. "Why would he bomb the forest entrance?"

"I can't see him as an eco-terrorist," said Pam. "Nor do I see him doing this on behalf of the tribes. He's not trying to blackmail anyone that we know of."

"Could there be a reason he wouldn't want us to find the bodies in the shack?" asked Floyd.

"If that's it, why not blow up the shack?" asked Dan Williams. "We'd have to know who was in the shack to know why he wouldn't want it discovered."

"It makes no sense," said Hoffman. "This guy wasn't even born when the people were killed at the shack. Why would he care?"

"Let's stand down until the team gets here from Minneapolis and I hear back from the bomb squad," said Hoffman. "We can all use a break."

"I agree. Pretty soon we'll be wondering if aliens and spaceships are involved," said Pam.

Floyd took out his cellphone and dialed the BCA. Laurie Lone Eagle, supervisor of the forensics unit, answered.

"Hi Laurie, Floyd here. "I've been working with Jeff and Sonny on the crime scene from the shack we found in the state forest. We think we may have a lead on the bomber. One theory is that the explosion was an attempt to keep the murder scene from being discovered. Jeff asked the U of M anthropology lab to do a virtual facial reconstruction of the victims. Do you know if they were successful?"

"I haven't heard from them," Laurie said. "Let me try to get Jeff on a three-way conversation."

After a series of clicks, Telker was on the line. "Okay, Laurie and Floyd. We have a probable ID on three of the men and we're looking for a match on the fourth. It appears that three of the men are the Cook County escapees, O'Connor, Darrow, and LaPorte. We've just pulled arrest pictures of some St. Paul gamblers who've been missing since the 1930s and the tech is in the process of attempting a match. Hang on one minute."

A few minutes later Telker said, "The fourth guy is probably Robert Steinhardt, who went by the nickname Frisco Dutch. He was a small-time St. Paul hustler who had a reputation for pulling together gamblers for poker games in places where the cops wouldn't bust them."

"Well, the shack was certainly a secluded spot where the cops wouldn't find them," said the sheriff.

"But none of those guys have links to Pine County," said Pam. "Who would care if their bodies were found or not."

"Maybe it's the woman," said Floyd. "Maybe she's the key. All we know is that she's a remote relative of Barb Skog. I'll have to give Barb a call to see if she can tie any threads together."

"Barb Skog? The DEA deputy director is related to the woman in the shack?" Hoffman asked, overhearing Floyd's conversation. Floyd hit the speaker button.

"She is," said Telker. "The U of M compared her DNA with Jane Doe and got a mitochondrial match. They're directly related somewhere on their mothers' side of the family."

"No shit," said Hoffman.

The sheriff's intercom clicked. "Sheriff, we have a group of ATF officers here. Where should I send them?"

CHAPTER 60

NORMAN TOWNSHIP
SUNDAY

P am and Floyd were parked on the shoulder of County Road 43 with several ATF agents suffering in the unusual warmth in their camouflage fatigues, helmets, and heavy tactical vests capable of stopping a rifle bullet. They were just out of sight of anyone driving down McNally Road. Another ATF agent was camouflaged in the underbrush fifty yards away so they'd have ample warning of any approaching cars.

Sheriff Sepanen and Dan Williams were parked at the other end of McNally road with Agent Hoffman and four additional ATF agents. It was early afternoon and they'd been in position for nearly two hours, waiting for something to happen.

During the planning, Agent Hoffman had made it very clear that it was an ATF operation the sheriff's department role was to back up the feds if things got out of hand.

"If Bruce really has all the explosives from Davidson's barn," Pam told Floyd, "I'm not sure I want to be anywhere near when the ATF stops his car. I felt the blast at the forest entrance and Hoffman thinks there could be four times that much explosive in Bruce Swanson's hands."

Floyd watched the ATF agents gathered around the hood of their black Suburban, poring over maps. "I heard something about a crater the size of a house. Even if we're not close, that's a lot of debris and shrapnel flying through the air."

Far overhead a small plane circled. "I wonder if Bruce knows he's being watched?" Floyd asked rhetorically.

"You've known Bruce a long time," said Pam. "Does he seem like the kind of guy who'd want to be an ecological martyr."

"Well, I don't see him as someone affiliated with any religious sect. He's a loner without many social connections outside of work. He's never been married that I know of. I've never even seen him in a restaurant or bar. The more I think about it, the more he seems to fit the profile of a psychopath."

"Well, that's encouraging," replied Pam, frowning. "I think I saw him in the grocery store with an elderly woman once. Didn't you say that he lives with his mother?"

The ATF agents were suddenly packing their gear and moving with purpose. The agent who had been hiding crawled out from the underbrush. He slogged through the ditch, dripping swamp water as he stepped onto the shoulder. The agents on the road were tightening the straps on their bulletproof vests, adjusting holsters, and rechecking their weapons.

"They're nervous," said Pam, watching the feds.

"They're putting on their game faces," replied Floyd.

The lead agent made a circling motion over his head, which meant the agents should gather around him. "Lock and load. The suspect is on the road." He said into a radio mic. He jumped into the Suburban and turned west. "East team, close the road behind him."

Pam took a deep breath and let it out, relieved. "We're off the front line," she said, climbing into Floyd's cruiser. "All we have to do is secure the driveway."

"You don't want in on the action?" Floyd asked facetiously as he buckled his seatbelt and slipped the transmission into drive.

"Not so much," said Pam, adjusting her vest and bracing the AR-15 against her leg as they raced down the washboard road. "I've had my share of suspect confrontations over the last two years, and there's no way I want to be anywhere near a rolling car bomb."

Floyd followed the ATF agents onto McNally road. The Suburban accelerated hard ahead of them, leaving a lazy dust cloud drifting across the road. Floyd stopped his cruiser, blocking Bruce's driveway, as had been the plan if the suspect went west.

He and Pam got out of the car, Pam with the AR-15 rifle and Floyd with a shotgun loaded with buckshot. They watched the Suburban disappear into the dust and waited. If the car had gone east, toward them, Floyd and Pam would have been braced behind the car, ready to support the feds, who would have blocked the road and engaged Bruce's car.

Out of the corner of his eye, Floyd saw a curtain move in the house. He stared, trying to determine if the wind had moved it, or if someone was watching them from the house. The radio came alive with chatter. In the distance there were shouted commands.

"Sounds out of control," Pam said.

"Every plan goes out the window as soon as the suspect reacts to the situation." He paused, then added, "There's someone in the house. I saw a curtain move."

Pam's head snapped toward the house, unconsciously putting the car between herself and the house. She studied each window of the old two-story structure. "I don't see anything."

"We have activity in the house," Floyd spoke into the mic on his lapel. "The suspect's mother may be home." Floyd rested the butt of the shotgun on his hip and started walking up the driveway. Unsure of his intentions, Pam hesitated for a second, then jogged to catch up.

"Shouldn't we make a tactical approach?" asked Pam, who was carefully watching the house and moving randomly from side-to-side.

"I'm more concerned about a tripwire on the porch or behind the door."

After carefully examining the porch for booby traps, they climbed the steps and stood on either side of the front door so a gunshot through the door wouldn't hit them, then Floyd knocked.

Creaking floorboards signaled the approach of someone. Both Floyd and Pam tensed. The door opened wide and an elderly woman looked at them through the screen. "Yes?" she asked.

"Please step out," said Floyd, trying to sound reassuring, but not loosening his grip on the shotgun.

The woman opened the screen door and stepped onto the porch. Her hair was white and chopped in a way that looked like she probably cut it herself with a pair of scissors. She was a hefty woman. Her weathered face looked weary. Floyd noticed the slightest resemblance to Bruce in her features.

"Are you armed?" asked Floyd.

"Hell no," she replied, with a raspy voice. "What's going on?"

"Is there anyone else in the house?" asked Floyd.

"Just a mangy cat."

Pam slid between the woman and the door to block her re-entry. "We want to talk to you about Bruce."

The woman's eyes narrowed. "Is he in trouble?"

"We've got some questions for him," replied Floyd. "What do you know about Pop Davidson?"

"Pop is a crazy old coot," said the woman. "He runs all over in his pickup. I think he spends more time gossiping than he ever spends blasting ponds or selling guns."

"What's your name?" asked Pam.

"I'm Sigurd Swanson," the woman replied. "I live here with Bruce. He works with you at the jail. Now tell me what the hell is going on."

"May I check your pockets for weapons?" Pam asked, slinging the rifle over her shoulder.

"I already told you, I don't have any weapons."

"Humor me," said Pam. "I'd like to check your pockets, just to be safe."

"Do what you've got to do," said the woman, raising her arms.

"We think Bruce may have taken some explosives from Davidson's farm," Floyd said as Pam gently patted the pockets of the woman's jeans, then patted her legs to the ankles. "Do you know anything about that?"

"Dynamite?" the woman asked.

Pam cuffed the woman's hands behind her back. "I think you'd better come along with us.," Pam said as they moved toward the cruiser. In the distance they could hear slamming car doors and orders being given over loudspeakers.

After a sharp right turn they saw a half dozen police vehicles parked at a jumble of angles, with Bruce Swanson's black Crown Vic in the center. ATF agents were taking cover behind Suburbans and cars. Two Pine County cruisers blocked the road fifty yards behind the Crown Vic.

"Where's Bruce?" Sigurd Swanson asked as Floyd braked hard, stopping far short of the apparent standoff.

"Does Bruce have dynamite in his car?" Floyd asked, as he backed up, taking a position out of the possible lines of fire.

"Why would he have dynamite in his car? That'd be stupid."

"Where is the dynamite he took from Pop Davidson's farm?" asked Pam.

"I didn't know he took anything from Pop. Why would he do that?"

"You don't know if he has any dynamite?" Floyd asked.

"I don't know nothin' about dynamite."

"Do you see all those cops with their guns pointed at Bruce's car?" Floyd asked calmly. "They think

Bruce's car is full of explosives and they want him to surrender without anyone getting shot or blown up. Do you understand what I'm saying?" Floyd asked.

Sigurd nodded, trying to look around the headrests to see the road ahead of them.

"Can you explain to Bruce that no one wants to hurt him and that he should give up?"

"Bruce doesn't listen much to me," she said. "He's always had a mind of his own. He barely tolerates me in the house and that's only because of my Social Security checks."

Floyd picked up his cellphone and dialed. "Sheriff, we have Bruce's mother in the car with us."

"What?" Sepanen replied.

"Bruce Swanson's mother is in my backseat. Maybe he'll talk to her."

"Hang on," said Sepanen. Floyd heard shouting and then silence. "Don't bring her any closer. Bruce is agitated and the feds are trying to talk him down from the brink. Stay on the line in case they want her to talk to him."

Pam opened the passenger door and leaned on the doorframe while Floyd sat behind the wheel. His phone vibrated. The caller ID said Salt Lake City, LDS.

"Hell of a time for the genealogist to call," he said to himself. He let it roll over to voicemail.

"Floyd, this is Hoffman. You've got Mrs. Swanson with you?" Hoffman asked over the radio.

"Yes. We're parked about a hundred yards behind your east team."

"Hold your position while I contact the suspect." The radio went silent again.

"Is Bruce okay?" Mrs. Swanson asked.

"I assume he must be if the feds are trying to contact him."

Floyd's cellphone rang. "This is Hoffman. I spoke with the suspect and we're going to back away, then he wants to speak with his mother."

The Suburbans and cars started to back away. The DEA assault team walked alongside as their vehicles moved, their guns still trained on the black Crown Victoria, but their fingers outside of the trigger guards.

"Sergeant Swenson, please disconnect this call. I'll have the suspect dial your cellphone. Have the mother talk. Monitor the conversation and if you sense tension or increasing agitation, just end the call and wait for my instructions."

Floyd opened the back door and knelt next to Sigurd Swanson. "Bruce is going to call my phone. I'll put it on speaker so we'll both be able to hear what he says. Please try to be reassuring and try to get him to settle down. We want him to surrender to the ATF agents without anyone getting hurt. Do you understand?"

Sigurd Swanson nodded just as Floyd's phone rang. He punched the speaker button and held the phone in front of her face.

"Bruce?"

"Is that you, Mom?"

"I'm in a police car down the road. They've got me handcuffed. I can see your car. Are you okay?"

"I'm as good as anyone who got stopped by a bunch of guys wearing camouflage with all kinds of guns."

"The cop says they think your car is packed with explosives. They want you to give up before you get hurt. I think you should listen to them. You're all I've got left."

Floyd leaned close to Sigurd and whispered to her.

"Bruce, do you have dynamite in your car?" she asked, at Floyd's prompting.

"That's what this is about? They think I've got dynamite?"

"That's what they said."

"I'm bringing your mother up so you can talk to her face-to-face," said Floyd.

"No! Stay back!"

Seconds later they heard, "The suspect is out of the car with his hands up." Hoffman announced over the radio. "Everyone stand down."

Two BATF agents advanced with their guns drawn. Bruce intertwined his hands behind his head.

CHAPTER 61

THE MINNEAPOLIS OFFICES OF PEABODY AND MARSDEN

Barb Skog and four BATF agents got off the Foshay Towers elevators on the twelfth floor and walked through the double doors with the Peabody and Marsden LLC logo painted on the frosted glass. The lead agent, Peter Flint, a trim man in a dark suit, stepped up to the receptionist's desk and unfolded his credentials, showing them to the surprised woman sitting behind a teak desk. The brass plaque on her desk said she was Susan Ledin.

The receptionist forced a smile and asked, "How may I help you, Mr. Flint?"

"Please take us to Garth McLeod's office," Flint said. When the receptionist reached for her phone he gently put his hand on the phone. "I want to go directly to Mr. McLeod's office."

"I'm not sure he's in," replied the receptionist. She'd been with Peabody and Marsden for twenty years and was polished, but unprepared for the five federal agents standing before her.

"Just take us to his office, please." Flint unfolded the search warrant. "We have a warrant to search his office."

"I'm sorry, but I'll have to contact Mr. Marsden. I'm sure he'll be able to help you."

Flint put his hand on the phone again. "No, Ms. Ledin, you're going to take us to Mr. McLeod's office. Either that, or we walk through the doors behind you and march down the hallway, looking into every office until we find Mr. McLeod's desk. I doubt that Mr. Marsden would appreciate the disruption that would cause."

"I'm sorry, but I can't allow you into the offices without Mr. Marsden's approval." She reached for the phone again, but Flint held it down firmly. He nodded to the other three BATF agents who walked to the double doors behind the reception desk.

"Wait! You can't just barge in there!"

"Then, Ms. Ledin, lead us quietly to Mr. McLeod's office."

"I have to release the electronic lock on the door," Ledin said, reaching for a button under her desk.

When she pushed the button the office doors automatically locked down and a light started blinking on Hector Marsden's desk. An alarm sounded in a console in the lobby and two security officers ran for the elevators.

Flint grabbed the receptionist's wrist from across the desk and pulled her up. "You're under arrest for obstruction of justice." He stepped around the desk and pulled her hands behind her back, quickly cuffing her wrists. The other agents went to the door leading to the offices, but found them firmly secured.

"Ms. Ledin, how do we release the door latch?" asked Barb Skog as Flint pushed her around the front of her desk.

"They're in lockdown until security or Mr. Marsden enters the code."

Barb Skog shook her head. "What's Mr. Marsden's extension?"

"I'm afraid that's confidential," replied Ledin.

"That's two counts of obstructing a federal officer," said Flint. "Each count is year in prison. Do you want to keep adding on, or do you want to cooperate?"

Hector Marsden pulled up the security camera view on his computer and saw four men and one woman, all in dark suits standing in the entryway. He watched as one of them cuffed his receptionist. Only then did he notice the badges hanging from lanyards around their necks. He rushed to the entry door and activated an electronic release. As the door opened, three agents pushed him aside and started walking down the hallway past rows of offices.

"What's the meaning of this?" Marsden asked, trying to stop the agents rushing past.

"We have a search warrant for Garth McLeod's office," said Flint, holding out the document. "Ms. Ledin refused to take us to his office, so we will find it ourselves.

"You'll do no such thing," said Marsden, as he pulled reading glasses from his shirt pocket, getting them briefly caught on his suspenders. "Our clients are entitled to private meetings with their attorneys and you can't just bust in here."

Two gray-uniformed security guards rushed out of the elevators with their hands on the butts of their pistols. "Stand down," said Barb Skog in a commanding voice and holding up her badge. "We're federal agents executing a search warrant."

"The proper procedure," said Marsden, handing the warrant back to Flint, "is to present the warrant to the security desk on the first floor. They would've called Susan, and she would've advised me. At that point, we would've sent an escort down for you and I would've met you at the door and led you to a conference room. We could've had a civilized discussion about the warrant, and then I would've led you to Mr. McLeod's office."

"That's very nice, Mr. Marsden. But we wanted to preserve as much evidence as possible and we would prefer to take Mr. McLeod's files, cellphones, and computers into custody before he has a chance to expunge or destroy anything," said Skog.

Marsden was shaking his head. "I'm sorry, but I can't allow you to access Mr. McLeod's computer or files until we've had a chance to remove any privileged client information."

"Again, that's a lovely protocol, Mr. Marsden, but this isn't our first rodeo. You'll be able to argue the confidentiality of files at Mr. McLeod's pre-trial hearing."

"That's not how we'd prefer to see this handled," said Marsden, through pursed lips.

"But that's what's legal," said Skog. "Considering the scope of the search warrant, I'd hate to have your firm blemished if it were determined that files were accidentally lost or destroyed."

Flint put up a finger and listened as someone spoke to him through his earpiece. "It appears that my associates have located Mr. McLeod and his computer. Would you like to have someone present while we search his office, Mr. Marsden?"

Marsden clenched his teeth as his face turned red. "Actually, I think I'll have someone film the search." He turned away, then paused. "What is your interest in Garth McLeod?"

"The search warrant explains that he's a suspected accomplice in the Pine County bombing."

"That's preposterous!" said Marsden.

"He'll have his day in court to argue those charges," said Flint.

Barb Skog leaned close and showed her credentials to Marsden. His eyes grew wide when he saw her title and the DEA logo. "In addition to the bombing charges, Mr. McLeod's alleged accomplices have also been charged with drug possession, drug trafficking, interstate transportation of a female minor, and Pine County is considering murder charges."

Barb Skog smiled as she watched Marsden consider the implications of even having one of his lawyers face those charges. She added, "You may be acquainted with Jane Simmons, the U.S. Attorney. She doesn't file charges unless she's pretty sure the case is ironclad. I can see that you're trying to figure out how to distance the firm from this whole matter, but it will be difficult when the local television stations film us leading Mr. McLeod from your offices, followed by FBI agents carrying boxes of evidence."

"Take the handcuffs off Ms. Ledin and let her find someone to witness the search," Marsden said through clenched teeth.

Marsden turned and walked quickly down the hallway to Garth McLeod's office.

Garth McLeod had been read his rights and was standing, handcuffed, in his office doorway watching an agent shut off his computer and unplug it. A second agent had taken McLeod's cellphone from his pocket and turned it off, and had just found the pre-paid phone in his suit coat hanging behind the door. The smug look on his face changed as he paled when he saw the agent plug a memory device into the pre-paid phone and copy the phone log.

"You can't do that!"

Ignoring his outburst, the agent calmly said, "Looks like you've made a lot of calls to Jeremy Pike," He shut off the phone and put it into an evidence bag.

"He's my client and our conversations are privileged!" replied McLeod.

"Really? His lawyer of record is Ira Rosen. I wonder where that leaves you?"

McLeod quietly stated, "I want a lawyer."

Agent Flint, standing behind him, said, "About ten of your colleagues are standing here watching the search. Would you like to choose one of them?"

"Garth, don't say another word," said Hector Marsden, who was standing next to Flint. "Take the handcuffs off of him."

"Sorry. He's under arrest. You can argue bail arrangements with the magistrate. Just so you know, those arguments will be much more challenging if the team searching his house and car find more evidence involving the Pine County explosions."

McLeod's eyes went wide and his mouth fell open. He glanced at Marsden, then looked away.

CHAPTER 62

PINE COUNTY COURTHOUSE
MONDAY

Bruce Swanson had been segregated in a single cell overnight to protect him from the other prisoners. He sat in the interrogation room wearing the rumpled uniform he'd been arrested in, his usual gray pallor accentuated by the harsh lighting and the lack of sleep.

Floyd sat next to Laurie Lone Eagle; Barry Hoffman sat next to Swanson on the opposite side of the table.

After the usual name, date, place, and circumstances had been recorded, Hoffman said, "For the record, you've been read your Miranda rights and you're willing to speak to us without an attorney."

"There's nothing to say," said Bruce. "I haven't done anything wrong."

Hoffman said, "We've examined your computer and you've been to some very dark places. You've been in contact with at least two militia groups."

"I'm not saying I haven't or that I disagree with some of those militia groups," said Swanson, "but that doesn't make me the Unabomber or anything. I just like to keep on top of what's going on in the world."

Hoffman was about to speak when Laurie put her hand on Bruce's arm. "I think you may be right," she said. "Agent Hoffman's people and my technicians have been all over the scene of the Nemadji forest bombing. It's obvious it was amateurish. It was a pure bush league job.

"We know that your MOS involved demolition," said Laurie. "No one with your experience would make a mess like that."

"I taught demolition! I know more about demolition than most BATF agents."

"So, you know how poorly it was done," said Laurie. "You'd never set up explosives like that. No expert would."

Bruce leaned his head back and stared at the ceiling.

"There's no way you'd botch a job like that," Laurie opined. "It was someone who just didn't understand the physics."

"I told you, I didn't set the explosives," said Swanson.

"Your car was the last vehicle leaving Davidson's house before the explosion."

Bruce sat up. "That's what this is about? Hell, if you check Pop's records you'll see I was picking up a new Taurus pistol I'd been waiting for. Pop was just fine when I left."

"You've seemed very interested when we've been talking about the bodies in the shack," said Floyd. "Is that related to this somehow?"

"Tell us about the bodies in the shack." said Laurie

"Well," Swanson he hesitated, looking at the people around him. "It's complicated."

"Take your time," said Floyd.

Bruce fidgeted. "My father's family were hardworking Swedish immigrants who came here to farm. But every family has a black sheep, and the Swanson's was cousin Abigail. According to my father, in high school she was pretty, flamboyant, popular, and pretty soon she was also pregnant, which was a really big deal back in the day. Once her condition started to show, her family kept her at home, in McGregor, out of school and hidden from the community, until the baby was born. The baby was given up for adoption. Everyone thought the ugliness had been put aside, but Abigail had too much spunk for that. By the '30s, she was tending bar in Pine Brook and was rumored to be doing other unspeakable things, which embarrassed the family.

"Dad had a steady job here, with Pine County, and when the bank foreclosed on the Tuxedo Inn, Abigail's father suggested that he and my father could combine their savings and buy the place from the bank. In Abigail, they had a talented manager, flamboyant enough to make the place financially successful, mainly through entertaining businessmen who came through on the train. Uncle Holger was happy that it got his daughter someplace more discreet than the Pine Brook bar, even though she was still a pariah. Rumors were rampant around town about the unspeakable Tuxedo Inn clientele and employees."

"What did your father do for the county?" asked Floyd.

"He was the head jailer. His name was Fred."

"So he had a steady county job that gave him regular wages when many others were losing their houses and businesses," said Floyd. "He chose to invest in a bar?"

"The family thought that running the inn would be enough to keep Abigail out of trouble, but she was serving liquor, entertaining businessmen from Duluth and the Twin Cities, and she kept in contact with relatives around the region. Dad said if one of Abigail's cousins was living in tough straits, she'd hop on the train and bring her back to work for her."

"Define tough straits," said Floyd.

"I don't know all the details, but I understand that one of the girls had a father who was taking liberties with her. Abigail was the one person who was willing to stand up to him."

"And what happened to him?" Asked Floyd.

Bruce squirmed. "His body was found in the hog pen the day after Abigail took his daughter away."

"Do you think Abigail killed him?"

Bruce shrugged. "No one ever talked about it. I heard that nobody felt too bad the pigs ate him."

"Go on," Floyd said.

"Well, Abigail rescued a few more cousins, sometimes from poverty, some from the orphanages, one from the State School, and her own daughter from her abusive adoptive father. She put them to work until they were old enough to get by on their own. Then she sent them off with some skills, and a few dollars in their pockets.

"Dad wasn't particularly happy about the clientele or her philanthropy, but as long as she made the mortgage payments and didn't get arrested, he didn't intervene, especially since the banks were closing and folks were losing their savings and farms."

"So how does that have anything to do with the shack?" asked Laurie.

"Abigail ran an orderly house, although it was rumored there were prostitutes there. At that time, no matter what was real, everyone believed what they heard. A few gangsters were seen at the inn. Dad said even John Dillinger had been there, but Abigail could handle them. But then Tommy O'Connor showed up. He was beyond ruthless, and even Abigail wasn't prepared to deal with his depravity and level of violence. She came to Dad early one morning bruised and bleeding. She explained that she had to sell the inn to O'Connor or he was going to kill her and take the girls to a brothel in Kansas City. Dad rounded up a couple of his buddies, planning to confront O'Connor at the inn. But O'Connor and his crew were gone.

"I don't know exactly how the next part worked out, but Dad hid something on one of the former county prisoners and he used the guy to arrange a poker game in the abandoned logging camp. Back then, the forest was hardly more than a bunch of seedlings except for the few acres of hardwoods. Dad found the shack one year when he was deer hunting and thought it would be the perfect place to deal with O'Connor. Dad hid out of sight, awaiting the arrival of the gangsters. When his spy signaled to him, Dad shot through the tarpaper walls and killed them all.

"Abigail was a hostage, and the spy who set up the poker game said she was sitting in a corner away from the poker game. Dad's plan was to shoot the gangsters, rescue her, and bring her back to run the Inn. After the shooting stopped, he looked inside the shack and found Abigail dead sitting beside one of the gangsters. Standing there, looking at the bloody mess, he knew he couldn't take her bullet-riddled body to a mortuary because it would raise all kinds of questions. So, he decided to leave her there with the scum who'd dragged her into the mess. I guess he thought the wolves would clean up the scene and no one would ever be the wiser.

"Okay, fast forward a few years. When I came back from Vietnam, I was a mess. Dad had been a Marine Corps private in World War One and a sergeant in the Pacific during the second war. He knew what I was going through. He took me camping so we could talk and maybe straighten my head out. We walked around the Nemadji State Forest for days and he guided me to the logging camp and the collapsed shack. He told me about the Tuxedo Inn, Abigail, and his final solution at the logging shack. He was emotional. The whole thing about Abigail had been eating at him for years so he spilled it all, and made me promise to help keep it a family secret."

"What happened to the tommy gun?" Floyd asked.

"Oh, you know about that, too."

"The shell casings at the shack have extractor markings from a Thompson machine gun," said Floyd. "There's one missing from the property room and I suspect it was the murder weapon."

"Dad's fingerprints were all over it. He stuck the tommy gun into a broken off hollow tree after the shooting. Back in '69, dad showed me the tree and told me as long as it was safely tucked away no one could ever tie him to the massacre at the shack. I went back to remove it, but I couldn't find the tree."

"Do you know what happened to all the women Abigail rescued?" Laurie asked.

"I have no idea where any of them went."

CHAPTER 63

SHERIFF SEPANEN'S OFFICE

The sheriff pushed the phone to the middle of his desk so he and Floyd could both be part of the conversation with Jane Simmons, the Assistant U.S. Attorney.

"The computer forensics people got past Garth McLeod's passwords and encryption last night. It seems he's been a behind-the-scenes militant environmentalist for some time. Not only was he scouring the internet for what he thought were environmental abuses, he was passing that information to teams of protesters and providing them with money. It's going to be a little tough to get through all the legal issues about the trust account he was using because of privileged conversations, but we know that he provided money to the protestors that were here for their travel expenses. Jeremy Pike, and the leaders of several other protest groups, had debit cards and McLeod regularly put money in their accounts. It appears the trust fund was also paying the legal expenses of any protesters who were arrested."

"Who was funding the trust?" Floyd asked.

"It's nearly impossible to say because the funds came from off-shore accounts and they're claiming attorney-client privilege. The one account we were able to trace belonged to a well-known Hollywood actress, who I'm not at liberty to identify. Because of the privileged nature of her relationship with the law firm, we'll never be able to tie her to any of the illegal activities, and I assume she didn't realize how militant some of the groups she was supporting had become."

"If the protesters were being funded by this trust, why were they prostituting the girls and selling drugs?" Floyd asked.

"After talking with the women, my guess is that their drug habits got out of hand and there wasn't enough money coming from the trust to cover anything more than gas, meals, and campground fees."

"You were able to tie McLeod to the explosions?"

"He was so arrogant that he didn't realize, or maybe didn't care, that he was being filmed by the television stations when he and his cohorts were racing around the sites of the explosions on their ATVs. McLeod's ATV had been wiped clean, but we were able to find dynamite residue on another ATV that we identified by the unique graphics we gleaned from the television coverage. The owner of that ATV was happy to throw McLeod under the bus in return for a reduced sentence at a minimum-security federal prison. He explained how McLeod found Pop's blasting business on the internet, and how three of them had ridden their ATVs to Pop's barn to steal the explosives. He was there when Davidson was killed, too, although it's going to be hard to separate which one of the three was the murderer."

"It sounds like you've got it all wrapped up," said the sheriff.

"I think so. We still have some forensic evidence to process but I'm confident that what we already have will be enough to put McLeod away for a long time."

"Thanks for the update," said Floyd.

After disconnecting, the sheriff leaned back in his chair and pulled a cigar from his pocket. He made a ceremony out of unwrapping it and inhaling the tobacco aroma. "I like it when a case comes together."

"We're not quite done yet," said Floyd.

"What's left? The bad guys have been identified and arrested, crazy Bruce is retiring, and we identified the bodies in the shack."

"We still haven't found Margaret Lane," said Floyd.

The sheriff was dialing Megan Winston's number as Floyd stood. "Megan, I've got the exclusive of the century for you," he said as Floyd closed the door.

CHAPTER 64

MONDAY AFTERNOON

B arb Skog met Floyd in the courthouse lobby. "I
can't thank you enough, Floyd," she said, shaking
his hand. "We found Abigail and the family can give
her a proper burial. I'll try to trace Abigail's daughter and the other women she rescued now that I know
they're my relatives too. I have their names from the
1930 Tuxedo Inn census."

Floyd patted his pockets for his cellphone. "Thanks
for reminding me. I missed a call from Salt Lake City
during the standoff."

He found the number and called. "Ms. Hartley,
this is Floyd Swenson, from Pine County. You called
yesterday." Floyd activated the speakerphone.

"Sergeant. I think I hit pay dirt. Margaret `Pixie'
Lane married Robert Allen Wickerson on October 14,

1946, in Fort William, Ontario. You probably don't have access to Canadian marriage records."

"Please repeat that," said Floyd. "Margaret's niece is standing next to me."

"Hi," said Barb Skog leaning close to the phone. "I'm Margaret Lane's niece. Thanks so much for the lead. Were you able to find other Canadian records for her?"

"No, but I found Carlton County, Minnesota, birth records for three children born to Robert and Pixie Wickerson, the first was born five months after the wedding, which might explain an out-of-town elopement. I'm inclined to think that Margaret's nickname was Pixie, or maybe she changed her name from Margaret to Pixie when they married. The handwritten records are shaky and subject to the interpretation of the reader. Perhaps the census taker knew the Wickersons personally and only knew Margaret as Pixie."

"Did you find a death record for Pixie Wickerson?" Floyd asked.

"Pixie's husband, Robert, died in 1982, but I haven't found a death record for Margaret or Pixie Wickerson. It appears their three children may still be alive too."

"Please give me their names," said Skog, excited.

"I'm sorry, but you know the quirk with Ancestry. com, it only tells you there are living relatives. It won't give the specifics unless you already know them."

"But the last name is Wickerson. Correct?"

"Yes," replied the genealogist. "They were all born in Carlton County, Minnesota. Perhaps that's enough of a lead for you."

Floyd ended the call after thanking her and found the number for the Carlton County Courthouse. After two transfers, he reached Travis.

"Hi, Travis. My genealogical mystery is coming to an end, but I need one piece of information. Can you find an old-timer around the courthouse and ask him or her if they know a Pixie Wickerson?"

"Sure, Floyd, but first let me do a quick search." Keys clicked as they waited silently. "Okay, there is a house in downtown Carlton that's owned by Pixie Wickerson, but her tax statements are mailed to a different address. Have you got a piece of paper?"

CHAPTER 65

CARLTON NURSING HOME

The receptionist directed Floyd and Barb Skog to a sunroom where three women were hunched over a jigsaw puzzle. One was a tiny frail woman with translucent white skin and white hair sitting in a wheelchair. Barb Skog took a chair and sat next to her.

"Excuse me," said Skog, her voice quivering, "are you Pixie Wickerson?"

The tiny woman looked up from the puzzle. "Do I know you?"

"My name is Barb Skog and I'm looking for my aunt, Margaret Lane. I think you may be the woman I've been searching for."

"I haven't been known as Margaret since I was a child. Everyone calls me Pixie."

Skog's eyes filled with tears as she took Pixie's frail hand in hers. "May I call you Aunt Pixie?"

"How am I related to you?"

"I'm your niece. I'm Frank's daughter."

Pixie turned her wheelchair so she was facing Skog. "I haven't seen or heard about Frank since we were in the State School. Where is he?"

"He passed away a few years ago, but he gave me the Lane family Bible and enough information about the family to keep me searching for you and your siblings. Your brother Karl joined the Marines and was killed in the South Pacific. Your sister, Esther, married and raised a family in North Dakota, where she died in 1967. She had four girls who are also your nieces."

"I didn't know I had any family," Pixie said, obviously overwhelmed by the news.

Skog paused, then asked, "Do you remember Abigail Corbett?"

"Abigail disappeared when the gangsters showed up. We thought maybe she lured them away to save us. You found her?"

"It's very long story, and I want to know more about the other girls who worked at the Tuxedo Inn. I understand all of them are our relatives."

"That's a secret," Pixie said, looking away and clasping her hands in her lap. "It was the last thing Abigail said to us before we were hustled out of the Tuxedo

Inn. She said, 'Carol, Florence, Mary, and Pixie, we're all cousins and we have to look out for each other."

"Did she explain how you were related?" Skog asked, excitement in her voice.

"I'm tired. Can you take me to my room? We can talk there."

CHAPTER 66

STURGEON LAKE, MINNESOTA
MONDAY EVENING

Travis and Pam were sitting on Floyd's couch sipping a sweet Riesling. Mary, sitting in an overstuffed chair with a brocade cover, had opted for water with a slice of lemon while they listened to Floyd's recap of the genealogy mystery.

"Within two hours of leaving the nursing home she was making plans for a family reunion so the newfound cousins could meet the rest of the fractured family."

"That's a really touching story," said Mary. "I know it's been uplifting for Floyd to be part of that." After a pause she added. "I saw Megan Winston on the five o'clock news announcing the arrest of the Pine

County bomber. Finding that lawyer and his accomplices must've taken some luck."

"Actually," said Pam, "I'm pretty sure he was at the Willow River campground when I chased the Rainbow People away from the feds. A group of guys were hanging around looking guilty. I thought it was probably because they were smoking pot, but thinking back about it, two of them grabbed backpacks and drove off on ATVs. I thought it was because of drugs but they may have had the explosives in the backpacks."

"What's happening with the logging?" asked Travis.

"A federal mediator was invited into the discussion to find some common ground. The tribes were more concerned about the negative publicity they were getting than they were interested in tapping syrup from the few remaining maple trees that were granted to them under the 1837 treaty. They agreed to let the loggers cut, but they claimed the right to the timber. The state forestry department has egg on their faces for missing the tribal rights to the hardwoods. They had to turn the cutting rights over to the tribe under the treaty terms. The tribe was happier with the protesters leaving the casino than they were about the symbolism of leaving the old growth trees to die naturally. The loggers got jobs, the tribe got cash for the logging rights, and the state got screwed for not doing their homework."

"Bring your wine glasses to the table," Mary said as she carried a bowl of salmon salad to the table and Floyd loaded toasted rounds of French bread into a basket.

"Let me top off the wine glasses," Travis said as Floyd set the basket on the table.

"Um, Floyd," Pam said as she dug a folded brochure out of her pocket. "Here's the real estate ad for that house I mentioned west of Sandstone."

"What house in Sandstone?" Mary asked as she sat down, snatching the brochure from Pam's hand.

"There's a one-level house out near the Audubon Center," explained Pam. "I told Floyd it would be the perfect neutral ground for you two. It's closer to work for both of you, and it's still a little bit rural."

"When were you going to tell me you were house hunting, Floyd?" asked Mary as she read the brochure.

"I wasn't house hunting," said Floyd putting his hands up. "It was Edna Purdy's idea. She saw the house and told me it would be perfect for us."

"It's time you consolidated into one house instead of pretending you're still living separately, piling miles of driving on your cars, plus paying double taxes and utilities," said Pam.

"What happened to the kids who barricaded themselves at the forest entrance?" asked Travis, seeing how uncomfortable Floyd was and grabbing the chance to change the topic.

"I got a call from the Assistant U.S. Attorney yesterday," said Floyd. "Susan Stevenson, the teenager, is struggling with her substance abuse treatment and is suffering a bit of Stockholm Syndrome. Her doctors said she can't testify against the guys. So Jane Simmons made some pretty lenient plea offers and I understand that all the defendants have agreed to the terms. The women will get treated for substance abuse and be on probation for a year. Two of the guys will plead guilty to drug possession charges and will spend a few years in prison. Only Jeremy Pike, who's already in prison finishing his previous term, will receive substantial prison time for transporting Susan Stevenson across state lines for sexual purposes."

"That seems awfully lenient considering the trafficking of the women and the drug sales," said Pam.

"I guess Jane felt it was the best she could get, and all of them now have a conviction on their records if they're rearrested in the future."

"Do you think they'll stay out of trouble?" asked Travis.

"The very best long-term treatment centers have a 'cure rate' lower than fifty percent, and involuntary programs without long-term follow-up are far less effective," said Floyd. "That tells me there's probably a ninety-percent chance they'll be back in front of a judge again."

"What about the D.C. lawyer?" asked Pam. "He was such a jerk."

"Judge Peterson sent letters to the Washington D.C. bar association and the head U.S. Magistrate, notifying them that he'd jailed Rosen for contempt of court and incompetent representation of a client. I don't imagine anything formal will arise from the bar."

"I would've liked to see him jailed for his misconduct," said Pam. "Not offering the plea agreements to his female clients to protect his golden boy was way out of line."

"I think all lawyers are slimy," said Floyd. "Some more than others."

Mary jumped up to answer the ringing phone while the conversation about lawyers continued.

"Turn on the television," said Mary, holding her hand over the phone. "The sheriff is going to be interviewed on WDIO in a minute or two."

An ad from the Duluth Trading Company extolled the virtue of their extra-long, butt-crack-covering underwear ended, the screen cut away to Megan Winston, standing next to Sheriff Sepanen in front of the Pine County Courthouse. Despite a hefty breeze that rattled across the microphone, Winston's hair didn't move. She had a Cheshire cat grin that showed teeth so white they looked like they had internal lighting.

"I'm here tonight with an exclusive interview with Pine County Sheriff John Sepanen." Sepanen's white shirt was freshly pressed and contrasted with his dark, close-cropped hair. "Sheriff, please tell us about the capture of the state forest bomber."

"Well, Megan, it was a multi-agency investigation. My department coordinated with the BATF, DEA, and BCA, culminating in the arrest of the man who has admitted to planting the fatal bomb at the Nemadji State Forest entrance, and also the murder of a local businessman."

"I saw video from our Twin Cities affiliate of a bomb-disposal trailer at the site of the arrest. Was there a bomb?"

"While executing a search warrant in downtown Minneapolis, the BATF agents found enough explosives in the trunk of the suspect's car to create a crater thirty feet in diameter and ten feet deep. They said that the explosives were old, degraded, and probably unstable. A bomb-disposal unit secured the explosives and removed them to a safe location where they were detonated."

"I understand that you also solved a cold case while pursuing the bomber."

"We recovered several sets of human remains from an old logging shack in the Nemadji State Forest and were able to determine that it was the site of a 1930's multiple murder. With the help of the Minnesota BCA, the deputy director of the DEA, and the University of Minnesota anthropology lab, we were able to identify the remains as four fugitive gangsters and a local woman they'd kidnapped."

"I understand one of the gangsters was quite notorious."

"Terrible Tommy O'Connor had been convicted of killing a Chicago policeman and was awaiting execution when he escaped from the Chicago jail in 1921. Other than a shootout with police in Hastings, Minnesota, he'd been missing since his escape." The sheriff paused dramatically. "In an interesting twist, we learned that the kidnapped woman who was murdered has a local extended family. They are now able to give her a proper funeral and bury her in the family cemetery plot."

"Thank you, Sheriff Sepanen, for this exclusive interview. We'll now return to the studio for the rest of your evening news."

Mary turned off the television. "John looks good on television," she said.

"I think it's amazing that he only mentioned the DEA once and BATF twice. That will probably put a burr under someone's saddle," said Pam.

"Really?" asked Travis. "Is there that much competition between the agencies?"

"Oh, yeah," said Pam and Floyd in unison.

Sonny Carlson and Jeff Telker, investigating a suspicious death in Willmar, were eating supper in their motel room while watching the Sepanen interview. Sonny's head was bobbing as the sheriff related the story of the bomber's arrest and the mention of the BCA's assistance.

"That ought to make our bosses happy," said Sonny. "We got mentioned on the local news. Maybe the network will pick up their interview for the national news tomorrow.

"I was thinking; we should probably write a book about all the investigations we've done. Each chapter could be a different investigation. After all the years we've been doing this and all the cases we've helped solve, it would probably be several volumes long. I bet my kids, heck, even my grandkids, would like to see all the things we've been into. It's been pretty incredible if you think about it. I bet we've been instrumental in solving twenty or thirty cases a year. I couldn't write something like that, though. We'd have to find a ghost-writer. Maybe my cousin, the one down in Stillwater, could do it. He's written . . ."

"Sonny," said Jeff, smiling.

"What?"

"Stop talking before your supper gets cold."

A NOTE FROM THE AUTHOR

This book is a work of fiction. The events, people, and places described are the fictional product of the author's imagination and any resemblance to living people or actual events is coincidental. Some locations and characters are used fictionally.

The Tuxedo Inn was real. It went out of business in roughly 1915. I have extended its life by two decades to provide the needed location for the purposes of the story. The real Tuxedo Inn was known as a "classy" resort, although my discussions with Pine City residents, a generation or two removed from the heyday of the resort, led me to believe that there may have been entertainment beyond the "classy" historical façade. Whether true or folklore, it's what some people believe.

ACKNOWLEDGMENTS

I have to first of all thank my readers. I've been met with polite enthusiasm in person and through on-line posts. Your interest and energy drives me. I must also credit my Pine City readers for providing the Pokegama Sanatorium and Tuxedo Inn as likely lo-cales for a mystery.

I offer special thanks to the numerous librarians and booksellers who have supported me through the years by promoting my books and keeping them on the shelves.

Many thanks to Gallen Kincaid, whose father was a State School graduate. Gallen's vivid description of his father's school and adult life planted the seeds for Pixie's life experiences.

Thanks to Bob Smith and Fran Brozo for your input on Barb Skog's genealogical search and your sugges-tions about the additional twists in the research, and the limits of that research. Thanks to Michele LaBrees Daniels, who coined the term "family wreath" when we spoke about my grandfather's New Brunswick, Canada, family and my great-great grandmothers, who were sisters.

Robert Dennis Arnold helps me make the police situations correct. He and his wife Barb, are also due recognition for their generous auction purchase of the character named Barb Skog.

Thanks to Pat Morris again for her encouragement, editing, support, and friendship.

Thanks to Brian Johnson for being the muse who helped me get restarted a few times when I'd written myself into a corner or off a storyline cliff. I appreciate being inundated with your off-the-wall suggestions that I sorted and distilled. You've helped me relocate the muse more than once. And, you make me laugh.

Thanks to my cousins Jeff Telker and Sonny Carlson for putting life into my BCA agents.

Thanks to my wife, Julie, Brian Stuckey, and Fran Brozo for your comments and constructive criticism of the early manuscripts. Your assistance was invaluable.

Thanks, Craig Kapfer and Natalie Lund for proofreading.

Cover design by Carrie Ayd.

Author photo by Michelle Reidel.

Made in the USA
Middletown, DE
30 July 2017